THE
DOWNSTAIRS
NEIGHBOUR

Helen Cooper is from Derby and lives in Leicester. She has taught English and Academic Writing in both Further and Higher Education and was Head of Learning Enhancement at the University of Birmingham. She has a MA in Creative Writing from Nottingham Trent University and has been published in Writers' Forum, Mslexia, the *Bath Short Story Prize Anthology* (2014) and the *Leicester Writes Short Story Prize Anthology* (2018). *The Downstairs Neighbour* is her first novel.

THE DOWNSTAIRS NEIGHBOUR

Helen Cooper

HODDER &
STOUGHTON

First published in Great Britain in 2021 by Hodder & Stoughton
An Hachette UK company

1

Copyright © Helen Cooper 2021

The right of Helen Cooper to be identified as the Author
of the Work has been asserted by her in accordance with
the Copyright, Designs and Patents Act 1988.

A CIP catalogue record for this title is available from the British Library

Hardback ISBN 978 1 529 33001 4
Trade Paperback ISBN 978 1 529 32998 8
eBook ISBN 978 1 529 32999 5
Audio ISBN 978 1 529 32997 1

Typeset in Plantin Light by Hewer Text UK Ltd, Edinburgh
Printed and bound in Great Britain by Clays Ltd, Elcograf S.p.A.

Hodder & Stoughton policy is to use papers that are natural, renewable
and recyclable products and made from wood grown in sustainable
forests. The logging and manufacturing processes are expected to
conform to the environmental regulations of the country of origin.

Hodder & Stoughton Ltd
Carmelite House
50 Victoria Embankment
London EC4Y 0DZ

www.hodder.co.uk

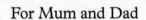

For Mum and Dad

Prologue

It feels intimate – wrong – to be in her bedroom when she's not home. The duvet is rucked up to expose the wrinkled corner of a sheet. The pretend-gold bracelet I bought her sits coiled at the back of her nightstand, no longer inseparable from her wrist. It looks cheap in this light, childish and flimsy, and my skin prickles with shame.

I turn on the spot, eyes roaming over photos and furniture that seem newly alien, knowing yet not knowing what I'm looking for. This room feels like a foreign country now. Out of bounds. I remember when there were no borders between her space and mine.

Isn't that how it's supposed to be, with children and parents?

Guilt stirs as I slide open the bedside drawer to see a black hairbrush, a packet of paracetamol, an out-of-date magazine. Turning to the wardrobe, I glide my fingers over the dresses and pretty skirts she never wears any more. I nose the soft fabrics, her scent trapped in them, like a memory.

Just as I'm about to retreat, my gaze falls on something at the bottom of the wardrobe. A wad of light blue fabric scrunched into the shadows of the back corner. I reach down to pick it up, but as it unfurls, shock makes me fling it away. It hits the mirror and drops to the floor, and I see it again: a dark lake of red encrusted on the front of a T-shirt.

I stand dazed. Heart thumping, I spread out the top on the carpet and stare at the dried blood, trailing my fingertips across the stain.

And that's the moment when I know I'll have to do something. The moment, really, that sets it all in motion.

PART ONE

I

Emma

If it hadn't been for a disruptive hamster and three nights of insomnia, Emma might not have found herself crouched in her under-stairs cupboard that night. She might not have heard the fear-pinched voice from overhead.

What had possessed her to buy the hamster in the first place? Rodents were for eight-year-olds who begged their parents for a pet, not broke, blue-haired women in their thirties. Had she really thought this ice-white creature with ink-spot eyes would offer comfort? During the day he submerged himself inside a nest of shredded paper, but when Emma went to bed he burst into life, rumbling on his wheel, flooding her small flat with relentless noise.

It felt like the soundtrack to her thoughts. Trundling around and around. Last night she'd shifted the cage into the living room, but back in bed she'd still been haunted by the cycling. She'd moved it into the kitchen. Still audible. So Gilbert's new home was this gloomy cupboard under the stairs, among dog-eared design books and unsold vintage hats.

It was 6 p.m. now – almost breakfast time for her nocturnal tyrant. Emma's flat had begun the various clicks and hums it always made as it warmed up and settled in for the night. It felt cold for mid-March, winter still clinging on, so she'd drawn her curtains and pulled on her pyjamas extra early, even by her recent standards. She was tipping sunflower seeds into Gilbert's bowl when a voice made her freeze. It was so clear and close that it seemed to be in the cupboard with her, as if Gilbert was acting as ventriloquist.

'Where *are* you?' it said.

Emma straightened where she knelt, bumping the sloped ceiling. She knew the well-spoken voice – knew it better, actually, than she knew its owner. It was her upstairs neighbour, Steph Harlow. She and her family owned the top two floors of the converted Georgian house, while Emma rented the little ground-floor space, squished in next to their shared hallway. There was a basement flat underneath, too, owned by a married couple, Chris and Vicky, but it had a separate entrance and Emma didn't hear or see much of them. She was often acutely aware of the buzz of life from above, though: the Harlows' footsteps and the flush of their toilet; the vibrant pitch of raised voices in the morning – *FREYA, time to go, love!*; *MUM, where have you tidied literally all of my belongings to?* And now Steph's voice felt right on top of her, as if there was no partition between them. Maybe there was something about the way sound parachuted down the staircase between their two flats, into this cubbyhole.

'Why's your phone off?' Steph said. 'I'm getting worried, Freya. Call me as *soon* as you get this.'

Emma's heart kicked in sympathy, recognising the gut twist of not being able to contact someone. She pictured Steph with her phone clamped to her ear, head dipped so her highlighted hair fell across her face, other hand absentmindedly smoothing her dove-grey suit. For that was how Emma would sometimes come across her in the hallway of their building, absorbed in checking her post or reading a text. Steph would spring out of her trance as soon as she noticed she wasn't alone, finding a warm smile and a compliment for Emma's latest combination of experimental hair/handmade earrings/pimped-up second-hand shoes. Something like *I could never pull that off!*

Emma would babble in response: *You don't need to! You've got the classic-elegance thing down to a T!*

And it was enviably true. Steph didn't need a fanfare of accessories to make a statement: her height, cheekbones and general aura did the job without fuss. But Steph would dismiss any attempt to compliment her in return, then whisk off to work or back up to her family before the conversation could progress. Emma would be left with the drift of her perfume in the empty hall, and a lingering curiosity about the woman she'd shared a front door with for nearly ten months. She didn't know what Steph did for a living, but assumed she was successful; didn't know how old she was, but guessed at early forties, and wondered whether forty was the point at which you stopped doing ridiculous things, like buying anti-social hamsters or generally making a mess of your life.

Steph had fallen quiet now. A drumming vibrated the dusty air, and Emma imagined her neighbour's hundred-quid heel tapping the floor above. She reached up as if to feel the beat in the low ceiling, jerked away at Steph's returning voice: 'Paul, pick up! Have you heard from Frey?'

Now it was Paul Harlow's image that filled her mind. Tall and athletic, maybe mid-fifties, his sandy hair a touch darker than his wife's creamy highlights and his daughter's white-blonde ponytail. Most mornings he rocketed past Emma when they were both out jogging by the Thames, his bulky headphones like a vice around his serious, determined face. He'd nod a brief greeting as he lapped her coming back the other way, and Emma would draw herself upright, trying not to look as exhausted as she felt.

Then there was Freya. The teenage daughter who apparently hadn't come home at her usual time, who'd upset the family routine that played out upstairs each evening. When Emma glimpsed Freya it was usually in full flight: running on deer-like legs for the bus, or sometimes racing her dad along the river path, overtaking Emma with matching ease. The girl oozed energy with her swinging, sun-catching ponytail, her Fred Perry rucksack bouncing on her shoulders. Emma had come to recognise her gait up or down their stairs: she'd take them in leaps or descend at a gallop, one of her parents trailing behind with a fond shout, 'Don't worry, Freya, I can manage all the stuff . . .'

Emma had to admit she'd taken to peeking out of the window when she heard the Harlows leaving or arriving. Had started noticing the various combinations in which they went out or came home: Freya-Paul, Steph-Freya, Paul-Steph, all three together. With or without Waitrose bags, or takeaway cartons (Friday treat), or fresh bread that would infuse the building with its smell.

Clearly, Emma didn't have enough to occupy her. Her once-busy days yawned empty and the Harlows' seemed endlessly, beguilingly full.

Was that why her pulse was soaring now? Why she was listening for Steph's next words, experiencing her neighbour's anxiety as a charge in the air? With a rustle of paper, Gilbert's pink nose emerged from his nest, as though he'd woken and sensed it too. Emma wondered whether she should run upstairs and offer to help. Her cheeks burned as she imagined explaining that she'd been crouched in a cupboard eavesdropping on Steph's phone calls.

She hunched into her dressing-gown. There was nothing but receding footsteps now, and a soft thud, as if Steph had walked to the other end of the flat and closed a door.

2

Steph

The smell of Heathrow's first-class lounge always clung to Steph after a long shift. Some days it was the lingering perfume of a traveller, who'd been polite and interesting, or the sweet vanilla scent of expensive sun lotion. On more stressful days it was the trace of her sweat inside her suit, or the champagne breath of an arrogant customer, who'd stood too close. Today the lounge had been packed with impatient VIPs, and Steph, as manager, had felt obliged to take responsibility for them. Her professional smile had creaked as she'd delivered single malts and dark espressos alongside updates on their flights. On the way home there'd been traffic, traffic, traffic, her make-up had seemed to slide off her face in one melting mask, and her headache had exploded across her skull.

And now Freya wasn't home.

Steph was sure she hadn't said anything about seeing mates after sixth form, and it wasn't the right night for volleyball or running club. She knew Freya's schedule as well as her own and she'd begged her always to stay in touch about what she was doing. It was a deal they'd recently struck: Steph would (in theory) stop being *quite* so over-protective, as long as Freya promised at least to text if she was staying out. She was seventeen. A bundle of leggy energy and hormones. No longer the little girl who would seek out her parents' faces in the crowd at all her sports matches, then snuggle between them on the sofa afterwards, drinking Steph's 'secret recipe' hot chocolate with a spoon. These days, Steph had to remind herself to let her daughter breathe, let her live.

So was she overreacting now? Was it so unusual for Freya's phone to be off? Steph checked the clock again – 6.20 p.m.: almost two hours beyond her normal home time. She couldn't stop leaving messages, anxiety strangling her attempts to sound breezy: *Drop me a text, Frey* . . . She inhaled slowly and cradled the breath in her lungs. At work when she needed to regain her calm, she'd stand at the giant window and watch a plane taking off, rising into the sky, her frustration somehow lifting with it. And she'd anchor herself to the floor below her feet.

She went to the tall sash windows of their living room, scanning for peaceful sights. The sun dissolving to pink on the suburban horizon. Silhouetted roofs of terraced houses, doorways flooding with light as people came home. For a moment she was comforted by her familiar slice of Kingston upon Thames, hovering between winter and spring. But as she leaned to see down the road, eager to spot Freya pacing along with a disgruntled bus-didn't-show-and-my-phone-died look about her, Steph's stomach clenched. The wind picked up, rattling the street's two rows of trees, which in a few weeks would sing with colour but now looked skeletal and stripped.

Paul wasn't answering his phone either. His gym nights had recently crept from three a week to four, helping him unwind after being cooped up in the office. He was like Freya in that way, like a kid who needed to be tired out, batteries exhausted, before they'd settle. Though Steph wasn't as sporty as her husband and daughter, she understood Paul's hatred of being manacled to a desk. She was always on the move at work, trying to give the impression of gliding serenely about when actually she was whirling between wine deliveries, staff short-ages and catering-related crises.

Now she made a deal with herself and her pounding heart. She would change out of her work clothes, pour herself a drink, chop the veg, and if she still hadn't heard anything she'd start calling round Freya's friends.

That wind was rattling the window frames now. Howling in the roof above Freya's attic conversion, or 'penthouse suite', as they jokingly called it. Steph hurried to close all their curtains, briefly comforted by the soft, weighty fabric dropping across darkening glass. In the kitchen, the steaks she'd taken out of the freezer that morning were seeping watery blood onto the break-fast bar. The oven clock flashed 18:50. Steph swallowed some wine, seized asparagus and a green pepper from the fridge. Then she cheated on her deal. Threw down the vegetables but didn't chop. Reached for her phone and started dialling instead.

Jess was the obvious first choice, though talking to Freya's best friend could be hard work. She was so different from Freya, so much flightier, and Steph and Jess always seemed at cross-purposes when they tried to chat. Steph prepared to cut to the chase as she dialled her home number. Jess's dad answered with a bark of their surname: 'McKENZIE!' He seemed disappointed that Steph wasn't a legal client he'd been waiting to hear from, and passed on the phone with a warning to his daughter not to keep the line engaged for long.

The conversation progressed in echoes from there, Jess repeating the last two words of each of Steph's sentences with added upwards inflection.

'Not *home?*'

'No *answer?*'

'Phone *off?*'

Steph eventually ascertained that Jess hadn't been in any lessons with Freya that day, so hadn't seen her since morning registration. They only had one A-level subject in common, business, on a Monday and Wednesday. Today – Thursday – Freya had psychology and PE.

Jess checked Snapchat. Freya hadn't been online since posting at 9.17 a.m.: *Not sure which to be more thrilled about . . . surprise test or explosion of bright green protein shake in my bag!*

'She's had her location turned off all day,' Jess said, as if Steph knew anything about how Snapchat worked.

'Really?' Steph jumped on this. 'What does that mean?'

'Oh, we all tend to keep it off, these days. I can let you know if she comes online?'

'Yes, yes, please do!' Steph ended the call, rushing on to the next. None of Freya's friends had heard from her, nobody whose number Steph knew anyway. No one remembered seeing her leave school, but her volleyball teammate Zadie said she often dashed for the 3.45 bus so she didn't have to cram onto the more crowded 4.05.

Where would Freya have gone without any of her friends? A brief *Back at 8* message would satisfy Steph now; she wouldn't get upset if there were no kisses on the end. Steph still signed off texts to her daughter with *Love you* or *LU*, but Freya's reciprocation had dwindled lately. She was growing up, and it was hard in lots of little ways that Steph had never anticipated.

She called Freya's school next, praying someone would still be there and cursing herself for not trying earlier. A security guard made sympathetic noises to Steph's garbled explanation, then managed to intercept an administrator just leaving for the night. After some pleading from Steph, she went back into the office and checked their register system, confirming that Freya had been in all her normal lessons. Steph thanked her far too profusely, but once she'd hung up she didn't know whether or not to feel reassured. She stared at her prized Family Calendar & Organiser (which Freya loved to make fun of), as though something illuminating might've replaced what she knew was there: *Freya driving lesson (lunch)*, and *Paul gym.*

Freya had scrawled a doodle of a Mini Cooper underneath: another unsubtle hint about the car she coveted. Steph had started drawing them, too, in the corners of the bank notes she gave Freya for her driving lessons: her way of telling her daughter that maybe, if she was lucky, they'd buy her one for her eighteenth.

Perhaps her driving instructor could shed some light. Maybe Freya would've mentioned something to him about going somewhere after school. And Chris lived two floors below, in the basement flat. Steph remembered when he and his wife had moved in, just over a year ago, she'd welcomed them with some half-joking comments about how handy it would be having a driving instructor in the building when Freya started to learn. When Freya *had* turned seventeen, Steph and Paul had felt obliged to send business Chris's way. And, actually, he'd built up a decent reputation by then, teaching several of the neighbourhood kids to drive.

There had been some tension lately, though. Steph cringed as she thought about the last proper conversation she'd had with Chris. At the prospect of asking him now for his help, her old shyness threatened to sneak back in, the tendency towards social avoidance she'd spent years training herself out of. She gulped her wine, squared her shoulders. A touch of awkwardness was nothing if it might help her track down Freya.

Pulling on the nearest coat, which turned out to be Paul's heavy wax jacket, she locked her flat and flew down the stairs. In the hallway she paused with Emma's door on her right, and the exterior door straight ahead, hit by another pang of nerves. The limestone floor made the hall permanently chilly. Steph rested her foot on the slab that had been wobbly for years, soothed by its familiar tilt, then shook herself and left the house.

The street smelt of evening meals being prepared behind dozens of glowing, shrouded windows. Steph swung through the iron gate that led down to Chris and Vicky's separate entrance. *Servants' entrance,* she remembered Chris quipping awkwardly when they'd first met, as he'd dragged a mattress down the narrow stone steps. It seemed extra dark down there now, the night pooling in the small, weed-riddled space in front of the basement door. There was a whiff of blocked drains, which would raise eyebrows among their more street-proud neighbours.

Steph rang the spluttery bell. Faint music leaked out as she waited – Pink Floyd maybe. She was about to press again when the door opened and Chris stood there in jeans and a grey hoody. He was slightly younger than Steph, with short dark hair, attractive eyes, and almost always a light spray of stubble on his face. On the occasions she saw him clean-shaven, she would puzzle over what was different. Now his hair and skin glistened slightly, as if damp.

He stood a pace or two back, as though braced for another reprimand. The memory of their last conversation bristled between them.

It must have been about a month ago. They'd seen each other on the street one morning, both de-icing their cars after a frosty February night. Steph hadn't intended to confront him but something had been niggling at her. She'd had a restless night, and her fingers were cold, her mood unusually grey.

Freya seems to have had an awful lot of lessons, she'd found herself saying, her voice sharpened by the chill in the air. She'd tried to lighten her tone as she'd added, *Feels like I've been handing cash over to her for months and months! Tell me she's ready to take her test.*

Chris had paused as he'd cleared ice from the logo on his navy car. His breath had clouded in front of him but no words had followed. He'd seemed to look meaningfully at Steph's BMW, emerging from beneath its own layer of white.

Eventually he'd said, *She's getting there.*

Steph had been able to hear his gritted teeth, grinding away any light-heartedness.

From what I can see she's pretty competent, she'd said. *I hope you're not spinning things out.*

Chris's expression had tightened and Steph had regretted being so blunt. She'd been thinking for weeks that maybe Chris was taking advantage of them, charging for unnecessary lessons, and Paul had agreed with her, in his own semi-distracted way. But once she'd blurted it out she'd begun to doubt herself.

That's not the way I do business, Chris had said, with more anger than Steph had expected. He'd always seemed a mild-mannered guy, always greeted her with the same quiet smile. Why was she creating this awkwardness? Why hadn't she just let it slide?

Something had stopped her backtracking, though. They'd stayed locked in the moment, the frost on her windscreen crackling softly as it thawed. Then Chris had got into his car – and had he slammed the door, or had the noise just been amplified by the freezing silence of the street?

She tried her best to smile at him now. To push aside the disagreement. 'Sorry to bother you, Chris. You saw Freya today, didn't you?'

'At lunchtime. Was there . . . a problem with the lesson?'

She flushed. 'No, no. I just wondered if she'd said anything about her plans for this evening. She . . .' her throat narrowed '. . . she hasn't got home yet.'

'Oh.' He passed a hand over his cropped hair. 'No, she didn't say anything.'

'And she seemed okay? She went back to school afterwards?'

'She seemed fine. Yeah, I dropped her off there.'

Steph paused. She felt she should ask more questions but her thoughts were a tangle. 'Thanks,' she said. 'Sorry, I'm letting all the heat out of your flat . . .'

As she retreated up the steps, he called after her: 'I could have a drive around if you like? Look for her?'

Steph stalled, almost at street level now. She glanced at his car parked nose-to-tail with hers – CHRIS WATSON DRIVING SCHOOL – and imagined it creeping through Kingston, headlights sweeping the darkness in search of her daughter. It was a scene from a TV drama. It dropped a shudder through her core.

'No,' she said, looking down at him. 'Thank you, that's kind. But it'll . . . She'll be back soon, I'm sure.'

'I'm sure.' Chris nodded, his brow creased as he watched her go.

Steph hurried to her own front door, a sudden longing for Paul piercing through her. He'd probably be showering at the gym now, trying to ease himself into relaxation mode, oblivious to her soaring anxiety. She fumbled with her keys, eager to get back to her phone. A cobwebby sensation brushed across her spine and she whipped around.

Nothing there. Just the street they'd lived on since Freya had started 'big school', the half-hexagons of bay windows making a geometric wave along the terrace, the black iron railings, which didn't normally look so jagged.

3

Paul

He hadn't intended to stay so late. As warm water sluiced over his head and shoulders, Paul's muscles groaned with what should have been the satisfying burn of a good workout, but smacked more of cramp and middle age. Hopefully, after a glass of wine at home, his exhaustion would cosy itself around him, like a sleep-inducing blanket. Or maybe he'd find himself in one of those states where his body felt drained while his mind was under-stimulated. These days, the closest he got to a mental workout was this shower spitting hot and cold, requiring deft nudges of the dial. Paul imagined he was trying to outsmart it, predicting and pouncing on its next temperature lurch.

Striding out of the gym, he glanced at his office building across the road, looking fittingly two-dimensional against the black sky. ANALYTICS SOLUTIONS blared neon above the rows of windows. How could a building with so many windows seem to have so little natural light when you were inside? Paul looked away, but realised too late that one of his younger colleagues was bee-lining towards him, his hand lifted in a static wave. As they walked together to the car park, Ollie kept mentioning that he'd been working late ('I just can't walk away from an incomplete spreadsheet, can you?'). Paul counted the number of buzzwords that Ollie sprinkled into his monologue, his favourite phrase seeming to be 'going forward'. *Going forward,* he reckoned they ought to have a regular spot for 'blue sky thinking' in all their meetings, and *going forward* he wanted to see what the new 'resource' in their team would 'bring to the table'.

Paul was a bit of a mystery to his colleagues, he suspected. And he had to admit that a part of him revelled in that. Even the co-workers he liked saw only a cardboard cut-out: Paul the semi-senior data analyst, a man of few words and an uncluttered desk, photos of his family nestling in his drawer. He gazed out of the window in meetings, never got involved in office politics, failed to show excitement about the layout of an evaluation form or a new policy on shredding. Yet he was unfazed by any task he was given, and had noticed how everyone leaned forward attentively on the occasions he did voice his opinion. Perhaps that was why he'd been promoted three times in his ten years there, despite surely appearing unambitious. He knew they all wondered what he'd done before joining Analytics Solutions, what he was like outside their open-plan office, which reeked of microwaved lunches and photocopier ink.

'Up to much tonight?' Ollie asked, as they prepared to branch off to their separate cars.

'Just the usual ...' Paul was about to elaborate, picturing Steph in her PJ bottoms, reading in a halo of light from a lamp; Freya strapping an icepack to her knee and dripping water all over the sofa; himself beside them trying to be in the moment, in the warmth of his home.

Instead he gave a vague smile and wished Ollie a pleasant evening.

Let them wonder.

In his car, he checked his phone. There were three voicemails from Steph, and he expected a message about picking up milk or bread, perhaps cherry-flavoured Lucozade, which Freya treated like a necessity. It was a surprise to hear Steph's higher-than-normal voice asking if he'd heard from Freya. Paul returned the call but it was engaged, so he tossed his mobile into the drinks holder, frowning at the time: 20:10. He'd get home as quickly as he could. Freya was probably back by now, in the doghouse for breaking a cardinal rule.

The traffic on the fringes of London felt like a personal insult. No matter how late he left work, every evening was a war of lane-changing and gambling on shortcuts. Sometimes he liked the challenge. If ever Freya was in the car he'd treat her to a commentary of his traffic predictions and genius workarounds, not that she was remotely impressed. Now, though, he wished he could cut through the congestion with a wailing siren. When he finally reached his street, he glimpsed Steph's familiar silhouette behind their curtains. If she was glued to the window, did that mean Freya wasn't back? He parked behind the driving instructor's car and sprinted inside.

There were no smells of cooking or murmurs of TV, no sounds of Steph and Freya chatting or calling out question-able song requests for Spotify. The apartment was quiet and dim: the many lamps that Steph usually switched on in the evenings were dark.

She turned from the window, mascara smudged beneath her eyes. 'I know she's practically an adult, but . . .'

Paul drew her in, her head slotting below his chin, the back of her hair giving off a strange heat. They didn't melt against each other for a few seconds of mutual rest, like they often would after a long day. Steph's body was rigid.

'Her phone's going straight to voicemail,' she said to his chest. 'None of her friends have heard from her – the ones I've spoken to, anyway.'

Paul swallowed. 'When did she leave school?'

'Normal time, far as I can tell. I've not actually been able to contact anyone who was in her last lesson with her. But the register says she was there, and her other friends reckon she usually leaves pretty sharpish for the bus. I spoke to Chris too

– everything was normal with her driving lesson. She didn't mention any plans for after school to him.'

'Snapchat? Instagram? Whatever she uses, these days?'

'No clues.'

'Have you had a good look for other people she's been connecting with or tagging or whatever they call it? She might be with a mate we don't know.'

Steph shook her head. 'I can't see her profiles any more, can I? Another condition of the infamous Freya's Privacy and Independence Bill. That's why I feel bad snooping around. I asked Jess and a few others to check for me. They said she hadn't been online tonight.'

'We'll give them another ring.'

'Are we making a fuss over nothing?'

Paul checked his watch. It was almost 9 p.m. 'Well, if she's going to give us radio silence, we're entitled to some light snooping.'

He fought to keep his voice steady, to balance out the fear in Steph's posture, her hands clutching the back of his shirt.

Paul phoned round Freya's mates for a second time, adding a few more as Steph thought of them, disguising his worry beneath a daft-dad performance that would have made his daughter cringe. He kicked off a phone tree of her volleyball and running-club friends, and asked Jess to read out every one of Freya's social media posts from the last month. Most were about loving driving, hating the stats part of her business coursework ('but, in a weird way, enjoying hating it'), and 'destroying' volleyball rivals. Some of the posts were funny and eloquent, though Freya would probably give him her best *whatever* look if he complimented her on them. She was surprisingly self-conscious about everything but her sporting abilities, her intelligence most of all.

Once they'd run out of ideas, Paul looked at Steph. It was a quarter to eleven. The heating had gone off and the flat was glacial, though they were only just noticing, rubbing their goose-pimpled arms. Paul didn't have to ask the question out loud. Steph nodded grimly and he reached again for his phone.

The on-duty PCs who arrived were young, the man still in training, Paul guessed. He said all the standard things – that these situations usually resolved themselves, and she wasn't officially missing yet – but he had an awkward manner, as if he was still learning his lines. The woman sat looking around their home, appraising their life. Freya's framed image decorated every surface, a gallery of different ages and haircuts: disappearing puppy fat and emerging cheekbones, freckles that came and went with the sun. She smiled from the blue-grey walls, too, closed mouth when she'd had her fixed braces on, flashing her liberated teeth once she'd had them removed.

When Paul took the police up to Freya's attic room, it had a tableau-like stillness. Her black Adidas kitbag hung from her favourite swivel chair. A glass of cherry Lucozade gave off a powerful scent from beside her bed. Pairs of snow-white sports socks were arranged with precision in the drawer, but her make-up spilled over the dressing-table and her en-suite was a bombsite of balled-up towels. The room was a scene of contradictions: meticulous in some ways and chaotic in others; simultaneously adult and childish, with weighty psychology textbooks next to threadbare teddies she'd had for ever. There was nothing obviously missing, apart from the handbag and jacket she'd taken to school – of course Steph remembered she'd been wearing her navy Puffa and Paul felt a failure for not having a clue.

Back in the living room, the questions began.

Who would have seen Freya today?

Does she have a boyfriend? (Paul and Steph shook their heads in unison, then glanced at each other with a silent appendix: 'Not as far as we know.')

Does she drink alcohol? ('She's more into fitness . . .')

Take drugs? (Steph's outraged 'No!' was directed right at the female PC's note-taking hand.)

And you're certain this is unusual behaviour for her? (Paul's voice rose at last, steely-edged: 'We wouldn't have called you if it wasn't.')

Right near the end, the woman caught him off-guard: 'I know this sounds extreme, but we need to get the full picture . . . Do either of you have any enemies? Anyone who might want to harm or threaten you? For any reason?'

Paul flinched, then froze. Steph must have felt it, sitting next to him, because her head turned his way. From the opposite sofa he saw the PCs' surprise at this break in the routine. Most parents probably dismissed this question in an instant: *Ridiculous, of course not.*

Steph was still looking at him. They all were. He shook his head and the police officers seemed to make a silent decision to move on, asking about Freya's recent state of mind. Paul stared at the photos on the wall and tried to deny the dread that was welling from his stomach.

Don't jump to wild conclusions. She's at a friend's, forgotten to charge her phone. She'll be back by morning and we'll make her promise never to scare us like this again.

Another voice wormed its way forward. *You complacent idiot, Paul. Of course something like this was always going to happen.*

4

Kate

Twenty-five years earlier

My socks slide down inside my shoes. Bag bounces painfully against my hip. I'm running full-pelt up the hill that separates school from home, and I'm not even trying to avoid the splats of grey chewing gum on the pavement. If I can just get back, I might be able to snatch ten minutes with Mum before *he* arrives. Ten minutes is better than nothing.

After the mammoth hill, the stairs in our tower block almost kill me – the lift's clapped out again. I duck under the line of washing that Joan from 310 always strings across the corridor, damp sleeves flapping in my face, and vault over a skateboard left at the bottom of the last flight of stairs. Then I burst into our flat, hoping he's not early.

'Mum?' I dump my bag, throw my coat in the direction of the pegs, rush through to the kitchen. She's standing at the window, staring out at our grotty view, the mottled window giving an impression of permanent drizzle. Or maybe she's not really looking at anything. She seems to do a lot of gazing into space lately. My cousin Becca reckons it's because she's in love, all moony and dreamy, but to me she looks lost in worries. Becca says I just don't want to admit she's been swept off her feet by a toyboy from the floor below.

Mum turns and I'm so relieved by the way she smiles at me, pleased to see me, that I run to her and hug her hard. She feels thin beneath her Post Office uniform. Is she losing weight to impress her boyfriend? The word *lovesick* snakes into my mind. It's so weird to think of her like that.

I go to fill the kettle. I always make the tea when I get home from school, and we have one chocolate biscuit each, sitting in the same places at the kitchen table – Mum at the end nearest the door and me to her right, where the storage heater chugs out its hint of warmth. That's the ritual. I hope we've got time to do it before Toyboy arrives. The kettle's so slow. I press my fingers against the sharp chips in the rim of the sugar bowl and feel steam kissing my nose.

At last we're sitting at the table, biscuit tin between us, Mum with her slim fingers wrapped around her mug and her dark hair tumbling over one shoulder. And I can't think of a thing to say. In the past this wouldn't have bothered me: I'd slurp my tea and drift into a daydream. But now I've got to make this daily ten minutes count for more than the whole evenings she spends with him.

'How was school, love?' she asks, seeming to break out of a trance.

I spray Hobnob crumbs down my front in my hurry to answer. 'Got a B in geography.' Suddenly it doesn't seem good enough, though I was happy with it earlier, especially as maps make me feel dizzy and dwarfed. The world's so huge and I've never been outside the Midlands. When the weather forecast does its sweep of the country I feel embarrassingly breathless, unnerved but mesmerised by the scattering of cities, the peep of Europe in the bottom-right corner of the screen.

'That's my girl,' Mum says, and I beam. She's still distracted, though. She's only nibbled half a biscuit, hasn't raised an eyebrow about the two I've gobbled before dinner.

'Amy got detention,' I tell her. For extra drama I add: 'Her third this week!'

Mum does an uh-oh face at me and I giggle.

'What did she do this time?' she asks.

'Miss Stone found fags in her pocket. But they were actually her nan's.'

'Didn't Miss Stone believe her?'

'You know Scary Stoney.'

Mum laughs mid-bite, and I feel like I've won a prize. 'Stern Stoney,' she says.

'Shouty Stoney.' I grin.

We're just warming to it, thinking of more S-words, when I hear the front door and my heart dives. Even the sound of him coming in and kicking off his shoes infuriates me. He doesn't knock any more. Leaves his trainers next to ours as if he's one of the family.

'Hi, girls,' he calls, in his posh voice – well, posh compared to us, anyway. He's from down south, somewhere. I think he moved up here for work. Even though he's been Mum's boyfriend for seven months now, and our downstairs neighbour for a few more before that, I know almost nothing about him.

He strolls over to Mum and kisses her. I can't help watching, can't help feeling he's squeezing her too tight. After they've pulled apart, his hand paws her hair.

'Cup of tea?' he asks, even though surely he can see we're in the middle of one.

To my surprise, Mum says, 'I'll have another, thanks, darling.' It annoys me that she calls him 'darling' when she calls most people 'love'. And that she's having another cup of tea just because he's offered.

'Can't tempt you?' he asks me, waggling the teapot. He always uses the pot instead of just plonking the bags into the cups like I do. Maybe Mum prefers it that way, doesn't want to hurt my feelings by saying so. Maybe she'll pour away the second half of the mug I've made.

I shake my head, mumble something about homework. Mum offers me a smile as I flee the room, but he doesn't glance at me. He's staring at Mum, like always.

5

Emma

It wasn't Gilbert's exercise regime that disturbed Emma's sleep that night. It wasn't even the phantom pings of longed-for messages on her phone. Instead it was movement and voices overhead, a dance of disquiet that suggested the Harlows' world had not settled back to normal since Steph's fraught phone calls earlier in the evening.

Emma probably wouldn't have been sleeping, anyway. Lately her worries were as nocturnal as her hamster, her brain churning with images that would make her reach for the note-pad next to her bed, drawing them in thick pen-strokes to try to purge them. She'd always been a compulsive doodler. A scribble in the corner of her schoolwork would escalate into a carnival of figures or a catalogue of designs. But, just like back then, there was a spiky anxiousness to the faces and shapes she now sketched.

She kicked her duvet aside and snatched her dressing-gown from its hook. Her phone told her it was ten past midnight. As she padded through her flat, the night turned her furniture into crouching lumps, her framed photos into colourless oblongs and squares. The rattle of Gilbert's wheel mingled with the sounds from above, creating the impression that he was controlling the neighbours' conversation, cranking it up, like an organ grinder.

She hesitated at the under-stairs cupboard. Told herself she was simply checking on her pet. When she opened the cage Gilbert didn't even pause, trawling onwards as though he had targets to reach. There was nothing else to do once she'd topped up his water (and marvelled at his total indifference to her), but Emma didn't move.

The voices were audible here. As clear as Steph's had been earlier. There were four now, though: Steph and Paul's were so familiar to her, but different tonight, distorted by anxiety, and it didn't take long to work out that the other two were police. A shiver rolled down Emma's spine. She hadn't been aware of the police arriving: she must've slept for a while after all. She'd heard Paul get home around 8.30 p.m. – car door slamming, footsteps shaking the stairs – and she'd been drawn again towards the cupboard: would he have news of Freya? What would he and Steph say to each other? Would they be pragmatic or panicked, bickering or united? Then her phone had beeped and she'd spun towards the sound, boomeranging back to her own life.

Only to be disappointed. It hadn't been the text she'd hoped for. Instead it was an email from one of her favourite suppliers, Mimi, who earned her living trawling antiques fairs and had sold Emma some incredible finds over the years. That jade-green beret with the flame-gold silk lining. The authentic flapper dress with pearls sewn into the black fabric, like stars in folds of night. Emma hadn't yet confessed to Mimi that she'd had to close her shop – or that there might be a delay in paying her final invoice. So she was still offering her things, this time a collection of 1940s Bakelite bangles in citrus shades. Emma had touched her wrists, imagining the feel of them clinking together along her arm, lime green against burnt orange against sunshine yellow. She knew just how to polish them up, how to stack them asymmetrically for display. Then she'd snapped back to reality, closing down the photo Mimi had sent. Suddenly she'd felt cold and exhausted and had dragged herself to bed without even cleaning her teeth.

Next time she'd woken she'd felt the change in the building. A sense that the top part of the house was vividly awake. Usually at this hour there was just her dead-of-the-night worries and the yowls of the neighbourhood tom cats. Now there was drama from above, a seductive diversion from her thoughts.

'I suppose she's been a bit . . . *short* with me lately,' Steph was saying. 'But she's been stressed about her mocks, and this big tournament . . .'

'Have you noticed her acting unusually, Mr Harlow?'

'Not really.' Paul's voice had a squeezed quality to it. 'But I admit I've been kind of distracted myself.'

'Any particular reason?'

'You know . . . work . . . life . . .'

Emma thought of how self-contained Paul often looked when jogging alone by the river, arms pumping at his sides. So different from when he was running loose-limbed with Freya, or laughing as they got into the car. But the same could be said for Steph, when caught unawares. Emma had several times glimpsed her entrenched in thought, blinking out of a reverie when her daughter or husband appeared.

Emma's chin jerked when she heard Paul add, 'Sweetheart . . . can I talk to the officers alone?'

He'd spoken so quickly she wasn't sure she'd heard right. The answering silence felt leaden, even from a floor below.

'What?' Steph sounded shocked. 'Why?'

'There's something I need to discuss with them.'

'Then discuss it with me, too!'

'Steph—'

'I'm your wife! Freya's our daughter! This isn't the time to—'

'I know.' Paul's voice was wound even tighter. 'Except . . . I need to.'

Emma imagined what was happening in the spell of quiet that followed. Paul reaching towards Steph, trying to placate

her? Steph staring at him in confusion? She could only picture
Steph in her suit and Paul in his dark running gear.

'Will you excuse us a moment, Officers?' Steph's usual
polite tone was suddenly back.

One of the PCs said, 'Of course.' Then there were footsteps
followed by more quiet. Emma strained to hear if the police
would say anything while Steph and Paul were presumably
out of the room. The officers talked in lower voices about how
they ought to proceed, given that they couldn't record Freya
as missing for another sixteen hours. 'Is something going on
here, though,' one of them hissed, only just audible, 'with the
parents?'

Before they could say more, the footsteps returned. Except
one set kept moving, over Emma, until the slam of a door
made the whole house quiver. A louder crash and a startled
cry had her leaping up, banging her head. The noise had
seemed to come from the stairs, or the hall. She scrambled out
of the cupboard and dashed to her front door. Steph was
sprawled at the bottom of the staircase, one hand flung against
the wall, her fingers as white as the emulsion behind.

'Oh, God – are you all right?'

Steph just lay there, her body at one awkward angle, her
head at another. *She's snapped her neck*, Emma thought, in
sheer panic. Relief coursed through her (with a snatch of her
mum's voice accusing her of a dramatic imagination) when
Steph sat up and began touching her face. Emma realised her
neighbour was on the verge of tears: the kind jolted out by a
slip or a shock but rooted in something else. Her cardigan had
dropped off her shoulders and a large tortoiseshell hair clasp
had landed on the stair behind her, its black teeth facing up.

Emma stepped closer. 'Are you hurt?'

Steph seemed dazed. The foyer light bulb flickered, adding
to the surreal atmosphere. 'I don't think so.' She prodded at
her ear and her finger came away stained with blood. Emma

had a strange flash of déjà vu, but before she could pin it down, the door to the upstairs flat opened.

'Steph?' came Paul's voice. His shadow stretched the length of the stairs, elongated by some trick of the light. 'Shit, are you all right?'

Steph stared ahead, her eyes pink. 'I slipped.'

'You're bleeding!' Paul rushed down towards her. He was wearing work clothes, but with no shoes, his shirt crumpled. He stalled when he noticed they had company and Emma felt him taking in her blue, bed-matted hair, the *Z* tattooed on her ankle. Her dressing-gown suddenly felt tiny and transparent, like a nightmare in which she realised she was naked in public.

Paul's eyebrows knitted but he turned away from her, reaching for Steph's shoulders. 'Darling—'

Steph moved so his hands grasped the air. 'Leave it, Paul. Go back to your *private discussion*.'

'Please, Steph. I know it looks bad . . .' As Paul implored his wife he glanced again at Emma, a look that made her feel like an intruder. She began to retreat into her own flat. Before the door swung closed, she saw Paul leaning towards Steph, and Steph jerking away, drawing up her knees, like a threatened creature curling into a ball.

Something flamed in Emma. A kind of recognition. Her heart boomed as she leaned against the inside of her door, failing to make out their murmuring voices. After a few minutes she turned the latch and opened it a crack. But the foyer was empty, the light bulb still flickering, Steph's hair clasp lying on the stairs with wisps of blonde hair in its jaw.

6

Chris

He must have travelled this route a thousand times. Usually in the passenger seat, his feet poised over his extra set of pedals, suburbia conveyor-belting past as his student drove excruciatingly slowly. The same tree-lined streets and chained-up bikes; the same cars in the same drives. Smug joggers and couples pushing elaborate prams.

Chris also spent a lot of time parked in various spots around Kingston, glimpsing snapshots of other people's lives while he waited for his learners. Sometimes he'd see a man in a designer suit taking crafty swigs from a hip flask, concealing it when his picture-perfect wife and son emerged from the pristine house behind. Or a homeless guy rummaging through the Waitrose bins, digging out a mushy avocado, shooed away by a self-important store manager. The divide between rich and poor, happy and miserable, genuine and false felt so flimsy around here. And Chris always teetered just the wrong side of the line.

Today Kingston felt watchful. Almost certainly it was Chris's imagination, his mood, but he'd sensed it from the moment he'd left home several hours before. Neighbours herding their kids into giant Volvos had seemed to blast glances towards his house – but maybe they'd seen the police parked outside the night before and didn't know who they'd been visiting. Even now, Chris seemed to catch the eye of every pedestrian as his student, Dylan, steered them haphazardly through the streets. He cut the lesson slightly short, needing to gather his thoughts before the next.

'Good effort, mate,' he said, when they pulled up with a bump of the kerb and a final stall of the engine. Dylan was a student at Kingston Uni, and one of the most timid drivers Chris had ever taught. 'Just need to work on that hesitation at junctions. The stalling's getting less frequent, though, hey?'

Dylan paid him and got out of the car, and Chris watched him trudge towards the student halls, his walk as apologetic as his driving. He wanted to shake him: *You're bloody lucky, you know. Young, free, privileged. Why hide behind that floppy fringe?* At the same time, there was a twinge of something – protectiveness, almost. Sadness? Chris gazed at the student block and saw people cooking and chatting behind the bare windows, toasting Friday night with their beers. Loneliness shivered through him, like a reflex.

Shifting into the driver's seat, he flipped down the visor against the low March sun and headed to Chantry High School. Kids of all ages were swarming out of the gates, unleashed for the weekend. Usually he was glad of his car's logo, separating him from the parents in 4x4s yet assuring everyone he wasn't some weirdo lurking outside a school, but today it made him feel conspicuous. He was glad when he spotted Jess's short legs in black tights weaving towards him. She was riffling through her handbag, checking her phone, oversized sunglasses tobogganing down her nose. Eventually she looked up and scanned for his car. He waved and moved back into the passenger seat, wondering how many times a week he did this shuffle-over, this relinquishing of control.

As soon as she got in, he could tell she was upset. She took off her shades and her maroon school blazer but just sat there, staring at her lap.

'Jess? You okay?'

She nodded, still didn't put on her belt.

'Ready to go? Shall we try a reverse-park again this lesson?'

At last she pulled her seat so far forward that her nose almost touched the wheel, snapped on her belt and set off. Jess was usually a pretty vocal driver, shrieking, 'Oooh, red light!' or 'Where's second gear gone?' at regular intervals. If he asked her to switch lanes or stop on a hill she'd act aghast: 'Chris, *really?*' She was silent today, though, and when she attempted the reverse-park she ended up jutting out almost perpendicular to the pavement, then clipped the shiny Audi behind. That was the final straw: she threw up her hands and dissolved into tears. 'I can't do this!'

Chris glanced behind to check there was no visible damage to the other car's bumper, praying there was no expensive bill to be covered. 'Come on, it's okay. Pull up over there and turn off the engine.'

She got herself under control and did as he said. They sat for a moment as the car exhaled around them.

'What's wrong?' He reached towards her shoulder but thought better of making contact, veering awkwardly away. Jess pressed her fingertips against her cheekbones, leaving oval prints in her make-up. 'If you're worried about bumping that Audi, it's a poser's car anyway.'

One corner of her mouth turned up. Slowly she lowered her hands. 'Haven't you heard?' she said.

'Heard?'

'About Freya. Nobody's seen her since yesterday.'

Freya's image flooded Chris's mind. Her confident posture when she drove. The healthy glow of her skin, which always made him feel flabby and light-deprived. He saw her vividly for a moment, eclipsing Jess as she sat six inches taller, shoulders relaxed, blonde ponytail fanned over the headrest. Infuriatingly confident, sometimes. Like she thought driving was no big deal.

'She hasn't turned up?' he said. 'I saw her mum last night . . .' He recalled Steph at his door, hunched inside an oversized man's jacket that had made her look somehow diminished. A different woman from the one who'd had the gall to challenge him in the street about her daughter's lessons.

'It's not like Frey to go off without saying anything,' Jess said. 'She's so on it with her training. Even with her school-work, though she doesn't admit it. She gets better grades than me every time, you know. We've got business coursework due on Monday . . .'

Seeing she was getting teary again, Chris patted her arm. She stiffened and he wished he'd stuck with his earlier decision not to touch her. It was hard to know what to do with a crying seventeen-year-old girl. Impossible to console her without overstepping the mark. Next month he'd be turning forty, yet in some ways he felt the same as he had at Jess's age. It was only the things and the people around him that had altered. Circumstances. Life.

'Her parents keep calling me.' Jess sniffed. 'But I really don't know where she could be.'

'Does she tell you everything?' Chris asked, then wondered if it was a weird question. He was suddenly conscious of the intimacy of being in a stationary car together, the usual conventions of a driving lesson stripped away. He stabbed at the button to roll down his window, air rushing into the car with the clamour of the street, a smell of petrol.

'I thought so. Maybe not so much lately. She's seemed a bit . . .' Jess made a mysterious, looping hand gesture, then turned to him. 'Did she say anything to you?'

'Me? Like what?'

She blinked, her eyes almost opaque with held-back tears. 'I don't know. Like, *anything*.'

'No, I . . . She seemed . . . normal.'

'In an hour she'll officially be a missing person. Frey! This can't be real, can it?' She shook her head and slumped forward, her forehead meeting the wheel, red hair cascading either side.

It felt wrong just to watch her cry. She *had* confided in him, after all. Driving lessons were so often full of mind-numbing small-talk in between 'Left here . . . Check your mirror . . . Try not to flatten that pedestrian . . .' And Vicky was so closed-off these days. Sometimes Chris fantasised about letting one of his students crash into the back of a bus, just to shake things up, just so he could phone Vicky from hospital and say, *Get down here. I've been in an accident.*

His hand hovered over the bumps of Jess's spine, visible through the thin white school shirt. She lifted her head and he withdrew.

'I . . . I'll drive you home,' he said. 'If you don't feel up to carrying on.'

She sniffed again. 'Thanks for being nice about it.'

'No problem.' He forced a smile. 'And try not to worry. Freya will be home before you know it.'

They swapped places and he drove back through Kingston, past upmarket pubs painted slate grey and olive green, coming to life with after-work drinkers sitting outside as if it was a carefree summer's day. As Jess became absorbed in her phone, Chris seemed to see and hear police sirens everywhere. But actually it was the flash of sun on a sapphire-coloured scooter; the wail of a car alarm; the bright blue hair of a woman he realised was his other neighbour, Emma, standing outside a vintage clothes store with a FOR SALE sign flapping beside her.

7

Emma

The fire-wave of anger caught her by surprise. It was the
starkness of her empty shop that brought on the white-hot
rush. She'd been calm up to this point, packing up swathes of
gauzy scarves, hand-sewn purses, dresses imbued with the
earthy smell of vintage clothes. Even when a rail had toppled
over and buried her beneath a mound of faux-fur coats, she'd
just lain there, blinking. But now that her shop was stripped,
ready for its new owners and new identity, Emma felt the air
whoosh out of her lungs.

'Jesus,' she murmured, pressing her fist against her breast-
bone. It *was* anger snatching her breath this time, rather than
that wearying sadness. She escaped into the fresh air, only to
be confronted by her livelihood sitting in taped-up boxes on
the pavement.

As she loaded her rented van, reversing the process she'd
gone through with such excitement six years before, the door
to the neighbouring café jangled and its owner, Lina, emerged.
Emma had watched Lina tidy away her one outdoor table and
'Best vegan scones this side of the Thames!' sign on countless
evenings. She observed her swishing through the routine now,
untying her apron, her braided hair gathered inside a scarf.
When Lina glanced over, Emma smiled. 'Hey!'

It was unmistakable. Lina froze. A look of wariness glazed
her features. Emma felt a hole open in her stomach as her
business-neighbour smiled thinly and darted back inside,
flapping her CLOSED sign into place. A blind unfurled over

the café window, juddering as it got stuck and Lina seemed to yank at its cord.

And how could Emma blame her? She'd behaved so badly on her last proper day in business, over a month ago now. Had forgotten her professionalism and let her personal life erupt in the street. Maybe Lina's customers had objected to having their afternoon coffees disturbed by drama from next door. Drama was something Emma tried to keep consigned to her outfits and hairstyles, these days. She liked to think they deflected it. But it seemed her armour was flimsy.

She dragged her eyes to her own shop, to the name, Threads, hanging over the door. It no longer evoked that tingle of pride. She felt she should apologise to the sign she'd designed herself, and the unsold treasures squished into boxes, and the regular (and in many ways *ir*regular) customers who'd kept her afloat and enlivened her work. It had never been easy to stay in business, had taken most of her energy, her focus, her self-belief, but until recently she'd seemed to have just enough of all those things.

She steered the van through Kingston's tight streets, half enjoying the looks of surprise on people's faces when they saw that White Van Man was actually Blue-haired Woman. The vehicle gave her a temporary feeling of height and breadth, as if she was in control of a parade float. There was nothing to fanfare about, though, as she crammed the van's contents into her tiny flat, which coughed up disgruntled clouds of dust in protest.

How could a place feel cluttered and empty at the same time? The more of Zeb's things she had to nudge aside to make room for her stock, the more she was forced to acknowledge that his left-behind trainers and toiletries had been in the same positions for a month.

Don't wallow. There's far worse suffering going on inside this house. Her thoughts lurched back to Freya and her gut did a somersault. She'd been missing for more than twenty-four hours now. All was silent above. Normally she'd smell the Harlows' dinner (always something super-nutritious, she'd imagine, trying to guess the ingredients from the scent), and hear them moving around, transitioning into their evening, pipes humming with showers and baths. She never sensed the same hubbub of activity from the basement flat, never felt anything like it inside her own any more. It was as if all the warmth and energy of the building rose to the top two floors. Or had done, before Freya's disappearance had extinguished it.

Emma went to her kitchenette and poured an Aldi gin with enough ice to anaesthetise her brain. Crunching the cubes between her teeth, she perched on her sofa and felt the silence bear down. She'd had to move some furniture to fit more boxes in, so the light and shade in her living room now pooled in different places, adding to the sense that everything was out of kilter.

The sound of an engine outside grabbed her attention. She rushed to the window and saw Steph unfurling from the back of a police car, looking more dishevelled than Emma had ever seen her, then running towards the house with her hand over her mouth. Paul followed, pausing to say something to the police officer in the driver's seat before hurrying to catch up with his wife. Emma's stomach knotted tighter. It was futile to keep watching, hoping Freya would bounce out of the same car and overtake her parents on the stairs, but she realised that that was what she was doing, her hands gripping the sill, her face inching closer to the pane.

Only her video-call ringtone pulled her from the window. A ray of hope shone through and she dived towards her laptop. Her eagerness drained when she saw it wasn't a Skype from Zeb. Instead her mum's image filled the screen, nightly wine in hand, the other waving in an exaggerated fashion as though to catch the attention of someone a hundred metres away.

'Hi, Mum.' She tried not to sound deflated.

'How are you?' Lately there was a tilt to Julie's head when-ever she asked this question. 'Just thought I'd give you a quick call while our dinner's in the tagine.'

'What are you having tonight?' Emma asked dutifully. Her mum had attended cookery courses based around every major national cuisine.

'*Kefta mkaouara* with Moroccan bread,' Julie reeled off. 'Have you had your hair cut?'

Emma touched her newish fringe. 'About a week ago.'

'Good to have a change,' Julie said. This made Emma feel like a breathing cliché, when in fact the restyle hadn't really signalled a fresh start. She'd asked for a fringe that shadowed her eyes and heavy layers around her cheeks and jaw, as though to hide as much of her face as possible.

Emma knew her mum wanted her to open up more. But she was afraid of what might pour out if she allowed herself to begin. Her tactic was to offer *something* early on in the conver-sation: something her mum could help with but that Emma could stand to talk about.

'D'you think you could store some stock for me?'

'Course, darling. Have you been clearing out the shop?'

Emma nodded. 'We're exchanging contracts on Friday.'

Julie's head-tilt returned. Emma knew her well enough to guess she was deciding not to comment that things would have been much easier if Emma had leased a shop rather than bought one. Something she was only too aware of.

'And have you heard from Zeb?' her mum asked.

Emma still got that feeling whenever she spoke about him. Like a trapdoor had opened beneath her feet. 'Not for a while.'

'You're not still doing weird things, are you?'

'I haven't done any weird things!'

'You almost suffocated yourself spraying Lynx around your place.'

'I just like the smell.' Emma's own scowl drew her eye, trapped in the mini camera-image in the corner of the screen.

'It's got to be dangerous in those amounts.'

'All right, Mum!' Emma resorted to a diversion tactic. She picked up her laptop and spun it outwards, moving to the cupboard to show Gilbert camped between a box of kimonos and a bucket of vintage walking sticks. She froze as a shout reverberated from above: 'Stop pushing me on this, Steph!'

'What was *that*?' her mum asked.

'The neighbours . . . Their daughter . . .' But her screen was buffering, chewing up her words.

'Sounds like they're having a barney,' Julie was saying, oblivious, as the connection resumed. 'Remember those neighbours we had in Clapham? Always screaming at each other. And didn't they keep some kind of iguana as a pet?'

'It was a snake . . .' Emma couldn't focus on her mum's chatter now that a storm seemed to be brewing overhead. 'Maybe I should call you back. I'm struggling to hear you.'

Julie needed to add the finishing touches to her Moroccan feast anyway, so she signed off in an unidentified language – had she re-started Mandarin lessons? – and the screen blanked.

The room darkened without the spill of blue light from the laptop. It was pin-drop silent until Steph soared into earshot: 'Don't you know how serious this is, Paul?'

Paul responded with something Emma couldn't make out. Heavy footsteps paced back and forth. She pictured Paul stomping from one end of their apartment to the other, and Steph with her back against a wall, as pale as when she'd been lying on the stairs. Emma slipped into the cupboard, hardly thinking about what she was doing or why. She twined her fingers around the bars of Gilbert's cage and heard him stir.

'I've never asked you about any of it,' Steph was saying. 'But now . . .'

'I will fix this.'

'Freya—'

'I know! God, do I know, Steph.'

'If she's in *any* danger—'

'I said I KNOW—'

There was a bang. The sound of shattering glass. Before she knew it Emma had thrown herself onto the floor with her hands over her head. A second later she unfurled, hot with embarrassment at her own jumpiness, still with her after years of trying to be fearless. She saw she'd knocked Gilbert's cage and he was awake and glaring at her. The noises above were suspended. Then Paul was saying, '*Shit . . .*' and there was movement, footsteps.

Nothing from Steph until her voice returned laced with tears: 'Where are you going?'

Another slamming door. Another tremor through the spine of the building. Emma crept out of the cupboard and to the window. It was Paul who'd left. She watched him stride off down the darkening road, coat on and hood up, the pale wash of the streetlamps gliding over him.

More footsteps drummed down the exterior staircase. Emma saw Steph burst out of the main door, glance both ways and yell something after Paul. She surged forward as if to chase her husband, but stopped dead and floundered in the road, already seeming like an unravelled version of the neighbour Emma had observed and envied. Steph's posture collapsed and she trudged back to the house. Emma strained to see if she looked injured from whatever had been smashed. Steph was stooped, crying, but Emma couldn't tell whether she was physically hurt.

She wondered again if she should reach out to her neighbour. How could she just sit there, knowing she was upstairs? What kind of person watched, listened, but didn't try to help?

She was edging towards her door, fizzing with nerves, when she heard an unexpected knock.

8

Steph

Steph no longer felt as if she was in her body. The sleepless night and nightmarish day had taken her to pieces. Part of her was still in the street, shouting, '*Where are you going?*' as Paul charged into the night. Another part was trapped in the surreal motions of registering their daughter as a missing person. Reciting her date of birth and her blood group, handing over her smiling photograph to be sealed inside a clear plastic bag.

Now, standing at Emma's door, Steph seemed to sway, untethered. None of this should be happening. She should be catching up on *The Apprentice* with Freya, discussing how irritating all the contestants were, Freya's feet lolling across her lap.

Panic swept her as she tried to remember the last time they'd actually sat like that on the sofa, actually watched an episode together. It had once been their never-missed thing, but for the last few weeks Freya had claimed homework and disappeared into her room, leaving Steph to press record and feel bereft. She imagined episodes stacking up on their Sky box, waiting for Freya's return, and the thought made her want to howl.

The door opened in front of her and she struggled to re-set her face.

Emma's outfit was more subdued than usual: knee-length grey jumper over mustard-coloured tights. A closer look revealed that her collar and cuffs sported tiny jewelled pineapples. Steph had never been sure of Emma's age. She was petite, with a youthful face and fashion sense, but sometimes there were glimmers of maturity. Once, for example, they'd seen each other in the street when Freya had just sprinted off for her bus, Steph was doing up the fiddly buttons on her long coat, and Emma was folding polythene-wrapped dresses into the boot of her battered car. Emma and Steph had swapped the usual pleasantries. Then Emma had nodded towards Freya, flying down the road with her phone at her ear, and said, *She's full of life, isn't she?* Steph remembered how it had made her pause, surprised and pleased at this insight into how others saw her daughter. But, also, Emma's observation had seemed to place her closer to Steph's age bracket than Freya's.

'Steph,' Emma said now, 'I . . . Freya . . .'

'She's gone missing,' Steph said, and the words enclosed her in dread.

Emma nodded, blinking. 'I'm so sorry. You must be so worried.'

You have no idea, Steph felt like saying. She wasn't exactly sure why she'd knocked on Emma's door. She'd had a thought that her neighbour might have seen something. Steph got the impression she was home during the day, more than she used to be: her Corsa was constantly parked in the street. The police would talk to all the locals but Steph had the chance to act sooner, faster, to *find her find her find her.*

More than that, though, she couldn't face being alone. Couldn't let herself think about the way Paul had reacted, where he might have gone, and how all the things they'd never properly talked about might somehow be linked to this, the worst day of their previously unspoiled family life.

Emma beckoned her into her flat. It was less than half the size of theirs but seemed to have twice the amount of stuff. Steph often wished for more storage space for all Freya's sports equipment, Paul's vinyl that he never listened to, her own books she never gave away. But Emma's living room

heaved with boxes, as if she'd never unpacked or was preparing to move, as well as an old sewing machine, scattered piles
of fabric and thread, and what looked like a giant wine rack
full of shoes. There was a noise just audible in the background,
like a turning wheel . . . *a hamster?*

Steph was sure a man used to live here with Emma. Or
maybe still did? She'd never actually met him, only heard the
muffled back-and-forth of their voices, and glimpsed them
together sometimes on the street.

'Were you at home yesterday?' she asked.

'Yes . . .' Emma perched on her sofa and fiddled with the
turquoise tassels of a throw, gesturing for Steph to sit down
too. 'I remember thinking the street felt quiet. The day seemed
to drag.'

'What about before that? Had you noticed anyone hanging
around? Ever seen Freya with anyone who seemed . . .?' She
shut her eyes at the horror of the questions, the inescapable
trains of thought.

'No, nothing like that.' Emma sounded pained, too. Steph
wondered what she must think of her. Who could let this
happen to their child? What kind of mother had to ask a neighbour, pretty much a stranger, whether she knew things about
her daughter?

'Who saw her last?' Emma asked.

'We don't know exactly,' Steph admitted, with another
wrench. 'She was in her final lesson of the day but the police
can't interview the teacher until first thing tomorrow.' It was
excruciating having to work to other people's schedules when
she'd been catapulted into this new sense of time. Even the
police search, which had been launched within half an hour of
them registering Freya as missing, was at the mercy of daylight.
Right now, Steph knew, the team were trawling the limited
CCTV footage from around Freya's school and bus stop.

'And her phone's off?'

'Yes. She's normally glued to it.'

As if on cue, a phone beeped. Steph's heart vaulted and she reached into her pocket before her brain could register that the chime wasn't one of hers. Still she opened her messages, WhatsApp, emails. Emma sheepishly picked up her own mobile.

'Sorry, that's me.' She moved to put it aside without reading the message, but seemed to change her mind, tapping the screen and frowning with distraction. Steph felt a vicious slash of jealousy. *What is it, Emma? Hair appointment cancelled? Friend wants to meet at a pub you don't really like? Boyfriend trouble?* She knew she was being unfair, but even the worst of other people's problems were enviable to her now.

She leaped to her feet. She was wasting time with a woman whose Friday-night drink was going flat, whose phone was buzzing with her own life.

Emma stirred, and jumped up too. 'You don't have to go!'

'I should be out there looking for her . . .' Steph glanced towards Emma's undrawn curtains. The night seemed to glisten and swell, like black water. Usually she loved night skies, the more vast and starry the better, but now she couldn't stand the thought of it, dark and depthless.

They were diverted by another ringing. Traditional this time, like a landline. Emma looked at the handset in the corner of the room, seeming surprised. Presumably her home phone rang as rarely as Steph's did, these days.

'Answer it,' Steph said. 'Just in case?'

Emma hesitated, then walked over and picked up the phone. 'Hello?'

There was a pause before she repeated: 'Hello?'

A chill touched the back of Steph's neck. She became conscious of that rumbling, hamster-wheel noise again, gathering momentum.

'Is anyone there?' Emma sounded perturbed now. '*Hello?*'

She replaced the receiver but kept frowning at it, rubbing her lips together with their traces of coral gloss. 'Wrong number, I guess.'

Steph watched her for a beat longer. Emma's face seemed to have paled. Her cheek was dappled by the moving shadow of a dream-catcher that hung from the ceiling. Was there something she wasn't letting on about the call? *No, of course not. Why would there be?* And even if there was, why would it be anything to do with Freya? It was already becoming impossible to distinguish between things that meant nothing and things she should seize on.

And then there were the things that made her brain power down when she thought about them.

Paul asking to speak to the police alone.

Paul flinging his water glass onto their kitchen floor rather than answer her questions.

'I have to go,' she told Emma again.

'Please, let me—'

'I really do.' Steph stumbled to the door. The hallway seemed to represent a fork: back upstairs, to do what, or back outside, to go where? She lurched towards the stairs, hoping she could collect her thoughts once she was in her own flat.

'If you need anything,' Emma was saying behind her. 'I'm – I'm just downstairs.'

Steph stopped and twisted back. Emma seemed young again, framed in her doorway, her blue serrated fringe in her eyes.

'Just keep looking out of your window,' Steph blurted. 'Look for . . . I don't know. Anything. Anyone.' *Tell me what Paul's face looks like when he comes home,* she wanted to add, *before he's prepared himself to come back upstairs.*

Tell me what you think of this street, our neighbours, this place that was meant to be safe.

Tell me, do you ever get the sense our house is being watched?

9

Paul

Bright spots of fear starred Paul's vision as he ran through Kingston's lamplit streets. His feet thudded out the mantra of his opaque promise to Steph: *I will fix this, I will fix this, I will fix this.* He arrived, gasping, at Surbiton station, lathered in sweat beneath his coat and jeans, just in time for the last train.

Other passengers shot him wary glances as he stumbled on. He suspected he looked wild-eyed, scarlet-faced, though his reflection in the black windows was translucent and featureless. Realising his hand was still beading with blood, he pressed his mouth to the cut. He couldn't forget Steph's expression when he'd thrown his glass onto the floor. He'd just wanted to break the momentum of her questions, the shrill ringing they set off in his head. But her eyes had blanked with shock and she'd stared at him as if he was a stranger, as if she couldn't predict what he might do next.

She knew his favourite brand of coffee, his annoying habit of absentmindedly singing a different song from the one they were listening to, where he liked to be touched and which politicians made him swear at the TV. But a black hole lurked behind all that familiarity, rarely acknowledged, and never in front of Freya, whom he'd always tried to shield from its shadows.

Fix it, the train's rhythm chanted. *Fix it.*

Paul got off at Waterloo and paced through the Friday-night streets. Though the evening was chilly, people were drinking outside bars, eating late meals at small crowded tables. He peered at every young blonde woman, earning some outraged frowns, but none was his daughter – none jigged her leg beneath the table with the restlessness Freya got from him.

He stopped dead in front of the police station. Cold blue light from its sign pooled over him.

Could he do this?

He *had* to.

His body stiffened in resistance as he strode up to the automatic doors. They sighed open at the last instant and seemed to suck him inside.

The foyer was quiet. A smell of cleaning products; a blast of hot air from the ceiling vents. Paul approached the desk, conscious of the sheen of drying sweat on his forehead. The officer behind the counter had a rugby player's build but a doughy, almost babyish face.

'I need to see DI Glover.' He was still based there, Paul was certain of that much. He sent Christmas cards, the odd email, though Paul usually threw away the cards, deleted the messages.

The desk officer cocked his head. 'Can I ask what this is about?'

'Tell him it's Paul Harlow. He'll know me.'

'Have you got any ID?'

He slid out his wallet, offering his driving licence. The officer picked up a phone. 'I'll try him. He may have gone home.'

Paul glanced around as he waited, to divert himself from imagining Tom Glover's reaction on the other end, but couldn't help listening to the one-sided call. *He didn't say exactly . . . Shall I ask him? . . . Oh . . . Oh, I see . . . Sorry, Inspector. Should I tell him to come back another time?* Paul thought about storming over and grabbing the phone, forcing Glover to answer to him rather than relay messages through this uncomprehending colleague. But the officer hung up.

'DI Glover says he'll see you.'

Paul raked a hand through his damp hair as he was led along a route he already knew. There were only small changes: new names gleaming on doors, a fresh carpet. The more familiar details became heightened: the slippery wood of the banister, the glare of the strip lights, the creaking weight of Glover's office door.

As Paul entered, Tom Glover stood up from behind his desk and whipped off his glasses. His eyes looked aged, and unmistakably guarded, but his suit was as well tailored to his trim frame as it had always been. In contrast Paul was shell-shocked and clammy, specks of blood on his jeans. As if he was still the unravelling man who'd practically crawled out of this station twenty years ago.

'Paul.' Glover's tone was questioning. Freya's case was obviously not yet on his radar, despite what Paul had disclosed to the two surprised PCs after he'd asked Steph for a moment alone with them.

Unless Glover was pretending not to know. When Paul had been put on 'indefinite leave' from his department, and had spent months self-destructing, then drifting, and finally recovering, he'd often got the sense that his former boss was keeping tabs on him. That he knew far more about his life than he would let on when he called to 'see how you are, old friend'. But that feeling had faded as Paul had got himself together, found the dull safety of an office job, married Steph, had Freya, and finally allowed himself to be happy.

Now that he was back in Glover's office, though, watching him select a facial expression from his disturbingly cold to overly warm range, Paul wondered if he'd been foolish to assume he'd lost interest in him.

'It's been a long time!' Glover clasped his hand, clearly opting for warmth. 'How are you?'

'I'm not good. I mean, I have been. It's not what you think . . .' Paul shook himself. *Get to the point.* 'My daughter's missing.'

Glover slid his glasses back on, appearing genuinely star-tled. 'Christ, Paul. When you say missing . . .?'

'Over twenty-four hours. Hasn't used her mobile or debit card. Friends haven't heard from her. No activity on her social media or . . .' He couldn't finish. The facts were brutal kicks to his stomach. If it had been somebody else's daughter, a case with no personal connection, he would have been working on the gravest assumptions. He saw Glover glance at a framed photo on his desk. Paul guessed it was a picture of his two kids, who'd been babies when they'd worked together. He hoped he could appeal to the fatherly side of Glover's person-ality to get what he needed. His old instincts for other people's motivations were waking, the subtle persuasiveness he'd once had in his toolkit.

'How old is Freya now?' Glover asked.

'Seventeen.' Paul heard the break in his own voice. Freya was feisty and smart, but there could be a naivety to her when she wasn't playing sport, when there weren't clear-cut goals to compete for. She could punch a volleyball in a way that would make Paul think, *That's my girl*, and she'd astounded him and Steph with her witty, charming acceptance speech when she'd won Players' Player at the school sports awards last year. But she also constantly lost things, closed her eyes at upsetting RSPCA adverts, became pensive or wildly indignant when they watched the news, as though she couldn't quite believe the things that happened in the world outside her safety zone. The thought of her out there in that world – in the parts of it he'd known – was terrifying to Paul.

'I need to see the Sanderson file.' He flinched inwardly as he said their former target's name. 'Especially any . . . updates.'

Glover sat back in his leather chair. Assessing something, though Paul wasn't sure what. Always calculating risk.

'I won't do anything stupid,' Paul pressed. 'I'll keep you informed of anything I need to follow up.'

'Follow up?' Glover's eyebrows jerked. 'You're worrying me now.'

'I wouldn't be here if it wasn't a matter of . . . It's my *daughter*, Tom.'

Glover stood and walked to the window, looking out at the floodlit courtyard to the rear. It was such a familiar move of his – striding to the window for a 'time out', keeping his back turned for just longer than was comfortable – that Paul shuddered with recollection.

Delicate was the word Glover liked to use about what had happened back then. It conjured up images of thin glass on the verge of shattering, fragile bones on the verge of breaking.

Tom turned back around. 'I can't give you access, Paul. You're not a police officer any more. There are no updates, anyway. You'll find nothing in those files you can't pull from your memories . . . if you choose to.'

Paul swallowed. Something prickled the base of his neck – instinct, warning? Glover was standing straight now, hands in his pockets.

'You must know where Sanderson is,' Paul said. 'Whether he—'

Glover held up a palm. 'Paul. Your head's all over the place. This is every parent's worst bloody nightmare. But you have to let Missing Persons find Freya. There's no point taking matters into your own hands, raking over things that are probably unconnected . . . things I *know* you don't want to dredge up.'

Paul felt the rise of fury only a split-second before it burst out. 'Well, what the fuck would you do?' He banged the desk, dislodging sheets of paper. 'Wouldn't you make the same assumptions as me, if it was one of your kids?' He seized the framed photo and held it towards Glover, who refused to look at it, his face shutting down. 'Wouldn't you do everything you could to make sure they weren't in danger because of what we did?'

There was a heated silence. Paul continued to thrust the picture at Glover, his grip so tight he was convinced either the frame or his knuckles would break.

Eventually Glover snatched it from him. 'What *we* did?'

Paul stared at him, still trembling with rage, tasting it in his throat. He couldn't believe he'd thought he could come here for help. He'd forgotten how smoothly his former boss could switch compassion on and off.

Glover called after him as Paul strode to the door. Paul stormed down the stairs without brushing the walls or the banister, unwilling to touch another thing in this place. Then he was back in the night, the London fumes less poisonous than the air inside the police station. He wanted to go back to Steph but he couldn't bear the hurt and confusion on her face. Something had been ripped open by Freya's disappearance, and what if there was no way to repair it? What if this was only the beginning?

As he collapsed onto a bench, his mind's eye began leafing through the file that Glover had denied him access to. Its pages would crystallise in his head if he let them, like pictures developing in a darkroom. Before he got very far, breathlessness grabbed him by the neck. His throat closed and he gasped, clawing at his collar. It had been years since he'd had a panic attack. But now here he was, fighting to breathe, breathe, breathe, tilting forward on the bench as people passed with barely a glance.

Even as the attack subsided, there was a slow swirling dread. That time, that place . . . He'd managed to free himself, heal himself, but what if it had come back for his little girl instead?

He sketched Freya's image behind his lids, testing himself with the detail, thinking of how people often said she had his eyes and how the cliché secretly pleased him, whether they really meant it or not. A falling sensation jolted through him as her face slowly dissolved into another. The girl from the pages of that file, the girl he had failed, and the mother whose dark hair and pale skin were emerging from the depths of his memory.

10

Kate

There's a knock on my bedroom door, and Mum's voice: 'Kate, you busy? Mind if we have a quick chat?'

For a second I think the 'we' is me, her and *him*. Then I remember it's Saturday morning and she's got work in an hour. He won't be coming round till later. I've got the day to myself but I don't fancy going into town or seeing who's on the rec. I just want to hide in here and read my library book.

'Come in,' I call.

'Can you put my hair up for work?' she asks, walking in. 'I'm so rubbish at doing it myself.'

She sits down at my little dressing-table, in front of the cracked mirror that Becca always deems bad luck. I stand behind and brush the frothy dark waves I've only semi-inherited – my hair is light mousy brown with a half-hearted kink. Mum closes her eyes. She loves me playing with her hair, though I'm not particularly good at styling and she doesn't really care what it looks like anyway. Becca's much better, of course, especially now she's finished her training. Auntie Rach wanted her to go to university and become a teacher, but Becca dreams of her own salon with gleaming surfaces and a galaxy of spotlights in the ceiling. 'You're not the boss of my brain cells, Mother!' she always says. 'I can use them how I like!'

I stick a row of kirby-grips into my mouth, spitting them out when Mum says, 'I know you're not keen on Nick.'

As I try to protest, she studies my expression in the mirror. 'It's okay, love.' She reaches back to put her cool hand over mine. 'It must be hard for you, having a man around after all these years of just the two of us.'

I shrug and blush, trying to focus on holding all her wild hair on top of her head. Strands break free, spill down to her neck. I notice again how narrow her back and shoulders seem.

'I haven't had a relationship since your dad left, have I? So I know it must feel strange.'

I'm squirming now. I don't like it when she talks about my dad – or lack of – at the best of times. Now she's using the word 'relationship', sinking my hopes that Toyboy Nick's a temporary blip in our lives. I wrestle a bobble around the thick ponytail and catch her reflected gaze.

'Will you make an effort to be nice?' she asks. 'For me?'

'I *am* making an effort.'

'More of one? I really need you to get along.' She smiles into the mirror, the crack bisecting her face, but something in her eyes sends a shiver through my body. For a split-second she doesn't look like herself. The light skating off the mirror carves hollows into her pale cheeks.

She forces her smile a little wider. 'You're my two favourite people, after all.'

My hand jerks and the ponytail collapses. So he's level with me now in her heart. I feel like she's thrown back her elbow into my stomach.

After she's gone I drift around the flat, watching dark-winged birds gather on our tiny balcony, then flap away over the city. Becca phones and gives me the latest from that side of our small family, the Derby clan. She asks how things are with us, and I can't even bring myself to tell her what Mum said about Nick. It's lodged in my chest, like a pain I can't quite shake, can't quite understand.

When Mum gets home, easing off her shoes and massaging her blisters, she announces that Nick's coming up and we're going to have Chinese. Takeaway would normally be a high-light of the month, but I find myself acting all negative, asking if we can afford it and claiming to be on a diet. She says Nick's treating us, and that I need to go on a diet about as much as Mrs Chalmers from 307 needs more cats. I try to laugh, try to show some enthusiasm for the menu that Nick arrives brandishing.

'Have whatever you want, girls,' he keeps saying. 'Spring rolls? Chips?' He's got his wallet out, waving it around in his huge hand, though we haven't actually phoned in the order yet. And even when he's talking to me he stands close to Mum, like they're invisibly handcuffed together. She looks small beside him. He makes suggestions about what she could order and she shrugs along with every one, as if making her own decisions is too much effort.

When the food arrives, I have to admit it smells incredible. Shiny red sauces and sticky battered chicken and fluffy egg-fried rice. Mum seems pleased to see me shovelling it down, as though enjoying the meal Nick's paid for is the same as liking him. With the glow of food in my belly, and the drop of cider Mum lets me have, I begin to soften. A couple of times I accidentally laugh at his jokes.

My smile dies when I notice that Mum's hardly eaten. Nick keeps looking at her plate too: 'Not hungry, babe?' I wonder if he's annoyed she's hardly touching the banquet. Mum says she's got a stomach-ache and he suggests she just have some plain rice, so she chews slowly while Nick watches every mouthful. I feel my own appetite nose-dive.

After tea I offer to do the dishes because I always do them on a Saturday; Mum usually dries. Tonight, though, Nick grabs a towel and orders Mum to put her feet up. She glances uncertainly between us. 'Well . . . I am a bit knackered . . .' Still she's hesitating, I wonder if she thinks I'm going to drop the friendliness as soon as she's out of the way. I long to do the dishes with her instead, hip to hip at the sink, slipping into a familiar washing–drying rhythm.

Nick makes a shooing gesture, and she relents. 'If you insist, then . . .' She leaves the room and I hear the TV crackle on as I plunge our plates into the lemony suds.

For a while the only sounds are the clink of crockery and the slosh of water, Nick humming something repetitive and tuneless. We're rarely alone together. The itchiness creeps over me, same as when I watch him cup his palm around the back of Mum's neck. I try to relax, try to recall the funny thing he said that almost made me choke on my black bean pork.

'You don't need to worry about your mum, you know.'

A cup slithers out of my grip and splashes back into the water.

'She's still not quite recovered from that bug she had,' he adds. 'That's all.'

I frown over at him. 'What bug?'

'She was under the weather last week.'

'I . . . I didn't know anything about it.'

'Well, she knows you worry about her. She probably didn't want to make a big deal of it. But that's why she seems a bit tired.'

I squeak my cloth around the inside of the glass, trying to cast my mind back.

'I'm just saying,' Nick continues, leaning on the edge of the draining-board, 'you shouldn't worry. Because I'm around now. I'm here to make sure you're both okay.'

Sourness floods my mouth, like a reflux from all the rich food. I yank the plug out of the sink, watching the murky water slip away.

★　　★　　★

Once all our mismatched dishes are dry, Nick goes through to the living room and I stay in the kitchen, staring out of the small window. The view makes me feel suspended in the black sky. Only if I move right forward and lean over the sink can I see the twinkle of the city below.

Mum and Nick talk in low voices in the living room. I shuffle closer to the wall but can't hear what they're saying, so I slip out of the kitchen and sneak up on them. They're standing now, though, sliding open the door to the tiny balcony. I hang back to watch them step through and light cigarettes, the glowing ends floating like fireflies. And I feel a twinge of satisfaction when I realise Nick's leaning on the spot where the birds always splatter their white goo.

Then I see him grab my mum's arm. See her step back, shaking her head. He moves closer, gesticulating, while she turns her face away. I stand watching the shadow-puppet theatre of their argument, a screen of stars behind them, and I feel that reflux again, that acid searing up into my throat.

Two days later I'm whirling about getting ready for school and Mum's racing around getting ready for work. The flat feels extra tight in the mornings. We're both disorganised, in a hurry. We keep colliding.

I know it's not the right moment to bring it up, but Nick's been here all weekend so this is the first time I've managed to get Mum on her own. As she's flinging things into her handbag, I ask, 'Were you ill last week?'

'What?' She's checking she's got her cigarettes and the shabby umbrella she carries everywhere.

'Nick said you had a bug, but I didn't know.'

'Nothing to know, really. Got your PE kit?'

'Yeah, I can't find my new shorts, though. The blue ones are too small . . .' I bend over to riffle through the washing-machine, discovering the newer shorts scrunched up inside, still damp.

Mum's face falls. 'I'm sorry, love, I completely forgot to empty it yesterday.'

I stuff them into my bag anyway, hoping they'll dry before second lesson. Then I glance sidelong at Mum, who's shaking her head, cross with herself. 'Nick said you're out of sorts because of being ill,' I venture.

She snaps alert, turning back to her own handbag, which has fallen onto its side and is spitting out loose change. 'I'm not out of sorts. I'm fine.'

She reaches to get her tea flask down from the shelf, and that's when I see it. I'm frozen as her Post Office shirt rides up, exposing her lower back. There's a shiny, plum-coloured bruise rippling across its width.

II

Chris

On Saturday morning Chris opened his door to two police officers, fluorescent against the rain-soaked steps leading down to his flat.

He'd been sure it would be them as soon as he'd heard the brisk trill of his doorbell while he'd been failing to eat a slice of toast. He'd just sat there at first, swirling patterns in the cremated crumbs, until he'd heard Vicky moving around in their bedroom and had leaped up to beat her to the door.

'Mr Watson?'

'Last time I checked.' He found himself speaking in the jovial tone he used for plumbers and electricians, which disguised his discomfort at being a home-owner, a bona-fide member of suburbia. Somehow, he always felt as though he was faking.

He tensed when Vicky's voice sailed from the rear of the flat: 'Who is it?'

'One moment . . .' he said to the police, abandoning them on his doorstep and hurrying back down their hall. 'Just a student!' he called to Vicky, once he was out of the officers' earshot.

He hoped that would appease her, but she appeared in the doorway of their bedroom. Chris put a hand on her shoulder to stop her getting any further. She looked startled – he'd grabbed her too hard. He loosened his hold and tried to smile. 'What shift are you on today?'

'You never remember.' At one time she would have said this affectionately, but now it came out toneless. 'I'm just doing eight till one to cover a gap. Should be back for lunch at Di's. I'll meet you there.'

She checked the watch clipped to the front of her tunic, and Chris remembered how it used to amuse him, for some reason, even though he knew it was part of a standard nurse's uniform. A fob watch seemed so stuffy and old-fashioned, so un-Vicky. Lots of things about her nurse's kit used to strike him as funny. The Bristol Stool Chart she often carried around with her, not least.

Glancing past her, he saw three new glossy magazines heaped up on their bed. Vicky wasn't a celebrity-gossip kind of woman, but she had a thing about snipping pictures out of magazines, keeping them in the drawer of her dressing-table, like tokens. He'd asked her about it once and she'd got defensive, saying he wouldn't understand.

Maybe he would, though, if she gave him a chance. When had they stopped acknowledging the things that had first drawn them together? The confidences they'd whispered as they'd squashed into her single bed in her grotty student halls, giggling and clinging to one another as they'd wriggled around trying to get comfy.

Fifteen years later they owned a flat with a Surrey postcode (admittedly one in need of a lot of work), Vicky had made senior nurse, and he had his own (not exactly thriving) business. Yet it felt like they had so much less. Sometimes he grew nostalgic for that lumpy single bed, for the stains on the ceiling that they would discuss as if they were constellations.

'Isn't your student waiting?'

Vicky was already walking back towards her dressing-table. He watched her squirt a blob of eczema lotion into her palms and wind her hands around and around each other, the ritual absorbing all of her attention. She was so introspective, these days, that she hadn't yet realised their teenage neighbour was missing. Thirty-six hours now. And Chris hadn't brought it up, hadn't wanted to make a thing of the fact that he'd taken her for a lesson on the day she'd vanished. With luck he could keep the police on their doorstep, keep the visit brief.

He steeled himself to go back out. The sick feeling that had kept him awake most of the night squirmed again. The police were murmuring to one another, peering at the upper flats, but when he returned to the door their focus snapped back to him.

'Would you come down to the station, Mr Watson? We need to ask you a few questions about your neighbour and student, Freya Harlow.'

The station. Chris hadn't been expecting that. They gestured up towards their car, which shimmered with drizzle behind the Harlows' his-and-hers BMWs. Chris silently fetched his coat. Outside, the street was quiet but the woman with the twins emerged from the large house opposite, gawping at him as she threw nappies into her wheelie-bin, and a wooden blind twitched in a bay window further down. He hoped Steph and Paul weren't staring down from their flat – he didn't dare lift his chin to see.

As he walked past his own car, he glanced inside. His eyes rested briefly on the glovebox before he followed the police onwards.

They insisted he wasn't being interrogated. But the marooned desk in the stark white interview room didn't exactly say 'cosy chat'. The woman and the man sitting opposite were not the two officers who'd come to collect him. They wore black suits and introduced themselves as Detective Ford and Detective Johnson. Ford had quick feline eyes and a prominent collarbone, like something trapped beneath her skin. Johnson was fresh-faced, handsome, but there was a petulant downturn to his mouth.

'How well do you know Freya Harlow?' Ford began.

Chris could feel himself slipping into a familiar mode. Censoring his words before he said them. He did it with Vicky, these days, he realised unhappily. Skirted around certain topics, no longer told her everything that was on his mind.

'I've been her instructor for six months,' he said. 'And her neighbour for a year and a bit.'

'Are you friendly? The two of you?'

Chris shifted in his chair. 'How d'you mean?'

'What do you talk about during your lessons?'

'Mainly her driving. As you'd expect.'

'Your last lesson with her was the day before yesterday.' Ford looked directly at him. 'The day Freya disappeared.'

She left a pause as if for his response. But she hadn't phrased it as a question. Chris was aware of breathing a little too heavily. He nodded, and she wrote something down even though he hadn't said a word.

'Did anything unusual happen?'

'Not that I recall.'

'Where did you drop her off?'

'Back at school. It was her lunch hour.'

'Did you see her walk in?'

Chris paused, picturing Freya's long stride, buoyant even when she was walking slowly, as though she was consciously charging each step with pent-up energy. 'Maybe not right in. But I saw her go up the drive.'

'Towards the main school? Or the separate sixth-form drive?'

All his saliva seemed to have deserted him. 'Um, the sixth form, I think. Could I get a glass of water?'

Johnson left the room. Alone with the woman detective, Chris felt her stare drilling into him. He shifted again in the narrow plastic seat. When Johnson returned, Chris gulped the water too fast and felt even more nauseous.

'How well do you know Freya's parents?' Ford resumed.

Chris thought of well-groomed Steph, with her polished smile, and sandy-haired Paul, who shouldered a huge leather gym bag at all times. He thought of how Steph would wave from the window if he and Freya were leaving for an evening lesson, how she'd often be watching from the same position when they returned, as if she hadn't moved in an hour.

Would the Harlows have told the detectives about the argument there'd been over Freya's lessons? Would it look bad if Chris didn't mention it? Would he even be able to talk about it without becoming hot with indignation?

He cleared his throat. 'Of course I see them around. Wouldn't say I know them well.'

He didn't add, *My wife and I used to call them the Wholesome Harlows when we first moved in. Or the Blond Brigade.* Chris didn't really see them like that any more, not since he'd started teaching Freya and everything had got so much more complicated.

Ford turned a page of her notebook. 'Who was your next student after Freya?'

He had tried to prepare himself for this one. Had thought about it on the way over, how important it was to answer nonchalantly. The reality was difficult, though, especially when his mouth was a vacuum.

'She was my last student of the day.'

Ford stalled, pen in hand. A change in atmosphere fell across the room like a shadow. 'Do you normally finish so early?'

'Depends who I've got booked in.'

'What did you do in the afternoon?'

'I went home, did some jobs.'

'Was anybody there with you?'

'No, my wife was at work.'

There was a loaded pause. Chris was sure he could smell himself now, smell his own anxiety.

'So you didn't see anybody else all afternoon?'

'Not until Vicky came home.'

'What time would that have been?'

'Around eleven p.m.'

Ford exchanged a flickering glance with Johnson, then made a note. She waited, scribbled something else, pursed her lips as if in thought.

Abruptly she leaned forward. 'Mr Watson.' Her tone was cool but something strummed his unease. 'Do you realise you were the last known person to see Freya?'

His face turned to rubber. 'Wasn't she at school in the afternoon?'

'We thought she was,' Johnson said, forcing Chris to shift his attention onto him. Was this how they were going to do it now? Turn-taking so Chris's head would swing from side to side? 'Freya had a free period after lunch and then psychology. The attendance records said she was there for psychology, but the teacher has since admitted he didn't take the register at the start of the class as he's supposed to. He filled it out from memory while the students were off doing research. He's not convinced Freya was actually there. It seems he wasn't exactly keeping tabs on his students while they did this "independent work". A lot of them have admitted the class is . . .' Johnson carved quote marks in the air '. . . "a total doss".'

'Sounds like you should be questioning this teacher,' Chris blasted back.

'We have done.' This was Ford again now. 'But since nobody can confirm Freya made it back from her lesson with *you* . . .' She let the sentence dangle.

Sweat gathered around Chris's neckline. For a disorienting second he felt a presence in the empty seat to his right. His feet pressed the floor as though he was braking.

'I dropped her off.' He peeled his collar from his skin. 'She walked up the drive. Maybe she doubled back, I don't know . . .'

'We'll need you to submit the exact route you drove with her that day. And your movements after you parted ways.'

'I don't know if I can remember the exact route.'

'You'll need to try.'

Ford stared at him for a few more moments. Chris tried not to shrink away from her eye contact as he wondered whether she had more to say. He sensed there was a question she hadn't asked, an angle she was saving. But she slammed her notebook shut.

'Thank you, Mr Watson. I'll ask somebody to take down those details before you leave. But if you think of anything else, please get in touch. Particularly any . . . *irregularities* from your lessons with Freya. Anything at all.'

He didn't like the way she teased out the syllables of 'irregularities'. It made him think of dodgy football managers or politicians under investigation. One of those euphemisms that meant somebody's net of secrets was about to unravel.

12

Paul

It was two days since he'd last seen his daughter. Since he'd said a hurried, distracted goodbye to her as he'd left for work on Thursday morning. Probably no more hurried or distracted than most weekdays, but still it pained him to think of it. He must've dropped a kiss on top of her head as she'd sat on the sofa with a bowl of milky Weetabix in one hand and her phone in the other. Had he wished her a good day at school? Done a subtle 'dad-check' of what was on the screen of her phone? He couldn't remember. Hadn't known, then, that he might need to.

Now he was sitting in her favourite sofa spot, unable to contemplate breakfast, staring at his phone. A reply to the message he'd sent during the sleepless early hours of this morning had just come through, making his heart quicken.

If Yvette was shocked to hear from him, she didn't say so. Her response was characteristically calm, and as concise as his original message had been.

Yes, we can meet, her text said. *Where and when?*

Paul glanced over at Steph, perched on the chair she'd drawn up to the living room window sometime in the last twenty-four hours and left in place, like a permanent lookout station. In her leggings, with her hair tied up, she looked painfully like Freya. Steph's ears stuck out the tiniest bit; normally she brushed her hair down over them, whereas Freya always had that life-of-its-own ponytail. Was that Freya's green scarf Steph had huddled around her neck, too?

He tilted his body so there was no chance Steph could see his phone. The action flooded him with guilt. He felt it widening even further, the gulf that had opened between them when he'd asked to speak to the police alone. It had grown when he'd left to visit Glover last night, and he'd been unable to close or even address it when he'd returned to find Steph printing endless MISSING posters with their daughter's face on.

As soon as possible? he typed. *Kingston Bridge?*

To his surprise and relief, Yvette came back instantly: *I can be there in half an hour.*

Did she already know about Freya? Or did she just realise that it must be important for him to contact her out of the blue?

Paul went to the bathroom, splashing cold water onto his face, shaking out his limbs, which had begun to prickle with nervous energy. Just the thought of seeing Yvette again was unscrewing things in his brain. Blocks that had been tightly, essentially, in place.

Returning to the living room, he said: 'I ... I'm going to pop out.'

Steph looked up, frowning. 'Where?'

'To look for Frey.'

'But *where?*'

He didn't answer. He reached for his trainers but the laces wouldn't tie: his fingers moved too fast for his brain.

'I'll come with you,' she said, standing.

He raised his head. 'No! No, you should stay here for when the family liaison officer comes.'

Steph gazed back at him through bloodshot eyes, pressing the scarf into her throat. Her cheekbones had already been sharpened by lack of sleep and food. He remembered the first time he'd ever seen her, almost twenty years ago: the curve of those cheekbones had stirred something in him, even though his head had been a dark, angry mess. He'd been going on a holiday that Glover had urged him to take, during the leave he would never return from. To break the exhausting cycle of his thoughts, Paul had struck up a conversation with the industrious woman serving drinks in the first-class lounge. He'd found himself observing her as he'd nursed a beer, watching her move expertly around the room, swerving chairs and tables without having to look. She had let him waylay her from her tasks, chatting to him with a touch of shyness but no obvious impatience. When he'd asked her about working in an airport she'd said it was like being in a bubble. That had appealed to Paul. He'd wanted to stay in the air-conditioned bubble of that lounge, pretending the rest of the world didn't exist.

Later, when she'd returned to her work, he'd heard her making an announcement about frequent-flyer cards over the tannoy. She'd paused halfway through, and when she'd resumed he'd detected suppressed laughter in her voice. Paul had spotted her through the door to the staffroom, holding the microphone to her grinning mouth while shaking her head at the colleague making her laugh. He'd felt he was glimpsing a different side to her and he'd smiled properly for the first time in months. Leaving his number on a napkin had just been part of the escapism. He'd never expected her to call, never expected to see her again, beyond that bubble.

He still loved it when Steph got the giggles and her usual composure would melt. Freya brought it out in her – they could lose it over something incomprehensible to anyone but the two of them, starting up again every time they caught one another's eye. His breath trapped in his throat as he thought about it now. When had been the last time?

'I'm supposed to just sit here?' Steph moved towards him.

'One of us should.'

'Tell me where you're going, Paul. Running away again. What the fuck's going on in your head?'

The word stalled him. She rarely swore, these days. They'd both tried to kick the habit when Freya was little because she'd been such a sponge, with a cheeky intuition for the naughty words. Paul had the urge to swear now, too, as ferociously as he could.

He put his hands on Steph's shoulders, moulding his fingers around their familiar shape. *You could tell her.* As the thought crossed his mind it was chased by dread. Steph seemed to change beneath his hands, her shoulders becoming thinner, her hair darker, those cheekbones warping into somebody else's. A different suffering mother desperate for answers. Paul reared away with an intake of breath.

'I'm sorry.' His hands tremored in mid-air. 'I don't even know what's in my head myself. I just need to get out, need to be doing *something*.'

She opened her mouth but any response seemed to evaporate. Paul walked quickly to the door, guilt tearing at his stomach.

'Paul,' he heard her say, but he thundered down the stairs.

Outside, every tree had his daughter's smile. Some of the neighbours had displayed the poster in their windows – Steph must've asked them to – and it was as if they'd imprisoned Freya in their tasteful living rooms. One poster had blown free from wherever it had been nailed and was pirouetting with new freedom down the road.

Paul battled an urge to chase it, dive on it. He yanked his eyes away as a taxi pulled up on the street and Chris Watson climbed out. Paul's jaw hardened. In the storm of everything else he'd almost forgotten about Watson, the last person to see Freya. Had he received his grilling from the police? The guy looked ruffled, yet somehow not ruffled enough. He walked to his door without acknowledging the posters of Freya, without seeming to notice her dad watching him all the way.

Paul thought about Steph's disagreement with Chris. How he'd seemed unwilling to enter Freya for her test even though she'd taken to driving as instinctively as she'd mastered catching and kicking a ball. How the school had fucked up the register and the CCTV had proven useless and there was a great blank space in the middle of Freya's afternoon.

He was so close to stalking Watson to his door: *What do you know about my daughter?* But still one thought roared louder than the rest, dragging his attention onwards.

Two missing girls, then and now.

As he strode along the Thames path, propelled by that ever-increasing nervous energy, Paul felt Freya bounding beside him. Doing the side-stepping thing she would do when she was in the mood to jog-and-chat, her hands shadow-boxing, eyes dancing. He'd long ago accepted that he and Freya didn't have quite the same brand of closeness as Steph and she had. Maybe it was an entrenched mother-daughter thing, or maybe because he was naturally more reticent, but Steph tended to be the confidante, the tear-drier, and Paul had to admit he left those things to her. But he had always been the one Freya wanted to race, or shoot penalties against, or compete with on the diving board during her swimming phase when they used to call her Flipper. She'd reawakened elements of him that had been diluted since he'd left the police: competitiveness, energy, drive. He needed to revive those qualities again now, and he prayed she was using them, too, that they were fighting their way back to one another.

He saw Yvette before she saw him. She was on the bridge, staring down at the water, the wind toying with the hem of her long red coat. Her hair was shorter than it used to be, with glimmers of grey. She still emitted an aura of calm – did all psychotherapists have that? Even the stretch of river flowing beneath her gaze seemed more tranquil than the fast-flowing bend further ahead. Paul's heartbeat settled into a less frenetic rhythm. Surely Yvette would be able to help him. And he certainly wouldn't resist her help, the way he had when he'd first been ordered to start seeing her as part of the police's 'duty of care'.

He thought of her therapy room with the beech tree outside and the window always fractionally open. The books about PTSD that filled her shelves; her patience as Paul had sat for long, silent stretches, finally beginning to cooperate near the end of each session. Nobody else knew so much about him. Not even Steph and Freya, who'd been like new limbs and a new heart after everything that had happened before.

Now he felt like one of his limbs had been hacked off as punishment for thinking he deserved to live normally again.

Yvette turned at the sound of his footsteps, and Paul realised she wasn't as calm as she'd first appeared. Her lined, worried eyes made his heart fire up again.

'Paul,' she said. 'What's happened? DI Glover called me yesterday and asked whether I'd heard from you. He wouldn't say why. Then I got your text. Something's wrong, isn't it?'

The wind whipped at her coat and she held onto its lapels. An old instinct made Paul follow her hands with his eyes. Many times she'd asked him to focus on their rhythmic, deliberate motion while she'd teased out his most troubling thoughts. Eye movement desensitisation therapy, they called it.

Now, as her hands disappeared into her pockets, the fears that had been piling up inside him tumbled out: 'You always told me I had to forgive myself. But what if Sanderson never forgave me? What if he's just been biding his time? Waiting to take everything from me . . . like he thinks I did from him?'

'Slow down, Paul. What's been taken?'

'My daughter. Freya. The one I sent you a picture of when she was a few weeks old.'

That was the last time he'd contacted Yvette before today. He'd sent her the photo eighteen months after he'd finished therapy, as a way of showing her he was doing okay. She'd sent him a note back – he still had it – saying Freya looked a perfect little livewire, her eyes already wide open, curious, alert.

Realisation appeared to be dawning in Yvette's face. Perhaps she'd heard something in the news but not made the connection with Paul. Perhaps half noticed a poster on the way here but not looked closely, not expected it to be the girl whose baby photo she'd once smiled over, thinking that one of her patients had found his happy ending.

13

Emma

'What do you mean, fallen through?' Emma roamed around her living room with her phone at her ear, banging into the boxes of stock that she still hadn't got used to having in her way.

'I'm afraid the buyers have changed their mind,' her estate agent told her, in a tone that made Emma feel as if he blamed her. Maybe she'd deterred her shop's buyers by being too openly sad about the sale. Perhaps she should've smiled graciously and wished them luck, rather than showing them round with a how-dare-you-buy-my-life sullenness. After all, it wasn't their fault. It was nobody's fault, as her mum kept reminding her. So why did she feel so furious?

'They decided to go another way,' the agent added.

'What does that even mean?'

'A different property, I assume.'

They were taking their second-hand electrics elsewhere. Probably to a place with cheaper overheads and higher footfall. Emma had never liked the idea of her shop being filled with rewired TVs, but she needed the money from the sale. Needed it to pay the rent on her flat and settle invoices while she searched for a job. To keep her afloat, in control, for when Zeb came home and everything would be okay.

She managed not to swear until she'd hung up. Then she flung her phone across the room, where it landed in a box of 1920s jewellery and sank into its glittery depths. Suddenly Emma felt suffocated, felt heat coming off the leather handbags lined up along every skirting board.

It took her a moment to realise her phone was ringing again. Its vibration sounded metallic against the brooches and hair-pins inside the box. She dug in her hand, praying the buyers had had a drastic change of heart within the last thirty seconds.

But it wasn't her estate agent.

'Zeb!'

She tried to tame her enthusiasm as she stabbed at the screen. There was no reply. A rustling came down the line.

'Zeb? Can you hear me?'

A buzz of voices now, faint and fragmented, and something like the clink of glass. Emma's spirits dived again. He'd clearly pocket-called her. Why did it sound like he was in a bar? *At eleven o'clock on a Saturday morning?*

'Hello?' Frustration rose through her. 'Zeb, are you there?'

There was a tinny echo on the line. She hung up and tried to call him back – once, twice, no answer – then sent a text: *Just want to know you're okay.*

She watched as the *delivered* notification appeared, but not the *read*. With a growl she deliberately aimed for the box of jewellery this time, torpedoing her phone to the bottom.

She needed to get out of the house. Pulling on her scruffy running gear (how did the joggers around here always manage to look so glamorous?), Emma stuck headphones into her ears, turned up her iPod, and escaped into the hallway.

'Oh!' She almost ran into two uniformed PCs just outside her door. 'Sorry.' She pulled the buds out of her ears, feeling disrespectful even for thinking of listening to a frivolous post-punk playlist when her neighbours were into their second day of hell.

'Emma Brighton?' the male PC with the earnest face asked.

She nodded, dropped her headphones, fumbled to scoop them up.

'Could we ask you a few questions?'

'Of course.' She stepped back inside and held the door for them. 'Please . . .'

They squinted around, as if wondering whether all her boxes were stuffed with knock-off DVDs. She'd spilled Gilbert's food earlier: seeds were crumbled on the carpet where the police stood in their regulation black shoes. The woman had auburn hair in a neat bun, the man a slightly gangly way of holding himself that reminded her of Zeb.

'You may be aware that your neighbour Freya Harlow is unfortunately missing.'

She swallowed. 'Yes. It's horrible. Have there been any . . .?'

'When did you last see her?'

'Erm, it would've been Thursday morning. I saw her out of my window, leaving for school.'

Her cheeks warmed at this half-confession of her interest in the Harlows. She hated the image of herself as a nosy neighbour or a bored spectator of others' lives. Was that what she'd become since her shop had closed, since Zeb had left?

'Did you notice anything out of the ordinary?'

Emma looked towards her window as if to recreate her last sighting of Freya. There she was in a navy Puffa jacket, ponytail flopping to one side as she paused to read something on her phone. Was Emma's memory tainted by the knowledge that Freya had vanished, or had the teenager really seemed subdued? Had she hunched her shoulders as she'd studied her phone?

She recalled now that Steph had come out of the house, calling after her daughter. Freya had looked irritated, shoving her phone into her pocket as she'd spun around. Steph had handed her what looked like a couple of twenties, and touched Freya's arm before she'd left. Did Steph remember that casual see-you-later touch? Had she been replaying it endlessly? Perhaps convincing herself, as Emma was now, that Freya hadn't responded, had maybe even shrugged her off.

'I guess I've seen her happier,' Emma said.

'Was she upset?'

'No, no. She just wasn't as full of beans as she sometimes seems.'

'Have you noticed other changes in her recently?'

'I don't really know her.'

'But you did notice she was less ... "full of beans" on Thursday?' The PC said it like Emma had coined the phrase.

'It was just an observation. I only saw her for a moment. And I ... I wouldn't like to say what's normal behaviour for her.'

But Freya's demeanour that morning *had* snagged her attention, even if she was only properly registering it now. Mainly because Freya's carefree bounciness had been a source of amazement to her for a while. Her own experience of being a teenager had been so different, so bogged down by self-consciousness and insecurity.

'What about her parents?'

Emma blinked. 'What about them?'

'Any observations about Mr or Mrs Harlow?'

She seemed to have been cast in the role of observer. But even before Freya's disappearance, hadn't her impressions of her neighbours often changed with her moods? Mostly their family life had appeared golden, but on her more bitter days, which she was ashamed to think of now, she'd been able to persuade herself it was all a front.

'They're going through something unimaginable,' she said. 'I've never even heard them argue before.'

The woman looked at her keenly. 'Does that mean you have since?'

'A – a few raised voices. Understandable in the circumstances.'

The man made a note and Emma felt uneasy again. Had she said too much, too little? Would any of this help Freya? Sometimes, lately, she feared she'd lost the ability to make the right judgements. She'd begun to question her own instincts, on everything from the decision to sell her shop to the wording of her texts to Zeb.

And the silent calls to her landline. She couldn't even trust her instincts on those. The first had come a few days ago, then another while Steph had been there last night and a third a few hours later, around 1 a.m. She'd been able to hear whispery breathing each time, painting her skin with goose-bumps. But that didn't mean they were a genuine concern, worth dwelling on amid everything else. Did it?

'One last thing,' said the male officer. 'Your other neighbour, Chris Watson.' He gestured downwards. 'Did you happen to notice whether he was at home on Thursday afternoon? Whether his car was here?'

Emma frowned at the change in focus. She conjured a mental picture of Chris, whom she'd had only a little interaction with since moving into the building. Approximately early forties . . . wife was a nurse . . . That was all she could muster. He and Vicky seemed to keep a low profile on the street, aside from Chris's branded car and the self-printed fliers he sometimes posted through letterboxes.

Or maybe she'd just never paid much attention to them, even though they lived beneath her. Evidently it was only the Harlows she'd developed a fascination with as her own life had deflated.

The police were waiting, pens poised.

'I can't remember,' she said. 'I'm sorry, I didn't notice if he was home or not. Is he . . . involved?'

'We're just asking about people who know Freya.'

Emma had so many more questions, but the PCs were preparing to go. They cast a final swift glance around, then subtly wiped their feet on her mat, perhaps to dislodge the hamster food wedged in their soles.

★　　★　　★

After they'd gone, she rescued her phone from the swamp of brooches, even more anxious than before for a reply from Zeb. There was nothing on the screen except a vicious-looking scratch. Emma slid her finger up and down it, her thoughts tumbling with Freya and Steph and Paul and Chris Watson and Zeb. As her temples began to throb, she decided to take a walk instead of a run, still craving the outdoors but feeling slower, heavier, as if the police's questions had added extra weight to her small frame.

As soon as she left the house she was confronted by Freya's face, enlarged and replicated in high-gloss, high-res, full colour. Her eyes were unnaturally blue, the medal round her neck the brightest gold, the flush to her cheeks the shade of strawberries. The effect was overwhelming, unavoidably reminiscent of the shiny, sporty girls Emma had half idolised and half hated at school. And the words shouting below that smile: HAVE YOU SEEN FREYA?

Emma suspected the police wouldn't have stretched their resources to these ultra-quality posters. She imagined Steph labouring all night after leaving Emma's flat, her printer in overdrive. *I could've done that*, she thought. *That's one thing I could've done.*

Her gaze flickered to Chris Watson's car. Its monochrome driving-school logo was like the antithesis of the vibrant posters. Emma dipped her head and hurried on.

Freya's image turned the corner with her, continued to punctuate her route until she smelt the river and felt guiltily glad to escape the teenager's dazzling gaze. The river path was one of the things Emma loved about living here. The rainbow of moored, swaying narrowboats; the pub gardens with fairy lights threaded into their fences; the German restaurant with outdoor benches and strong beer, where she'd been for lunch with Zeb and her parents a few times. But today the gloom of the sky was reflected in the water, the whole scene a rolling wash of grey.

She walked as far as Kingston Bridge, where she'd once seen a MO WILL YOU MARRY ME? banner hanging from the railings. She remembered how she'd grinned, imagining the story behind it, the unknown Mo's reaction . . . but as she approached the bridge today, she stopped dead.

Paul Harlow was in the middle of it, talking to a woman in a red coat. The pair stood a small distance apart, their backs to Emma, staring downriver. They could have been mistaken for strangers who happened to have stopped in the same spot, but she could tell by the angle of their heads and the movement of their bodies that they were talking. As Emma watched, their conversation grew more animated. The woman reached for Paul's arm but he yanked away and stormed off towards the opposite bank.

The woman stayed on the bridge. She leaned both palms on the pale stone barrier, watching Paul go. Then her head turned to stare down at the water and her shoulders shook as if she was crying.

All the way home, Emma pondered what she'd seen. Was the woman connected to Freya? Did Steph know about the meeting, which had seemed so emotionally charged? Emma thought of the shouting from last night, the smashing glass. And the evening before that: Steph at the bottom of the stairs and Paul's shadow stretching down towards her.

She didn't know what to make of any of it.

As she let herself into the house, she peered up at the Harlows' windows, then down at Chris's, seeing no movement in either. Her pulse hopped when she pushed the main door and it hit something on the other side . . . some*one*, in fact. Steph was standing behind it, reaching into the mail basket attached to the reverse of their letterbox. She drew back, holding a small white parcel.

'Steph,' Emma said.

Her neighbour's face was ashen, emerging out of the loop of a green scarf. Emma tried to compose herself to ask, *Are you okay, any news, what did the school say?* but stalled as her neighbour dug her hand into the envelope she was clutching, and pulled out a hardback book.

'Did you order this?' Steph asked.

Emma was taken aback by her urgent tone. 'Erm . . . no.'

'It isn't yours?'

Emma squinted at the title. Confusion made the words blur a little. *How to Be a Better Parent.* The cover showed a woman in a yellow dress and a boy in his early teens, facing each other in opposite armchairs, the woman leaning towards the boy, as if listening earnestly.

'I don't think so,' she said.

'It came through the door, but it isn't addressed to anybody . . .' Steph's eyes glazed as though her thoughts were galloping. Emma glanced at the book again, a flame of anxiety igniting in the back of her mind.

She hadn't ordered it. That much was true. So why was it making her feel so strange?

Steph opened it, and gasped as orange liquid dripped out of its middle. Emma jerked back, clapping a hand over her mouth. The rest of a crushed raw egg slopped out of the book's pages and spread in a sticky puddle at Steph's feet.

'What the *hell*?' Emma said, into her palm.

The sight of the egg sliming their hall floor, some still leaking from the book in Steph's hands, brought back a sickening memory from years before. Steph was like a statue, holding the book open, staring at the blobs of yolk and fragments of shell clinging to its pages.

'I don't . . .' Steph's voice was soft and hoarse. 'What does this mean?'

'I have no idea.' Emma wondered whether her neighbour could tell her heart was booming, paranoia creeping up around her neck. *There's no reason this would be aimed at you,* she told herself. *The Harlows are the victims here.*

'Our doorstep was egged two weeks ago,' Steph said.

Emma snapped to attention. 'Really? I never saw that.'

'I didn't think anything of it at the time.' Steph's voice was shaking now. 'I assumed it was a random prank so I cleaned it up straight away and forgot about it. But now . . . This can't be a coincidence, surely. And this book . . .' She slapped it shut and stared at the title. 'Maybe it's trying to tell us something. That this is our fault.' She closed her eyes, dropping her chin as if something had landed on her shoulders. 'Oh, God,' she whispered.

'Maybe it's just some nasty stranger stirring up trouble.'

Steph opened her eyes. Her pupils were huge. 'I have to call Paul. And our family liaison officer.'

Emma nodded. She wasn't sorry that Steph now seemed eager to wrap up the conversation: her insides were still churning. Neither was she sorry when her neighbour suggested they didn't disturb the egg in case the police needed to examine it.

She was lightheaded as she watched Steph run up the stairs clutching the soiled parenting book. The door to the upper flat slammed. Emma found herself checking her hair and clothes, even though the egg hadn't touched her. She hurried into her flat and washed her hands until they were scarlet.

14

Kate

Twenty-five years earlier

The tower block seems to sway towards me. Clouds scud overhead and I gaze at the aerial on its very top, pointing into the sky, until I'm too close and it vanishes. As I drop my eyes they home in on a familiar denim jacket. Nick is pacing back and forth on the litter-strewn grass verge outside the main entrance. He's started appearing at ours earlier and earlier, so I've been pushing myself to get home sooner, but it's never enough.

Why's he smoking out here instead of on our balcony, or his own? He's stomping over the brown grass, flattening the weeds, tapping his cigarette so ash flies away on the wind. I'm sure he sees me but he acts like he doesn't, staring towards the road as if watching or waiting for something.

I wish I could lock the main door behind me, keep him out of the entire block. By the time I've dashed up the stairs, sweat is leaking in tentacles down my back. I dump my rucksack and shout for Mum.

She doesn't answer. She's not in the kitchen. There are two un-drunk mugs of tea on the table. I burst into her room and find her lying on her side on her bed, scrunched up like one of the pale blind puppies Auntie Rach's dog gave birth to.

'Mum?' I'm out of breath. 'Are you okay?'

Her eyes are red-rimmed, face white as flour, dark hair spread across the pillow. 'Hello, love.'

'What's wrong?' I perch on the edge of her bed, wanting to yank up her work shirt to check for more bruises.

She eases herself into a sitting position, cautiously as if everything aches. 'I'm just knackered. Long day.'

'Why's Nick outside?'

'He's on his way to the shop. We're out of milk, toilet roll . . . basically everything. I've been a bit useless. Thank God for Nick, eh?'

I can't bring myself to agree. *Thank God for Nick.* 'Have you two argued?'

'Course not. I just needed a lie-down and he offered to pop out. Now, are you going to make some tea?'

'You haven't drunk the ones out there.'

She adjusts her position and there it is again, the wince of pain, but she forces chirpiness into her voice. 'I'd forgotten about those. Better make some fresh, eh?'

Reluctantly I go back to the kitchen. As the kettle boils I hear next door's kids squealing, and Mrs Begum watching a game show on the other side, the volume so high her speakers become a death rattle. Outside the window a plane draws its frothy trail across the sky and I wonder about the people on board, who they are and where they're escaping to.

I can't find the mug that Mum likes her tea in, the purple one with the daffodils on that I bought her for Mother's Day. It makes me cross, frustrated. Nothing's going right, nothing's as it should be. I give up and use her second favourite, but when I chuck away the teabags I catch sight of a glinting purple shard inside the bin. I reach my hand in deep. Carefully I dig out smashed pieces of crockery, painted yellow petals: Mum's favourite mug, broken.

The kettle peaks and falls silent. Still staring at the rubbish, I tune back into the noises in our own flat. Mum moving around her room, opening her wardrobe, the rustle of clothes. She's getting changed. This is my chance. I drop the shards back into the bin and tiptoe to the slightly open door of her bedroom. And though I feel weird about spying, I put my eye to the gap.

Ever since I saw that bruise I've been frantic. Watching her. Watching him. The way she sometimes flinches when he touches her, the way he pulls back and they both look at me. At school, as it gets to the time he usually finishes work in the big BT office on the industrial estate, I can't concentrate for thinking about what might be happening at home. Even in English class, which I usually don't ever want to end, all I'm doing is waiting for the bell, trying not to feel sad that I'm disappointing my favourite teacher with my distraction.

I do my best to minimise the time they have alone together. It's hard to stop them going out to the pub or spending the night at his flat, though. I feel out of control if they disappear off there, even though it's just downstairs, and when Mum comes back her movements seem even more slow-motion. I've tried pretending to be ill so she'll stay, and sometimes she looks like she might, but then he appears, asking if she's ready, drawing her away.

We need a bit of time to ourselves, Kate, she'll say, tucking my hair behind my ear. *You'll be okay for a few hours, won't you? Put a film on? I'm just downstairs, love.*

I sit there watching reruns of cheesy old sitcoms, wishing he'd picked somebody else's mum in this block of flats to ask out. Why mine? Why us? And why did she say yes to that first drink, then to another, when we were happy as we were? Before long it was dinners at our place, his bare feet in the mornings and his razor next to the sink.

Two nights ago, when Becca rang, all my fears about him came pouring out. For a while there was silence at the other end of the line. Then an uncertain little snort: 'Your mum wouldn't stand for that!' But she hasn't seen Mum lately, doesn't know how she's changed. I told her it could happen to anyone, and if she could feel the atmosphere ... When I started crying I think it shocked her into taking me seriously. 'I'm sorry, Kay-Kay,' she said. 'How 'bout I come stay with you next week? I need a break from this bloody job-hunting, anyway ... It's all right, Kate, everything will be all right.' I felt better, then. Becca's eighteen, older than me. Those two years somehow give her more power to fight this with.

Mum is standing in her underwear, leaning against her wardrobe in a moment of private stillness. And I can see that nothing I've tried to do over the last fortnight has been enough. There are bruises on her stomach, her legs, her arms. Some are yellow-green, like islands of mould, others fresh and dark, like stains of red wine. I clap a hand to my mouth and stumble back. Behind me the front door opens, and I turn to watch Nick's tall silhouette eclipsing our hall.

15

Chris

How well do you know Freya Harlow?

Are you friendly? The two of you?

Since nobody can confirm she made it back from her lesson with you . . .

Chris stood in his hall, staring blankly at the hideous floral wallpaper they hadn't got round to stripping and repainting in some acceptable neutral shade. His eyes traced peach petals and lime-green leaves as he replayed his interview with the police from a few hours before. He began to feel woozy. The peeled-off edges of the wallpaper revealed crumbling plaster beneath.

He jumped out of his skin when his phone rang.

But it wasn't the police calling back. It was Tamsin Spence, who lived at number 82 on the street and whose daughter Chris also taught. He cleared his throat and tried to switch into business mode, stuttering out his name as he answered.

'I'm afraid I'm going to have to cancel Lily's session with you on Tuesday,' Tamsin said shrilly.

Chris swallowed. 'Oh . . .' He did his best to keep a grip on his professionalism. 'Do you want to reschedule?'

Tamsin muttered something about getting back to him and the line went dead. Chris blinked at his phone, reeling from her abruptness, unease curling in his gut. Had word already got around that he'd been whisked away by a police car earlier?

Vicky's voice startled him again: 'Who was that?'

He turned to see her standing behind him in her work tunic and a baggy cardigan. Her short hair was styled differently from earlier. It looked nice, but at some point in recent years he'd lost the knack of telling her so. She was clutching a half-knitted scarf. What was with the knitting lately? Who was going to wear all these scratchy-looking scarves?

'A student,' he said. 'Why aren't you at work?'

'I forgot my ID card. Had to pop back in my break.'

Had she heard anything about Freya? Surely she'd noticed the posters that Chris hadn't been able to look at as he'd arrived home from the police station in a taxi. Vicky's face was so expressionless these days. Sometimes when she was lying on the sofa watching TV he'd become genuinely afraid she wasn't breathing. He found himself thinking often about the Vicky he'd first met. Fun-loving, witty, acerbic. She could open beer bottles with her teeth; at parties people used to hand their San Miguels straight to her. He'd been flattered when, after a few encounters at the parties of mutual friends, she'd made it obvious she liked him. And it had been gratifying to discover her more vulnerable side: the idea that someone like her might want or even *need* someone like him.

'I thought *you* had lessons all morning?' she said.

There was a silence in which they both seemed to register that neither had expected to bump into the other.

'Just grabbing a coffee.' He nodded at the orange wool dangling like a dead creature in her hands: 'What are you knitting?'

He didn't catch her answer because his eye was drawn to something sparkly on her wrist. A silver bracelet with white gems and tiny pearls. Not her usual style. Not the kind of thing she'd ever buy for herself.

He was still staring at it after she'd finished speaking. She tugged down her sleeve and walked away into the kitchen.

Chris followed. He knew he had to be careful with his words, his tone, but it was hard not to grab her arm and yell.

'New bracelet?' he said casually.

She had opened a cupboard and was gazing at rows of jars and tins. She swivelled a couple so their labels faced her and Chris heard the bracelet slide along her arm.

'Di gave it to me.'

'Oh, right.'

'I should take it off before I go back on shift.' He saw how she couldn't help touching it, couldn't resist a quick look before she smoothed her sleeve back down.

'Real diamonds?'

She snorted. 'Di's not made of money. More so than we are, for sure, but not *diamond* level.'

With a small dissatisfied noise, she closed the cupboard she'd been peering into and opened the next one along, contemplating a pack of biscuits. Chris didn't know what she was searching for, what she wanted but apparently hadn't found.

As he turned to leave, she said, 'Did you know the girl from next door's missing?'

Chris wheeled back to face her. She was looking at him, her posture and eyes suddenly alert, like a different person. He nodded.

'I feel awful now,' she said. 'For calling them those names when we first moved in.'

'We didn't mean anything by it.'

We were just developing our in-jokes, he wanted to add, *back when we still had them. Back when we used them to cling together if we felt like fishes out of water.*

He *did* have lessons booked for the rest of the morning – Saturday was always busy – and there was nothing to do but forge on with his routine. The sense of a street made of eyes was more oppressive than ever as he left the house for the second time. Still he couldn't look up at the Harlows' even for an instant. He ducked his head into his car like a celebrity – or a criminal – avoiding the press.

Something made him flip open the glovebox and check it yet again, reaching his hand to the back and patting his way around the carpeted emptiness. He sat back and fastened his seatbelt but the jitters wouldn't settle. This car used to feel like a haven. His domain, where he was in charge, the expert. He'd liked being alone in it, listening to nostalgic soft rock and swigging coffee from his travel cup, but he'd also liked the ebb and flow of students, the way he could allow them in for prescribed blocks of time. Recently, though, he'd felt trapped if he spent too long sitting there, felt like he was running out of air.

His mind returned to his conversation with Vicky, the bracelet glinting from her wrist. It was possible her sister *had* given it to her. Chris knew he shouldn't ring Di and ask, but the compulsion to do so was taking root. He needed to get to his next appointment, find a distraction. He'd see Di later at the weekly lunch. Maybe he'd—

He sat bolt upright. A navy Puffa jacket was moving towards him along the street.

Seconds later his vision adjusted, but his heart still charged. Red hair not blonde, scurrying steps not long, athletic strides.

Jess, not Freya.

And, in fact, the coat was black rather than navy, different from Freya's now that he saw it properly.

Jess spotted him and faltered. Struggling to recover, Chris lowered his window. She stopped but he noticed she didn't come too close, which made him feel grubby, tainted.

'You okay?' he asked her.

She shook her head, her eyes filling.

'Sorry,' he said. 'Stupid question.'

'I've come to talk to Steph.'

She looked younger than usual and Chris realised she was wearing no make-up. There was a childishness about the way she was standing too, with toes pointed inwards, hands clutching opposite elbows. He felt a sudden sharp twist of sorrow. 'Has there been any news?' he asked.

Her chin thrust out. 'I thought *you*'d know more than me. Judging by what the police have said.'

Chris flinched as if she'd spat through his window. Not for the first time, he wondered how much Freya had told Jess about him. Her eyes were wide with accusation, but she couldn't seem to keep them trained on his face. Lines marred her forehead; the overall effect was more confused than confrontational.

'Jess . . . I don't know what the police have been implying. Of course they'll be checking out my story, testing other possibilities – that's their job. But as far as I knew she'd gone back to school after our lesson. I *really* thought she had.'

There was a silence. Recycled air blew from his dashboard heaters. Jess didn't seem to know what to think. Her lip had started to tremble.

'Seriously.' He leaned forward. 'I wish I knew more. Wish I could help.'

She let out a sigh that inflated her bare cheeks. 'Fuck, this is all so weird. Sorry for the language.'

'You don't have to apologise.'

He smiled at her and she eventually smiled back through her tears, her body language softening. Chris found himself wanting to keep the conversation going, wanting to secure her as an ally, pathetic as that was. Why should her opinion matter? Yet somehow it did.

She wound a rope of hair around her fingers and glanced towards Steph and Paul's flat. Chris finally dared to look too, squinting at the upstairs sash windows with their heavy taupe-coloured drapes. The sun flashed and he thought he saw a pale face between the curtains, the whip of a blonde ponytail, but as he caught his breath it was gone.

He took in the Harlows' immaculate paintwork, noticeably brighter than his own, the house seeming to wither as the eye travelled down. Anger swept him, like a flare of heat. It was old resentment rolled in with something new, a kind of outrage with a ball of fear at its centre. Steph and Paul had everything and they'd never appeared grateful. And they didn't know their daughter, any more than she knew them. They'd accused him of milking them for money, when really it had been Freya who'd wanted more sessions . . . *It came from her . . .*

'Oh, before I forget.' Jess broke his thoughts, holding a crumple of cash towards him. He had a memory-surge of Freya doing the same: those banknotes with her mum's little car drawings in the corners.

'What's that?' He stared at Jess's offering, sliding his hands beneath his thighs to flatten their trembling.

'For yesterday's lesson. I didn't pay you.'

He shook his head. 'Don't be silly. We didn't really have a lesson in the end.'

She shrugged and put it away. 'Thanks, Chris,' she said, and he felt an unexpected flood of affection. Perhaps a displaced feeling, perhaps a reaction to hearing his name said without hostility.

Jess leaped back as the house's main door opened. Chris felt his own body jolt, the seatbelt snapping tight around his neck.

Blue-haired Emma emerged, rather than one of the Harlows. His breath gushed out and the belt slackened. But he could see that Jess was rattled to have been caught talking to him, even by Emma. Was he already the enemy?

Jess fled without saying goodbye. Emma's gaze lingered on him as she held the door for Jess, then got into her own car. When Chris caught movement again in the Harlows' window, he started his engine. Freya's frozen image watched from every tree as he accelerated away.

16

Steph

Freya's old one-eyed teddy was number eight. Her multi-coloured psychology revision notes – left halfway through a sentence – were number twelve. A half-full bottle of her favourite Lacoste perfume was seventeen.

The police had re-examined her attic room, leaving small numbered labels on everything, even the towels in her en-suite. Now that she was allowed to touch things again, Steph inhaled the perfume, pressed her face into the teddy, thumbed through the train tickets on the white-painted desk. Maybe there would be something nobody had yet spotted, something whose significance only she would recognise. Or maybe just by touching these things she could pull Freya back into reach.

She wished she could lay out her thoughts around the room and number them, too, to have any chance of making sense of them. Paul wasn't back, wasn't answering her messages. Even when he was here his mind was blatantly elsewhere, his face frighteningly shuttered. In his absence, the police had come to look at the smashed egg and had seized *How to Be a Better Parent* for testing. But not before Steph had caught glimpses of its advice.

Be open and honest with your child.

Give them explicit permission to lay the worst at your door; let them know that nothing they might want to talk about is off limits.

Don't avoid topics just because they're difficult.

Every word had felt like a wagging finger. *But we used to talk*, Steph had wanted to whisper back to the pages. *She used to tell me things.*

She'd seen nothing that said parents had to be limitlessly honest with their children in return. Or with each other. But her brain had pencilled it between the lines.

A visit from Jess, just after the police, had only heightened her guilt. Jess had swung from insisting she would've known if Freya had been upset or in danger to bursting into tears and suggesting that Freya *had* been different lately. She'd thrown around words like *moody, distracted, hyper, secretive* without seeming to realise they were making Steph's head spin, her heart hurt.

Now Steph rippled her fingers over the spines of Freya's books. Freya was known for her sportiness, but there was a bookish side to her, which Steph treasured. She'd given her the Ursula K. Le Guin novels she'd adored when she was a teenager, and hoped her daughter would be captivated by them too – hoped so much, in fact, that she hadn't yet asked her about them, just in case she wasn't. The shelves were mainly devoted to Agatha Christie and Sherlock Holmes: Freya had long had a thing for detective fiction. But it was a dog-eared Harry Potter that currently lay next to her bed, bringing a lump to Steph's throat. She knew Freya reread Potter whenever she needed comfort, and used the soothing murmur of the audio books to lull herself to sleep.

I keep thinking about the last time I watched her play volley-ball, Jess had said. *She was amazing as always, but . . . she seemed kind of livid. Every time she punched the ball I actually winced!* But Steph had been at that match, too. She hadn't seen Freya as angry, only determined, powerful. She and Paul had cheered rather than winced. Were they deluded?

She hasn't even seemed that excited about our uni applications recently, Jess had also flung into the mix. Steph had bitten back her protest: *Course she's excited!* Because what if Steph was the one who'd actually been excited, at the idea of Freya doing what she hadn't? The numerous prospectuses she'd ordered for her daughter were cowering at the back of Freya's desk drawer, seemingly untouched. Perhaps Steph had requested far too many. Perhaps she'd ignored the fact that Freya had hardly reacted each time she'd presented her with a new one.

Perhaps she'd ignored a lot of things.

Her hands moved faster now. Opening drawers, lifting lids off boxes, flipping pillows. She caught sight of herself in Freya's mirror: bent over, burrowing, desperate. Surrounded by the drooping heads of the daffodils she'd bought Freya last week. Watched by the photos Blu-tacked to the wardrobe: groups of friends at sleepovers and bowling alleys; Jess's dog, which Freya doted on; Steph, Freya and Paul on their American road trip two summers ago, the marbled colours of the Grand Canyon rippling behind them.

Buried underneath, to Steph's surprise, was one of her and Paul's wedding photos. The picture Freya used to giggle at when she was little, when she'd had a fascination with her mum's long lace veil and her dad's dated haircut. So this was where it had got to.

The door buzzer broke her thoughts. Steph dropped the wedding photo into her pocket and rushed to the living-room window to see out. Before even checking who'd buzzed, her eyes snapped to the empty space on the street where Chris Watson's car was usually parked.

What do you think of him? she'd asked Jess. *Did Freya like him? Do you think he's telling the truth about her going back to school?*

Jess had seemed to grow even more muddled, her cheeks flushing, eyes widening, then scrunching. *I guess I like him ... I don't know ... I think Freya liked him okay ...* She'd crumpled again into tears and Steph had found herself hugging her, trying to pretend she was Freya but she wasn't, nothing like, and she'd had to pull away before resentment had overwhelmed her.

Her gaze shifted to take in Paul's parents waiting on the pavement. Heather's lips moved incessantly; Brian spun his watch around and around his wrist. Steph felt a blast of love, as she always did when she saw them, especially because she had no living parents of her own. But today she wasn't sure she could cope with their emotions as well as hers.

She took a breath and went to let them in. The hallway smelt of bleach where the egg had now been cleaned away. Steph's stomach flipped at the memory of it slithering from the book. She thought again of their egged doorstep a fortnight ago, before she'd had any reason to pay it much notice, before the line between meaningless and sinister had become blurred. Other things had started to niggle at her, too, like those three rotten banana skins impaled on their railings about three weeks before. Was it a pattern, or were these just things that happened all the time?

As soon as she opened the exterior door, Heather was upon her. She wrapped her solid arms around Steph in such a heartfelt way that she felt something break inside. *Please don't be nice to me, don't be too motherly.* Brian hovered behind, always more restrained. Like Paul, he was an ex-policeman, and often struck Steph as an older, less complex version of his son. But perhaps she was being unfair with the latter part of that judgement. He kissed Steph's cheek and clasped her hands with such gravity that again Steph almost crumbled.

A confused thought flashed through her mind: *Frey will be disappointed to have missed them.* She regressed in age when her grandparents visited, let them ply her with ginger cake and call her by pet names she'd long outgrown.

'Oh, Steph,' Heather kept saying, tears slipping out of her eyes as if she was no longer aware of them.

Upstairs, her in-laws gazed bemusedly around them. The flat did feel alien without Freya in it, even though her leggings were still on the radiator and her Ugg boots were in a heap next to the sofa where Steph had repeatedly asked her not to leave them.

'Where's Paul?' Brian asked.

'He's gone out.'

Heather looked at her. 'Where?'

'I'm . . . not sure.'

'Oh . . .' Heather blinked behind her owlish glasses. Steph had never seen her look so lost. She was an ex-social worker, gutsy and level-headed. She sat down and immediately stood up again, the wire frames sliding along her nose. 'What have the police said? What are they doing to find our Freya?'

It was an ordeal to talk them through everything, to relay facts that felt as if they were about someone else's daughter, neighbours, family. Steph watched Brian for a reaction when she mentioned the police's questions about whether she or Paul had enemies. He started twisting his watch around his wrist again, its strap catching on his dark hairs. There was an odd expression on his face, glazed yet intense, reminding her of Paul when he disappeared into himself.

You know something, she thought, with sudden conviction. *Not about Freya, perhaps, but about your son. Do you know something I don't?*

The three of them sat in the living room and each took up a task. Steph pored through her address book for anyone she hadn't yet thought of who might have heard from Freya. Heather did the same, with her wider circle of family and friends. Brian had a long phone conversation with their family liaison officer, then reverted to detective mode, making a timeline of the day Freya had last been seen. Another back-to-front thought occurred to Steph: Freya would have loved to help him with this. Writing down clues, following a trail, solving a puzzle. She used to say she wanted to be a detective when she grew up, until she'd got older and had seemed to pick up on her dad's reluctance to talk about his police career.

So much for no topic being off-limits, Steph thought again, the parenting book's words still vivid in her mind.

As soon as Heather left the room to make some calls, she turned to her father-in-law.

'Brian, why did Paul leave the police force?'

He looked startled.

'I . . . Well, I thought you . . .' His fingers plucked at the knees of his once-smart trousers, his hands just like Paul's. 'Why do you ask?'

He seemed to mean, *Why do you ask* now?

Steph didn't answer. Let her question float between them. She remembered it had taken months to get to know Paul when they'd first met. To peel back the layers of him. There had been so much he wasn't allowed to tell her about his job, about why he was on indefinite leave from the force and seeing a therapist once a week. But back then she'd become convinced she'd found the real soft core of him. She hadn't cared about anything else. Perhaps the idea of a fresh start, no looking back, had appealed to her too.

Yet on certain nights, when they'd made love, or lain facing each other in a moonlight-striped bed, she hadn't been able to escape the feeling that Paul was reliving something in his mind. They'd spoken tentatively about previous relationships and Paul had always claimed, 'Nothing serious, not until you.' But she'd begun to suspect that there *had* been something, and that it had been serious in ways she hardly wanted to imagine. How it connected to his police career, she didn't know. She hadn't wanted to push it, and at some point it had become too late and too difficult to ask.

They'd moved forward nonetheless, and they'd been happy, especially when Freya had come along in all her distracting, demanding glory. Paul was a besotted dad, and Steph had felt safe and blessed. She'd stopped sensing the past like a third party in their marriage. Freya had become their third party instead. Freya had become everything.

At the same time, though, a particular question had begun to plague her – and still did – whenever she saw a veil return to Paul's eyes or noticed him twitching restlessly, unable to just sit in peace with his wife and daughter. She could never ask this question, for too many reasons. But it came at her now and again, as did the answer she thought she knew, which she was so afraid of.

The question she'd asked her father-in-law should have been easier.

'Did something specific happen?' Steph persisted. 'He never talks about it. And he seems to think . . .' The words jammed in her throat. 'It's like he thinks it's connected . . .' She gestured at the Freya timeline surrounded by Brian's notes.

Her father-in-law stared at what he'd written as if he didn't recognise it. He lowered his head and plaited his fingers, and if Steph hadn't known him better she might have thought he was praying.

She pressed her hands over his. 'Please, Brian. Tell me what you know.'

His head lifted. 'There's only one thing I know for sure, Steph. Before his final assignment with the force, Paul was hardly scared of anything. He thought all things were reversible, mendable. He broke his ankle when he was young but it healed and he was straight back on the football pitch. His first girlfriend gave him the elbow when he was eighteen but he got over it and he was off to university, his next adventure. Life seemed to slide right off him. Freya's the same, isn't she?'

Steph's eyes burned. She couldn't entirely agree. Things affected Freya more deeply than people realised. She didn't correct Brian, though: this was the most she'd ever heard him talk – about his son, about anything.

'Even in his early career, he didn't let the cases get to him,' Brian continued. 'But then he got picked for that operation . . . We didn't see him for *three years*, Steph. Couldn't even phone him. We were told that if we ever happened to pass him on the street, we should ignore him, in case we blew his cover—'

'Hang on.' Steph stared at him. 'His cover?'

Brian's eyes met hers. He blinked twice. 'Well . . . yes.'

Slowly, his words sank in. Steph felt as if she'd been punched in the stomach, felt heat flaming in her cheeks. The humiliation of not knowing this major thing about her own husband. Her picture of Paul shifting yet again.

'He was undercover?' she said.

Brian looked stricken now, clearly realising the information had come as a shock.

'I'm sorry, love,' he said. 'I assumed . . .'

'It's not your fault. Of course you'd assume I knew. Paul should've told me!'

Brian rubbed at his temples. Steph pulled Freya's scarf across her chest as though to help her feel less exposed. Why hadn't Paul ever said anything? She couldn't get her head around the implications, the questions. What had he been investigating? Where had he lived, and who with, who *as*? For *three years*. Not long before he'd met her.

'These kinds of operations tend to be highly confidential,' Brian said. 'Perhaps he thought it was safer to say nothing at all.'

Steph didn't respond. A chunk of her husband's life had just been made unfathomable. Even more so than before. And what did this mean for Freya? Were unfathomably bad people involved, too?

'I don't know the details of the operation,' Brian stumbled on, as if he felt he had something to repair. 'Only that when he came back he was changed. More serious, cautious, quiet. Then you came along, love, you and Freya ... and brought him back. But, still, I think he's spent the whole time feeling like he doesn't deserve you. Worrying that something will take you away from him.'

Steph let her tears spill. 'What if Freya *has* been taken away from us?'

Brian leaned forward. 'Then we'll fight every day and search every bloody place we can think of, and we'll bring her back.'

Steph hid her face inside the scarf. Suddenly the search seemed bigger than she could handle, the fight far beyond her. Freya and Paul were receding from her at alarming speed, their fingertips slipping from her grasp.

17

Kate

Twenty-five years earlier

Becca is here. Her hair products line the sides of the bath in their blackberry-coloured bottles and her heavy, glossy copies of *Vogue* cascade across the floor of my room. She is a different Becca from the one I saw at Christmas. Sleeker and sharper. Her hair is in a shining bob, shorter at the back than at the front, veering up the sides of her head. She has smoky eyes and vampish lips and she stares at headshots of models, her fingers snipping the air as she imagines how to recreate their hairstyles. Straight away she wants to give me a trim to cheer me up, and I try not to take it personally as she plans a style that will 'liven up my look'.

There are remnants of the old Becca, though. She still loves banana milk at breakfast, despite pretending to 'prefer a black coffee, these days'. She sleeps rolled up in a sleeping-bag next to my bed and we whisper into the night like we used to when we were young. Becca talks about her ambitions and urges me to get some of my own, something more concrete than just wanting to write stories, use words. Best of all, her presence seems to keep Nick away. I'm starting to wonder if Mum's told him not to come up while she's here. Maybe she thinks my cousin's shrewder than me, will work things out. But then he reappears.

Us three girls are sitting round the kitchen table, a sunset glow filtering through the blinds. Becca's trying to persuade Mum to let her remodel her hair into a 'layered bob, very now', and Mum's poured us each a small glass of wine. The atmosphere has brightened in our flat these last few days, and I've let myself get swept up in it, my worries beginning to shrink. When I hear him opening the front door, the dark shadow returns.

'I'm guessing that's Nick rather than a burglar,' Becca says, as we listen to clattering from the hall.

'You can meet him at last,' Mum says shrilly. 'I bet you were starting to think I'd made him up!'

'Your toyboy's the talk of the family in Derby.' Becca grins and I wish she'd stop – wish she wouldn't talk about Nick in such a flippant way.

He walks into the kitchen, the collar of his denim jacket turned up around his ears, and as usual goes straight to Mum's side, gathering her hair between his hands as though he can tell Becca was only just entertaining plans to chop it off. Then he turns to Becca with a slow smile. 'So, you're the brainy rebel of the family, by all accounts.'

'My reputation precedes me.' Becca's laugh seems genuine and her eyes linger on Nick.

I see her continuing to appraise him as they shake hands. My stomach bends with anxiety. I don't want her to be taken in by him, don't want her to like him even for a second.

He raises the plastic bag he's brought. 'I got some champers to celebrate Becca being here.'

Becca hoots and Mum's expression lifts a little. Nick makes a big show of popping the cork so it cannons across the room. We haven't even finished the cheap bottle of wine that Mum bought specially from the corner shop, but he floods our glasses with champagne instead.

The bubbles catch in my throat. Becca and Mum seem giddy after only a few sips – Becca especially. Nick starts to tell a story about buying the champagne. He uses the phrase 'wine merchant' and Becca creases up, Mum smiling too.

'Wine merchant!' Becca clearly likes it even as she mocks it. 'That's an offie round these parts, right, Kate?'

I shrug, pinching the stem of my glass.

'Okay, I admit, it was a jumped-up offie.' Nick laughs along. He's playing with Mum's hair again, twirling it round his hand. I imagine him pulling hard, her neck snapping back.

I retreat to bed early but their gales of laughter carry through the wall. Becca starts advising Nick about haircuts, offering him a trim; I picture her fingers sliding over his scalp. Mum's voice seems to fade as the night stretches on. It's all Becca and Nick, Becca and Nick, hurling banter back and forth. When Becca finally comes to bed, I crush my face into my pillow and pretend to be asleep.

I wake disoriented in the night, my sheets twisted, a nightmare fading, along with a childish urge to cry out for my mum. After a few groggy moments I remember that Becca's asleep on my floor.

Except she isn't. The sky is black through my thin curtains, as black as it ever gets in this city, but Becca's sleeping-bag is empty.

Nick's got her, I think feverishly. He's charmed her, flattered her, made her think he wants to swap Mum for her.

I scramble out of bed and stand in the middle of my room. When I hear the gush of a tap, my shoulders release. Of course, she's gone to the toilet. I'm about to return to bed when I catch the sound of retching.

'Bec?' My voice is low as I creep to the bathroom. 'You okay?'

'Come in, Kate,' she whispers back.

I glance at the door to Mum's room, imagining Nick's body draped around hers, thinking of long-ago mornings when I used to fly in and launch myself onto her sleepy form, burrowing under the covers to snuggle against her warm back. Now a horrible feeling of shyness and exclusion prickles over me. I don't know who she is when she's with him. She doesn't seem to belong to me.

In the bathroom, Becca is crouched over the toilet. Chunks of pale sick float in the bottom of the bowl. The smell makes me stretch the collar of my pyjama top over my mouth and nose.

'Sorry,' she says. 'Gross, I know.'

'How much did you *drink*?'

'Not loads. But it doesn't mix too great with my tablets. Makes the side effects worse. Plus the meds turn me into a major lightweight.'

'Oh,' I say, remembering. 'Do they work?'

'They've had me on a few different combos. These seem to do the trick. Side effects are annoying, though.' She yawns widely. 'The drowsiness does my head in.'

I'm distracted now, recalling a steaming-hot afternoon five years ago, in Auntie Rach and Uncle Jack's back garden. When it happened, all the adults were inside drinking beers, pressing the fridge-cold bottles against their cheeks, Uncle Jack's records turned up loud.

Becca and I were outside playing catch. Seeing how long we could keep throwing the ball without it hitting the ground. I was never very good at it, Becca was always better, but we'd almost broken our own record this time. I remember the unnerving moment when I threw the ball to her and it landed at her feet because she was standing rigidly still. I giggled, thinking she was messing about, but then she tipped backwards onto the lawn and began to jerk. Eyes rolling. One arm smacking the ground. Lips tinged blue. I screamed for the grown-ups, and tried to stop her hurting herself by slipping my hand underneath her head. When I yelled again, one of the neighbours appeared over the fence. 'Call an ambulance!' I shouted to her. 'Please!'

Becca came round looking confused and sleepy. The paramedics said I'd done all the right things, and that my cousin was going to be fine. She'd be tested for epilepsy, treated if necessary. Later, all the adults praised me. They felt guilty for not being there, not hearing me as they'd chatted and danced just inside.

I guess Becca and I have been closer since that day, protective of one another. She often ruffles my hair and jokes that I saved her life, that she owes me, but it's not really true. I can still see it so clearly, though. The red ball we were playing with sits on the top shelf of my wardrobe. I don't know why I've kept it, why I get it out sometimes and roll it in my palms.

'Do you still have fits?' I ask her now.

'Haven't for a while. I'm hoping I've not just vommed out my latest dose.'

'You should be careful, Bec.'

She smiles at me. Liquid glistens around her mouth. 'All right, Nurse Anxious.'

She hauls herself up, splashes her face, uses her finger to rub toothpaste into her tongue. Her trendy hair is all matted and moist. She flushes the toilet, then flips down the lid and sits on it. 'You were right,' she whispers.

I perch on the edge of the bath. 'About what?'

'*Nick.*'

I look at her in surprise. 'I thought you were getting on with him.'

'He *is* charming.' Becca fiddles with her earlobe. 'And good-looking. I can see why your mum—'

'Urgh,' I break in. 'Don't.'

'Is that why you went to bed? Were you pissed off with me?'

I shrug, not wanting to admit how I'd thumped my pillow, almost cried into it with frustration.

'Oh, Kay-Kay, I forget how sensitive you are.' Becca pinches my cheek and I blush, flapping her away. 'I was just sounding him out,' she continues. 'And there's something . . . I don't know. The way he's always watching your mum.'

My annoyance evaporates. 'You noticed that too?'

'And when I went to the toilet, I came back to them stood by the kitchen window, whispering. As soon as they saw me, Nick gave your mum this look and they both shut right up.'

I nod urgently. She's on my side, after all, and I have to keep her there, have to make her see. 'They often stop talking when I come into the room.' My voice wobbles with the relief of having an ally. 'And her bruises . . .' Tears push into my eyes.

'Have you spoken to her about it?'

I shake my head. 'She won't talk to me like she used to.'

'You have to try. Or . . . I could, if you want?'

'You'd do that?'

Becca slides off the toilet and crawls over to where I'm sitting on the damp bath edge. She lays her head on my knee and hugs me around my middle. I can see the porcelain skin on the back of her neck where her hair rises to its shortest point.

'Don't worry, Nurse Anxious,' she says. 'We'll sort this.'

18

Chris

'More chicken, Chris?'

Di pushed the enormous bird his way, then seemed to notice his plate was still half full of meat and gravy-drowned mashed potato.

'Not hungry?' she asked, and her eyes narrowed – or did they? All afternoon he'd been looking for signs that Vicky's sisters were treating him abnormally, but he could wring meaning out of anything when he was feeling paranoid – a glance exchanged between Jane and Di, a casual question about what he'd been up to.

The first part of the meal had brimmed with discussion about Freya. Chris should have anticipated that she'd be the talking point of this week's lunch, should have come mentally prepared. Instead he'd been dumbstruck as Di's iPad had been passed round the table, the local news story on its screen, Freya's photo beneath a smear of fingerprints.

'It's awful,' Di had kept saying, her face stretched into a mournful expression, 'just awful.' Chris had bristled with anger. She didn't even know Freya. Why was she acting so upset? Whereas Jane, the younger sister, could barely hide her excitement at the fact that the missing girl was her sister's neighbour, her brother-in-law's student.

He'd been relieved when the others had picked up their cutlery and the iPad had been set aside. But now the spotlight was shining on his lack of appetite.

'Dieting?' Jane asked.

Chris's hand reflexed to his middle and he was dismayed, as ever, by the soft paunch that seemed to have developed almost overnight when he'd hit his late thirties. Along with the thinning patch on his crown, which he would wince at in unflattering photos or mirrors at the wrong angle. That was why he shaved his hair short, these days. Was it also why Vicky didn't seem to find him remotely attractive any more?

'I had a big helping,' he lied.

'Belly bigger than your eyes,' Di's six-year-old daughter, Polly, diagnosed.

'Other way round, Pol,' Di said, 'Eyes bigger than your belly.'

'Nobody's eyes are bigger than their belly. Not even Anna and Elsa's and they've got *huge* eyes . . .' Polly demonstrated by widening hers, fluttering her fingers on top of them like lashes.

'Anna and Elsa?' Chris said distractedly.

'From *Frozen*!' everybody else at the table replied, looking at him like he was an alien.

Di began pushing the chicken towards other people. Vicky took a whole leg and bit straight into it. She ate ravenously whenever they came here. Maybe it was a habit from childhood, the three sisters fighting over food at the dinner table. Di had done the cooking from a young age because their mum had rarely been up to it. Vicky still became emotional if she had to talk about the last meal they'd eaten together before they'd been placed with different foster families. She couldn't even look at macaroni cheese – as Chris had found out on their third date when he'd made it for her, oblivious to its significance, and had seen behind her tough façade for the first time.

He watched her now, chicken grease glistening on her lips, and felt a pang of affection. Maybe she sensed it because she actually smiled at him, then wiped her mouth with a napkin and laughed at her own table manners.

The moment was broken when Jane said, 'So what's she *like*, Chris?'

'Who?'

'The girl! Freya. You must've got to know her a bit, teaching her to drive?'

He trailed a finger in his cold gravy. 'Not really. There isn't much chit-chat during a lesson. I'm generally just trying to keep us both . . .' He caught himself before he said *alive*, and an uneasy silence fell.

'Her parents must be worried sick,' Jane said.

'Well, maybe they should've taken better care of her.' This was Di, suddenly indignant, aggravating Chris again, even though part of him wanted to agree.

'That's harsh, Di,' Vicky said. 'Horrible things can happen to anyone.'

There was another silence, a twang of tension, and Chris sensed their history swirling between them, sensed that they were half talking about their own parents now, and their different levels of forgiveness.

It was Di's husband, Gav, who defused things, scooping up plates and blathering about pudding. The man couldn't cope with serious conversation for longer than a few seconds. Chris was grateful to him tonight, though. The atmosphere adjusted with the clatter of crockery and a discussion about treacle sponge. He felt Vicky's eyes on him, but when he glanced up she wasn't looking at him at all: she was twisted away, talking to Jane.

Di never let anyone help her clear up after dinner. Chris hated the martyred air with which she retreated into the kitchen, washing every dish and putting them all away, loudly urging her guests to relax. The other sisters thought nothing of it: this had always been Di's role, Chief Grown-up, and now that she had the biggest house it seemed even more entrenched.

On his way back from the bathroom, Chris poked his head into the kitchen. He normally avoided asking Di if she needed any help, reluctant to offer her an extra chance to decline heroically, but tonight he had to talk to her.

'Want a coffee, Chris?' She began filling the kettle with her left hand, scouring a baking tray with her right.

'I'll make them.' Chris managed to wrestle the kettle from her, and got out the mugs, which had the same speckled pattern as his and Vicky's cups at home – Di had donated her spares. He decided to use this as a route into the conversation he wanted to have. After stumbling over a line about Di being generous, always giving things to others, he segued into 'That bracelet you gave Vicky is nice.'

Was there a pause? Did she clang a saucepan to buy herself time?

'Yeah, I thought it would suit her.'

He stared at Di's profile, bent over the sink. Her lips were pressed together, accentuating her overbite, and her dish-scrubbing had become more vigorous.

Chris didn't know what he'd hoped for. Of course Di would pick up on the need to cover for Vicky, even if the bracelet hadn't come from her. The three sisters had a shared radar for defending one another.

It doesn't suit her, he wanted to snarl. *Not at all.*

'Did you buy it for her, or was it yours?'

'I bought it.' Her brush scratched manically at the saucepan. 'Thought it might cheer her up a bit.'

'Cheer her up? Is she . . . Has she said something to you?'

'She's just seemed a bit down since switching wards, don't you think?'

'Switching wards?'

'Oh . . .' Di stopped her assault on the pan, her cheeks flushed. 'I thought you knew.'

'No, I—'

They were interrupted by Vicky walking into the kitchen. She looked from one to the other, seeming to detect an atmosphere. 'Everything okay?'

Di leaped in: 'Fine! Chris is kindly making coffee.'

Vicky arched an eyebrow. The post-dinner coffees used to be his regular role, back when he'd had the energy and inclination to insist. Chris wondered if Vicky was thinking of the day she'd first brought him round here, how anxious he'd been for acceptance, and how they'd kissed in the car afterwards, laughing about Chris calling Gav 'Garth' and Di interrogating him about his intentions.

Now Vicky glanced at her sister and at Chris again, before her face smoothed into that exasperating blankness.

'Which one's mine?' she asked, nodding towards the drinks.

Chris was relieved when Vicky suggested they head off. As usual there was a lengthy goodbye process, new conversations budding on the doorstop, Polly throwing a tantrum because she didn't want her aunties to leave. Chris waited on the pavement. He'd once asked Vicky whether she and her sisters found it hard to say goodbye because of being separated when they were young. She'd grinned, pecked his cheek, and said, 'Nah, we do it because it drives our husbands up the wall.'

As Polly began performing diversionary handstands, Chris gazed around the street as if to test whether this one, two miles from his own, gave him that same sense of being scrutinised. The house opposite had its curtains open, revealing a couple lounging at opposite ends of a sofa, reading different sections of the same newspaper, their feet entwined. With a stab of sadness, Chris turned away towards his car.

He froze when he clapped eyes on it.

There was a piece of paper on the windscreen, tucked beneath the wipers. A chill zipped down his spine. His eyes swept the street again, before settling on the note. It couldn't be . . .

Vicky appeared beside him. 'You all right?'

'I'm fine.' He walked on, tripping slightly on an uneven paving slab. Vicky pulled out her phone and seemed preoccupied, reading messages. Then she lifted her head and noticed the note. 'Oh, what's that?'

Chris snatched it before she could, and kept it out of her line of vision as he unfolded it.

He almost choked on a rush of outward breath. It was just a message from one of Di's fussy neighbours, asking 'whom it may concern' not to park in front of their house. Chris tore it in half, relief and irritation clashing together.

'There aren't any parking restrictions here, mate,' he mumbled, glancing at number 52. 'You don't own this spot.'

Vicky rolled her eyes – at Chris or at the neighbour, he wasn't sure – and prompted him to unlock the car.

As they drove home Chris felt shaken, hoping Vicky hadn't noticed his reaction. She turned up the radio but Chris turned it down again and she looked at him in surprise.

'Why didn't you tell me you'd moved wards?' he asked.

This was where a lot of their conversations seemed to happen: driving to and from places, each the captive audience of the other.

'Didn't I?'

'Don't play dumb, Vic. It doesn't suit you. When was it?'

'Three weeks ago.'

'Where are you now?'

'Cardiac outpatients.'

He glanced towards her, but she was staring out of her window. 'Did they make you move?'

'*No.*'

'Then why?'

'I fancied a change, okay?'

'Did something happen?'

'I said, no! Stop interrogating me.'

'I just wish you'd tell me stuff.'

She made a small sound through her nostrils.

'What was that?' he asked.

'What?'

'You made a noise. Like a nose-sigh.' In the past, his spontaneous invention of the term might have made them both chuckle, dissipating the tension.

'I'm just breathing,' she said. 'I assume that's allowed.'

She flicked the radio back up. Chris drove on auto-pilot, his mind whirring. How many times had he driven between Di's house and theirs? Past the florist where he'd bought Vicky tulips that one impulsive time; past the record shop where he'd once bumped into Paul Harlow and made painfully awkward small-talk. How would he feel if somebody told him he'd never do this journey again, that the routines he often bemoaned could vanish in a flash?

'Slow down, Chris,' Vicky said.

He realised how fast he was driving, his hands tight on the wheel. Yet he didn't slow. In fact, he swung around the next corner without braking, and Vicky lurched sideways. 'Chris, for fuck's sake.'

'Did something happen?' he repeated, his face hot. 'On the ward?'

'No! Aren't you listening?'

He accelerated again. He wanted to shake her up, *wake* her up. Then he caught sight of her stricken face, her fingers gripping the door handle, and felt a surge of shame. His throat filled with bile as she morphed for an instant into Freya. He thrust his foot onto the brake to slow the car right down.

'You don't tell me everything either,' Vicky said, once he'd been driving normally for a while.

'What are you talking about?'

'I don't keep nagging you about why you're so jumpy and weird lately,' she said, 'so don't nag me about what's going on at work.'

Chris let his hands slip to the base of the wheel. It was as if she was offering him a pact. Let's agree to keep secrets. Agree to pretend. He wondered how far such a deal could possibly stretch. What would it take to shock them both out of their denial?

19

Paul

Paul only realised how far he'd walked when the huge bulk of Richmond Hill loomed ahead. Checking his watch, he was shocked to find it was almost 2 p.m.: two hours had passed since he'd left Yvette on the bridge. He'd been striding aimlessly along the river, fighting to get his head straight, to figure out what to do next.

There were six messages from Steph on his phone, asking where he was. The final one said, *Your parents are here. Come home*.

Paul spun around, almost colliding with a woman on a bike, and ran back in the direction of Kingston.

Even the familiar sensation of wind streaming past his ears couldn't obliterate his guilt. He'd achieved nothing for Freya. He'd added to Steph's worry. And, on top of everything else, why had he lost his temper with Yvette? There had been a time when he'd considered her his only real friend. He knew it was in her job description, but she'd been the one person who'd actually seemed to get it. What it was like to be undercover, what it could cause you to do.

She'd cried as Paul had told her about Freya's disappearance. But, when it came down to it, he'd only been interested in whether she knew where Sanderson was. His emotions had got the better of him when she'd claimed Glover told her very little about cases or targets, past or present, only as much as she needed to counsel the undercovers. He had been particularly cagey about the Sanderson operation, she'd added, and though Paul knew that was true he'd still stormed away from her, reverting to anger and mistrust. The old paranoia had him in its clutches again: who was on his side? Who was *real*?

Do you think there's any chance Sanderson still lives in Nottingham? he'd pressed her. *Still on the same estate, even?*

Yvette had eyed him with concern. *You're not thinking of going there?*

Paul hadn't answered. He'd long ago promised himself he'd never go back.

As he ran past the boats and paddling swans that were the landscape of his current life, he couldn't help seeing the Chainwell Estate superimposed over it. Graffitied play-grounds, boarded-up pubs, vandalised bus stops. And the tower block that had been Paul's parallel universe for three years. His mind's eye dived through an upper-floor window, disturbing a flurry of memories. Mostly everyday domestic scenes, but always with something slightly amiss, a glance or a silence or an atmosphere.

Sanderson's oppressive presence. The sorrow that had weighed in the air.

Nathalie silhouetted in the kitchen window, biting her shredded nails.

Nathalie, Nathalie, Nathalie. If he allowed himself to think of her it was usually in fragments: green eyes, thin wrists, dark hair on a white pillow. But lately the dots had begun to join up, the gaps to infill . . .

It's been pulled down, Yvette had told him: the one piece of information she'd had. *The tower block. It was deemed unsafe. Nottingham City Council demolished it a few years ago.*

Paul had been ambushed by emotions, hearing that. Relief that he wouldn't have to go inside it ever again; exasperation at another dead end; a swell of unhappiness he didn't want to make sense of. He'd tried to destroy that place in his memory, and now he couldn't fight the idea that he'd somehow made it happen for real.

Yvette had suggested Freya's disappearance might be unconnected to his past. In a different way from how Tom Glover had phrased it, with different motives, Paul hoped – but still with no effect. The symmetry between then and now was beginning to consume him. Yet he was no closer to tracing his daughter, to making sure she never became one of the tragic unfound.

As soon as he got home, he smelt the Elizabeth Arden perfume his mum had worn for years, which Paul bought her unimaginatively every birthday. The scent was a burst of short-lived comfort. He could hear his parents' voices from the spare room – so familiar, and sounding upset – but he went first into the living room, looking for Steph.

It was empty. He stared at the papers scattered on the coffee-table. Lists of names and phone numbers with ticks or crosses next to them. An annotated timeline in his dad's writing: *7.50 left for school (Steph waved her off, gave driving lesson money); 8.45 met Zadie outside gates (normal); 1 p.m. driving lesson; 2 p.m. CW dropped her off (nobody saw); 2–3 p.m. free period (unclear whether anybody saw her); 3 p.m. maybe not in last lesson (register in doubt).* A flipbook of Freya's last-known movements seemed to whir across Paul's vision, tears pricking at his eyes.

He jolted when he heard a loud clatter above his head, followed by what sounded like Steph crying out. As he dashed to the attic stairs he heard other sounds, scuffling and creaking, seeming to come from Freya's bedroom.

'Steph?' he shouted. 'Is that you?'

His mum came out of the spare room, following him up the stairs. 'Paul, you're back! What's going on?'

Paul pushed the door to Freya's room. It wasn't unusual for

Steph to spend time there at the moment, among their daughter's things, but now she was leaning over Freya's bed frantically tearing off the sheets. Paul's stomach pitched when he saw that the bedlinen was soaked red. Steph panted as she stripped off two layers, the mattress below also stained crimson.

'What the hell?' Paul's voice emerged loud. 'Are you hurt?' He studied her for cuts or wounds, but could see only dots of red on her sleeve.

'No,' she said, 'Urgh, *stupid* me . . .'

Then he spotted the overturned tumbler on the bedside table. A glass of Freya's favourite cherry Lucozade had sat there since before she'd gone. Steph must have knocked it off, spilled it over the bed. She mopped with a balled-up sheet as tributaries of Lucozade trickled everywhere. Paul's mum righted the empty glass – a pointless gesture, really, but Paul wished he'd thought of it, instead of just standing, watching, his arms spread and empty.

'Here, let me, Steph,' he said.

'No, I'll do it,' she snapped, and dragged the bed away from the wall so she could wipe down the side.

As she did so, something dropped onto the floor.

'What's that?' Paul stepped forward and picked it up.

Both his mum and Steph paused, looking towards him, and he realised it was because he'd become totally still, frowning at what he'd found. It was a glossy strip of images taken in a photo booth. Freya was on the right of all four pictures, smiling, sticking out her tongue in the final one, but with something unfocused about her eyes. It took Paul a moment to identify the man with her. Arms slung round shoulders, the pair seemed pretty familiar with one another. In two of the shots, their cheeks touched.

'Who *is* that?' said his mum, while Steph stood in shocked silence beside him.

Paul grappled to put a name to the face. He hadn't really met him properly, hadn't seen him around for a while, but remembered he was called something unusual.

It was Emma's partner. The guy who lived downstairs with her, or used to at least.

Paul's skin grew hot. Why would Freya have this man's picture down the side of her bed?

PART TWO

20

Kate

Twenty-five years earlier

Our opportunity comes sooner than expected. I hear Nick telling Mum he's got a 'work thing' on Tuesday night so he probably won't be round. Becca says I should make myself scarce, let her handle things, so I tell Mum I'm going to a friend's house to work on a homework project after school. Part of me feels jealous that Mum might open up to Becca rather than me, but hope overrides it. This could be our only chance.

Actually, I don't have many friends at school. People don't want to partner with me because they think I'm a daydreamer: I melt into my own thoughts too often. They don't realise that when I'm one-to-one with somebody – like Becca, say – it's as if my 'on' switch has been pressed. Sometimes Becca and I laugh until we cry at pretty much nothing. And when we put our minds to it, like now, we can achieve things too.

I leave school and walk in the opposite direction to home, wandering through the area with all the colourful fabric shops, spicy smells, sari-clad women fluttering through the streets. Soon I'm crossing green fields rimmed by broken fences, the grass cool through my thin soles. When buildings loom in the distance, I realise I'm on the outskirts of the airport. A plane takes off on the horizon, silhouetted in the orangey twilight; another follows and I imagine them queued up, waiting to launch themselves into the sky.

I think about what might be happening back home, and cross my fingers tight. For a second I waver: *Can I trust her?* Becca's been so nice to Nick's face these last few days, but when he turns his back, her eyes are like steel. The switch is kind of unnerving. But I have to trust her. I *do* trust her. Aside from Mum, she's my best friend in the world.

The next plane seems to be heading a different way. As it rises I see both its wings, spanned as if to hug me, and I realise it's going to sweep right over my head. I feel the gust and hear the roar, and then I'm craning my neck as it cloaks me in its shadow. Just as I'm thinking that's the first time I've seen the belly of a plane, something crazy happens. There's a crackling noise and the sky seems to ripple, to churn. It's like there's an earthquake up above rather than on the ground, or like I'm inside one of those balls of electricity we experimented with in science. A sensible part of my brain tells me it must be turbulence, or the plane interfering with the atmosphere, or *something*. But another part thinks this is what the end of the world feels like.

Then, abruptly, it's over, like a storm that's passed so quickly you think you've imagined it, and calm settles, like a clean sheet.

When I get home I'm cold and tired, but my head sings with what I've seen. The way that plane tore up the sky, the way everything was normal again seconds later. How can the atmosphere stay intact if it gets thrown around like that every time a plane blasts through?

As soon as I walk into the flat, I realise something's changed the atmosphere in here, too. There's tension in the air. I backtrack through my memory: I'd been lost in thought approaching the tower block, but had I seen Nick's car parked outside? What if he came back unexpectedly and heard Becca talking to Mum about him? My breath quickens: why didn't I pay attention? *Daydreaming again, Kate.*

I look at the spot where he normally leaves his trainers. They aren't there. Hearing sounds from my room, I hurry through to see Becca aggressively rolling up her sleeping-bag. Her rucksack sits by her feet, bulging with clothes.

'Are you going?' I ask, with a spark of panic.

'No choice.' She tries to bully the sleeping-bag into its impossibly small cover but it keeps unravelling, won't be tamed.

'Why?'

'She didn't like my interfering.'

I blink at her. 'Mum's making you leave?'

'Fuck's sake ... How did this ever fit in here?' Becca punches the polyester while it balloons out the other side. 'I said we were worried about her. We thought she didn't seem herself ...'

'Did you mention the bruises?'

'I hinted. She went all pale and said she often bangs herself at work.'

'She only works in a post office!'

'I don't think she realises you've seen them all over her body.'

'What else did ...?' I trail off and glance behind me as I remember that Mum might be nearby.

'She's on the balcony,' Becca whispers.

I tiptoe to check she's still outside, and see her profile in the dark, framed by curls of smoke.

Back in my room, Becca's given up with the sleeping-bag and is sitting on my bed. When I sink down beside her she grabs my arm. 'We need to help her, Kate. I could see she wanted to tell me something, but it was like she was afraid. So instead she got mad, said I'd got a bloody cheek ...'

'Did you mention Nick?'

She flushes. 'I might've got a bit carried away there.'

'What d'you mean?'

'I wasn't going to push it, just ask if he was treating her right and hope she'd realise what I was getting at. But she wouldn't take the bait. She just clammed up. So I said I got bad vibes from Nick. I said he made me uncomfortable . . . I might've called him sleazy . . .'

'I thought you were going to be subtle, Bec!'

'I tried. But she was so fucking careful in what she was saying. She won't hear a bad word against him. And I just know it's because she's scared. I could see it in her face.'

The thought is unbearable. My brave mum who used to protect me from nightmares, from nasty kids in the playground, from monsters under the bed.

'You can't leave,' I say desperately. 'I'll talk to her.'

'She's mad with both of us.'

My heart plummets. I hate Mum being angry with me, hate when disappointment pulls at the corners of her mouth. I'll do or say almost anything to make her smile at me again.

'We'll apologise,' I say. 'We'll act like we didn't mean any of it and think of a new plan.'

Becca shrugs. 'Worth a shot.'

'I'll go to her now.'

I venture into the living room, looking through the smeary glass at my mum still outside, cigarette finished. She turns and our eyes lock. There it is: disappointment, anger. But something else, too. I feel those eyes are pleading with me.

She slides back the door and steps into the room, slow as a moonwalker.

'What's all this about, Kate? Honestly!' But it's like she's just playing the part of a stern mum, confident in her crossness. The hollow ring of her telling-off frightens me even more.

'I'm sorry, Mum. We obviously got the wrong end of the stick.'

'I've told you not to worry, Kate. I know things feel stressy round here sometimes, and me and Nick have the odd . . .' she pauses as if selecting the right phrase '. . . tiff. But you need to keep that imagination in check. And stop letting Becca encourage you.'

'It wasn't her fault. Please don't make her go.'

'She gets you all wound up. Puts these ideas in your head. I know you idolise her . . .' she glances at the wall, drops her voice '. . . but I don't think she's the best influence. She's going to cause trouble if she keeps saying . . . well, things that just shouldn't be said.'

'We made a mistake.'

Mum rests her hands on my upper arms. Her own arms are covered by her cardigan. I can't remember the last time she wore a short-sleeved top. 'I don't need you to rescue me or worry about me, Kay. That's the wrong way round! I want you to focus on school and your exams, make more friends . . .' Her fingers squeeze. 'I want you to have all the chances I never did. To get out of this place one day.'

I look down at my feet. My shoes are bobbled with clumps of wet grass. 'Just let Becca stay a bit longer. Please.'

Mum sighs and hoops me in her arms. 'I'll think about it. If you *promise* to drop all this.'

I creep my hands round her waist, wanting to cling on. If I hugged her for ever, he'd never be able to push his way between us.

'And one more thing,' she murmurs into my hair. 'One more promise you need to make.'

'What?'

'Don't . . .' Her arms tighten and her voice vibrates at the side of my head. 'Don't mention any of this to Nick. You mustn't . . . He'd be upset.'

I feel my heart swooping again, her muscles tensing as our hug stretches on.

'Promise me you won't accuse him of anything, Kate.'

Gently I flatten my palm against her back, listening for her stifled gasp of pain. She stiffens and I know the bruises are still there. I can sense them beneath her clothes, urging me not to give up.

21

Emma

Emma was sketching when they arrived, sitting in the chair that had somehow inched closer to her window in the last thirty-six hours and stayed there. She drew a hamster's wheel with blurred, in-motion spokes; a tortoiseshell hair clasp abandoned on a stair; Zeb's old trainers, which were still in the corner of the room, laces trailing . . .

When she heard footsteps descending from the Harlows', she paused. Her eyes rebounded to her pad and she was shocked to see that she'd also drawn the face of an alien-like girl, with wide eyes, trying to lure her back to the past. It was a kind of self-portrait. A version of herself that, until recently, she was sure she'd left behind.

She dropped her pencil. The footsteps had come to a halt outside her door. She heard two people murmuring to one another – Steph and a man with a Welsh accent, possibly the police officer Emma had heard around the building a lot lately. An older couple had also arrived yesterday; Emma had guessed from the resemblance that they were Paul's parents. She'd glimpsed them only briefly from her window, but their devastated faces had fed her insomnia for another night.

It didn't feel like a springtime Sunday. It was the third morning of Freya being gone.

Just before she answered the door, Emma remembered she had three strings of glass beads around her neck and an ostentatious ring on each finger. During the night she'd been sifting through her stock, fishing out things she'd managed to sell back to her suppliers, and had begun draping herself in her favourite pieces of jewellery as though to become a walking embodiment of her shop. Hastily she shed the necklaces, slipped off the rings before opening the door.

Steph was wearing the green scarf again, but unwound, its ends swinging. There was a wildness to her bloodshot eyes, while the man was neat and composed next to her. Emma had never thought *neat and composed* could ever be used in contrast to Steph. Her neighbour seemed about to speak but the man took over, introducing himself as George, the Harlows' family liaison officer.

'Could we come in?' he asked.

They'd hardly made it through the door before Steph spun towards Emma. 'Your partner . . . where is he?'

'My partner?'

'Boyfriend, husband . . .' Steph blinked with impatience. 'Doesn't he live here any more?'

'Steph,' George said, 'maybe we should all go and sit down.'

Steph ignored him. 'Do he and Freya know each other?'

'What?' Emma felt like she was in the wrong conversation, a misunderstanding she couldn't disentangle herself from because she couldn't quite get a footing in it.

Steph reached into the pocket of her cardigan and drew something out, shoving it at Emma.

It was a strip of photos. Emma's confusion bled into shock as she held it by its edges. *That's . . . But they . . .* She struggled to comprehend the series of snaps taken in a booth. Zeb. And Freya. Squashed together in the four square frames. Playful poses and drunken eyes.

Her heart started to thud.

Steph jabbed a finger at Zeb's face. 'Why's my daughter having photos taken with your partner?'

Emma's eyes slid up to meet her neighbour's. Her head was still fogged, heart still booming, but a tiny part of the puzzle was inching into place. 'Oh . . . no,' she said. 'Zeb's not my partner. He's my son.'

A surprised silence filled the room. Awkwardness shimmied up the back of Emma's neck. It wasn't in anticipation of the explanations she'd have to reel off, wasn't because she cared that Steph might gape at her as people often did, scandalised that she, with her petite stature and electric blue hair, could have a six-foot eighteen-year-old son. It was because it suddenly looked as if she'd kept Zeb a secret. Emma hadn't let on that she had what her neighbours feared to lose, if not in touching distance then at least within some kind of reach. It hadn't seemed appropriate, or kind, to bring it up in any of her recent conversations with Steph.

'I thought . . .' Steph's eyes moved around the room, clocking the photos of Zeb she obviously hadn't studied the last time she'd been there. Emma felt something expand from her chest as if to envelop all the pictures, all those reluctant, self-conscious, precious smiles.

'I had him when I was fifteen,' she said. 'He looks older than he is. And I guess I look younger . . . as long as you don't peer too closely.'

Steph drifted around, nudging framed photos, like somebody spoiling for a fight by prodding a rival in the shoulder. Emma wished she would stop, but how could she deny her anything, this woman whose child was even more lost than hers?

'I don't think you ever properly met him,' Emma tried to explain. 'He was at art college, and he worked in a comic-book store at the weekends, so he was out a lot. And now he's . . .' she hugged her elbows '. . . away.'

Steph spoke at last. 'How old?'

'Eighteen.'

Steph echoed the number, gazing at Emma's son who had been her whole life, really, since before she'd even grown up herself. They'd lived with her parents until he was thirteen; rented a house with a garden and a plum tree while the shop was doing well; swapped it for this flat when profits had started to fall. And then everything had seemed to go very wrong, very quickly, both with Zeb and her business, as if the two were as intrinsically connected as her heart and brain.

'I didn't realise,' Steph said. 'Didn't realise you were a mum, too.'

It was as if Emma had added to her neighbour's grief with this secret she'd barely been conscious of keeping. Then Steph seemed to snap out of it, whirling around and pointing again at the photo strip, which Emma was still holding. 'What was he *doing* with Freya?'

Emma's hackles rose at the way Steph said it. But jumbled with the instinct to defend her son was a flutter of nerves. She hadn't been aware that Zeb and Freya were friends, either. *More than friends?* They seemed such different teenagers: Freya social and sporty; Zeb more introverted, creative, obsessed with obscure bands and Marvel films.

'I've no idea,' she admitted.

George cleared his throat. 'Could you contact your son, Miss Brighton?'

'Yes,' Steph said, that wildness back in her eyes. 'Call him.'

Where was her phone? As Emma scanned the room she saw her sketchbook still open on the table. She prayed Steph wouldn't recognise her own hair clasp among the drawings. And the windows around the edges of the page – Emma couldn't stop sketching windows.

Spotting her phone on the sofa, she grabbed it and pulled up her recently dialled list, dominated by Zeb's name. After weeks of longing to talk to him, she wasn't sure she wanted him to answer this time, with Steph and George staring. Her mind raced as the phone rang: *Zeb and Freya? Zeb and Freya?*

'No answer,' she said, hanging up.

'Please keep trying him,' George said. 'Could you supply us with a phone number and current address for him too?'

Emma nodded, her palms moist as she tore out a page of her sketchbook to write them down. Steph's traumatised face made her maternal anxieties surge to the surface with renewed force. She should never have let Zeb go. Should have fought harder. *How to Be a Better Parent,* the book that had come through their door was called, with a mother and an adolescent boy on its cover. Emma had kept seeing that cover ever since, likening the boy to a younger Zeb, paranoia overtaking sense.

Did the book contain any advice that might have helped either Steph or herself hold on to their children?

Steph extended her hand and it took Emma a moment to realise she was asking for the photo strip back. For a second she felt territorial: it featured both their kids so why should Steph get to make demands? But she was being ridiculous: they were Freya's pictures. And perhaps they were evidence now. A shiver zipped through her. *Evidence of what?*

Left alone, Emma dialled Zeb's number three more times, anxiety soaring again when there was still no response. She sent him a text: *Need to speak to you, Z. It's urgent.*

To distract herself she turned to a clean page and began to sketch him. The velvet-haired baby; the rampaging toddler; the gangly adolescent with a mop of curly brown hair. She found it harder to sketch him as he was now. The nuances of his face kept eluding her: sometimes grinning and guileless, at others withdrawn, unfamiliar. She'd experienced something like grief even before he'd left, feeling him pulling away, their relationship fraying. That was why she'd caused such a scene outside her shop on the day he'd dropped his bombshell. She winced as she remembered half the street looking on, Zeb walking away shaking his head, like he was ashamed of her.

Her hand stilled as an image popped into her mind. A sketch, but not one of hers. She leaped up and went to Zeb's room, where the scent of Lynx and musty maleness lingered. She hadn't stored any stock there in case it jinxed his return. Some of his clothes still hung in the wardrobe, band T-shirts and black jeans: a reason to hope, or an indication he'd left in a hurry? Emma imagined Steph sitting in Freya's room, gazing at her things, her teenage life. The shock of finding unexpected photos.

She took Zeb's sketchbook from his drawer. The wellbeing officer at his college had suggested he use his love of drawing to help with his 'anger issues'. Emma still became dry-mouthed when she thought about that phrase, so at odds with the baby Zeb she'd been sketching. It was probably temporary, his tutors had told her. A response to stress, to becoming an adult. And didn't Emma know how hard that could be?

Zeb mostly used charcoal, giving his drawings a dark smokiness. Emma turned the crisp pages, drinking in the skilful pictures she'd studied many times in his absence. She flipped past a hand with fingers curling into a fist. A jacket caught on a bush, its sleeve torn, the shrub starred with flowers and thorns.

Eventually she reached what she was looking for today. The drawing was larger than the others, and he'd filled in the backdrop with dense strokes, so the figure in the foreground rose off the page. It was a girl of around Zeb's age, sitting on the edge of what looked like a roundabout in a playground. She had a pale ponytail and wore a jumper and leggings, slim arms stretched above her head. Zeb hadn't drawn her face in much detail, only closed eyes and the smudge of a mouth, but she was suddenly so familiar that Emma's heart skipped.

She dropped the book when the home phone trilled. Another silent call? She'd had five in total now. Each time she would consider not answering, but each time she'd think,

What if it's Zeb calling from a pay phone? What if he's changed his mind about everything, but lost his mobile, needs rescuing? And hadn't she just asked him to contact her urgently?

She rushed to the handset in the living room.

'Hello?'

There was no reply. Barely any sound.

'Who is it?'

No background buzz. Just soft, slow breathing.

'Say something,' Emma hissed, angry now.

That fear was rising, same as when the egg had slopped out of the book: a dread of being targeted. She told herself yet again that there was no evidence of a link between the calls and the parenting book. That she didn't need to fear the lines being drawn between present and past ... between her son and Steph's daughter ... between her own problems and the Harlows' ordeal ...

'Leave me alone!' she yelled, slamming down the phone.

22

Chris

Chris emerged from the bathroom deep in thought, vigorously towelling his hair as if to dislodge trouble from his head. When he lowered his arm he saw Vicky in their bedroom, misted by the cloud of steam that had followed him out of the shower. She was wearing one of his old shirts, with jeans and slouchy socks. The shirt dwarfed her – she always hid her body from him, these days – but Chris felt pleased to see her in his clothes, like it showed they were still a couple. As if this was a normal lazy Sunday.

Oddly, though, she was standing at the mirror applying bright red lipstick. She rarely wore much make-up so the slash of scarlet looked surreal. Chris watched as she painted her lips, then pressed them together and inspected her handiwork. He moved closer and saw a shiny gold Chanel logo on the side of the lipstick.

'Bold colour,' he said, unable to bring himself to compliment it outright.

She clicked the lid back on. Their gazes met in the mirror, the rest of her face ghostly white. He saw her startle when their doorbell chimed.

'I'll get it,' she said, slipping away before he could object.

Chris was left staring at his own unhealthy reflection, his damp, patchy chest hair in the V of his dressing-gown. There was a smear of lipstick in the corner of the mirror; he licked his finger to rub it off but it only smudged and streaked, like blood.

'There are some police here to see you.'

Chris froze. Vicky had reappeared in the corner of the mirror, blinking worriedly.

'Really? Uh . . . I'll get dressed.'

His skin was clammy as he wrestled on a T-shirt and jeans. Vicky watched him, her pale gaze asking: *What's going on?* Chris pushed past her and stumbled down the hall, his damp feet slipping on the garish carpet they'd deemed so-awful-it's-awesome when they'd first moved in.

'Hello!' he said to the detectives, who were hovering just inside the flat, peering brazenly into the nearest rooms. He wished, now, that he'd told Vicky all about their previous enquiries. He could have played it down – of course they'd want to talk to him, the missing girl's driving instructor.

She had followed him. 'What's this about?'

'Freya, I'd imagine.' Chris tried to strike the right tone: concerned for the girl, not for himself. 'Happy to help,' he chirruped to the detectives. 'Would you like to do this at the station?'

They left him hanging, all three of them silent. Then Ford said, 'That won't be necessary.' She opened her notebook as Chris caught his breath. 'It's about the route you took with Freya on March the fifteenth.'

'Hang on,' Vicky said. 'Was this the day the Harlow girl actually *disappeared*?'

Chris tried to talk over her. 'The route . . . I submitted it . . .'

'You *taught* her that day, Chris?'

'Vicky.' He glanced towards her, a pulse thumping in his neck. 'Can we talk about this later? The detectives must be very busy.' Turning back to them, he spoke in a panic: 'It's a common driving-lesson loop.'

'So you're certain that's the way you went?'

'Yes.'

'Would you take another look?' Ford thrust a piece of paper at him. Chris cast his eyes over the street names swimming on the page. He was aware of Vicky peering over his shoulder; he glanced at her and the red lips surprised him again.

'You stand by this?' Detective Johnson asked.

'As far as I remember. I teach a lot of students so the lessons sometimes blur.'

'Anywhere else you think you might have been?'

They were giving him a chance to save himself from whatever had brought them back here. But Chris couldn't think clearly enough.

'I . . . really don't remember.'

Ford snatched back the paper. 'We just wanted to confirm.'

They turned to go, and Chris wiped his palms on his jeans. But it was almost like a deliberate feint on the detectives' part: Ford paused halfway out of the door, swivelling back. 'Actually, while we're here, could we look in your car?'

'My car?'

'If we could do it with your cooperation . . .'

'Why?' Vicky broke in. 'What do you need to search his car for?'

'We're just covering all bases.'

Chris felt Vicky studying his reaction. He shrugged, nodded, made a meal of locating his keys. Following the officers back up to street level, he felt as if he was emerging out of a bunker, squinting and wary. He willed Vicky to stay in the flat but of course she wouldn't. So much for their unofficial pact to leave one another to their own messy affairs.

He unlocked his car and the detectives shone torches inside. Their beams probed under the seats and into the foot-wells – places even Chris rarely looked. It was as if they were examining him internally. The houses of the street seemed to crane forwards to see into the car, too, and Chris's spine tingled with awareness of the Harlows' place looming overhead. The police asked him to open the boot, the glovebox. He had a sudden fear that a completely empty glovebox was abnormal.

That his car was too clean. *A spotless vehicle is part of my profes-sionalism*, he prepared himself to explain. They said nothing, though, and abruptly they were gone, a promise to be 'in touch' trailing behind.

Slowly, Chris faced his wife. She was staring at him as if he was a stranger she half-recognised and was trying to place. A stranger who made her skin crawl. It was crushing, to have her looking at him that way. Worse than the police's interrogations.

'You never said you had a lesson with her that day. Or that you'd been asked to submit your route.'

Chris grabbed her arm. 'Can we not talk about this out here?'

'Why?' She pulled out of his grip. 'Afraid of people overhearing?'

'Do we really want to be the couple that hollers their private business to the entire street? The neighbours already think we're a bit rough.'

'It's not private, it's the girl who lives right *there.*'

Still he wouldn't look up, couldn't look at Vicky's face, either, as she seemed unable to tear her eyes from the Harlows' windows.

At last she shook her head and stalked past him down their steps.

Inside the hall she became subdued. She scratched a dry patch on her hand and he noticed she wasn't wearing the bracelet.

'You taught Freya . . .' finally, her gaze returned to him '. . . on the day she vanished into thin air?'

'She had contact with lots of people that day. I bet their spouses aren't looking at them like they killed someone.'

'What makes you think she's dead?'

'It was an expression! Jesus.'

'Are you a suspect?'

'No! Thanks for having faith in me.'

She let out a long sigh. 'Honestly, I don't think I do any more.'

Chris felt something shift deep inside him. He could sense the conversation inflaming into something much bigger. He wasn't sure whether he wanted to stoke the fire or extinguish it. 'That's rich,' he said.

'What's that supposed to mean?'

'You know, Vicky.'

She lifted her chin, her face pink. 'Stop deflecting.'

'Weren't you the one who suggested we don't "nag" each other about what's going on in our lives? Our *separate* lives, where we're apparently just two miserable people who share a house, and act vaguely like a married couple about once a year . . .'

'Is it that often? I hadn't noticed.'

'Well, that's the point!' He spread his arms, aware of trying to make himself larger, wanting to fill the space in front of her. 'You barely notice me, except when—'

They were interrupted again by the doorbell. This time it was loud in the hall, making them both jump. Neither moved for a moment, then Vicky went to the door. Chris exhaled when she opened it, never so relieved to see his sister-in-law.

Di looked from one to the other, presumably seeing flushed faces, sensing tension. 'Am I interrupting something?' she asked. 'I was just passing.'

Vicky smoothed her hair. 'No, no, come in, sis.'

Di was still peering questioningly at them as she stepped inside, but Vicky distracted her by asking where she'd been. They began talking about Di's shopping trip – she always had some story about terrible customer service – and Chris slunk away on the pretext of making coffee. Once he'd delivered their drinks to the living room, he lingered outside the door. Would Vicky tell Di what had happened? He thought back over Ford and Johnson's questions. It terrified him that he didn't know what they were thinking, who they were talking to, what they might have been told and how it might seem.

Not to mention what they might do next: search his flat, look into his finances?

The idea drove him into the bathroom, where he locked the door and delved into the cabinet. Finding the box right at the back, he emptied it of shaving paraphernalia and out tumbled the notes he'd stashed beneath. It was insane to have kept them. He tore them up, threw them into the bath and turned on the tap. Freya's words bled in black streams, the paper wilting to mulch as he forced it down the plughole.

Next he rushed across the hall to the glorified cupboard he called his study. He tried to be quiet, but couldn't help gathering speed as he gutted every box file from this year, scattering tax documents and lesson records across the carpet. Aside from the sorry state his business had been in for longer than he cared to admit, what else might his accounts reveal?

A noise made his head spring up. Di was peeking at him through the slightly ajar study door. How long had she been there? He hadn't heard her come down the hall. The toilet cistern gurgled in the bathroom behind her.

Chris knelt among the storm of papers and files, wondering how crazed he must look. Di snapped her eyes away when she realised he'd seen her, and disappeared out of sight.

23

Steph

Zeb Brighton, Steph typed into their family iPad, tapping her foot hard on the kitchen floor. The search found nothing relevant to her neighbour's son. She wasn't even certain he'd have the same surname as Emma. Heather hovered at her shoulder, asking questions Steph didn't have the answers to. No, she didn't know anything about this boy who'd pressed his cheek against her daughter's. Or about his mum, apparently: the impressions formed in the few months they'd shared a building had now been torn up, reshuffled. Her downstairs neighbour, who'd appeared to have more vintage coats than responsibilities, also had a teenage son.

A son who was nowhere to be seen. Who knew Freya more intimately than any of them had realised.

She rubbed her palms together. What to type next? To her shame, and Freya's endless amazement, Steph was bad with technology. There wasn't much call for it in her job, which was about high-end service, about maintaining standards and smiles. Strange, really: she had never thought of herself as a 'people person', but apparently she was, or had taught herself to be.

If you're planning on doing a uni course you'd better get down with the tech, Mum, Freya had teased her a few months ago, when Steph had shared that she was considering a part-time degree. Steph had teased in return that she'd follow Freya to her first-choice uni and live in the same halls. Even as she'd said it, she'd felt a deep pang at the prospect of Freya leaving home. Now, though, she'd give anything for the privilege of missing her in that bittersweet, part-of-life way.

'Try adding a location,' Heather urged. 'Type Zeb Brighton, Kingston upon Thames.'

This time, a link to Emma's vintage clothes shop appeared, but when Steph clicked on it, the page told her it was no longer in business. That explained why Emma was home so much. But there was still nothing about Zeb.

'Try just Zeb, Kingston,' Heather suggested, 'in case he's got a different surname. It's an unusual first name, isn't it?'

Nothing again. Steph raked her memory for anything she could recall about him. All that had really stuck was the deep voice she'd sometimes heard in the ground-floor flat, which had made her assume he was older. She hadn't been paying attention, consumed by her family life and her own preoccupations, her neighbours just figures on the fringes. Now it felt like these once-minor characters were laying claim to pieces of Freya. Hours spent alone with Chris in a car. Photos taken with Emma's son.

She grabbed her mobile and pulled up Jess's number. Paul and Brian were talking to George in the next room, pressing him about the analysis of Freya's phone records. Steph tried to tune into their conversation as her phone rang in her other ear. Her thoughts flickered again to what she'd learned yesterday about Paul. It had been elbowed aside by the discovery of the photo strip, but it still pulsed at the back of her head.

'Steph?' Jess answered, sounding breathless, hopeful.

'Can you do something for me?' Steph dived straight in.

'Course.' Jess's voice faded a little as she seemed to realise this wasn't the ecstatic we've-found-her-safe-and-well call.

'See whether Freya's friends with anyone called Zeb on her social-media accounts?'

'Zeb?'

'Have you heard of him?'

'I would've remembered. Does he go to our school?'

'No, he went to art college, I think. But now . . . well, I don't know. He used to live downstairs from us.'

'Hang on . . .' Steph could hear Jess typing, yelling to her dad that she was on the phone, then typing again. To her right Heather was still on the iPad, deftly trying different searches.

Even Gran's better with that thing than you, Mum, Freya had said, laughing, on one of Heather's visits.

And why wouldn't I be? Heather had challenged, with a grin.

Steph drew in a breath as Jess came back on the line.

'Frey's not friends with anyone called that. I've just asked a few people on WhatsApp whether they know him. I've got some mates at the art and design college up the road. D'you think that's where he went?'

'I don't know.'

'Hang on . . .' Jess said again. 'DAD, I'M STILL ON THE PHONE! IT'S FREYA'S MUM! GO AWAY!'

Steph suddenly remembered when Jess's mum and dad had split up, around three years ago, and Jess's mum had gone to live in Cornwall with her new partner, Freya had come home from school in tears, begging Steph for reassurance that that would never happen to them. And, of course, Steph had sworn that *nothing* would destroy their family. She wanted to shake that past version of herself, with her hollow promises.

Jess's voice changed as she said, 'Someone's already replied . . . My friend Lee says he knew a guy called Zeb Brighton at college.'

'Really?' Steph's foot tapped again. 'What does he know about him?'

'Not a lot. He's friends with him on Facebook but nobody actually uses that any more. I'll get Lee to have a look, though. Is he . . . What's the deal with him?'

'I don't know that either,' Steph said. 'That's what I need to find out.'

'Okay, Lee's looking at his profile now . . .'

Steph pictured an invisible network of lines, connecting Zeb to Emma, Emma to her, her to Jess, Jess to Lee and back to Zeb. Where was Freya in this web?

'He's only posted twice in the last year,' Jess said, 'and it's kind of weird . . .'

'Weird?' Steph's tone made Heather look up from the iPad.

'The first one was about three months ago. Lee's sent me a screenshot . . .' Jess cleared her throat as though to make a speech. '*Random request alert: does anybody know a Robin Lyle? Think he might live out towards the South Downs. Any info massively appreciated.*'

'Robin Lyle?' Steph looked at Heather, who took her cue and began to search for the name.

'His second post, about a month ago, was a link to Robin Lyle Construction. No explanation.'

'Robin Lyle Con—' But Heather had already found the website and was holding the iPad towards Steph, showing a man in his early to mid thirties, with long brown hair, wearing a hard hat and high-vis jacket.

Steph stared at him, her throat tight. She'd never seen him before. How could she know whether the network expanding out from her daughter contained this man? How could she know how far it stretched in miles, people, time? Or whether the answer was actually so nearby that she was failing catastrophically to see it?

24

Kate

Twenty-five years earlier

I can't let this happen. Can't let them go away together for a long weekend. Imagine what he could do to my mum in three whole days far from home.

He sprang the idea on her, just after I'd persuaded her to let Becca stay. For the past week, Becca and I have been pretending we've forgotten all about our suspicions. Becca's been on her best behaviour, trying not to upset Mum, but an atmosphere hums in the air. Mum is sometimes subdued; sometimes falsely, painfully cheery. Nick's moods are up and down, too. Some days he acts like our protector: he fixes things in the flat, deals with dodgy-looking people hanging round the tower block, insists Mum puts her feet up while he cooks tea. Other days I'll get home from school to find they've sent Becca out for chips, and Nick will be smoking on the balcony while Mum's in her room or in the bath, door closed. And I'll know they've been arguing.

And now this.

A surprise break, an early birthday present. As Mum sits at the kitchen table and tells me about it, she tries to seem excited but her eyes are empty.

Don't go, I long to say. *Please don't go.*

'The Cotswolds,' she says, smiling vaguely. 'Lovely, hey?'

'I thought we might do something special for Becca's last weekend,' I say.

'Well, you two can. You'll have more fun without us.'

Doesn't she remember the fun we all used to have together, before him? Creating our own cinema by turning off the living-room lights and heating up popcorn. Going to the library café for banana milkshakes when Mum and Auntie Rach had been paid.

'She said Auntie Rach might come up to fetch her,' I lie. 'Don't you want to be here when she comes?'

'I thought Becca was getting the train back.'

'Rach wants to see you.'

She fixes me with a searching look, then stares towards the window, two grooves etching the bridge of her nose.

Don't go, don't go, don't go. You don't want to, I can tell.

'Rach will just have to see me another time,' she says briskly. 'Nick's gone to a lot of trouble to arrange this.'

Becca and I try to hatch a plan. We consider involving Auntie Rach, maybe asking her to phone up and persuade Mum to stay at home, but Becca isn't keen. She's not getting on with her mum at the moment, she admits. They're always butting heads, these days, going through spells of arguing or not speaking (while Uncle Jack keeps well out of it), but I'm too stressed to ask her what it's all about this time.

None of our plans seems fail-safe. Some are ridiculous. The one we keep coming back to is telling the police.

'All they'll do is talk to your mum, though,' Becca says, in the worldly way that sometimes reassures me, sometimes drives me mad. 'And if she won't admit anything, there's nothing more they can do.'

'They could arrest him!'

'It doesn't work like that, Kay. And do you even know where the police station is?'

I stall. Of course not. I don't know anything. I'm useless.

I stand up and look frantically around my room as if it might be hiding among my things. 'We could phone 999?'

'That's for emergencies.'

'This is an emergency! He could kill her!'

'Kate.' Becca leaps up and puts her arms around me, rocking and shushing, telling me it'll be okay. I sob into her shoulder, wetting the thin fabric of her dress.

I barely sleep for the rest of the week. On Thursday Mum's on an early shift, so she kisses me goodbye and goes off to work while I'm still in my pyjamas and Becca's still in bed. Nick left even earlier. The mornings feel lighter when he isn't at the breakfast table. In the quiet that Mum leaves behind, I slip into her room.

It feels intimate – wrong – to be in her bedroom when she's not home. The duvet is rucked up to expose the wrinkled corner of a sheet. The pretend-gold bracelet I bought her sits coiled at the back of her nightstand, no longer inseparable from her wrist. It looks cheap in this light, childish and flimsy, and my skin prickles with shame.

I turn on the spot, eyes roaming over photos and furniture that seem newly alien, knowing yet not knowing what I'm looking for. This room feels like a foreign country now. Out of bounds. I remember when there were no borders between her space and mine.

Isn't that how it's supposed to be?

Guilt stirs as I slide open the bedside drawer to see a black hairbrush, a packet of paracetamol, an out-of-date magazine. Turning to the wardrobe, I glide my fingers over the dresses and pretty skirts she never wears any more. I nose the soft fabrics, her scent trapped in them, like a memory.

Just as I'm about to retreat, my gaze falls on something at the bottom of the wardrobe. A wad of light blue fabric scrunched into the shadows of the back corner. I reach down to pick it up, but as it unfurls, shock makes me fling it away. It hits the mirror and drops to the floor, and I see it again: a dark lake of red encrusted on the front of one of her T-shirts.

I stand dazed. Heart thumping, I spread out the top on the carpet and stare at the dried blood, trailing my fingertips across the stain. Vomit surges into my throat as my thoughts scatter, crazy and panicked. *My mummy, my mummy, my mummy.*

Now I know I have to act. I stuff the top into my schoolbag and charge out. I'd feel braver if Becca was with me but I can't waste any time, don't want my nerve to fail.

I ask four different strangers before I find someone who knows where the police station is. Reciting the directions over and over, I stumble through the streets until I reach the grey building with one-way windows. I hate going into any place I don't know: I'm never sure how to introduce myself, what I'm meant to do. I remember my first day at secondary school, when I accidentally walked into the staffroom and a dozen teachers' heads swivelled towards me.

Pushing through the front doors, I stand for a moment in the foyer. My vision is full of bright spirals and I'm burning hot from the rush to get here. To my left is a waiting area where two people sit in tired silence. One has a plaster cast on her wrist and the other is aggressively chewing – I can't tell if it's gum or the insides of his cheeks.

I shuffle up to the wide reception, which has clear glass panels right the way along, like in the post office where Mum works but higher and wider. The people behind are surprisingly far away, sitting at separate desks typing busily. I try waiting until someone notices me, then eventually tap on the window. A woman glances up and heaves herself out of her chair.

'Can I help?'

'I'm here to . . . I need to talk to a policeman . . . or -woman.'

'You're looking at one.' Her tone isn't nasty, but I blush and my tongue knots.

'I just need to tell someone . . .' My hand flutters towards my bag, where Mum's bloodied top is balled up beside my school things.

'Have you witnessed a crime?'

My hand shies away. 'Not exactly.'

'Have you done something?' She cocks her head. 'Is there something you want to admit to?'

'No, no!' I shake my head, choked by tears. 'I don't want to say it out here,' I whisper.

I'm not sure whether I imagine her cluck of impatience. She goes over to her desk and returns with a clipboard and a piece of paper.

'Why don't you fill out this form?' She nods towards the chairs, and I recoil from the chewing man and the broken-armed woman.

Normally I'd jump at the chance to write things down. I'm much better with words on paper. But the boxes and the dotted lines look so confusing: how will I know I'm ticking the right things? Will it go on a permanent record?

'Can't I talk to someone in private?' I ask.

The woman sighs. 'Wait here. I'll see if one of the interview rooms is free. Can't promise anything, though. I keep telling them these facilities aren't up to scratch, we need an extension . . .' She wanders away.

At first I breathe out with relief, but while she's gone I mull over what she said. *Interview room.* I picture two police officers firing questions at me, leaning in close, doing good-cop-bad-cop. Rationally I know it won't be like that, but sweat breaks out on my face.

I imagine them taking Mum's top and sending it away for tests. She'll know I've been in her room, rummaged through her things. They'll send someone round and she'll get upset and angry, and her refusal to admit what's going on will make me look like a liar. Nick will see how easy it is to crush my attempts to help her. Confirmation, once and for all, that Mum won't betray him.

A photocopier on the other side of the screen starts to snarl and beep. The man in the waiting area shouts, 'How much fucking longer?' Suddenly the girl with the broken arm sits forward and pukes onto the floor, the smell instant and horrible.

This isn't right. It no longer feels right.

Before the policewoman has even returned, I am gone.

25

Emma

Zeb's Skype profile picture was frozen on the screen, mocking her with its stillness as the 'calling Zeb' icon danced in the centre. Then, like a miracle, the static image vanished and was replaced by a moving, breathing Zeb. His hair was longer, and his face seemed thin – though his shoulders looked more muscular. There was a window behind him with a view onto a dusty yard. It was as if he'd been cut-and-pasted onto an alien backdrop.

She blinked back tears, wishing she could shed her unease. This was her son. Her Zeb.

'Hello, stranger!'

'Hey, Mum.' It didn't help that his voice was out of sync with the movement of his mouth, tilting their conversation off-balance.

'How are you, Zebbie?'

'I'm . . . good.'

'Yeah?' Emma leaned forward, eager for reassurance. She tried to keep her eyes on him rather than the background, but it was hard not to wonder who else was around. 'Really?'

'Yes, Mum, really.'

'Well, that's great.' There were so many questions she wanted to ask, but each seemed fraught with possible conflict.

'How 'bout you?' He surprised her by reciprocating. 'You said there was something urgent?'

Emma wondered where to begin. Her eyes scoured his face, looking for other changes, her breath becoming choppy as she felt the distance between them, the barrier of the screen, the weak signal.

Suddenly she noticed a dark pink mark on Zeb's hand. She pointed, frowning: 'Hey, what's that?'

'This?' He lifted his hand and she saw it properly: a wide, deep cut across his palm.

'How did you get that?'

'Cutting open a box.'

'Zeb, it looks bad! Did you go to hospital?'

'Had a couple of stitches.' He dropped his hand. 'Looks worse than it is.'

She knew it was just a cut but it seemed to represent all her fears. *You shouldn't be there. You should be with me.*

As she tried to stop staring at his hand, she saw movement behind him. Someone had appeared in the yard: a man with long brown hair, wearing navy overalls, was dragging a bag of gravel towards a shed. Emma's heart turned over. *Robin.* Zeb must have noticed the slip in her attention because he twisted around and the two men waved at each other. Emma composed herself, so that when he turned back she could be rational and calm.

It was difficult, though. Her mouth was so dry.

'Zeb.' She focused on him, not the yard. 'You know Freya who lives above us?'

Zeb's attention swung back. 'The blonde girl?'

'Yes.' She glanced towards her own window. The two rows of trees were head-banging in the wind, the posters of Freya clinging on tight. 'Have you ... seen anything about her online?'

'I haven't been on much. The connection's crap here. Why, what about her?'

'She ... she's gone missing.'

The screen blanked, making her jolt in surprise.

'Oh! Zeb, you still there?'

There was a crackle and his image reappeared. 'Think we lost video for a second,' he said.

'Yeah . . .' She was discombobulated. Part of her wished the picture had remained blank. It might be easier to do this blind. She knew she needed to see his face, though. *To be sure he's telling the truth*, a tiny part of her acknowledged before she shoved it away.

'Freya's missing?' Zeb seemed to say her name with greater familiarity now. 'Really?'

Emma nodded. 'Three days.'

'Shit.' Zeb rubbed the back of his hand across his mouth, the cut visible again. His fingers were calloused, too, with white plaster dust on their tips. Emma's gaze darted towards Robin in the background, now leaning on a spade contemplating a stack of paving slabs.

For a moment he seemed to look straight at her. She jerked her eyes back to her son.

'And her mum found some photos,' she said, all in a rush. 'Of you and her in one of those photo booths. Which confused me, because I didn't even know you were friends.'

'We're not.'

Emma's arms grew cold. With an almost subconscious gesture she reached to her left and turned up the thermostat. She should be thrifty with her utilities, but this spring day suddenly had bite.

'We only . . .' Zeb said '. . . we spent one night together . . . not like *that*.'

She made herself stay quiet, waiting, steadying her breath. But when Zeb clammed up, she couldn't help prompting him: 'What happened?'

There was another long pause, before he launched into his explanation at last.

'It was a couple of months ago. I bumped into her in the park. I was sitting on a bench, thinking about stuff, and so was she by the look of it. I wasn't going to say anything more than hi, but then I realised she was *totally* pissed.'

'Was she?' Emma couldn't imagine Freya drunk. Healthy, golden Freya. Zeb's sketch flashed into her mind: the girl on the roundabout with her arms in the air.

'I thought I'd better check she was okay. She was clearly upset – she was saying all this stuff, it didn't make a lot of sense . . . She had a bottle of gin and asked me to have a drink with her.'

'What was she upset about?'

'I couldn't work it out at first. I got the impression she hadn't talked to anyone else, but maybe I was able to rel—' He stopped. Emma looked at him. He'd been about to say he could relate to Freya, to her troubles. Before she could ask how, he hurried on: 'She got kind of giddy after a while. She sat on the roundabout in the play area and she was laughing, saying she'd got a plan . . .'

'You drew her.' It popped out before she could think it through.

Zeb paused, his face clouding. 'You looked at my sketches?'

Emma flushed. 'I didn't think you'd mind. They're really good, Zeb. But I just wondered about—'

'Don't go through my stuff, Mum. My sketchbook was in the drawer. It's not like it was just lying around.'

She saw him take a breath, eyes closing, lips tightening. Was he counting to ten? Had he learned that in his anger-management sessions?

What had happened to the little boy who used to have air-guitar contests with his grandparents, who'd held the end of a tape measure for hours when Emma had been fitting out the shop, who'd told his nursery teacher he was going to marry his mum when he grew up, as if it was a viable option? And what had happened, even, to her teenager who loved music and cooking and comics?

You happened, she thought, seeing Robin's fuzzy outline in her mind, anger and fear blooming again.

Zeb opened his eyes. 'I haven't got much time,' he said, curt now. 'There's stuff to finish in the garden before it goes dark.'

It was so tempting to swerve the conversation towards something easier for their last few minutes. She *had* to hear the end of his story, though. What he knew about Freya.

'What else happened, Zeb?'

He gazed out of the screen, not quite meeting her eye, though it was hard to tell whether that was a side effect of Skype or a deliberate avoidance.

'We messed about on the play area for a bit longer, drinking and racing each other up and down the climbing frame. Then we decided to head home. We had those photos taken in the booth at the station, just for fun. But on the train she got really upset again. Started talking about her parents . . .'

'Her parents?' Emma glanced at the ceiling as if she'd be able to see into the Harlows' flat. There was a creak of floorboards, the tapping of a pipe. Zeb seemed pensive now. For a moment the light silhouetted him completely, like a television interviewee with their identity protected.

Emma thrust away the mental image of Robin hovering at the edges of the frame.

When Zeb looked back at her, his eyes were wide. 'Parents think they can keep secrets from their kids. But we find stuff out and it's even more shitty because of the lies.'

She felt like she'd been slapped. As Zeb ploughed on, explaining the rest of what Freya had told him, she had to work hard to concentrate. She knew how important it was but she just wanted to sob at his pointed comparison, to defend herself, to apologise, to rage.

26

Chris

Di had finally left, with a semi-threatening shout of 'Speak soon, Chris!' along the hall. Vicky had gone for a lie-down without another word. Chris had slipped away and was driving through a flurry of wind and rain towards Freya's school.

He wouldn't linger there, of course. He just needed to start at that location so he could retrace the route they'd taken three days before, checking for CCTV cameras that might have picked them up that afternoon. The escalating rain made it difficult. His wipers shrieked each time they swept across the glass – he'd been meaning to get some new blades for weeks. He used to take an embarrassing amount of pride in maintaining his and Vicky's modest cars. It was the one thing he was good at, and he'd especially liked doing it for her. She'd always rolled her eyes when he'd lectured about oil levels and preventing clutch wear, but she'd liked it really, he could tell. These days it was harder to please or amuse her, harder even to know whether she was happy or sad.

A heaviness dragged at his body as he recalled how she'd looked at him after the police had left. He'd once believed she loved him unconditionally, that they were fundamentally the same person. Now that naïve theory was being put to the test in ways he'd never imagined.

His phone started to ring. Di's name appeared on the hands-free display. Alarm spiked through him – did *speak soon* have to mean this soon? He fumbled with the controls.

'Hi, Chris.' Di's voice sounded different coming through the speakers.

'Di,' Chris said. 'Everything all right?'

There was a pause. He kept one eye on the passing streets, his fingers beating a nervous tempo on the wheel.

'Well . . .' Di said '. . . actually, I was going to ask you the same question.'

He swallowed. 'What?'

'I mean . . . is everything okay with you and Vic?'

His shoulders tensed. 'I don't—'

'Money-wise.'

After the initial surprise of her question, he didn't know whether to be relieved or worried. If Di had asked him about their finances a few months back, he would have gone straight on the defensive. Even now, he answered abruptly: 'Why would you ask that?'

'Well . . . I saw you in your office today. Going through your accounts. You looked very . . . *anxious*.'

Of course she couldn't just not mention it. Always had to stick her nose in. 'I was looking for something,' he said. 'Something I needed for my tax return.'

'You can tell me if there's a problem. Gav and I would like to help.'

'You've told Gavin about this?'

'Erm . . .'

'Did you mention it to Vicky?'

'No, no, I wanted to speak to you first.'

Chris gritted his teeth. 'Di, Vicky and I are doing fine. I do take care of her, you know, despite what you and Jane might think.'

'I didn't mean to imply—'

'I have to go. I'm in the car . . .' He talked over her as she tried to cut in once more. 'I'll see you at lunch next week. Or, no doubt, before.' The last part came out more nastily than he'd intended.

As he disconnected the call, his wipers let out a particularly high-pitched squeal. Chris realised he was lathered in sweat. Who the hell did Di think she was? He was furious with himself, too, for not being more discreet, for letting his panic overwhelm him.

His heart was galloping now. Alarmingly fast. His whole body was alive with the feeling that somebody else was in the car. Freya was in the passenger seat, watching him drive, her gaze drawing goose-bumps to the surface of his skin. She was in the back, leering over his shoulder, her breath in his ear, then on the wet bonnet staring into his eyes through the windscreen. She had things in her hands, sparkly trinkets that seemed to swell in size, and she was wearing Vicky's bracelet, Vicky's new blood-crimson lipstick . . .

He could hear her voice crystal clear. He saw her laughing, tossing her hair, making him laugh, too, with her surprisingly sharp humour. But then cold, as if a switch had been flicked, or angry, gesturing with both long-fingered hands off the wheel. Chris pulled over and curled in on himself, gasping for breath as the wipers continued to scream.

I can't stand this.

Reaching for his phone, he went to the number he should have deleted, and jabbed at the call button.

It rang and rang.

Pick up, pick up, pick up.

Of course there'd be no answer. It was reckless to try, but he needed . . . He didn't even know what. He just knew he was almost at his limit. Flinging his phone onto the passenger seat, he twisted his rear-view mirror towards him, and stared into his own red-rimmed eyes.

Pull. Yourself. Together.

His phone beeped with a message and he leaned over to read it. *My parents won't let me have lessons with you any more. I'm sorry. Jess.*

Chris sat back and closed his eyes. His chest rose and fell heavily. A feeling of numbness began to steamroller over him.

He jumped alert when he heard, then spotted, a group of police officers emerging from the park entrance across the road. They all wore gloves and held clipboards, German Shepherds trotting beside them, sniffing the damp air. Was this one of the search teams who were combing the area for Freya? Not wanting to provoke any questions, Chris started his car and moved quickly on.

He looped back towards the street he wished they'd never moved into, back towards his wife, who'd started to eye him with as much suspicion as all the others.

He couldn't think of anything else to do.

27

Emma

After her Skype call with Zeb, Emma wandered around her flat with an unsettled cloud in her stomach, eventually ending up back in her son's empty room. She lay on his bed, looking at the framed Deadpool poster on the wall, trying to unpick everything he'd said to her.

Why couldn't she stop thinking how strange Zeb and Freya's encounter in the park seemed? Or fight the feeling that there was more to it than Zeb had revealed? Even though he'd been so angry with her for looking through his drawings – among all the other things he was angry about – she got up and retrieved his sketchbook from the drawer. She studied the picture of Freya until the girl seemed to come to life on the page, crying and confiding as to why she was upset.

It was this 'why' that Emma now had to pass on to Freya's parents, despite its sensitivity, despite the many questions it would spark. *So do it,* she chided herself. *Stop procrastinating.*

She closed the sketchbook and then guiltily, without quite knowing why, opened Zeb's other drawer to peek inside. With a twinge of sorrow she noted its bareness: just a few folded T-shirts, a Sherlock Holmes book (since when was Zeb a fan?), and his keys to this house, which he'd obviously decided he didn't need. She moved on to his wardrobe, in denial about the fact that she was now actively snooping, and half smiled at the skateboard propped up in a corner, a summer-long fad from a few years ago. In his bedside cabinet, the box of artists' charcoal she'd bought him last Christmas also made her pause. Emma touched the slim pencils, the thicker charcoal sticks, the solid blocks. Then she noticed something down the side of the box: a long, glossy rectangle of white.

As she plucked it out and turned it over, she already knew what it would be. Zeb and Freya grinned up at her from a strip of photos just like the one Steph had brought round that morning. Four times over, laughing with heads together. In one picture Freya was tipping a vodka bottle into her mouth, looking more like a hardcore socialite than a blossoming sports star.

So Zeb had a memento of their meeting, too.

Emma tried to convince herself it wasn't *hidden*. It was just in his bedside cabinet. There was nothing wrong with that. Her pulse was rapid as she put it back and left the room.

Her nerves only grew as she rapped on the Harlows' door. She'd rarely ventured up these stairs in the past and she wished now that she'd done so more often, for pleasant neighbourly reasons. Maybe then this wouldn't feel so daunting. Their door was painted a smart, clean ivory, a shiny brass C in its centre.

Her heart sank when Paul answered. She'd really hoped to talk to Steph alone. He looked exhausted, but still so unreadable, even as Emma blurted, 'I've spoken to Zeb about Freya.'

He led her wordlessly inside. She'd been right in thinking their flat was much bigger than hers. They went through to a large living room and Emma was diverted by the feeling of space and light, the expanse of varnished floorboards, the lampshades hovering above, like satellites.

The brightness seemed to fade, however, as she took in the people sitting around the room. Steph was hunched in a chair beside the window, almost a mirror image of the one Emma had pulled close to her own window a floor below. The family liaison officer, George, was distributing cups of tea while an older woman fussed with coasters on the coffee-table.

A grey-haired version of Paul sat clutching a wad of paper and a pen, staring into space. The atmosphere was hushed but expectant, like the morning of a funeral.

'Emma's here,' Paul announced, and all the heads pivoted, their anxious anticipation suddenly centred on her.

Steph stood up. 'Have you spoken to your son?'

Emma nodded. Her heart was hammering again. She wasn't sure she could say the thing she needed to in front of all these people. George looked as though he was going to speak, but the woman with the round glasses cut across him. 'What does he know about our Freya?'

Emma had mentally rehearsed how she was going to summarise her conversation with Zeb, but now her thoughts scrambled. She didn't know who to look at, so she focused on a print on the wall: the swirls of Van Gogh's *The Starry Night*. Her gaze was compelled towards the photo of Freya beside it. She looked sunlit and happy, her smile unguarded. It was hard to imagine her necking vodka, hard to comprehend secrets or problems that might have led her away from this clean, comfortable home. Especially not the one she'd shared with Zeb, now trapped in Emma's throat.

'He . . . he and Freya bumped into each other one night in the park. They got talking, had a drink together, nothing—' She stopped herself from saying *nothing untoward*, not wanting to plant ideas. 'Nothing major.'

'When was this?' Steph asked.

'About two months ago, a Friday night. Freya was supposed to be staying at a friend's but apparently she hadn't felt like going. Zeb said she was . . . upset.'

'Upset? *Why?*'

Emma shuffled her feet. 'Well, Zeb said that it . . . it was related to something she'd found out . . .' she motioned towards Steph, then broadened the gesture to encompass Paul as well '. . . about her parents.'

There was a shocked silence. Steph stared towards Paul but he was looking down, pressing his temples, seeming to sway back onto his heels.

'What do you mean?' Steph's tone was sharp but breathy.

Paul stepped towards Emma. 'Freya found out something about one of us?'

'Yes.'

'What?'

'I . . . don't know.' As the lie came out, Emma pinched the edges of her cord dress. She just wanted to get out of there now. Compose herself, come back later. She could listen for when Steph seemed to be by herself, and tell her privately, let her absorb it first. 'Maybe I should talk to him again.'

'He'll need to make a statement,' George said.

'Okay.' Emma edged towards the door. She felt as if they were all crowding in on her but in fact they were stationary in their positions, watching her inch away.

When she was almost there, Steph's voice stalled her. '*Both* parents?' She was fiddling with the zip below her chin, moving it a centimetre up, a centimetre down, small scratchy noises. 'Which parent did Freya mean?'

Emma tried to signal to her that she'd return. 'I don't know,' she said again. Her stomach tipped as she wondered if this counted as withholding information. The awkwardness of the situation rolled itself in with her unease about Zeb, about glimpsing Robin, about coming across another strip of photos in her son's drawer.

How could she stand in front of this audience and reveal something that might pull the Harlows apart?

28

Steph

Once Emma had left, silence cloaked the room. Steph noticed distantly that their ceiling light had two bulbs out, making one half of the living room darker. Everybody else seemed to be on the illuminated portion of a stage whereas she was in the wings, the shadows. She shut her eyes to complete the darkness, trying to grasp what Emma had said, feeling that it was what she hadn't said that was vital.

'Have you any idea what Miss Brighton's son might be referring to?' George asked them.

Nobody answered. Steph turned to Paul. 'We need to talk.'

Paul nodded. His skin was grey and there were half-moons of exhaustion beneath his eyes. Steph's glimmer of sympathy was overridden by a quick wave of fear.

'Let's go for a walk,' Paul said.

'I'd like to discuss this with you both,' George said.

'We need a moment.' Steph left the apartment before George or her in-laws could protest further. Paul caught up with her outside. He'd brought her coat and he slipped it around her shoulders. They walked briskly, without speaking at first. There was a charge in the air as if another downpour was imminent, and the buzz of a police helicopter in the bruised sky. Steph stared at each car and pedestrian that passed them, and noticed Paul doing the same. She had the fleeting, terrible thought that this could be their life from now on: looking for their daughter in every turned-away face or shadowy window.

'I promise you,' Paul said, 'whatever Freya found out about me, wherever it took her, I'll bring her home.'

The words *dead or alive* knifed through Steph's head and she pushed them violently away. She glanced at Paul, his clenched arms, the intensity in his face. What was he carrying that made him so sure he was to blame?

'What is there to find out?' she asked, as spots of rain landed cold and soft on her forehead.

She watched for his reaction. Did he know what his dad had let slip? Would he be honest with her now?

The rain gathered urgency. Streams ran beneath her collar, drops sticking to her eyelashes.

'Let's duck in here,' Paul said, pointing towards the church.

They darted up the path. The door clanged shut behind them and the silence inside was chilly but peaceful, Sunday-morning service long finished. Rain dripped from their clothes as they walked down the aisle in a parody of a wedding.

Sitting in the front pew, with blue light slanting through the stained-glass window in front of her, Steph felt The Question rising from her core. The one she'd stopped herself asking him, all these years. It seemed even more pertinent now she knew the true nature of his police work.

Yet still she swallowed it, and instead said: 'You were under-cover. For three years.'

His head swung towards her. 'How do you know that?'

'Your dad told me.'

Paul pressed a hand against his face and she heard him exhale.

'I wish *you*'d told me,' Steph said.

He stared at the floor. 'I couldn't.'

'I know the details must be classified but you could've at least—'

'I couldn't talk about it, Steph!' His voice surged. 'And I don't just mean because it was classified.'

She felt tears behind her eyes. Paul moved his hand as if he was going to touch hers, but he didn't: he ran his fingertips along the worn edge of the pew.

'What was your name?' she asked quietly. 'Can you at least tell me that?'

There was a pause before he said: 'Paul Darren Jacobs.'

'Paul?'

'It's better to use your real first name if possible. Less scope for slip-ups.'

'Oh.' Even this small insight made her feel overwhelmed. Clueless.

'Things went wrong,' he said, 'when I was undercover. I thought it was all in the past, but now . . .'

Dread shivered through her. 'Wrong how?'

'I . . . deceived people. Made bad choices. Lost control . . .' He seemed to coil in on himself on the pew, long legs bent, his spine a question mark. 'And there were consequences.'

Steph felt her pulse in every part of her. 'Was it to do with drugs?'

He shook his head. 'In a way I wish it had been. Drug deal-ers, straightforward villains – perhaps I would've dealt with those better. But it was more complicated than that. It was more . . .' He seemed to grapple for the right word, then choked out, 'It was hard.'

'Did you have a relationship?' Steph asked, replacing The Question with one that had troubled her almost as often over the years – for different reasons, perhaps, and without realis-ing, then, that Paul might have been with someone who didn't even know his real identity.

She felt the pew move and creak. 'What makes you ask that?'

'I've always had this feeling . . .' She gazed towards the stained-glass window. In it, three people were lying side by side. Steph couldn't tell if they were praying or sleeping or dying. '. . . that you loved someone before me. Someone you didn't want to tell me about.'

He seized her hand. 'I love *you*. And Freya. You're my world.'

Sadness exploded through her. The man who'd learned her favourite passage from *Jane Eyre* for their wedding, who could still make her tingle by kissing her neck, who'd had damp eyes on Freya's first day of school, he was receding from her again. Or maybe it was her who was retreating. Shutting down because it was all too much.

Paul stood up and paced back and forth, like an impassioned minister delivering a sermon, except that he was murmuring, '*Fuck*,' over and over. His curses echoed in the crest of the ceiling, as if they were collecting up high.

'Did you kill someone?'

The Question had broken free.

Paul stopped abruptly. 'What?'

Steph didn't want to repeat it. She was already regretting asking, but she was also breathless to hear his answer, as though she was detaching herself from the conversation, watching two unknown people and wondering, *What is he going to say now? And what will she say?*

Then she looked at her husband and recognised what he was doing. His shoulders were drawn forward. There were pain lines in his face. He was trying to keep himself upright, like someone who'd been struck in the stomach and didn't want to fold.

Steph stepped towards him but he flinched away as though wary of a second blow. Suddenly all she felt was blistering guilt. 'Paul, I . . .'

He straightened and they looked at one another. Then a loud beep startled them. It was just a text message alert, coming from Paul's pocket, but the acoustics of the church and the tension of the moment made it feel like a small explosion. Paul blinked as if waking from a confusing dream. His hand hovered towards his pocket, his gaze still on Steph. Finally he broke eye contact and drew out his phone. The moment seemed to cave in.

'I have to go,' he said, staring at his screen.

'No, Paul—'

'I'm sorry.' He was already moving towards the church door. 'But I really have to this time. I've just had some information . . . Steph, I don't want you drawn into this. Please go home, stay safe. And I'll be back, I promise. *With* Freya.'

She saw how his face had now transformed. He was fired up, reawakened, but all it stirred in Steph was a new rise of panic. Paul thrust open the church door. As he disappeared yet again, intent on reversing whatever damage he was convinced he'd caused, a chill of doubt spread beneath Steph's skin.

'Wait!' she called, but her legs were shaking too much to follow.

29

Kate

Twenty-five years earlier

Friday arrives. The day that Mum and Nick are due to go away for the weekend. At school I can't concentrate, can't eat, can't remember anything about algebra or the Second World War or even *Romeo and Juliet*. When the bell goes I hurtle home, not even bothering to pick up my untouched lunchbox when it tumbles out of my bag. I'm not sure why I think I might be able to stop them leaving at the very last minute. Maybe if I pretend to be ill again. Or maybe if I don't come home at all, they'll have to postpone their trip to look for me. I halt in front of the tower block, imagining Mum frantic and fraught, searching the neighbourhood. Phone calls to my teachers and the mums of my classmates. Could I really set all of that in motion?

A wild plan forms in my head. But then I lift my eyes and see Nick, framed in our window, staring down at me. Waving. There's a giant lump in my throat as I wave mechanically back. And nothing to do but walk inside.

Their luggage waits in our hallway. A smell of bacon leaks out of the kitchen as I drop my rucksack beside Mum's over-night bag. Last-chance thoughts of destroying their suitcases parade through my mind. I could throw them out of the window, watch them plummet four floors.

'Hi, Kate,' Nick shouts from the kitchen.

Why is *he* greeting me, not Mum? Is she not here? And where's Becca? My nerves dance as I push the kitchen door.

Nick's frying bacon on the stove. The air is full of the sizzling noise, the meaty smell. He's whistling, cheerful today, glugging a beer.

'Where is everyone?' I ask.

'Your mum got held up at work. She'll be home soon and then we're heading for our train. I'm starving, though.' He grins and flips the bacon, beads of fat spitting from the pan, then cracks two eggs against the rim of a bowl.

'Becca's having a shower.' He beats the eggs, fork rattling. 'You two looking forward to having the place to yourselves?'

'I guess.'

He turns and looks at me. The fork's in his fist with slug-trails of yellow dripping from its prongs. 'Your mum really needs this break.' There's a warning there, his smile shrinking: *Don't stand in our way.*

I feel tears building, and hurry out of the room before he sees them. Sitting on my bed, I run my finger up and down a ladder in my tights until Becca appears, wearing my dressing-gown, a towel wrapped around her hair. As soon as I see her, the tears burst.

'Kay-Kay.' She sits beside me. The towel slips from her hair and water spatters my arm. I see she's been dyeing her hair dark purple – the white towel is stained with indigo streaks.

'I've *got* to do something,' I say.

'The police?'

'No, no, you were right about that.'

'I could come back with you, help you explain . . .'

I shake my head, shuddering at the memory of my failure yesterday. Nick's got us trapped in a corner and I'm too pathetic to haul us out. I hear him whistling again from the kitchen, and the carefree tune makes me want to explode.

Then my gaze snags on something. A small plastic tub on the bedside table. 'Your pills.'

Becca glances at the clock. 'Oh, you're right, I'm due some.'

'No . . .' I pause, forming the sentence in my head before I let it leave my mouth. 'Couldn't we give him a couple?'

'What?'

I remember Becca vomiting into the toilet the first night she stayed with us, blaming it on the combination of alcohol and tablets. 'We could put some in his food or beer. If he's sick, they won't be able to go tonight.'

'Kate—'

'It would buy us some time.'

'But—'

'One dose won't do any harm, just upset his stomach, right?'

'Probably.' She tilts her head like she's reassessing me. For better or worse, I'm not sure. 'I don't know. I'm no expert. I just take them.'

'Did you get sick the first time?'

'I think so, a bit.'

'It might shake him up,' I persist. 'What with the pills and the beer . . . They might stay at home, at least for tonight. Then we could work out another plan, a proper one.'

Becca's eyes travel towards the bottle of tablets. 'Kate . . . it's *poisoning*.' Her lips smack around the word as though she doesn't know whether she likes the taste of it or not.

'He'll just think he's got a bug.' I grab her hand. 'If we let him take her away, I've got this horrible, horrible feeling she won't make it back.'

'Jesus, Kate, I'd do anything for you and your mum, you know that. But this feels . . . extreme.'

I'm almost proud. Bet she never thought I'd be willing to go this far. It's rarely been *me* convincing *Becca* before. All our life she's been the one with the bold ideas, while I'm usually the hesitator.

I grab for the pills but she gets there first, holding them to her chest. 'Kate, come on.'

'You said you were here to help.'

'For fuck's sake, I am. But spiking a guy's drink?'

'He's not just *a guy*. He's . . . he's . . .' My tears surge back and Becca reaches out to me: she never could stand to see me cry. But I blink my eyes clear and take my chance to snatch the pills. 'He's the guy who gave my mum a hundred bruises.' I close my fingers around the tub and for the first time in weeks, perhaps the first time ever, I feel powerful.

30

Paul

Paul charged towards home, the rain still hammering down, his car an exasperating distance away. On his street, the coloured ink was bleeding out of the Freya posters, making grotesque rainbows in the puddles. He took several down and folded them gently inside his coat as if to keep her dry. Glancing up at his flat, he imagined his parents and George inside, wondering what was going on. There was no time to explain. Where would he even begin?

Paul got into his car and reread the text that had interrupted his talk with Steph.

It's Yvette. This is my personal number – use this from now on. I did some digging. Sanderson still lives near the Chainwell Estate. Don't say anything to Glover. Please be careful. I hope I'm doing the right thing here.

She'd followed it with an address and postcode. Paul keyed it into his satnav, still disbelieving even as the location was confirmed. Sanderson had moved barely two miles from the old tower block, had stayed close to the memories all this time.

Thank you, Paul replied to Yvette. *So much.* His chest swelled with gratitude and hope, temporarily masking his dread of the journey he now had to make. As he set off, anxieties old and new swarmed in. The echo of Steph's question in the stillness of the church.

Did you kill someone?

Once this nightmare was over – and he had to believe it would be – how could he make his wife and daughter understand, and forgive him? How could he even describe his former life of confused identity, confused loyalties? Buddying up with a man who'd potentially committed an unforgivable crime; getting closer than he should have to a woman who had no clue who he was. Freya and Steph would surely see him differently if they knew, just as he'd always feared.

His whirling thoughts accompanied him along the motorway and distracted him from his approach to Nottingham. Then, suddenly, his destination seemed to be moving towards him, rather than the other way round, and he was falling into a once-familiar part of the city, becoming enclosed by dilapidated buildings and burned-out social clubs. Perhaps it was the years that had passed, or the life Paul now lived, but the estate seemed sadder than ever. Paint peeled off the houses like flaking eczema; the whole place reeked of blocked drains.

He parked where he could and sat for a moment, afraid that as soon as he got out he'd be someone else. Someone capable of causing irreversible damage. He thought of Freya, of Steph, of the clean smell of home and the breeze along the Thames. Until he felt calm enough to get out of the car.

As he discreetly followed his phone's directions, his eyes sought blonde ponytails, navy Puffa jackets, trainers with mint-green soles. Instead he saw the landmarks of his former life, like objects from a dream: the streets he'd stalk at night when insomnia plagued him; the corner where a phone box had once stood, from which he would call in his updates to Glover. He passed the closed-down pub where Sanderson used to drink, and Paul, too, once he'd managed to befriend him. Countless hours spent trying to get his target drunk, trying to tease out confessions, hints, *anything*. Some nights, when he could, Paul would take Nathalie there alone. They'd play dominoes in the back room, shooting smiles at one another, touching knees beneath the table. And Paul would forget, too often, to ask her things relevant to the investigation. Would forget he had any other purpose but to try to make her happier for a few hours.

Pain seeped across his chest. He rammed his fist against it and counted his breaths. He couldn't have a panic attack now. Couldn't run away, like his mind was shouting at him to do. *Chin up*, he used to tell Freya at half-time in under-11s football, if her head was dropping with defeat. He saw her pushing her fringe out of her eyes, straightening her blue-team bib, never one to give up without a fight.

She'd had permanently grazed knees at that age. When Paul thought of her childhood, he thought of endless jungle animal plasters. He imagined sticking one over his thrashing heart now, his messed-up head. *Patch yourself up and press on.*

The outer fringes of the estate were less familiar. He found himself in a maze of sleepy terraces, punctuated by shops that weren't obviously either open or closed. Then Google Maps told him, matter-of-factly, that he'd reached his destination. An unassuming cul-de-sac with a faded NO BALL GAMES sign. Paul took a deep breath and pulled up his hood, trying to remember how to become invisible.

Ducking behind a tree, he stared across at number 18. A small, unremarkable house. He didn't know what he'd expected. He used his phone camera to zoom in subtly, seeing no lights or movement. When he panned up towards a dark window in the roof, he wasn't sure why it sent a zip of adrenalin through his blood, an urge to holler his daughter's name. *Freya, are you in there?* He could feel her everywhere now, even in this place where she didn't belong.

What now? Wait, watch? Paul had almost forgotten the periods of anxious limbo that were a big part of investigating. The constant, smouldering fear – of discovery, of failure. He didn't even have the cushion of a false identity any more, the support of listening ears at the end of a wire. In fact, he felt gut-wrenchingly alone.

He had only one lifeline. In the shadow of the tree, he speed-texted Yvette: *Do you know if Sanderson works? What are the chances of him being out right now?*

Then, more waiting. Staring at his phone, at the house, left and right along the street. Spooking at every sound.

Finally, a reply: *He works in a garage. Taylor's. I don't know his working hours but according to their website it closes at 6.*

Paul checked the time: 4:40.

Tom Glover's voice filled his head now, ordering him away. But Paul was far beyond caring about the consequences for himself or the police. Further down the street he found a small alleyway, overgrown with weeds, which led him round the back to a row of locked gates. He counted until he reached the right one, his gaze sweeping the rear of Sanderson's house.

Stripping off his coat, Paul was reminded of how he'd felt after the Sanderson job had come to an abrupt end and he'd finally peeled off the clothes he'd worn while 'in character'. He'd taken a long bath in searing-hot water, as though to burn away the last of Paul Jacobs, but afterwards he'd felt empty. The real Paul hadn't been waiting for him after he'd shed the snakeskin of his false persona. As months had passed he'd feared he'd never find him again, until he'd met Steph and she'd slowly helped him believe he still had substance, without even really knowing she was doing it.

Thoughts of her fired his determination. He reached up to grip the top of Sanderson's fence. Pull-ups had once been his forte, but now they got harder with each passing year. He gritted his teeth, bounced on the spot, used all his strength to heave himself up. The wood was sharp as he grasped for purchase. His left leg caught and he almost dropped head-first, but managed to tumble sideways onto a damp lawn. He lay panting, bones groaning, and squinted up to see if he'd alerted any neighbours. There were no stirrings, so he crept to Sanderson's back door.

Locked. Paul didn't want to have to smash a window. He'd have to rely, if possible, on his knowledge of Sanderson. On the fact that he was a man of habits, who would never risk the indignity of being locked out of his own house.

Paul crawled around the patio, testing its slabs; none lifted. He patted the back wall but found no loose bricks. Once he'd checked the neglected plant pots, he turned his attention to the small shed. It was built on a wooden platform with a narrow gap between that and the ground. And there it was: a glimmer of metal. Paul found a stick and poked it beneath the shed, exhaling as he manoeuvred a silver key towards him.

He hurried to the back door, slid in the key, and he was inside. Standing in the kitchen of the man who hated him most in the world, looking at a dark blue coffee cup in the sink, a leftover bread crust on a plate.

After more than twenty years, he had infiltrated Sanderson's life once again.

31

Steph

Steph wasn't sure how much time had passed. She'd been sitting in the church growing colder and colder, a swampy odour rising off her damp clothes. The stained-glass window had darkened in front of her, as if the figures it depicted had been put to bed.

She was haunted by Paul's collapsed face when she'd asked her question. Had she hit on the truth, or was he just devastated she would think that of him? His phone kept going straight to voicemail, reminding her of Thursday evening, the start of it all, when she'd been trying to reach Freya. A similar feeling clawed at her now, a sense of menace she couldn't quite pin down. And a rising undercurrent of guilt.

Leaving the church, she walked back through the relentless rain. With every step, the guilt swelled. *Hypocrite*, the trees seemed to say, as the wind shook their wet leaves, showering her with even colder droplets.

Paul's car was gone from their street. Steph hesitated in the hallway of their building, hearing Heather and Brian's voices above, gathering herself to go up.

She jumped when the door to the ground-floor flat opened, and Emma emerged.

'Steph?' she said. 'I saw you come in – God, you're *soaked.*'

Steph wasn't sure whether the moisture on her face was mostly rain or tears. Her muscles had begun to shiver uncontrollably. She felt too exhausted to protest as Emma ushered

her inside her flat and settled her on a sofa. A mug of chamo-
mile tea was pressed into her hands, its heat bringing sensation back to her palms. Steph wrapped Freya's scarf around
the outside of her knuckles, like a bandage.

Then she felt something soft brush her ear. With surprise
she realised Emma had fetched a towel and was squeezing the
wet ends of her hair. The gentleness made Steph want to lean
against her. For the first time she saw her neighbour as motherly, and felt a twinge of regret that they hadn't been friends
before. It was surely impossible now. Their lives were inter-
twining only in the worst way.

Why haven't you got any friends, Mum? Freya had once
asked her, quite casually, but the question had taken Steph
aback.

I have friends, she'd said. *I've got my colleagues, and other
mums from school . . . and my book club . . .*

But in truth she wasn't close to any of those people, and
she'd only been to the book club twice before realising she
liked to read and think about books much more than she liked
to talk about them while eating breadsticks.

Anyway, you're my best friend, she'd said to Freya, with a
smile. *You and Daddy.* Freya had been thirteen then, still just
young enough to look pleased by that comment rather than
roll her eyes. *Three sides of a triangle,* they used to call themselves, telling Freya that it was the strongest shape, building
pyramids of cards or bridges of straws to demonstrate.

Where did that leave Steph now, though? With nobody to
confide in except her downstairs neighbour, a near-stranger,
whose son had become inexplicably involved.

There *was* one other person she had considered calling in
the midst of this crisis, but she'd always stopped herself. That
was separate, that was . . . She couldn't even think about it
now.

'Steph,' Emma said quietly. 'I need to talk to you.'

She moved the towel away and a draught snaked into the gap. Steph nursed her tea, noticing for the first time that the mug had a picture of Frida Kahlo on the side, looking fiery and fierce.

'My conversation with Zeb . . .' Emma said. 'What I told you all, earlier . . . There was more to it, but I wanted to see you alone.'

Steph's fingertips met around the mug. 'What do you mean?'

Emma was flushing now, hesitating. Finally she said, 'Freya thought you were having an affair.'

Steph's lips parted. For a second she couldn't speak. Then, 'What?' she said stupidly, aware of her mouth hanging open.

Emma twisted the towel around her fingers. 'She told Zeb she saw you somewhere when you were supposed to be at work. Maybe more than once. And that she'd noticed you acting strange, being secretive with your phone, telling little lies to her dad. I think she started trying to investigate . . .'

'Where?' There was a tight vibration inside Steph's skull. 'Where did she see me?'

'One time was during a driving lesson. She saw your car heading out of town.'

Steph felt like she was falling.

When you were supposed to be at work.

Telling lies to her dad.

Heading out of town.

'Zeb said she talked about getting her own car,' Emma went on, 'as soon as possible, so she could follow you—'

'*Follow* me?'

'I think so. I don't know much more, I'm afraid . . .' Emma's head jerked as if she'd just remembered something else. 'Except she mentioned a plan. Apparently she got upset, said there were parts she wasn't proud of . . .'

'Was the plan to follow me?' Steph was short of breath and it distorted her voice. 'Was that what she meant?'

'I don't know. And I'm sorry I didn't share this earlier. It's just . . . all those people. I thought you'd want to know first.'

Steph raked a hand through her hair, pulling at the knots. The sneaking doubts that had chilled her as Paul had left the church were now surfacing as waves of nausea. Everything was shifting, reshaping.

It was *her* who Freya had felt let down by, her side of the triangle that had given way.

Not Paul. You.

Freya had been trying to follow her. For a moment Steph was sure she was going to be sick. As if she could tell, Emma passed her the towel. Steph held it over her nose and inhaled.

'She really told Zeb all of this?' she asked. 'In that one night?'

'It seems so.'

'Where *is* Zeb?' Some part of Steph was trying to discredit the information, digging for a hint that Zeb was unreliable. Trying to shift the focus to Emma's relationship with her child instead.

Because if this was true, it meant she'd failed in ways she couldn't even comprehend right now. And Paul had absorbed the blame, was out there acting on it, when perhaps this was all on her. She had done this to their family and had refused to face up to the possibility.

'He's staying with his dad,' Emma said. 'They're . . . getting to know each other.'

There was something guarded about the way she said it, but Steph was too dazed to process what it might be. Robin Lyle, she recalled hazily. Was he Zeb's dad? The man in the hard hat, another stranger Steph had painted her own guilt onto. She stumbled towards the door, reaching for its handle, as though for an escape lever. When she got there, she paused and turned back. 'Thank you for telling me,' she said.

Emma's blue hair glowed like a gas flame beneath the lights. 'I just hope she comes home, Steph.'

Steph felt tears building deep inside: the kind that might tear her in half if she let them out. 'Could I . . . could I ask you not to say anything about this to anyone? I'll take it from here.'

Emma nodded, and to Steph's relief, she didn't press for any more information. They looked at each other for a few more seconds, a silent contract forming between them.

Steph fled into the hallway and stood wheezing for breath, the potential scale of her misjudgements starting to take hold. She forced herself upright, walked out of the house and got into her car. As she accelerated away, she ran through recent conversations with Freya, occasions on which she might have spotted her mum 'somewhere she shouldn't be', or seen her shielding her phone, hiding a bank statement. Suddenly Freya's silences at breakfast weren't just late-onset teenage mood swings. The disappearance of kisses from the end of her texts was not simply a side effect of her growing up, or the petering-out of their duvet nights in front of *The Apprentice*, their chats about books, their chats full stop.

And Paul was not the only parent with secrets that mattered.

How could she have been so blinkered as to think he was?

Steph was under no illusions about what it might have done to Freya, if she'd feared a threat to her parents' marriage. She thought again of little Freya wearing her wedding veil around their first flat, accessorising it with a pair of Paul's shin pads, tripping over the trailing lace every few steps. And how she'd been so upset, so scared when Jess's parents had split up – the first time it had happened to someone she was close to.

She still had one of our wedding photos in her room. Had Freya taken it from the album recently, while she'd been stewing over her suspicions? Or had she had it for a while, just because she liked it?

The deception would have wounded her, too. The thought that her mum had been lying to her, to Paul, and at the same time cheerfully buying Freya daffodils, trying to continue with their mother–daughter TV nights, their banter about applying to the same universities . . .

As cars flashed past her on the motorway, Steph realised she was slowing. Because she was no longer sure this was the right thing to do, the right place to go. She kept imagining Freya behind her, in a Mini Cooper like the ones they used to jokily draw for one another.

Following her.

How far, exactly, might she have got?

At the next junction, Steph turned off. She circled an island and rejoined the M3 to speed back home. All the way, she irrationally scanned the landscape for some kind of sign from her daughter. If she'd been blind before, now Steph had to open her eyes.

32

Paul

Paul searched Sanderson's house, on high alert for sounds of him arriving home. He imagined spotting Freya's school blazer hanging in a cupboard, a long blonde hair shimmering on the carpet. Breathing hard, he hurried up the stairs. The rooms were soulless, nothing particularly personal or sentimental anywhere. Yet little touches of luxury suggested Sanderson had some money. A flatscreen TV in the bedroom; a super-kingsized bed, which looked slept-in on one side only. Perhaps he still had part of the appallingly huge pay-off they'd been forced to award him. But nobody, it seemed, to share it with.

The attic staircase was steep and narrow, like climbing up a dim, dusty tunnel. Different from the gentle curve of the wooden steps up to Freya's attic room. When Paul reached the top of Sanderson's, he hesitated before groping for a light switch.

Then he staggered backwards.

She was in here. She was everywhere. Photos of Nathalie papered the walls: smiling, biting her lip, hiding from the camera, walking away and towards. The expressions on her face were achingly familiar, yet at one remove in their age-faded colours, like seeing somebody who vividly resembled her. Her wide green eyes, the fall of her hair, the pucker of the skin above her nose.

Paul flinched away as sadness barrelled into him. But other images took shape, took on a life of their own, filling in the parts the photos couldn't show. Nathalie smoking alone outside the tower block; Paul approaching her for the first time, walking another man's walk, offering a light. The hurt she always seemed to carry in her posture, the dreams that would trouble her eyelids as she slept. Yet her openness, too: always so open-hearted and hopeful, despite everything.

Paul's eyes went to a photo of her and Sanderson. Sanderson seemed to glare out of the picture, wary and possessive, his arm clamped tight around Nathalie.

And suddenly Paul couldn't actually think of him as *Sanderson* any more, the way Glover and other colleagues had referred to him as they'd hovered at the edges of the operation. He couldn't stay detached enough from the feelings of hatred and guilt and confusing nostalgia that were stirred up when he looked into Daniel's eyes.

He's just an over-protective big brother, Nathalie used to insist. *Especially after everything we've been through.*

There was only one photo of her daughter up here. Daniel's niece was framed separately from the rest, a miniature Nathalie with long dark lashes and unravelling pigtails. Billie. Her young eyes seemed to plead with Paul, and to reproach him, and to speak in desperate harmony with Freya: *Find me.*

Paul fought to control his breathing. White spots blotted the darkness behind his eyelids. If he could just keep them still, stop them swirling . . . He flailed to the rear window and pushed, relieved when it opened and fresh air burst in. Paul held his face to the coolness, but when he opened his eyes he got another shock.

Because he hadn't realised. Hadn't got his bearings, hadn't remembered the geography of the area well enough.

You could see the woods from here. A few miles behind the house, they stretched out like a dense carpet, the twilight casting them in a violet glow. The trees seemed to huddle closer together than ever, as though closing ranks, protecting their secrets.

Nobody goes near the woods any more, Nathalie had once told Paul.

And it wasn't so hard to understand why the locals had steered clear ever since what had happened, or how they could believe, in the absence of any other explanation, that the black spaces between the trees had swallowed the little girl who'd never been found.

In truth, Paul had no idea what had happened to five-year-old Billie in those woods, almost twenty-five years ago. A day that had changed his own future, though he couldn't have known that as he'd watched the story unfold on the news. The only witnesses, Nathalie and Daniel, said Billie had strayed too far in while playing. The search of the woodland had lasted months. The wider search for Billie had continued indefinitely – along with the stream of donations to the search fund Daniel had set up in aid of his niece.

From the moment Billie's disappearance hit the news, Daniel Sanderson had had everyone in his pocket. The public were all behind him. The press ran campaigns to *Find Our Beautiful Billie*, always featuring quotes from her distraught uncle. Nathalie had shied from the limelight, would duck her head behind Daniel's shoulder as the press photographed them leaving their block of flats. Paul still remembered thinking at the time, when he was just an ordinary police officer in south London: *There's something about her, about the two of them.* But mostly: *There's something about him.*

And, as he'd later discovered, the Nottingham police had thought so too. Except they'd found it impossible even to question Daniel as a suspect – such was the power of the public's support, the press's attention. Daniel had built a narrative around Billie as a working-class child, claiming that people never cared about kids like her, that deep down everybody believed her family must have brought it on themselves.

Donations poured in from individuals anxious to show they weren't like that.

The donations had soared each time the police had interviewed either Daniel or Nathalie, too. The papers went to town on police prejudice, victimisation of a suffering family. Daniel had managed to secure a forcefield around himself and his sister, strong enough to make the police back away.

They never took their eye off Daniel, though. Never stopped attempting to monitor his *Find Our Beautiful Billie* fund, wondering what all that cash was really being used for, whether Beautiful Billie had suffered something terrible at the hands of her doting uncle. Several years on, when Paul had finished his undercover training, he'd been approached by DI Tom Glover about a job he'd thought Paul would be perfect for.

Not drugs or gangs or activists, like most UC assignments. This was a missing-child case that couldn't be solved with traditional methods. It involved getting close to a family, and it was sensitive, needed to be handled just right . . .

Now a noise broke Paul's thoughts, making him leap back from the attic window, then freeze in place.

A car door slamming out front. Footsteps and the jangle of keys.

33

Kate

Twenty-five years earlier

I crush two pills in advance, shake the white powder into a little tub that previously held cotton buds, and hide it in my pocket. When I give Becca the nod, she pauses and I think for a moment that she's going to back out. Leave me alone with this plan after all. But I know she won't, really, know her instinct to stand by me is too strong. She sucks in a breath and lets out an impressive shriek. There's a delay, then the sound of Nick's footsteps.

He bursts into my room. 'What's going on?'

Becca hops onto the bed. 'Spider!'

He rolls his eyes. 'Thought someone had been killed.'

'Oh, God, I can't *stand* them. Think it crawled under the bed. I won't be able to relax until I know it's gone.'

'Good Lord,' Nick grumbles, but he's in the right mood to be the hero. He grabs an empty tumbler from the bedside table and drops to his knees.

He's soon absorbed in his mission so I sidle out, catching Becca's eye as I go. I need to work fast, don't want to leave them alone for too long. Can't rely on Nick's good mood lasting.

I pull the kitchen door shut behind me. The plan is to slip half the powder into his beer and half into his food. Pouring crumbled pills into the neck of a glass bottle is trickier than I'd anticipated, especially with trembling hands. I do what I can, and use the handle of a long spoon to stir as quietly as possible. Then I glance around again. The bacon's cooling in the frying pan but I can't see the scrambled eggs. I yank open the microwave to find a bowl in there, the yellow mixture starting to solidify. Luckily there's enough liquid to dissolve the remainder of the crushed tablets. Putting back the bowl, though, I'm struck by doubt. What if a normal dose of pills won't make him sick? He's much bigger than Becca: they might have nowhere near the same effect. And what if he doesn't eat all the scrambled egg, or drink enough beer? He could end up with only a fraction of the powder in his stomach, and I'll have to watch him take my mum away.

I jump at the sound of his returning footsteps, leaping away from the microwave as the kitchen door creaks.

'Couldn't find it,' he says, strolling back in. 'She'll live.'

I can't speak. My cheeks are on fire. Nick looks at me curiously, then his eyes move back to his bacon, cold and fatty on the stove. 'Don't feel that hungry any more.' He lifts the hem of his T-shirt to wipe some dust from his face.

'Mum'd be cross if you wasted it.'

'True! Don't want to start the weekend on a sour note.' He grabs a plate and sticks a couple of rashers onto it. I think he's going to stop at that, but to my relief he takes the eggs from the microwave and tips out the whole lot, splattering them in brown sauce before sitting down at the table.

He pauses as his fork heads for his mouth. 'Want some?'

I shake my head.

'I'll leave you some money.' The forkful hovers. 'You can have a takeaway on me later.' In it goes. Will there be a strange taste, a gritty texture? He chews slowly, then follows it with another mouthful, washing it down with a swig of beer. I realise I'm watching too intently, and busy myself clearing pots. The sounds of him eating and drinking continue behind me. I mumble something about Becca and flee the kitchen.

Just as I'm about to go back into my room, the phone in the hall rings. I don't want Nick to leave his food to answer it so I grab the receiver. 'Hello?'

'Hi, love.' It's Mum. My heart judders. What would she say if she knew what I'd just done? Would she be horrified? Grateful?

'Just picked up some shopping to keep you and Becca going this weekend,' she says. 'The bags are heavy. Could you ask Nick to come down to Costcutter and help me? Ask *nicely*, though, Kate.'

I glance at the kitchen door. 'He ... er ... he's busy. I'll come.' Before she can object, I hang up. For a few seconds I stand there, too much breath in my mouth, not enough in my lungs.

I poke my head round my bedroom door and whisper to Becca, 'Got to help Mum carry some shopping back. Won't be long.'

'Did you do it?' She's pale, as though she really is afraid of a lurking spider.

I nod, holding up crossed fingers.

'Is he eating it?'

I nod again. 'Now we'll just have to wait and see.'

As I walk off I'm light-headed, suddenly euphoric, and a blade of evening sun leads me down the corridor.

34

Steph

Steph sat in her car outside her house, her windscreen slowly steaming up, black skeletons of trees disappearing behind the veil. Back from her aborted mission, she was at a loss as to what to do next.

She couldn't stop thinking about that first night, when Freya's absence could be measured in hours rather than days, and the PCs had asked whether Steph or Paul had any enemies. Paul's conscience had clearly tortured and driven him ever since. But Steph had refused to join the dots between her own secrets and the protective sphere she'd tried to hold around her family, like a spell. If they did somehow connect, the picture they would form was everything she'd ever feared.

There was something to grasp onto now, though. A sign that she had to join those dots, face the unthinkable. She seized her phone and scrolled to a number she'd called 'Work 2' in her contacts. Her finger froze on the screen as she was hit by the same doubts she'd had while driving along the motorway just now. Attacking this head-on seemed too risky. There were risks to every plan she thought of: risks to Freya and Paul, to herself, her whole existence.

Risks if she was wrong, risks if she was right.

Minutes later, she was pounding on Emma's door. She knew she was knocking too loudly, that it was getting late, but they were far beyond neighbourly etiquette. And Steph was beyond worrying what Emma thought of her, even beyond worrying whether she was completely trustworthy. She had nowhere else to turn.

Her neighbour peered out into the hall. 'Steph?'

'I need you to do something for me.'

Emma blinked and beckoned her in.

Steph didn't waste any time. Adrenalin was flying around her body. She thrust forward a piece of paper. 'Take this to the police.'

Emma looked startled. 'What?'

Steph swallowed. 'It – it's an address. Urge them to watch the place, keep their eyes on it. But don't mention any connection with me.'

Emma blinked several more times. 'I don't know if I—'

'Please!' Steph interrupted before she could restrain herself. She'd hoped to keep her emotions in check, but now she sensed her desperation was striking a chord. Her neighbour stared at her for a long moment. Steph could hear that creaking sound again, the turning wheel, this time a haunting soundtrack.

'Can't you give it to them yourself?' Emma said, in a low voice.

'No . . . no.'

'They'll ask me a load of questions.'

'Call the tip-line anonymously,' Steph said. 'Just be sure they take it seriously. Say you saw a teenage girl in a navy Puffa jacket going into that house. I can't risk them recognising my voice.'

There was another pause. The wheel continued to rattle. Steph couldn't tell which direction it was coming from and it was starting to get to her now, like it might actually be cogs inside her head. She rubbed the ends of Freya's scarf, her comfort blanket. 'I wouldn't ask if I didn't have to,' she said.

'What are you afraid of, Steph? Is it Paul?'

'What?'

'Are you scared of him?'

'No, of course not! I love him, that's why I . . . why I can't . . .'

'I want to help, but you have to tell me the whole story.'

'I'm not having an affair. It's not that.' Steph felt another volley of fear. She stepped closer to grab her neighbour's hand. Emma tensed but didn't pull away. Her fingers felt as small-boned as Freya's used to, in the days when Steph would grip her hand to cross the road or walk through the park. Even as a little girl, Freya had resisted Steph's over-protectiveness. Perhaps she'd always sensed her mum's subconscious fears, running deeper than regular parental anxiety.

Steph tried one last appeal, pushing the address into Emma's palm. 'Please. I know you understand what I'm going through. This could save my daughter.'

35

Emma

Emma closed the door behind Steph and leaned against it, expelling a long breath.

She unfurled the address in her clammy hand, and a crush of responsibility bore down on her. Should she carry out Steph's request, in the secretive way she wanted? Or go to the police and tell them everything, hand over the burden? Why did the thought of the latter make her hug the address protectively to her chest?

Maybe Steph wouldn't have put so much faith in Emma if she knew she was hiding a mess of secrets and troubles, too. Or maybe she'd chosen her for that very reason. A strange affinity seemed to be developing between them, impossible to walk away from.

Taking out her phone, she searched on Google Maps and Street View, zooming in on an ordinary terrace near Chertsey, only twelve miles away. She couldn't think of a way to find out anything more. Couldn't forget Steph's wide, desperate eyes, her hands fretting at the fabric of that green scarf . . .

Something made her pause. What had just tapped at the back of her brain? The scarf . . . Steph had been wearing it ever since Freya had gone missing, but Emma had seen it somewhere else recently too.

She followed her train of thought into Zeb's room, grabbing his photo-booth strip from the bedside cabinet. Freya was wearing the green scarf in those pictures. It made sense that it was hers, that Steph was clinging to it in her absence . . .

and now that she thought about it, Emma had seen Freya with it before. But that wasn't what was nagging at her.

She was sure Freya *hadn't* been wearing it in the photo strip Steph had shown her only that morning. As Emma cast her mind back, other differences began to bother her. Hadn't Zeb been wearing his brown winter coat in Freya's version but his leather jacket in the pictures she was now studying? And wasn't Freya's hair slightly different, too? Emma wished she could trust her memory, wished she could put the strips side by side to compare. Each time she swung towards thinking she was imagining things, something else would swing her back. Freya was drinking vodka here; Zeb had mentioned gin in his story. Were they, in fact, separate occasions? Had Zeb lied about the number of times he and Freya had met? If so, *why*?

Emma left the room and paced around her cluttered flat, something she seemed to have done too many times lately. She went to the window, inching it open to feel the cool night air on her face. The rain from earlier made the dark pavements look varnished, the puddles under the streetlamps like pools of golden oil. When the home phone began to ring, she jumped even more violently than usual, then felt a rush of combustible anger. She'd had enough of these intrusive calls. Enough of *everything*.

She stomped to the kitchen and snatched the receiver. This time she didn't even say hello, meeting the other person's breathy silence with her own. A long, intense moment pulled tight between them.

'Robin?' she demanded.

She expected the click of a hang-up. Instead the caller's breathing quickened. Perhaps Emma would have hung up herself, if her emotions hadn't been swirling, climbing. What was Robin trying to do to her, even after all this time? She wasn't fifteen any more. And in messing with her – the parenting book, the eggs, the calls – he was also messing with a couple who were going through the worst possible ordeal.

She didn't even want to follow her fears to their very end. To the connection between what she knew of Robin's character and what she was starting to worry she *didn't* know about Zeb.

'This has got to stop,' she said into the phone, heat flooding her cheeks. 'Stop fucking with my head. Stop sending things to this house. And . . .' her voice was rising, uncontrollable '. . . and *give me back my son.*'

She shouted the last part much louder than she'd intended. Threw the phone against the wall with a crack. She stood panting, and cringing, but filled with a sense of release. Then she heard footsteps down the stairs again. She gulped air as a knock came on the door, and Steph's voice: 'Emma?'

Emma slumped into her window chair. She couldn't face Steph now.

'I'm okay,' she shouted. 'Sorry.'

She heard Steph lingering at the door. Her head felt as if it was going to explode. She laid her brow against the cold windowpane, letting it freeze away all sensation until her neighbour retreated.

36

Paul

Paul was flattened against Daniel's attic wall, listening hard, his heart thrashing. Someone, presumably Daniel, was wandering around downstairs, doors creaking and closing. His movements seemed unhurried, as if he was as yet oblivious to the intruder.

Paul eyed the rear attic window. It was still open a crack where he'd gasped for air, and would probably open further, but how would he get down the back of the house? He peered out and glimpsed the woods again, the furthest trees now silhouetted in a spiky curve along the horizon. Creeping back across the attic, he stared instead down the narrow staircase, his brain fritzing with options.

His muscles tightened when the footsteps grew louder. Daniel was directly below now, on the first floor. Paul held his breath and pressed himself into the wall again. A toilet flushed and a vibration of pipes enveloped the attic. Then the swing of a door, a brief pause, the sound of receding footsteps.

Paul edged his way down the stairs to the first-floor landing. There was a burning in his chest. He could hear the hum of a television, and when he risked a peek over the banister he saw the living-room door was closed. Could he make it out of the front door while Daniel was in there? He snuck down the final flight of stairs, two groaning beneath his feet, but froze when he heard the squeak of sofa springs and a cough.

He was three or four paces from the front door now. His eyes did a speedy assessment of its latches and locks. It looked a simple case of twisting the top latch upwards and pushing the handle down.

So why wasn't he diving towards it?

He knew from past experience that wavering over a decision could mean the difference between escape and discovery. You had to keep your head, make rational choices, then act on them swiftly and confidently. It wasn't fear of failure holding him back this time. It was a much greater force, Freya's voice again in his ringing ears. Why had he broken into Daniel Sanderson's house if only to slink out?

Then a shout came from the living room, leapfrogging across decades: 'Who's there?'

For a second, the years seemed to concertina. Paul almost called back as Paul Jacobs, as if strolling into Daniel and Nathalie's flat: *Only me! Picked up some beers for us all.*

As time bounced back, his fists balled tight. A cold draught emanated from the front door as if to remind him how close it was.

'Who's *there?*'

Paul threw up his hands as Daniel crashed into the hall brandishing a cricket bat. He stopped dead when he saw Paul. A bubble of shock seemed to form around him, fixing him in place, like a bronze batsman on a trophy.

'What the . . .' For a moment his defences seemed weakened. That would have been the time to rush at him, disarm him, but Paul's composure was blown too. He took in the face he used to study endlessly for signs of untruth. The face he used to catch staring at Nathalie sometimes, with a look that was somehow both tender and cold, intimate and calculating. Now, Daniel must have been fifty-three but the shadows beneath his eyes had a look of permanence, as if he was tired of being himself. He was still broad, though, and strong-looking, dressed in grey overalls with some kind of logo on the breast pocket.

Daniel's face twisted with prolonged shock, then settled into an expression of dark loathing. 'What the *fuck* are you doing here?'

Paul kept his hands up. 'Drop the bat.'

Daniel stepped forward, holding it over Paul's head. Paul tried to gauge whether he could grab it, block it, but it didn't swing down, only hovered. 'I should knock you out. I should kill you.'

'But you won't.'

You won't if you've got my daughter, because you won't want a scene. Equally, maybe you won't if you haven't touched Freya, because you must wonder why I'm here, after all this time, after everything.

'We've an agreement,' Daniel said. 'I'm not under investigation any more. You spying bastards admitted you were in the wrong.'

'I'm not here for that.'

'What, then? Not done enough damage?'

'My daughter.' Paul watched for a reaction, but there was only a flicker: possibly surprise, possibly knowledge, possibly imagined. He was long out of practice at reading what Daniel was thinking.

'We could talk calmly,' he ventured, as Daniel stayed silent, 'or you could hit me and see what happens. Either way, I'm not leaving till you've answered my questions.'

Daniel lunged forward and pushed the bat against Paul's throat. Their bodies lined up squarely as he pinned him to the wall. There had been a competitive edge to their past 'friendship', which had seemed to come from their similar builds, and perhaps from the fact that Paul had made an effort to mirror Daniel's body language and way of speaking. It was something they taught you in training, how to make someone take to you, but it could work the other way too, could set you up as a rival.

Their gazes met, almost exactly level. The wood bit into Paul's neck.

'Where's my daughter?' he wheezed. 'What have you done?'

Daniel slammed his weight behind the bat. '*You*'re the bad guy here. I can't believe you've shown your face.'

Paul's vision slipped in and out of blackness. He closed his eyes, sucked in shallow breaths.

'You don't even feel bad about my sister,' Daniel said, 'do you?'

Paul blinked open his eyes. 'Every day,' he choked. 'I loved her.'

The fist took him by surprise, punching him in the stomach before he'd registered that the bat had lifted from his Adam's apple. Air shot into his throat just as it was thumped out of his abdomen, a mix of heady relief and deep, low pain.

'Don't disrespect her even further by lying,' Daniel said.

'I'm not lying. I loved Nathalie.'

'*I* loved her.'

By controlling her. By using her grief to your advantage. But hadn't Paul done the same? Hadn't he thought he was so *smart*, using her as his way in? Nathalie hadn't shared Daniel's guardedness, that was the thing. You could tell just by observing her that she'd suffered a loss and was desperate to plug the void. So, when Paul had been dropped into his new life on the Chainwell Estate, trained and prepped, ambitious and naïve, he'd set out to befriend her first. To keep 'bumping into her' when her brother wasn't around, and patiently to gain her trust. He'd been the odd-job man, who'd turned up to fix the fridge in the café where she'd worked; the fellow smoker ready with a light outside the tower block; the cheeky chappy making her laugh even when her eyes were still so sad. Then Paul had used everything in his skill set to overcome Daniel's wariness of his little sister's new boyfriend. Painstakingly, he'd established himself in their lives, their flat, their family, watching and listening for any clue as to what had really happened to Billie. He hadn't noticed the growth of his feelings for Nathalie until it was too late. He'd been blinkered, fixated on his task . . . and he'd never been in love before. Didn't know how it could coil itself around you while you were looking the other way.

Paul saw the next punch coming but didn't duck. Let it smash him full in the face. This was the kind of punishment he could take: an attack on himself, not Freya, not Nathalie. He stood firm as Daniel hit again and pain splintered across his cheekbones.

'She was my sister,' Daniel roared. 'And you were nothing. Nobody. A pig. A liar. A *murderer.*'

The final word made a fist around Paul's heart. There was another second of dizzy reprieve, before the cricket bat struck his knees and he folded to the floor. Daniel kicked him in the ribs and Paul let himself go limp. His head spun with voices, mingling with Daniel's stream of accusations.

Nathalie saying, *Who the hell* are *you?*

Steph saying, *Did you kill someone?*

Freya saying, *Dad, you're not giving up?*

And he was so close to giving up. Closing his eyes and accepting what he deserved. But how about what Freya and Steph deserved? What about everything Yvette had tried to do for him, to help him see that he had made mistakes but he wasn't evil?

The next time Daniel came at him, Paul hauled his torso up and head-butted him in the face. The agony of the movement brought bile into his mouth. He'd managed to unbalance Daniel, though, so he jerked his leg into his shin, making him stagger against the wall. Paul swayed to his feet. His ribs felt shattered. He lurched towards the door, but Daniel was back upright, blocking the way. Paul flailed towards the kitchen instead. Daniel followed, his face purple, brandishing the cricket bat streaked with Paul's blood.

Paul felt as if he was moving through water as he strained for the back door. The bat thudded between his shoulder-blades, doubling him over. He grasped a kitchen worktop, twisting around to find himself once again cornered, Daniel's face blurrily close, further accusations forming beads of saliva at the corners of his mouth. *Liar. Traitor. Failure. Killer.*

Something inside Paul gave way. He couldn't take one more blow, one more shouted declaration of his crimes versus Daniel's self-proclaimed innocence. Old instincts had already caused him to do a lightning-quick check as he'd stumbled through to the kitchen. He knew where his exits were, but he'd also clocked the set of knives clinging to a magnetic holder on the wall. As Daniel swung the bat again, Paul reached side-ways and his fingertips brushed metal.

37

Kate

Twenty-five years earlier

The neighbourhood fuzzes past as I trace the familiar route to the local shops to meet Mum. My instinct is to rush, but at the same time I want to slow things right down, return home only once the pills have worked. I imagine Nick bent over the toilet bowl, clutching his stomach and groaning that he's not well enough to go on holiday.

Mum's waiting for me outside Costcutter, the sea of carrier bags at her feet wrinkling in the slight breeze. I'm too nervous to make conversation as we wander back. Mum seems quiet too, trudging along, tired from work, she says. The bag handles cut grooves into my palms and the evening feels humid and sticky.

'You'll be okay this weekend, won't you, love?'

'Yes,' I mumble. 'We'll be fine.'

Halfway home we bump into Linda, the Irish lady who lives below us, next door to Nick. I've sometimes thought about asking her: *Do you ever hear anything? Noises that don't seem right?* But surely Nick's too clever for that.

We chat to Linda for what feels like ages. She and Mum talk about Linda's son, who's nineteen – Becca flirts with him whenever she comes to visit. I can't stop looking towards the tower block, wishing for telescopic vision, until finally the conversation ends.

It takes us a while to climb the stairs because the lift's still broken. I grab another bag from Mum to lighten her load. The whole of our floor reeks of Nick's bacon and egg. Mum sniffs the air and I can barely keep my tone casual as I explain he made himself a snack.

She goes in ahead. My whole body's braced: will the plan have worked, or will Nick come whistling from the kitchen, asking Mum if she's ready to hit the road? How fast might the pills take effect, if at all?

Mum calls out a greeting but nobody responds. A second or two later, Becca comes out of my room. She still looks pale and her smile doesn't bend right. I try desperately to read her expression, catch her eye. I'm hot again and the label on my school shirt is niggling at my neck.

'Where's Nick?' Mum asks.

'Bathroom,' Becca says.

My heart speeds up. Does that mean . . .?

'Have you coloured your hair, Becca?' Mum asks, as I try to listen for noises from behind the bathroom door.

'Yeah,' Becca says distractedly, twirling a purple strand around her finger.

Mum's gaze moves to the towel lying rumpled on my bedroom carpet. 'Hope the stains come out of that,' she says, in the tight voice she's started using more and more lately. It's almost like she chooses Becca to take out her stress on, like she's afraid to provoke Nick, and she's habitually soft on me, so somebody has to bear the brunt.

Today's exchange doesn't get a chance to escalate. There's the sound of a flush, and a lock being drawn across, the bathroom door opening.

And there is Nick. Looking normal. Fine. Smelling of minty soap.

He smiles at Mum and kisses her. 'Was wondering where you'd got to. Ready to go?'

★   ★   ★

I watch from the kitchen window as they leave. Two miniature figures walking away from the tower block towards a taxi. Nick somehow manages to carry all the luggage while keeping one arm around Mum's shoulders. If other people are watching from the flats, they're probably thinking what an attentive boyfriend he is. I press my face against the steamed-up pane as the taxi door closes behind them.

'We tried, Kate,' Becca says. 'Maybe it's for the best that it didn't work. It's only three days . . . Your mum will be okay.'

I say nothing, just stare at the frying pan and the bowl that held his scrambled eggs, now dripping slow bubbles onto the draining board.

We channel-hop our way through the evening. I don't want to use the money Nick left us for a takeaway so Becca digs a pizza out of the freezer. We leave it in the oven too long; it tastes like ashy cardboard. She drinks one of Nick's beers and the smell makes me feel like he's in the room.

Why hasn't Mum rung to say they've got there okay? Did she promise she would? I can't remember now. Everything's muddled. I search the kitchen for the address of the B-and-B they're staying at. Where did Mum say she would leave it? I wish I'd concentrated. I was just so intent on stopping them going.

'I can't find the address,' I say, banging drawers open and shut. 'I don't even know where they've gone!'

'Kate, you're exhausted.' Becca pulls me away from the drawer I'm riffling through, closing it gently. 'You should go to bed. I'll find the address.'

She's right. I'm so tired. I sleepwalk through my bedtime routine, but when I wriggle under the covers my brain refuses to rest. I'm having a feverish conversation with Mum inside my head, telling her to get far away from him, begging her to come home.

Becca comes into the room not long after, smelling of the almond oil she slicks through her hair every night to keep it glossy. The dark room fills with shuffling noises as she adjusts her sleeping-bag. Her breathing smoothes out almost instantly, and I wonder if she's really as anxious as me, or if she's just been enjoying the drama. As the night crawls on, my waking worries and half-asleep nightmares smear together: I see Nick standing over my bed; I hear a violent argument in the next room, can't move any part of my body to stop it.

And Becca sleeps. I'm just beginning to get really worked up, convinced that her deep, dreamy snores are some kind of betrayal, when I hear her voice: 'Kate? Kate?' A sound of covers being thrown back, floorboards creaking, and then I feel her climbing into bed beside me, warm arms squeezing me close. That's when I realise I've woken her with my sobs, and she's wiping tears from my face, kissing my cheek. I cuddle against her like I used to with Mum in those early mornings, just the two of us, and I realise it's not Becca I'm mad at, it's myself and it's Nick and it's Mum and it's everything.

I don't know what time it is when I next wake. There's milky light at the windows and Becca is still beside me, our limbs tangled together, her almond-scented hair tickling my nose. It takes me a few moments to realise that the phone is ringing from the hall.

The phone is ringing.

In a heartbeat I'm up, scrambling over Becca, who mumbles and stirs. I glance at the clock as I streak past. Five a.m. It's not good, it can't be good. My head roars as I grab the receiver.

38

Emma

Yet again, Emma had not made it to bed. She sat cross-legged on her living-room floor, encircled by photos, occasionally lifting one up and angling it towards the light.

Intermittently there were footsteps from above. Steph was still awake, too, maybe listening to Emma's movements just as she was hearing Steph's, feeling the other woman's presence and trying to predict what she was thinking. Emma glanced at the Chertsey address lying just beyond her moat of photos, a reminder of the decision she had to make. It seemed even more complicated now that she suspected Zeb hadn't told her the whole truth about Freya. She kept picking up her phone to text him, then putting it down again. *I'll Skype him in the morning. Look him in the eye and ask calmly.*

The pictures she was sifting through were mostly of him. In one, he was six months old and she held him on her knee, still a kid herself, the baby seeming physically to overwhelm her. Perhaps most parents divided their existence into the era before they'd had children and the era after, but Emma often got the feeling she'd lived her life on shuffle. At times she felt ancient compared to her friends, who used Tinder, drank fifteen-pound cocktails and never seemed afraid. Other times she would try to embrace her early thirties: she'd allow herself to be set up on dates but would usually chicken out, telling herself she was a mum and a businesswoman, no room for romance.

She stalled over a picture of herself in school uniform, year ten, not long before she'd fallen pregnant. Automatically, she started picking faults. Her arms were awkward twigs, her chest was concave, eyes too big for her face. Suddenly she was that girl again: that spiky, slow-to-develop teenager, who felt as if a layer of her skin peeled off each time she was taunted by the class bully.

Not even the *class* bully, in fact. Her own personal bully, or so it had seemed, who would relentlessly single her out, always accompanied by two silent, smirking disciples.

Alien Girl, he used to call her. He would draw cartoon aliens with goggle-eyes and pinched faces, leaving the sketches on her desk or sticking them to the back of her school jumper. They really did bear an uncanny resemblance to her – Emma could see it and so could their sniggering classmates. Sometimes he would point at her braless chest, in front of everyone, and declare that her species obviously didn't have tits. *Maybe all your species are actually lads, even the ones pretending to be chicks. What have you got down* there, *Alien 'Girl'?* She recalled how his eyes had dropped towards the hem of her skirt, how he and his two mates had roared with laughter when she'd hovered a protective hand in front of her crotch.

One lunchtime – and Emma's stomach still liquefied at the memory – he'd crept up behind her while she was eating sandwiches with her small group of friends, and she'd felt something cold and wet touch the back of her neck. She'd let out a shriek of surprise, but her bully had stayed silent for once, his fingers delving into her hair, spreading slimy wetness. She'd tried to pull away but he'd pushed her head forward and ground the gunge into her roots. Only as he'd extricated his fingers had she heard his familiar guffaw, cueing the obedient snickers of the other two.

Later, she'd discovered that it was a large blob of 'alien ectoplasm' from a joke shop. Green and sticky with a strong rubbery smell. She'd spent the rest of the day in the toilet trying to get it out of her hair, crying as she'd snapped her friend's comb and the knotted, gluey mess had just got worse. Eventually she'd been forced to hack into it with a pair of blunt school scissors, leaving bald patches that she'd covered with a hat for months.

She'd felt powerless, not wanting to tell her mum or the teachers, even assuring her friends it was all fine, quite funny, really. But whenever she reached the limits of what she could laugh off, he would decide to be nice to her for a while. Perching on her desk, calling her 'Em' and asking if she knew what this quadratic-equation bollocks was all about. After months of humiliation, one friendly word could melt her into a puddle of gratitude. She'd never known how long these interludes would last, though, could never predict when she'd next find her chair drowned in black ink ('Alien Girl blood'), or adorned with a dead frog that had been squeezed to make its eyes bulge like hers.

She remembered the day he'd followed her home from school. The thrum of her heart as she'd sensed him on her heels, the shock and relief as he'd caught up with her and behaved like they were buddies. When he'd offered to carry her bag she'd been sure he would bowl it into the river; when he'd flirtatiously poked her ribs she'd waited for some comment about her figure.

She'd been spellbound with fear and fascination. That knife-edge of pride and dread as she'd gone into a pub with him, as he'd managed to get served, as cheap vodka had bubbled through her veins and he'd asked if she'd got a boyfriend.

Uh ... no. I haven't. She had to admit, it had flattered her that he'd even thought she might.

A slow smile had spread across his face. *Good.*

Her heart had started to pound, the vodka setting off stars in her head.

Good, he'd said again. *Because Robin really likes you.*

She hadn't understood at first. The tipsiness had slowed her brain. Her bully, Andy, had nodded towards the corner of the pub and she'd followed his gaze to notice his two loyal followers sitting there. When had they come in? Emma had often thought of them as one entity: Andy's audience who validated his bullying with their devoted attention, their emotionless laughter.

For the first time, across the pub, she'd contemplated them separately. Robin was the quieter of the two, with brown hair and freckles, not the redhead whose gormless grin exposed the fillings in his back teeth.

Emma had returned her gaze to her lap. *Yeah, right.*

I mean it, Andy had insisted. *He thinks you're really fit. And he likes how clever you are at school.*

She'd wanted to believe that part. Often she'd fantasised about a boyfriend who would admire her intelligence instead of mocking it, but who would fancy her too, be proud to be seen with her. Nervously, she'd considered Robin again. He'd been looking at Andy but he'd glanced at her and their eyes had met. She remembered how he'd shuffled, seemed awkward; she'd recognised that awkwardness and, somewhere in her woozy head, had convinced herself they had things in common.

Andy had beckoned Robin over. He'd hesitated, and Emma had considered bolting, to save herself from any possibility of humiliation. But she'd felt glued to her sweaty seat as Robin had approached and Andy had urged them to sit next to one another, widening his legs on their shared bench to force them closer together. Of course, looking back now, she could see that Andy had been revelling in yet another game of control. But she'd lapped up the attention, blushing as Robin had paid her compliments under Andy's instruction.

You like how smart she is, don't you, Rob?

Maybe Robin's next words had been the real turning point. Eyes to the table, he'd mumbled: *Yeah, and good at art.*

The warmth in her cheeks had deepened. Robin had noticed she was good at art? She'd been pretty sure that hadn't been part of Andy's script. But clearly he'd thought, *Nice one, Rob*, because he'd stood up then and declared he was going to stop playing gooseberry now.

Emma had seen his suggestive wink as he'd left. Could replay it to this day. But at the time, her skin still aglow from Robin's comment, she'd chosen to ignore it.

An awkward silence had fallen once they were alone. Robin had moved a few inches away, especially when a group of popular girls from school had sauntered in. Emma's glow had started to die. Memories had returned: the frog on her chair . . . had Robin sourced that for Andy? The ectoplasm: had Robin been the one holding her still as Andy had mashed it into her scalp, or had it been the other guy, or had she imagined the hand on her arm? Goose-bumps drove any last warmth from her skin and she'd come close to fleeing, until Robin had murmured something.

Sorry about him.

Emma hadn't known what to say. 'Sorry' didn't cover it, not even a fraction, but still there'd been a power in hearing it that had almost made her burst into tears. She'd felt light and soft and strange, and when he'd asked if she wanted another drink she'd nodded.

Let's sit outside, he'd said. *It's too hot in here.*

They'd perched on a wall in the pub's deserted garden, chatting quite normally. Then he'd stubbed out his fag and shuffled closer. The kiss had been clumsy at first but he'd seemed to relax into it, and she'd tried to as well, tried to calm the tornado of her thoughts. *This is okay. He's not like Andy. He said he was sorry. He thinks I'm good at art.* She'd even giggled as they'd rolled off the wall and lain behind it on the cold concrete, shielded by a row of stinking bins.

She'd been so nervous about going back to school the next

day. Excited, though, about seeing him. Surely others would be able to tell how last night had changed her. Surely they'd guess she felt both ashamed and alive, that she hadn't been able to look her mum in the eye, that she'd cried in the shower but hugged her secret close.

In the form room, people had started tittering as she'd arrived. Shooting glances her way, grinning behind their hands.

There'd been a new drawing on her desk. The usual goggle-eyes and tiny twig body, but this time Andy had made the lips bigger, poutier, redder. Emma had started to panic. More laughter had rumbled as she'd grabbed the drawing and screwed it in her fist, breaking her normal policy of not reacting. She would never usually sit down without checking her chair first, either, but she had done that morning, straight onto a condom blown up like a balloon.

The room had erupted. The effort of holding back tears had made her cheekbones throb. She'd gripped the edges of her desk and only when she'd been sure of not crying had she lifted her eyes to seek out Robin. He'd been looking at her, his face solemn, unreadable. Ashamed, perhaps? Of what was happening now, of what they'd done last night, of being associated with her at all? Emma's expression had become pleading, but when he'd noticed Andy observing them, Robin had turned abruptly away. He hadn't laughed with everybody else, but he hadn't stopped the laughter either. He'd spared her just one more glance before they'd returned to their places in the social order.

From then on Robin had ignored her. Wouldn't look at her, speak to her, continued to watch Andy make her days a misery. Emma's shame had brewed hot and angry. She felt like she'd fallen for their final trick. As if the loss of her virginity on grubby concrete had been the culmination of his mission – Andy's, or Robin's, or both.

By the time she'd discovered she was pregnant, it was too late to do anything about it. And year ten was over, the stress of school had melted into listless summer. All her peers were shopping for bikinis and trying not to think about GCSEs. Emma, instead, was plucking up the courage to tell her parents she had something alive and terrifying wriggling inside her belly. Her own alien baby. Her dad had been the one to fixate on who the father was, but Emma had refused to give a name, or to tell Robin he'd got her pregnant. She'd wanted to leave that school and never see him again.

And then there was Zeb. Zeb, with his little star-shaped hands reaching out from beneath a cloud of blankets. Zeb, with the tender swirl at the back of his head, the miniature feet that would kick as if air-swimming. Zeb, whom she wanted to pretend was nothing to do with bullies, or a patch of concrete behind a wall of bins.

They'd lived for almost eighteen years in their little bubble, Robin never knowing of Zeb's existence, and Zeb seemingly content with his mum and grandparents and only a question mark of a dad. Emma should have known the bubble would burst, but she hadn't expected it to happen quite so spectacularly. Five months ago, Robin had bumped into an old classmate who knew why Emma had moved schools and, assuming Robin knew too, had casually released the secret Emma had kept for so long. Robin had tracked Emma down and had been bombarding her with emails ever since, insisting they should talk, meet, even asking where she lived, pushing for photos of Zeb. Each new message in her inbox had triggered the kind of panic she hadn't experienced since school. *Delete, delete, delete. Pretend this isn't happening. Pray it will all go away.*

What she hadn't realised, though, was that Zeb had made a discovery of his own. As he'd grown up and started college, branching outside their bubble, he'd begun to wonder about his father. Thinking back now, Emma realised he'd tried to ask her about him, but she'd shut down every discussion. So he'd resorted to snooping for clues, eventually learning Robin's identity by eavesdropping on a conversation between Emma and her mum.

At the same time as Emma had been deleting Robin's emails, feeling nauseous even at the sight of his name on her screen, Zeb had been googling that name, posting it on Facebook, trying to find the man Emma was so keen to erase.

Except she hadn't even erased him well enough. She'd left one of his emails in her inbox, her laptop open in the living room, and she'd heard Zeb's shout as she'd been putting away washing in her room. *What the fuck, Mum?* She still remembered freezing while hanging up her favourite 1970s blouse, letting it slide off the hanger as she'd realised her mistake.

How could you have denied me a dad? Zeb had said during the awful argument that had followed, or maybe even a subsequent one – they all merged now. *How could you not tell me he's been emailing you about me, while I've been scouring the fucking internet to find him?*

It's about the worst thing you could've done.

After that, things had slipped out of her control. Zeb had Robin's email address and was determined to make contact. When he'd come to her at work, already packed, and announced he was moving in with his dad to help renovate an old remote house, Emma had lost her cool. She'd clutched at straws to explain why she wouldn't let him go, her voice getting higher and louder in the street outside her shop. The house didn't sound safe, the dust would aggravate his asthma . . .

After he'd gone, Emma had cried on her mum's shoulder and Julie had tentatively suggested that maybe Robin was a different person now. But Emma wouldn't be fooled again. He'd taken her son and he was sending her messages: that she was in need of a parenting book; that she could be unravelled by some heavy breathing down a phone, or a raw egg that was surely supposed to remind her of the ectoplasm. Just as easily unravelled as when she was fifteen.

She put down the school photo, blinking back tears. Her eyes were tugged again to the address Steph had given her, and guilt crashed over her for sitting on it, not doing *anything*.

After I've spoken to Zeb, she promised, her stomach a ball of nerves.

The sound of a vehicle pulling up outside diverted her. She returned to the window, where dawn was rolling back the night and George was climbing out of a police car. Emma frowned as she noticed his face, drawn and sombre. Maybe he was just exhausted, maybe he'd been up all night too, but something about his demeanour made hairs rise on her arms.

She watched him straighten his posture and step up to the house. Heard the buzzer trill in the flat above, the beep of the exterior door being released, George's heavy tread on the stairs. Moments later, a terrible sound came from overhead. It pierced down through the ceiling, tearing across the memory of everything she'd ever heard from upstairs before.

It felt like more than just a cry: it seemed to have its own colour, even a texture, dark and raw.

It was Steph, howling as if her heart was broken.

All the air left Emma's lungs and her arms lifted towards the ceiling, as though to catch her neighbour if she fell.

PART THREE

39

Kate

Twenty-five years earlier

I slide the receiver back into its cradle. The hall floorboards feel icy under my bare toes. The dawn light picks out a furring of dust on the mirror, and the ticking clock sounds like someone clucking their tongue, a steady beat of disapproval.

There's a pad of footsteps and Becca appears, rubbing her eyes. 'What time is it? Was that the phone?' At the sight of my face, her hands drop. 'Has something happened?'

'That was Mum.'

She jerks her head.

'Nick's in hospital.' My words and mouth feel disconnected. 'He's in a coma.'

Becca stares. Her lips purse like she's going to say, *What?* or perhaps *Why?* But nothing comes out.

I stumble on anyway. 'They got to the hotel okay but he was ill in the night. Drowsy and dizzy, then sick, and he got a rash on his skin . . . I think that's what Mum said . . .' The phone call already seems hours ago. 'And then he started having trouble with his breathing. Mum called a taxi to Casualty. He fell unconscious on the way.'

Something is casting a dappled shadow across Becca's face. The clock seems to get louder, nipping at the silence.

'What . . . caused it?' Becca asks at last.

'They're running tests.'

Neither of us wants to say it. I don't even want to think it.

'It couldn't be,' Becca murmurs: the closest we can bring ourselves to facing the possibility. 'It was only—'

'Exactly,' I cut her off, turning slightly away. 'There's no chance.' I stare into the kitchen, picturing myself at the counter tipping crushed tablets into a bottle. 'Anyway, he'll probably be okay. Surely he'll be fine.' My legs buckle and I sink onto the floor, head between my knees.

'Even if he is, what if the tests show . . .?'

'I don't know. I don't even know what kind of tests they'll do.'

'*Shit.*' Becca kicks the skirting board with her bare foot. 'Oh, shit, shit, shit.'

'A coincidence,' I say, like a chant. 'It's just a coincidence.'

'I told you this was a bad idea.' She's pacing now. I can see her feet going back and forth along the hall, chipped purple varnish on her toenails. 'You had to talk me into it . . . crying, making me feel awful . . .'

I leap up. 'I wasn't faking that, Bec! Remember why we did it in the first place!'

She comes to a halt. Her shoulders droop and she presses a hand against her mouth.

'We did it for Mum,' I say, in a tiny voice. 'We only meant to shake him up.'

She nods, her head hanging. My eyes sting, my stomach feels scooped-out.

'It might help them treat him,' Becca says.

'What?'

'If we tell them.'

Fear surges through me. I know she's right. But the thought of confessing makes me want to run away and crawl under my bed.

'We could ring the hospital,' she says. 'Do 1471 on the phone.'

I grab her arm. 'What would we say?'

'I don't know. That we think he might accidentally have taken some of . . .' She stalls as she looks into our bedroom, past her rumpled sleeping-bag, towards the tub still sitting brazenly on the bedside table '. . . my pills?'

We both stare, breathing heavy and hard. I tell myself again that it can't have been them, not a reaction so strong. Imagine if we confessed and it was nothing to do with us. Imagine what Mum would think of me, Auntie Rach, my teachers . . . Would I ever be allowed back to school? Would we go to *prison*?

'They won't believe us.'

'We could tell them we've just noticed some missing. They won't know it was us.'

'They *will*.' My fingers tighten on her arm. She doesn't blink as she peers at me, a lattice of pink lines on her eyeballs.

Then she slides her arm free and smoothes her pyjama sleeve. She smoothes mine, too, unnecessarily, the gesture a minuscule comfort to us both. There's a long pause as I watch her weighing things up. My own thought processes are gagged by fear.

'I'm going to make us some tea,' she says hoarsely.

She walks into the kitchen, her footsteps soft, as though she's tiptoeing. The tap hisses and a cupboard door swings. I lean against the rutted wallpaper, shivering in the draught.

We sit dumbly at the kitchen table, sneaking glances at one another as if afraid of what we might talk ourselves into, or out of. My tea's too hot, then too cold, but I sip it anyway, at intervals, when I remember it's there. It's daytime now but the sun is more like moonlight, white and cold. Next door's kids wake up and start yelling; traffic noise rises from the streets below.

The phone rings again at half past seven. I scramble to my feet, Becca following me into the hall, her breath in my left ear as I press the phone to my right.

'Hello?'

'It's me,' Mum says.

Footsteps of dread patter up my spine. 'How's Nick?' I manage.

'He's . . .' Mum falters. 'He's gone.'

Something in my brain blocks the full meaning of her words. 'Gone?'

'He didn't make it.'

There's a suspended moment, almost an anti-climax, until the reality of what she's just said smacks me on the back of the neck.

'Oh, my God, Mum.'

'He seemed to be improving, almost stable, but then . . . Then he stopped breathing. It was all so surreal . . . doctors rushing in. Like on TV, Kate.' She sounds spaced-out. 'Except they didn't save him. They usually do, in the programmes, don't they? Everything went so still. I could see through the door. I saw the moment they all gave up.'

'Why did it happen?'

'They don't know. There'll be a post-mortem.'

Becca's doing an agitated dance beside me. I hold my hand up because I want her to stop, I can't get any words together.

'Do you want us to come down there, Mum?'

'I . . . no. I'll come home as soon as I can. I have to go now. There're things to sort out . . . God, such a lot to sort out. I can't believe it. It doesn't feel real.'

Her breathing comes soft and slow down the line, an echoey hospital bustle in the background, before the dial tone hums.

I drop the phone with a clatter. Becca's eyes widen and I slowly nod. She releases a string of swearwords, then stuffs her knuckles into her mouth. I start to cry and sway on the spot. Someone who was alive only a few hours ago is now dead. And there's a strong possibility it's because of us. Me.

Becca doesn't comfort me, like she has all the other times I've sobbed in front of her. She pats at the blotches that have broken out on her neck. 'Fuck,' she says. 'Oh fuck, oh fuck, oh fuck.'

I cover my face, squeezing my fingers together so no light can sneak through the cracks. I remember coming home last night, staring at Mum and Nick's luggage in the hall, all those desperate plans reeling through my head. If only I'd chosen one of them instead.

Perhaps he deserved it. Maybe he would've killed Mum, eventually, if he hadn't died today.

I want to believe it. Want to comfort myself with the idea that Nick's death saved my mum's life.

'Bec?' As I lower my hands I realise she's panting scarily fast. Rasping something I can't make out: the word *pills* and maybe *police* or *promise*.

Her body stiffens and then bucks backwards. I'm slow to react, until everything snaps into focus and I see her convulsing on the floor. Blue seeping into her lips. Her limbs jerking even faster than I remember from last time.

I crash onto my knees. As I support her head, its weight and warmth are so familiar, the silky texture of her hair. Should I call an ambulance? I remember Becca saying that it isn't really necessary any more, not unless she doesn't regain consciousness. But today it feels like anything can happen.

I close my eyes again.

When I open them, I want none of this to be true. I want to be standing at my dressing-table helping Mum with her ponytail, hardly aware that men like Nick even exist.

I think of the plane that day, soaring over me, the raked-up night sky followed by the beautiful calm. I'm back there and I'm gazing upward and I'm never going to move.

Becca's seizure is slowing. Her face is soft and sleepy, with drool running down her chin. Eventually she lies still. I see her chest rising normally, find a pulse on her wrist, and drop my head in relief. As she comes round, I almost envy her because she's temporarily forgotten everything that's happened. She's been granted a few seconds of absence.

I settle her on the sofa. The seizure has zapped her energy and given her an excuse to stop thinking, stop deciding what to do. Recovering from her own small ordeal, she can just sit. And so I do the same.

40

Chris

Chris's flat had never felt more claustrophobic. Another sleepless night had triggered a constant sickly motion behind his eyes, and his entire living room was lit with images of Freya that seemed to carousel around him. She was on his TV, which Vicky's sisters were glued to; on Di's phone, supplementing the TV; on the front page of the *Surrey Comet*, from which Jane was loudly reading extracts. The whole street could probably hear her penetrating voice, including the Harlows two floors above.

'"Following last night's discovery,"' Jane said, her chewing gum moving around in her mouth, '"the search for Freya Harlow, missing since Thursday evening, has reached a critical point. Police are appealing again for anyone with information—"' She broke off and stared at Chris. 'Hey, are you okay? You're green.'

He was trying to breathe through a tide of sickness. 'Fine,' he croaked.

His eyes floated to Vicky, who had said hardly a word all morning. She was sitting by the window, gazing up at the street, where reporters had now started to gather, attracted by the increased urgency of the case. She had been on shift last night but hadn't gone to bed since; she'd kept frowning at Chris, asking why he wasn't at work. He didn't want to tell her he'd had three more cancellations in the last twenty-four hours. And that they'd actually come as a relief.

He wished he could stand up and go to her, touch her wrist and feel the grounding thump of her pulse, with no un-Vickyish bracelet in the way. But he was trapped on his sofa with one of her sisters at either side. Why were they even *here* on a Monday at midday? Didn't they have anything else to do with their lunch hours? Jane was chain-chewing gum, texting news links to her workmates and her on-off boyfriend; Di was bossily shushing them all, even though they were silent, as Detective Ford came on the TV wearing her sharpest suit.

'Tests are being done but the jacket *is* thought to be Freya Harlow's,' Ford said, her face grave. 'And regrettably the stains are thought to be blood.'

Chris let his chin sink towards his chest, lower and lower, until the doorbell made him freeze.

'I'll get it.' With another pitch of his stomach, he flapped to free himself from the sister-in-law sandwich. He dashed across to the kitchen to take a subtle peek out of the other front window, and his fears were confirmed.

Except he hadn't been as subtle as he'd intended. The two PCs in uniform had seen him. Chris went back into the hall, kicking shut the door to the living room to stop Vicky and her sisters getting wind of the situation. He took a second to try to pull himself together, but his brain and body refused to sync.

'Mr Watson, we need you to accompany us to the police station.'

Chris's voice was thick but his words came out oddly formal: 'In what capacity?'

'We need to re-interview you, on the record, about Freya Harlow's disappearance.'

Chris couldn't move. His T-shirt sucked against his back. Then he heard a door swing open behind. He'd given Vicky and her sisters enough time to wonder what was happening, and now they were spilling into the hall, and he couldn't bring himself to turn and see their expressions.

'What's going on?' This was Di, of course, taking charge.

'Chris?' Jane sounded giddy.

Vicky said nothing.

Chris stepped towards the police officers. He wanted to say something to his family, something reassuring but appropriate: *Just doing my bit for the investigation.* But he didn't trust himself not to misjudge it.

He prepared to walk up the steps onto the unforgiving stage of the street. Maybe it would have turned into an amphitheatre, with high stands full of neighbours baying for his blood. He glanced back at Vicky and her sisters, and realised what an idiot he'd been not to make that reassuring comment. His silence had hushed them all, too, even Jane. They were watching as if something momentous was happening, and Vicky was holding onto the edge of the hall table looking utterly lost.

41

Emma

Emma sat in her chilly car, engine off, watching the curtained upper window of a small maisonette. She'd been there for half an hour and seen no movement. The house radiated a shut-down air, exacerbated by the fact that the lower floor was boarded up. In fact the whole street seemed lifeless, the bricks and pavement an unbroken grey.

The maisonette's address lay on the passenger seat beside her. She couldn't stop glancing at Steph's handwriting, remembering her eyes as she'd pressed the note into Emma's palm. Remembering, as well, Steph's howl the next morning, when she'd been told, as Emma had later understood, that Freya's bloodied jacket had been found buried in a ditch thirty miles north.

The new discovery had thrown everything into confusion, including Emma's own conviction about what to do with the address, even how to approach Zeb. Steph's feral roar had rattled her soul. The harrowing mental image of Freya's famil-iar Puffa jacket soaked in blood had seemed to raise all the stakes. What had happened to her? Why was Steph keeping secrets from the police, from Paul? Why was he keeping secrets from her? And if Zeb *had* lied about the amount of time he and Freya had spent together, how might that muddy the waters of the investigation, even if it was entirely innocent – as hopefully, *surely*, it was? Then Emma would loop back to worrying about Zeb in general, imagining more cuts on his hands, convincing herself he was slaving under unsafe condi-tions while Robin turned him irreversibly against her.

She'd had to escape the house, the street.

Now something made her stare more attentively towards the maisonette. Was it just the shifting light? She waited, her breath shortening, then glimpsed it again: a shadow behind the tatty upper-floor curtains. It seemed formless at first, striping across the window, until it stilled and took on the outline of a person. Emma lifted her phone and snatched a photo. The shadow moved and became fluid, melting into the general darkness of the interior.

She waited. The shadow didn't reappear and the house became lifeless again. Should she go and knock? Her nerves revved at the thought, and the longer she sat without seeing anything further, the more she wondered if she'd been duped by an optical illusion. *Go home, tell the police, back away.* But she was here now. She needed to understand what this place was that had wound Steph into such a frenzy.

Her palms were clammy as she crossed the road and stood before the house. She counted herself down like she used to at school when she was working up the courage to step into her form room. Different scenarios motored through her head, options for what to do if somebody answered. But nobody did. Not at the second knock, or the third.

And the photo on her phone was hopelessly blurry. The shape she'd captured could have been a woman or a man, could have been a stain, could have been a ghost.

When she returned she found a crowd of journalists on the street, drinking coffee and talking into mobiles, a much larger group than the one or two who'd been hanging around earlier.

'Miss Brighton,' one hollered, as she approached. It unsettled her that they knew her name. She tried to push past but a microphone was thrust into her face.

'Do you know where Paul Harlow is?' the journalist asked.

Emma couldn't help pausing. 'What?'

'He doesn't appear to be at home. We're wondering why that is.'

'Is he being held in custody?' another reporter butted in.

She checked the space where Paul's car would usually be. It was true, she realised. He'd been gone since the previous afternoon.

'I don't know.' Pressure was escalating in her head. Even in her state of confusion about whom to trust, a defence of the Harlows erupted out of her: 'Just leave them in peace, won't you?'

'What about Chris Watson? Has he been arrested?'

'I said I don't *know*! Why would I?'

She shoved through the throng, made it into the house and slammed the exterior door. At the same moment, a smell hit her nostrils. It was the pungent scent of a certain area of the local park, the whiff of something nasty dragged home on the bottom of a shoe. She checked the soles of her boots, but they were clean. Her eyes watered and she stoppered her nose as she looked around the hallway.

A package was half wedged through the letterbox. She could tell instantly that the envelope was soft and moist, little flecks of brown seeping at the corners. When she tugged at the very edge she felt its horrible squelch, and as it came free of the jaws of the letterbox she yelped and dropped it to the floor.

Dog shit now? Really, Robin?

Disgusting. Childish. Pathetic.

Except she couldn't even use these words to diminish her own horror. This package was the thing that finally made her tears erupt.

42

Steph

Steph knew she had to listen to what George was asking her, as he leaned forward from her sofa while she hunched in her window seat. But there was chaos in her head, white noise in her ears, grief in the pit of her stomach and anger at the grief because a bloodied jacket *did not mean the end*. It wasn't helpful to Freya to think the worst, to howl with loss, to stop breathing every few seconds because some irrational part of her feared she was stealing breaths that should have been her daughter's . . .

'Steph, I'm sorry, I know this is hard . . . but do you recognise this?'

George was holding his iPad towards her, with a picture on its screen. Steph didn't want to look. The last thing he'd shown her, early that morning, had been the photo of Freya's jacket for her to identify. Crudely buried, bloodstained, folded over, like somebody lying on their side. Steph had been convinced that the next words out of his mouth were going to be about body parts or bones. She understood, now, what people meant when they talked about time stopping. It had been the worst moment of her life.

Now George expected her to contemplate another image on that screen.

Intervening thoughts scissored across her mind. She had to get to the maisonette, should have gone days ago. She'd been so cowardly leaving it to Emma. Each time she opened her mouth to tell George to send his colleagues there, fear froze her stiff, thinking of everything it would unleash. If only she could slip away from all the people who seemed to be constantly around her . . .

And Paul was still gone. Unreachable, oblivious. She kept thinking she saw him in the street, her heart contracting with hope, but it was just a journalist who looked a little like him, fooling her every few seconds.

'Steph?'

Finally, she looked at what she was being shown. At first she thought it was just a photo of a twenty-pound note, until she spotted the doodle in the top-right corner and all her fractured attention rocketed towards it.

'That's . . . Freya's driving-lesson money.' She lurched forward and grabbed the iPad from George. 'I always draw a car in the corner of the notes I give her for her lessons. It's just a . . .' she stared at her own silly sketch of a Mini Cooper '. . . a thing I do. It's an ongoing joke that Freya loves Minis.'

George nodded. 'There were several banknotes folded up in her jacket pocket, with this same drawing on each. Amounting to almost three hundred pounds.'

'*Three hundred?*'

'Do you tend to give Freya the money in advance?'

'No, on the day,' Steph said. 'I don't understand . . . Why did she have so much on her?'

'We were hoping you might be able to tell us.'

Steph had to look away from her doodle, her eyes raw. Chris Watson's face now leered into her mind. Hadn't Freya been paying for her lessons? Or hadn't the lessons been taking place at all?

George moved closer and swiped at the tablet still in her hands. Colours skidded across her vision. 'What about this?'

It was a photo of a round silver box, a cluster of jewels decorating its hinged lid.

'What is it?' Steph asked.

'You don't recognise it?'

'Should I?'

'It's a solid silver pill box. It was also in Freya's coat pocket.'

Steph planted two fingers on the screen and zoomed in until the image was as pixelated as her thoughts. She shook her head, feeling faint.

'Did Freya take any regular medication?'

'No.'

'Could this have been a present?'

'Not that I know of . . .'

She imagined George looking up sharply and saying, *Well, perhaps you wouldn't know. Because perhaps you didn't know her as well as you thought. And maybe she learned her deceptiveness from you.*

43

Kate

Twenty-five years earlier

When Auntie Rach arrives to stay with us, the flat becomes instantly cramped. She's almost as wide as she's tall, with a shelf-like chest and a frizz of hairsprayed curls. She hands out sorrowful hugs and I let myself lean into the doughy comfort of her body. Becca does the same, but only for a second: clings to her mum, then pulls away as if remembering they fell out before all of this happened. I sometimes wonder how Becca copes with the constant rollercoaster of war and peace between her and Auntie Rach. Not to be speaking to my mum, to have her ringing up her sister to moan about what a 'nightmare' I am, I wouldn't be able to stand it like Becca does.

Auntie Rach insists on sharing Mum's bed with her, saying she shouldn't be alone. Imagining Mum teetering on the edge while her sister takes all the room would normally make me laugh, but I doubt I'm ever going to find anything funny again. I wonder whether Mum sleeps in pyjamas, hides her skin, whether Auntie Rach will spot the bruises. I wonder who has the side of the bed that used to be his.

As far as I can see, Mum still hasn't cried for Nick. She stares at his things lying around the flat, picks them up and examines them, like pieces of moon rock that have somehow found their way in.

The cause of his death hasn't been confirmed. The first stages of the post-mortem were inconclusive, so now there'll be a toxicology report. Auntie Rach tells us this one morning, after a phone call from the coroner's office or maybe the police: I'm losing track of all the people involved. I've never heard of a toxicology report but I can guess what one is. I shoot my eyes towards Becca: she's staring into space, unblinking.

I want to ask exactly what they'll test for. Exactly how it works. But I press my lips shut, my pulse hopping.

Auntie Rach lays a palm on Mum's shoulder. 'It could take four to six weeks.'

Mum sinks her head into her hands. 'What about the funeral?'

'Once they've collected all the samples they need, they'll release his body back to the family. Apparently it's the analysis that takes the time. We should be able to have a funeral.'

The family. Since Nick's death I've realised he didn't exist in a vacuum, didn't appear out of nowhere just to make our lives a misery. He has a dad and a brother who live somewhere down south. Mum murmurs on the phone to them, awkward and unsure because she doesn't even know them; they're having contact only because they were all connected to someone who's dead. I try to listen in, try to guess whether his dad's crying, whether his family loved him. Once I hear a raised voice at the other end, and afterwards I catch Mum whispering to Auntie Rach, 'They want answers.'

At the moment I get most of my information from eavesdropping. I hoover up overheard fragments, one-sided phone calls. Neighbours pop round with steamed-up Tupperware boxes of food, and I lurk in the background, wondering what they'd think if they knew even half the truth. The police ask us questions about the weeks leading up to Nick's death: had he been ill or acting oddly? To my relief, Mum mostly keeps me out of it. My legs go soft each time I see the flash of a uniform through the peephole in our door.

About a week after his death, the word *anti-depressants* starts cropping up in the hushed conversations Mum and Auntie Rach have when they think Becca and I are asleep. At first I wonder if Mum's started taking them: I check the bathroom cabinet but there's only a gnawed red toothbrush and a bar of dusty white soap. The next night, I hear them discussing it again and I manage to grasp the thread this time. I scurry over to Becca and shake her.

Her eyes fly open. We're both on a knife-edge at the moment. Always waiting. Some days I can convince myself no one will ever know what we did. Other days a confession prickles like ground-up glass on my tongue.

Becca snaps into a sitting position. 'What is it?'

'Nick was taking anti-depressants. The police found them in his house.'

She frowns. 'What?'

'Maybe it was a reaction to *them*,' I whisper, 'not to . . . to what we . . .'

Becca is silent. I can hear her breath coming in little bursts.

'Don't you think?' I ask.

'Maybe.' She draws up her knees, hooks her arms around them. 'It's possible.'

I shuffle back to bed but can't escape my thoughts. I wish there was somebody I could talk to, somebody who knows about medicine and post-mortems and inquests. Who would answer my questions and never tell a soul that I asked.

Soon Auntie Rach has to go back to work, so she and Becca prepare to head back to Derby.

Tears fill my eyes as I press my face against my aunt's big shoulder and smell the mousse in her crispy perm. Without Becca I'll feel totally alone, but perhaps I'll be able to think for myself. Maybe things will be clearer. We hug loosely, her body skinny and cool compared to her mum's, and she squeezes my wrist, like a signal of solidarity.

Then it's just Mum and me, like it always used to be. Except I still feel echoes of Nick. I still jump at tall shadows, hear the jangle of his keys, catch phantom drifts of frying bacon in the air.

We rarely mention his name, which is weird in itself. But he's still around.

One Friday evening, Mum comes into my room. It's stripped of Becca's things now: I can pad right across my carpet without having to stretch over her sleeping-bag, and my books have resurfaced from beneath her heaps of fashion magazines. Her meds no longer sit on the bedside table; they haven't been there since the day after Nick died, when Becca whisked them away as if getting them out of sight would solve everything.

Mum stands on the spot where Becca slept for almost three weeks. Spreads her arms as if suddenly noticing all the extra space.

Releasing a breath, she says, 'I've arranged for you to have Monday off school.'

'Monday?'

'Nick's funeral.'

An uncomfortable silence falls. I think she's going to walk away, but she lingers near the door. 'I'm nervous,' she says eventually.

'About the funeral?'

'I don't know why. Maybe the thought of all those people. And I still feel so ... I mean, funerals are supposed to give closure, aren't they? But we won't really have that. Not until we know why it happened.'

I blurt: 'What's the toxicology report for?'

'To test for anything he might've had in his system. The doctors think he had some kind of reaction.'

'Like an allergic reaction?'

She plucks at her cardigan. 'Possibly.'

'Could it be . . .' I know I should stop but I can't '. . . his anti-depressants?'

'How do you know about those?'

'I heard you and Auntie Rach.'

There's a pinched look to her face. The blue discs under her eyes resemble bruises, making me wonder if the real ones on her body are still there, whether they're fading now, faster than the memories.

'They're not sure,' she says quietly. 'The analysis takes a while when they don't really know what they're testing for.'

It's one of the longest conversations we've had since he died. Part of me wants to keep it going – I've missed her and I don't want her to leave. Another part fears that if we keep talking, I'll tell her everything.

She moves to go.

'Was he in pain?'

I didn't mean to say it.

Mum stalls. 'What?'

'When he got sick.' My voice is almost a whisper. 'Did he seem like he was in a lot of pain?' I don't even know what answer I want to hear.

Mum lifts a chunk of her hair and studies it. Thin threads come away in her fingers. 'Oh, love . . . it's all a blur.'

44

Paul

A jacket of pain seemed to have replaced Paul's ribcage. When he tried to peel open his eyes, his face threatened to crack. There was an expanse of white above him, a searing pain in his skull. He shifted his legs. He was in a bed beneath cool white sheets. A voice was saying his name, but the heaviness of his eyes became irresistible and he let them settle closed again.

The next time he woke, he must have cried out. Concerned faces were peering down at him, coaxing him to lie back against the pillow. He was still mouthing something. Perhaps an echo of whatever he'd shouted that had brought people running.

Freya, Freya, Freya.

'It's okay.' This was a nurse with a soft smile. 'Do you remember where you are?'

Paul glanced around and slowly nodded. He was on a ward now, rather than the chaos of A&E. It was daytime. How long had he slept?

'What time is it?' he asked, his swollen tongue mashing his words.

'Two thirty p.m.,' the nurse said, as she took his temperature. 'Just another manic Monday! You'll still be drowsy from the painkillers. You need to get some rest.'

'No ...' He was groggy, and in pain, but the last thing he could afford to do was rest. 'Freya ... Steph ... Daniel ...' He wasn't even sure he was saying the names out loud, but the nurse was nodding dutifully.

'We'll get in touch with your family, don't worry.'

'No, you don't understand. My daughter, she's . . . and my wife . . .' The frustration of not being able to articulate it made the pain in his head intensify. 'I have to call . . .' He twisted towards the bedside table, amazed to find his mobile there. His relief was short-lived as he saw that its screen was shattered.

'I can call someone for you,' the nurse said.

'My wife. Steph.'

'Do you know her number?'

Paul scrunched up his face, then croaked out the digits that were more familiar than his own. The nurse poured him some water but he gesticulated at the number she'd written down.

'Please hurry,' he said. 'Tell her I'm okay, but not to come. I'll get home. And . . . ask her about Freya. Any news.'

She stared at him curiously, then nodded and turned to leave.

'One more thing,' Paul said, trying not to cough: his ribs were agony. 'I think another man arrived at the same time as me? Daniel Sanderson?'

He didn't want to add, *With a stab wound?* Or ask whether the police had visited while he'd slept.

'I don't know, I'm sorry. It was just you brought up from A&E. I'll see what I can find out.'

'Don't worry,' Paul said quickly. 'Leave it, it's fine.'

She hesitated again before she left, flinging one more querying look over her shoulder. Paul struggled to sit up, a wave of protest sweeping through his muscles. He was exhausted. Close to breaking in a way there was no going back from. He couldn't, though: he had to get out of here.

Now that he was alone, his head gradually clearing, he thought back over what had happened. The explosive sense of release as he'd sunk the knife into Daniel's shoulder, followed all too quickly by panic and regret. Then a frantic attempt to stem the bleeding, a call to 999, a spiralling fear that he'd made things a thousand times worse. He *couldn't* be responsible for another death, no matter how he felt about Daniel. There was already so much guilt to bear.

The nurse returned sooner than he'd expected, startling Paul out of his thoughts.

'The number was engaged,' she said. 'I'll try again later. Are you all right? You look extremely pale.'

'I'm okay.' Paul sank into his pillows, his heart thundering. He felt a deep twist of longing for Steph, wishing everything was as it had been only a few days ago, that maybe he'd just had a minor accident, like the time he'd come off his bike, and she was rushing from work to fetch him . . .

'One of the receptionists gave me this,' the nurse said, handing him an envelope with *Paul Harlow* written on it. 'Apparently a woman dropped it off about an hour ago. She didn't want to stick around, but asked us to pass it to you when you woke.'

Paul stared at it. Who on earth knew he was here but wouldn't stay? He waited until the nurse had moved politely away before tearing open the envelope.

I'll be waiting on the far side of the Blue Car Park.

45

Emma

She could still smell it. The dirty, sickly stench. She didn't know if she was really smelling it any more, or whether the memory was trapped in her nostrils.

Her first impulse, of course, had been to throw the revolting package into a bin far from her house. But then it had occurred to her that she might need the evidence. As repugnant as the idea was, she had to keep the stinking parcel, now quadruple-wrapped in plastic bags, until she had an opportunity to talk to the police.

Because she *was* going to tell the police now. It made her ill, the idea that Robin, father to her son, might actually have gone to the lengths of scraping up dog shit, forcing it into an envelope, posting it through the door . . . And Zeb was living with him, being influenced by him. Just as Robin had clearly been influenced by Andy's approach to intimidation all those years ago.

She tried to busy herself by checking through the post and emails she'd left neglected for the last four days. But it was just bills that would plunge her into her overdraft, an email from her estate agent asking whether she wanted to relist her shop for sale, and an invitation to a job interview – depressingly, at the shop where she'd been working when she'd first entertained the idea of buying her own. Emma didn't have the headspace for any of it. She buried her laptop under a pile of scarves as if it had offended her as much as the dog dirt.

The next time a police car pulled up, she peeked out of her window. Two officers in uniform got out and went to address the mob of journalists. Emma wondered whether any of the reporters had witnessed the horrible delivery. An argument seemed to bubble up; one of the PCs stayed out on the pavement while the other came into the building, irritation scrunching his face.

Before she could change her mind, Emma stepped out of her flat.

The PC was in the foyer murmuring into his radio. Emma hovered awkwardly, glancing up the stairs towards the Harlows' door. When he slipped the radio back into his belt, she found her voice: 'Excuse me, could I ask your advice?'

He looked preoccupied, but not unfriendly, sweat glistening beneath the brim of his hat.

'I . . . I need to report some potentially threatening mail I've been getting. And . . . other things too. Phone calls . . .' She thought of what Steph had said about their doorstep being egged a fortnight ago. 'Vandalism . . .'

She had his attention now. 'Is this related to Freya Harlow?'

'I don't think so. Not exactly.' Emma watched for a reaction, convinced the interest had slipped from his face. 'I can't be sure, but I think it's . . . my son's dad. We have a difficult history and I think he's trying to unsettle me, or punish me. I know you might not be the right person to tell, and the last thing I want is to detract from the investigation . . .'

He looked thoughtful. Emma worried that he was going to fob her off, send her away, and perhaps rightly so. But he reached into his coat and brought out a notebook. 'Can you say more about this mail you've been getting?'

'He sent a book a few days ago. A guide to being a better parent, with a raw egg smashed inside. I'm pretty sure that's been reported to the police already. Steph Harlow thought it was meant for her and Paul, but I think it may have been aimed at me . . .'

The officer started scribbling. Emma followed the jerky movement of his pen on the page. Things were meshing together; she didn't know what was linked and what was separate, coincidental. The exterior door opened and the other PC came in. Emma was glad of the brief interruption so she could collect her thoughts. But her head snapped round as she glimpsed, through the closing door, a familiar figure standing beyond the press pack, staring around at the once-quiet street that now thrummed with the mayhem of a missing teenager.

Surprise flooded her with such force that she ran outside. A few reporters clicked their cameras, as if they thought surely she must be flying towards the missing girl, because otherwise why would her arms be straining forward? Why would there be tears on her cheeks?

46

Chris

Chris had found himself plunged into a spiral of repeated questions. All the same ones they'd asked about Freya before, but with a new gravitas hanging over them, and a camera now recording from the corner of the interview room. And there was extra stuff too, personal stuff. They seemed to know exactly which nerves to hit when it came to his marriage and his insecurities.

Now his 'alleged route' from his last lesson with Freya was being waved around again. Chris felt beaten-up. Why didn't they just get on with whatever they wanted to say about it?

Eventually they did.

'Your number plate was picked up by a speed camera,' Ford said, 'at thirteen forty-two on March the fifteenth. Three miles from where you should've been at that time, according to your version of the route.'

Chris shifted. 'I told you my memory might not have been completely accurate.'

'But shouldn't you have been heading back towards Freya's school at that time? Instead, you were going in the opposite direction.'

His mind swam. Would a speed camera have been able to tell who was driving? Would it show two figures arguing in the front of the car?

How much could a camera reveal about the relationship between a driving instructor and his student?

Chris resorted to sarcasm. 'I'm not sure how much you know about driving lessons, but the idea isn't to take the most direct route to where you want to go. The idea is to practise driving.'

'You wouldn't have had enough time to get back to Freya's school for two p.m.'

'We were running a bit late, as it happens.'

'You didn't mention that before.'

'Didn't I?'

'No. Is there anything else you've failed to mention?'

The sarcasm drained out of Chris. He dropped his hands to his knees and shook his head.

Just as he thought they'd exhausted every last detail, there was something else. Ford reached for an iPad and showed him their trump card: a photograph of a crumpled, dirty bank note. Chris recognised the doodle in the corner and his breath truncated.

'Why did Freya still have three hundred pounds' worth of the money that was meant for her driving lessons?' Ford asked. 'Why was it in her pocket?'

'I have no idea.'

'Shouldn't she have been giving it to you?'

'Yes . . . She did.'

'So she had been paying for her lessons?'

'Of course.' There was itchy sweat in his eyes. 'Maybe this was for future ones.'

A thick silence followed. Chris bit the insides of his cheeks.

At last, Ford put down the iPad. She placed her hands at either side of it, palms on the table, as if she was wanting him to draw around her fingers.

'I think you're hiding something, Mr Watson.'

Chris tried to stare her out, but fear was filtering through him. 'I want a solicitor.'

'Fine.' A smile played on Ford's lips, as though this was what she'd wanted him to say. As though it was an admission of guilt.

It was Vicky's face that came most strongly into his mind now, rather than Freya's. Vicky pulling him up to dance, at a party full of raucous student nurses sometime in the distant past. Vicky staring into their bedroom mirror yesterday, painting her mouth with scarlet Chanel lipstick, and today, holding on to the hall table as she'd watched the police lead him away.

The duty solicitor, Ms Beaumont, arrived within half an hour. She had unmoving black hair and a brisk, efficient manner. When Chris faced the two detectives with her at his side, it felt like a fresh start, of sorts. Having someone next to him equalled things up.

'It seems my client has been asked some irrelevant questions about his personal life,' Ms Beaumont said. 'There will be no more of that.' She sounded like she was reprimanding two naughty children. 'And please inform my client whether he is under arrest.'

The detectives exchanged a glance. Ms Beaumont's head was cocked expectantly, her hair like a black metal helmet. But as Ford opened her mouth to respond, the door to the interview room creaked and a tall man with pouched eyes appeared. 'DI Ford, a quick word?'

'We're just wrapping up here,' Ford said, sending a wash of relief through Chris's body. 'Can it wait?'

The man looked at Chris, then back to Ford, a subtle signal in his gaze. 'Not really.'

Ford stood and left the room. Chris turned to Ms Beaumont for reassurance, but an M-shaped frown creased her forehead. He rocked back in his chair, feeling its legs bow beneath him. Finally Ford returned, brandishing a second iPad and moving with new purpose as she retook her seat.

'The team has finished going through Freya's iCloud storage,' she said, and Chris felt the drop of his stomach, the clean slide of a dreaded but inevitable outcome.

Of course she'd have backed up her photos to the Cloud. Sometimes it felt like nothing could be contained any more. Secrets floated in cyberspace, beyond your own reach and control. He thought of Vicky cutting out pictures from a magazine, or touching the bracelet on her wrist as if to check it was real. Was she trying to make things tangible? Trying to keep control, one ownable item at a time?

Chris looked at the photo on the iPad. It was hard to believe that its collection of sad-looking bric-a-brac spilling from a glovebox had embroiled him in this.

'If I'm not mistaken,' Ford said, 'this is the inside of your car.'

47

Kate

Twenty-five years earlier

We leave in darkness on Monday, the first bus of the day rumbling us through traffic-free streets. Mum is dry-eyed and distant. I have to nudge her alert when we get to the station, then guide us to the right platform, focusing on practical things until we're on the train and my blood starts to hiss in my ears.

Daylight leaks into the sky as the train rushes through a spectrum of colours, ink to pale amber to blue. My black dress crumples beneath my thighs. Mum fiddles with the armrest, flipping it up and down, and checks her watch and rubs her eyes and, as we chug into Basingstoke, clasps my hand with all the dread I'm trying not to show.

My heart turns over when she tells me we're heading to Nick's brother's house first. We've been invited to travel in the proper funeral car with his family. I suppose I shouldn't be surprised, Mum was his girlfriend after all, but I still feel like we're outsiders.

We freeze in unison as we step out of the taxi. The man striding to greet us is so much like Nick. He moves like him; he has the same eyebrows and mouth. When he introduces himself as Richard his voice is similar too. It's like shaking hands with a ghost.

Richard's house is big but there isn't much stuff in it: 'minimalist', Becca would say. I wish there was more clutter to camouflage against. I feel too visible as we stand in the living room and are introduced to Nick's dad and two cousins. Nick's dad has the same family resemblance, less striking because he's older. It's almost a relief when the two black cars arrive and a flurry of activity distracts me. But then I glance out of the window and am embarrassed by my own jolt of shock.

Of course one of the cars would have a coffin in it. Of course we'd be riding to the funeral with Nick himself. What did I think would happen?

The only other funeral I've been to was my grandad's. That was in a church, with hymns and readings from the Bible. I was only seven but I remember being fascinated by the man playing slow tunes on the organ. Nick's funeral is in a crematorium surrounded by trees. A small crowd of people gathers outside, but when we get out of the car there's no rumble of conversation, only silence. The coffin is carried through the middle and we walk behind with our heads low.

During the service I learn more about Nick than I did the whole time he was with my mum. He wanted to join the RAF but his eyesight wasn't good enough. He used to like boxing when he was younger – I have to clamp my mouth so as not to react to that. His brother does a tribute and his voice wobbles twice. Every anecdote that's shared and every song that's played makes me more confused.

And I can't stop staring at the coffin. I remember thinking that my grandad's looked small – even to me as a kid. But Nick's coffin is long and broad, the cherry-dark wood gleaming.

After the service we go back to Richard's clean, empty house. People loosen their ties, speak a little louder; I pick at a triangular sandwich and feel like my legs won't hold me up.

Eventually I shut myself in the downstairs toilet, splashing cold water onto my wrists.

When I get back to the living room I see Nick's dad heading towards my mum. I arrive at her side at the same time as he arrives in front of her. He glances at me, then locks eyes with Mum and says, 'I'm very sorry.' It seems an odd thing for him to say to her. He's lost his son, after all. And there's something about his words, something I can't puzzle out.

Mum bites her lip. 'So am I.'

'Could we have a quick talk?' he asks. 'How about some air?'

Mum shifts her black handbag from one shoulder to the other. 'Will you be all right for a minute, Kate?'

I nod, but I don't think she sees. She pats my arm and Nick's dad gestures towards the door.

On the way home I ask her what they talked about during those fifteen minutes, when I could see only the tops of their heads through the living-room window. 'Nothing, really,' she says. 'Just Nick.'

I daren't push it. I'm just relieved to be speeding home, rocked into a trance by the train's bumpy gallop.

Even after the funeral is over, the suspense thickens every day. There are so many things that make my pulse fly – the ringing phone, visitors at the door. Becca and Auntie Rach come back whenever they can, usually at weekends, Auntie Rach bringing dirty potatoes from a friend's garden or little bottles of brandy for her and Mum to share. Becca and I try to catch moments alone, but it's impossible in the flat, and I'm not sure what we'd say to each other anyway.

We're all in the kitchen eating breakfast when it finally happens. The only sound is teeth crunching burned toast. It doesn't seem like we can get much quieter, but all noises evaporate as a knock thuds on the door. It's as if we know this isn't just another neighbour with a watery chicken stew.

Auntie Rach answers it and comes back with two police-men. They introduce themselves but I don't take it in – I'm not even sure if they're the ones I've met before. I notice, distantly, that I've dropped my toast jam-side down onto my plate.

'We're here following the post-mortem and toxicology report for Mr Nicholas Wood,' one of the policemen says. 'We need to ask you about some medication found in his system.'

I grip the edges of my chair. I don't know where to look, how to make my legs stop twitching.

'Anti-depressants?' Mum asks.

'Well, yes, a low dosage of anti-depressants *was* found. Analysis of Mr Wood's blood and urine, combined with his medical records, suggests he'd been taking those for around four weeks. But it's unlikely that was the cause of death.'

It's Auntie Rach who asks the question. 'Then what was?'

'After several rounds of testing, the toxicology team also found an anti-convulsant in Mr Wood's system. They estimate he ingested it around eight to twelve hours before he fell ill.'

I make myself focus on the police, a slight frown on my face, hoping a deep flush isn't bleeding into my cheeks. The fridge is buzzing like an insect in the corner, the noise it makes when it's on the blink.

'An anti-convulsant?' Mum echoes.

'Carbamazepine.' The name of Becca's medication takes on a new emphasis in the policeman's voice. Auntie Rach shifts as if she recognises it, but says nothing. I look towards Becca, expecting her to look back at me, expecting this to feel like the inevitable end. She stares squarely ahead. Then I real-ise that everyone has followed me in turning towards her, and we've formed a ring of expectant gazes with her at its centre.

'Do you know of any reason Mr Wood might have taken this drug?' one of the officers asks. 'It's most commonly used to treat epileptic seizures.'

I snap my eyes downwards, hoping everybody else will do the same. Auntie Rach's gaze slides away from her daughter, but Mum's still staring in Becca's direction.

'My niece has epilepsy.'

Becca straightens. 'But I don't take that drug.'

My eyes boomerang to her. Does she really think she can get away with lying?

'Look.' She leaps to her feet and goes to her handbag, rummaging through and producing a packet of pills: sodium valproate.

I feel as if I'm seeing things. Maybe I was mistaken. Maybe she's been taking these all along. But that would mean the toxicology report was wrong.

More likely she's changed her medication. For a genuine reason? Or in some crazy attempt at a cover-up?

What have you done, Becca?

'Have you always taken those?' one of the policemen asks, accepting the packet and studying it.

Becca sits back down. Her neck is blotchy. 'Actually,' she screws up her face as if remembering, 'I *did* used to take carbamazepine. But I've been on these for a little while now.'

'Were you taking carbamazepine when Mr Wood fell ill? Might there have been some in the flat he could've accessed?'

She shakes her head firmly. 'Nope. I actually wasn't taking anything then. I was between meds.'

Between meds? I dare to glance at Auntie Rach: her face is full of confusion. Becca looks pale now too, as if regretting going down this road.

'We'll have to follow this up, Miss Fielding. With your cooperation, I hope? And we'll also consult with the toxicologists, to confirm how sure they are about the exact type of anticonvulsant in Mr Wood's system.'

'How much was found?' Mum asks.

'It can be hard to measure levels in the blood, but they've been estimated as quite high.'

'Did it kill him?'

'The toxicology team and our medical experts think he died from a strong adverse reaction to that drug. The anti-depressants might have increased its effects, and made the levels of carbamazepine appear higher. With alcohol in his system also, the synergistic effect of all three . . .'

I try to breathe evenly through my nose. I can hear Becca cracking her knuckles beneath the table. Auntie Rach is very still, unusually quiet. Mum frowns at Becca's pills in the policeman's grasp.

Chair legs shriek on the lino as one of the officers stands. 'We'd like to talk to you all separately. It would be easier to do this at the station, if you would follow us there?'

I risk a final glance at Becca. She's slumped now, as if in defeat. As if she knows that lying about her tablets is yet another decision we can't take back.

48

Paul

Paul told the ward staff his pain was down to 'a two or a three'. Forced himself to sit and stand, eat and drink. All so they wouldn't protest when he said he wanted to 'get some air'.

In reality, his ribs screamed when he walked too fast, and his jaw clicked as if it would never be quite right again. Approaching the Blue Car Park, he clutched his side and glanced in every direction. He thought he'd recognised the writing on the note that had been left for him, but he couldn't be sure.

Then he saw her, standing close to the overgrown bushes on the far side, wearing a tan leather jacket rather than the scarlet coat from last time.

How had she found him? Why was she here? Up close, Paul struggled to guess what was on her mind and realised he'd never tried to before – never had to. Yvette had done so much for him, knew so much about him, and he couldn't say the same in return.

His life felt full of one-way relationships. He was never allowed or able to give enough of himself. Even to his daughter, his wife.

Yvette hugged him gently, shaking her head as she took in his injuries. 'I should never have given you his address. I should've known it would end badly.'

'This isn't your fault,' Paul insisted. 'I was determined to find him. It would've driven me crazy if I hadn't.'

'What happened?' she asked, at the same time as he said, 'How did you know I was here?'

'Glover called me in a rage,' she said, 'swearing down the phone at me, asking if I'd told you where to find Sanderson, if I knew how much shit I'd caused. Typical Glover – the soul of discretion until he truly loses his temper.'

Paul nodded. He'd always had the impression Yvette shared his dislike of Glover, but as his therapist she'd been too professional to say so. Now all pretence was dropped.

'Anyway, I knew something must've happened,' she went on. 'I kept looking at Nottingham news online, but there was nothing. Eventually I decided to take the risk and drive to Sanderson's address. One of his neighbours was outside, all pumped up because there'd been an ambulance on the street. That got me even more worried, of course. I managed to track you down, but I didn't want to come right to you, in case Glover was hanging around.'

'But how did Glover know anything had happened?'

'I'm not sure. He makes it his business to know everything when it comes to Sanderson. Constantly terrified of the truth getting out ...' She paused, drifting into thought. When her gaze returned to him, she scanned his bruised face again. 'Did Sanderson do all this?'

Paul nodded, looking down. *But I did worse to him.* 'Do you know if he's in this hospital?' he asked, ducking the real question: *Do you know if he's alive?*

She shook her head. 'Was he hurt too?'

Paul nodded again. He could still feel the force of Daniel's blood as he'd crushed three tea-towels against his shoulder wound. The warmth, and the smell, and the alarm in Daniel's eyes, which should've been satisfying but wasn't. Help had seemed to take hours to arrive. There'd been no time for explanations or interrogations as the paramedics had sped Daniel away in the ambulance, and Paul had been taken to hospital in their smaller vehicle, without the blue lights wailing. He'd kept expecting the police to turn up at his bedside, asking questions, but there'd been nothing yet, and somehow that was even more unnerving.

'I stabbed him,' he finally answered Yvette, and heard her surprised intake of breath. 'And then I tried to save him. But I don't know if I succeeded. It's a fucking mess.'

As he'd knelt there trying to prevent Daniel from bleeding out, the adrenalin that had inflamed their confrontation had begun to fade. And Paul had been left with a heavy conviction that this had all been for nothing. Daniel's reaction to seeing him again had been so strong, Paul could no longer reconcile it with a calculated revenge plan. It had been pure bottled hatred, unexpectedly unleashed by a visitor from the past. If Daniel had taken Freya, wouldn't he have been prepared for Paul's arrival?

Slumped against his kitchen cabinets, his skin grey, Daniel had slurred: *I haven't touched your daughter.*

And then, *I didn't hurt Billie either. I didn't.*

He'd looked smaller, sadder, his head hanging. It was hard not to believe a man who clearly thought he might die. But if Paul did choose finally to believe him, it meant the whole operation had been pointless. Lives had been ruined on theories that had never been true.

In the aftermath of Nathalie's death, he used to torture himself by mentally listing his crimes.

He had deceived a woman who was trying to grieve for her missing child, and whose only source of support was the brother Paul had been sent to investigate.

He had broken every rule of undercover ethics: he'd kissed her, fucked her, made promises to her. He had let her stand naked in front of him, let her show him photos of Billie as a baby, let her fall in love with him, even though her heart was already broken. And he'd barely told her a single honest thing about himself.

He'd sworn to keep her safe, promised that one day they'd go away together, somewhere far from Nottingham and all the things that had happened to her. He'd half meant it too, even though he'd known simultaneously that it was impossible. He'd told her he loved her – and maybe that was the one truthful thing he'd ever said to her, but even that wasn't a pure truth.

And, above all, he still hadn't quite trusted her. He'd succumbed to a creeping suspicion that she might know more about what had happened to her daughter than she was letting on.

Those trips she'd started taking, slipping off early evenings once or twice a week. By then Paul had known the smell of her hair after a shift in the café; the lullabies she'd sing when she was sad; the way she'd fiddle with her left earring when nervous – particularly around her brother, it had always seemed. But he'd had no idea where she went on those just-popping-out-for-a-bit nights.

In a way, it had redressed the balance. She'd known nothing real about him – she thought his parents were dead, that he had always done odd jobs for a living – so perhaps it was only fair she had her secrets too. But Paul couldn't have let the mysterious outings pass without investigating them, especially when he'd noticed Daniel slipping her money before she left. It had been his duty to find out what she was doing. So he'd told himself many times since.

Paul closed his eyes and saw the remote outbuilding he had followed her to one night. His heart pumped as hard as it had at the time, watching her go in, fearing the worst about whom she might be visiting. He'd experienced a brief flutter of excitement at the prospect of a breakthrough in the case he'd nearly lost hope of solving, but it was quickly drowned in dread. Nathalie couldn't be involved. It was supposed to be Daniel, not her. She was innocent, and she would be free once they'd exposed her brother. That was what he'd clung to throughout their relationship.

The other times he'd followed her, he had hidden much better. That time, perhaps he'd subconsciously wanted her to see him. He'd been so desperate to know what was inside that building, what she was doing there.

And, of course, when she'd spotted him on her way out, she'd wanted to know the same.

'What the hell are you doing here, Paul?'

He'd had his explanations prepared, just as he'd been trained to, but he'd frozen for a second too long.

'Did you follow me?' she'd asked, looking so incredulous that Paul had begun to fear he'd got things very, very wrong.

'Why would you do that?' She'd kept asking questions because he hadn't been answering. All he'd been able to think was that he didn't want to lose her, wished he could turn back the clock in every possible way.

His eyes must have strayed to the building she'd come out of. Nathalie had looked round too. When she'd turned back he'd been unable to read her face, half lit by a glow from the narrow windows of the hut. Paul couldn't resist glancing back at it, trying to see inside.

'What is this place?' he'd asked, finally recovering his voice.

Afterwards, he'd convinced himself that if she hadn't acted evasive at that point, everything might have been okay. The way she'd squinted, fiddled with her earring, it had made his police instincts kick back in, merging with his intimate knowledge of her nervous tics.

He'd taken a step towards the building, watching her reaction, asking again what was there.

'What – you think I'm having an affair or something? Don't you trust me?'

Did he trust her? Did he trust anyone?

'You sneak off here most weeks,' he'd said. 'I've even seen Daniel giving you money beforehand.'

'So what?'

'So . . .' He could still remember how light-headed he'd felt, how he'd known he was on a cliff-edge: he could either tip over or haul himself back.

An outside force had seemed to snatch the words from his mouth before he'd fully decided whether he should, or could, say them: 'Is it something to do with Billie?'

All the muscles had tightened in her face. She'd looked so different in that slow, drawn-out moment, staring at him. 'What do you mean by that?'

'It's okay.' Paul had tried to touch her arm but she'd jerked away. 'You can tell me.'

'Tell you what?'

'If . . . if Daniel made you do something. If he dragged you into his plan.'

'*Plan?*'

Paul had felt himself tumbling over that imaginary cliff-edge, falling in blackness. He pictured telling Glover, *I thought it was time. Time to push her a bit on the Billie thing. I'd secured her trust and hoped she'd tell me the truth.*

'Whatever happened to Billie, maybe it was an accident. I know it would've been Daniel who saw an opportunity to make money from it. Not you. Or maybe she's still alive, maybe someone's taking care of her . . .' His eyes had flashed again to the outbuilding. 'Maybe you feel trapped now, like you can't undo it. But you can. I can help you. I love you.'

She had begun to shiver violently. It had seemed to last for ever: Nathalie standing there, trembling, her chest rising and falling hard.

When she'd finally spoken, it had been in a low, alien voice. 'How could you think that about me?'

'That's what I'm trying to say. I know Daniel must be behind it—'

Her volume soared. 'How the fuck can you think that about either of us? He's your friend, and I . . . I . . .'

'He's not my friend.'

That had reduced her to silence. Paul instantly knew he'd said too much. Nathalie had stared at him again and he'd taken deep breaths, trying to rein himself in, to remember his training and how much was at stake.

'Who the hell are you?' she'd asked.

The question had seemed so inevitable it was like déjà vu, like they'd already had this conversation in multiple parallel existences. It was always bound to come down to this.

Stay in character at all times. Talk, walk, feel and dream in character.

Stick to your story unless you are absolutely certain your cover has been blown.

Have explanations ready for when anybody doubts or questions you. Recite them in your head before you go to sleep, when you wake, when you shave and shower and sit on the toilet . . .

'You're not who you say you are. Are you?'

'Of course I am, baby—'

'Don't call me baby!' She'd thrown up her hand to ensure he didn't move any closer. 'I'm not the only one who sneaks off places.'

'What?'

Always pre-empt. Know where the danger is coming from even before it arrives.

But Paul had no longer been sure what he was most afraid of: losing Nathalie, or destroying the whole operation. Were they one and the same? Glover's voice had kept coming into his head, then falling away again as soon as he'd looked at Nathalie and felt his heart wrench.

'I've noticed something lately,' she'd continued, her voice growing stronger, but still with a tremor. 'You go off to use the phone box at the same time every week.'

He'd feigned half-amused confusion. 'Do I?'

'*Exactly* the same time.'

He'd been spending far too much time with her. Letting her stay in his flat more often, rather than hers. Enjoying the morning warmth of her in his bed.

Giving her a chance to observe his routines.

'I'm a creature of habit.'

'And you never use the nearest phone box. I followed you once too, remember – that time you forgot your wallet and I thought you'd need money for the phone. You were using the one on Howe Street.'

'I thought that was the nearest.'

She hadn't even seemed to be listening to his excuses any more. Later, he'd realised she'd been working things out even as they'd spoken. Grasping the significance of all Paul's little slip-ups, here in the moonlit wasteland he had trailed her to.

'Last week, when you came back from the phone box, you hid a piece of paper under your mattress. I saw you do it, and I looked at it later. Who's G?'

'Are you accusing *me* of cheating now?' Paul had hoped to divert the conversation that way. Another woman was a better explanation for his weekly check-ins with Glover than the truth.

'Nobody does things like that unless they've got something to hide. I shrugged it off at the time, but now . . .' She'd almost run out of breath, her palm pressed to her throat. 'Now . . .'

'Nat, let's go home and talk. Please. It's getting cold, we're both tired.'

'I'm not tired.' She'd drawn herself up tall. 'I want to know why you've followed me. Why you're asking questions about Billie. Why you make secret phone calls, and write notes in weird code, and why you never talk about yourself. You always change the subject when I ask about your family or . . .' Her words had disintegrated into tears then, and Paul had realised, with a plunge of his stomach, that she knew. He'd let her get too close and he'd made bad choices, and they weren't even balanced on that cliff-edge between truth and lies any more. They were sliding into a ravine below.

'I love you,' he'd whispered.

'Who are you?'

'I want to protect you.'

She'd screamed: '*Tell me who you are.*'

He'd touched her just to try to calm her down, but she'd screamed again and beaten her fists against his chest. He'd grabbed her wrists, tried to hold her. She'd twisted away and he'd felt the friction-burn of her skin under his grasp.

Stepping back, he'd realised he was crying too.

'You're with the police,' she'd said.

Paul had let himself have one more moment of borrowed time, before he'd nodded.

Nathalie had bent at the waist, hands covering her face. 'Oh, my God.'

'I'm sorry. I'm so sorry. Please believe I never meant to hurt you.'

'So all of it ... the last three years ...' She'd thrust her fingers into her hair as if to stop her skull exploding.

'It wasn't you I was investigating. It was your brother, and the search fund. He made himself untouchable. It was the only way ...'

'Oh, God.' Her hands over her face again. 'You bastard. You *bastard.*'

'My feelings for you are real,' he'd said desperately. 'So very, very real.'

'Three years of my life. All the things we ... the things I ...'

'I love you. I promise I love you.'

'Stop *saying* that! I can't believe a word that comes out of your mouth.'

'Nat—' But he'd stopped short because of course she'd been right. Nothing he said had any credibility any more, or ever could again. He'd been trained to lie, and now she knew that. It was the only thing she knew about him.

Abruptly, she'd grabbed his arm. He'd found himself dragged towards the outbuilding, stumbling with surprise. Nathalie had banged on the door and they'd waited until it creaked open, casting a quarter-circle of orange light out into the gloom. A woman with a fountain of dark curly hair had stood there. A lacy shawl around her shoulders, long black dress with red embroidered roses.

'Nathalie?' she'd said, kohl-lined eyes darting towards Paul. 'Are you all right?'

'Tell him who you are,' Nathalie had said.

'And who is *he*?'

Nathalie had snorted with humourless laughter. 'Good question. He's my boyfriend. He's a stranger.' Her voice had cracked on the last word, the uncharacteristic sarcasm dissolving. 'He wants to know why I've been visiting this place.'

If the woman had been perturbed or confused, she hadn't shown it. She'd looked from Nathalie to Paul, then moved to one side so Paul could survey the candlelit room behind. He'd tried to take it all in: the gauzy drapes; the bowls of glimmering white crystals; the cards on the table.

'Emilia is a clairvoyant,' Nathalie said. 'I'd heard she'd helped others. I had to try something . . .'

'I don't understand,' Paul said.

'I thought she might be able to tell me where Billie is.' Nathalie had started to sob again. 'Because, clearly, nobody else can.'

It was as if somebody had thrown scalding water into his face. Nathalie had been visiting this woman with her cards and her crystals: one last pitiable attempt to know what had happened to her daughter. Paul was the criminal, not her. He was the liar, the one who deserved to feel burning shame.

After Emilia had closed her door, Nathalie had seemed to cry herself out. And that was when the anger had returned. She'd said Paul's behaviour was disgusting. Claimed she'd never really loved him anyway – she'd just been lonely, he could have been anyone. Insults had spewed out, designed to wound him, and he'd let her rage until her voice became hoarse.

The last words she'd ever said to him were, *You're going to regret what you've done.*

The last he'd seen of her, she'd been running away from him in the moonlight, hair bannering behind, fists clenched as though she was ready to fight if he tried to follow.

49

Emma

Zeb didn't speak as she ushered him inside. He looked dazed by the transformed atmosphere of the street, the police and press, everything he'd been cut off from at his dad's rural house. Even inside their flat, he offered one-word responses to Emma's questions and her garbled updates about their missing neighbour. She chose not to notice that he had no luggage. Surely her boy was back and everything was going to be all right.

She began making him a cup of tea, hoping he still liked it strong with half a sugar: it felt too awful to have to check.

'How could you, Mum?'

The spoon wavered in her hand. 'What?'

'The last text you sent me. Accusing Dad of all sorts.'

She dropped the spoon into the mug with a sinking feeling. At the height of her panic, tipped over the edge by the latest revolting delivery, she'd tapped out a desperate text to Zeb, a stream of reasons he had to come home. And she'd still left out the things she needed to ask him about Freya. Now he was in front of her and she couldn't put them off any longer.

'You seriously think he put raw egg through the door? And dog shit?'

'I—'

'Why the hell would he do that?'

Because clearly he's angry that I never told him about you. And he knows how to rattle me. He observed it first-hand for a long time.

'Is this another attempt to make me stop seeing him?'

'No—'

'I want him in my life, Mum! He's my dad! The last few weeks have been so great, getting to know him at last. I honestly can't believe you never let me have this before.'

He looked so sincere, it crushed her heart. She'd never realised, or never wanted to acknowledge, how much he'd lacked a dad. She'd believed she was enough, and the realisation that she wasn't had seemed to carve cracks into every part of her life. Alien Girl couldn't raise a son, run a business, wear peacock-feather earrings and stick up two fingers to her schooldays. How stupid to think she could.

'Has he been nice to you?' she couldn't help asking.

Zeb stared at her as if she was mad. 'Of course he has. I don't know why you hate him so much. He only says good things about you.'

Emma turned cold. 'He's talked about me?'

'You think we act like you don't exist? He says he wishes you and him could be mates.'

Emma recoiled from the idea, and Zeb must have seen it in her face.

'Seriously, Mum, what's your problem with him?'

'I . . .' Every time she started to explain, the words curled up. She was afraid it would sound like trivial school nonsense, rather than a period of her life that had affected and changed her so profoundly. 'I just don't trust him.'

'You don't even know him!' He jabbed a finger at his chest. '*I* know him now. And you trust *me*, don't you?'

His question made something tighten inside her. It suddenly felt like the worst part of all of this, that the answer was no longer, *Of course I do. Always. Unreservedly.*

'You've only known him a few weeks,' she said.

'Long enough! I feel like I've known him all my life. Except I haven't, of course. You made sure of that.'

'If you'd known him all your life maybe you wouldn't have such a high opinion of him.'

'Don't you think people change?' Zeb raised his voice. 'Is it one strike and you're out with you?'

'That's not fair.'

'In your text you said you were going to tell the police on him!'

'Well, I was *scared*!'

As she flung it out there, she realised how true it was. The last few days, and even the weeks before that, had been underscored by fear. She thought of her conversation with the police officer, left unfinished when she'd spotted Zeb, and wondered whether they would follow it up. Whether she wanted them to, now she'd seen how furious Zeb was.

Her admission seemed to stall him, though. No matter how angry, she was heartened to see that the idea of her being frightened bothered him. She took the opportunity to step closer, brush his arm. He no longer smelt of Lynx but of something DIY-related, like WD-40.

'I don't want us to fall out,' she said. 'Especially with everything that's been happening to our neighbours.' She watched his face as she said this, pained again that she felt the need to. He was looking at the floor. 'You're so precious to me, Zeb. But it's just been so ... disturbing. Things through the post. Silent phone calls—'

'The calls were me.'

She withdrew. 'What?'

Zeb squared his shoulders, but his cheeks had reddened and he couldn't meet her eye. 'I've been calling you.'

Her heart began to thump. 'And ... hanging up?'

He pressed his fist to his Adam's apple, rubbing the stubbly skin there.

'I just wanted to talk,' he said gruffly.

'You can talk to me any time, Zeb.'

'Not about Dad. We've never been able to talk about him. Even the Freya thing. It's been on my mind, but ...' He scratched harder, at his chin now.

Emma found herself looking at the home phone, goose-bumps mottling her arms as she remembered how she'd felt each time it had rung. Late at night. Early in the morning. Soft breathing down the line. 'I don't understand,' she said.

'I bottled it every time. Always ended up tongue-tied. So I'd wait a few seconds, hoping I could get my shit together, then start panicking about the silence and eventually hang up.'

'But ...' she struggled to take it in '... the number was always withheld.'

'Must be a setting on Dad's phone. There's pretty much no mobile signal out there so I usually used the landline in his office. I didn't want to talk to you over Skype – it's too awkward. I didn't mean to scare you or anything.'

Emma pulled back her hair and flattened it beneath her palms. She was trying to stay calm. Trying not to shout, *Well, you did scare me. For God's sake, I've barely slept.*

Gilbert had woken. She could see Zeb frowning at the snuffly noises coming from inside the cupboard, trying to work out what they were. He hadn't even met her sad little attempt to make the place feel less empty. Probably thought she'd acquired a rat problem.

'What about the other stuff?' she asked.

He exhaled through his nostrils.

'I have no idea. I'm just certain it wasn't Dad. He wouldn't do that. Please, can you drop your campaign against him?'

She clasped his hand. 'I was only ever trying to protect you.' Even as she said it, she wondered how true it was. Had she been protecting Zeb or herself? She couldn't help thinking of Steph again: who was *she* protecting with her secrets?

Zeb let her hold his hand for a moment, looking down at her, so tall and grown-up yet still with that potent teenage angst. Then he slid his arm free and turned towards the door.

'You're not going?' she said in alarm.

His head was dipped as if he was already prepared for the flashing cameras. 'I've said what I needed to.'

'Wait, Zeb! I have to ask you something!'

He paused, turning back. He was twisting the cuffs of his hoody around his thumbs, a habit he'd had since he was young.

'Did you and Freya meet up more than once?'

His eyebrows lowered as he seemed to absorb her question. Then he shrugged, and released his cuffs, adjusting his hoody with a tug of the hem. 'Yeah, actually.'

Emma breathed slowly in and out.

'We became mates, sort of. Used to meet up sometimes. It was no big deal.' There was a slight catch in his voice, and he glanced up at the ceiling.

'Why did you say you'd only spent that one evening together?'

Another shrug. 'I wanted to keep things simple, I s'pose. I didn't think it mattered. I told you all the important stuff, all the stuff that might help . . .' She saw his throat move as he swallowed. She wanted to step closer again but she didn't dare. It was all she could do to keep her voice even.

'So you don't know any more than you said?'

'No, of course not! Why do you have to be so *suspicious*?'

'I'm only asking.'

'First Dad, now you're starting on me!'

Suddenly Emma felt herself snap. When would he stop demonising her? Idolising Robin at the expense of everything else?

'You're *not* going back to your dad's,' she said. 'You're going to stay here and help the police.'

'No, I'm not.' He turned again to go. 'I've done what I can. I'm going home.'

'This is your home.' She rushed forward and grabbed his arm. 'I've had enough of this, Zeb!'

He shook her off. As she glimpsed his face, she recognised the signs that he was about to cry.

'Zeb—'

He slammed out of the flat. Emma started to chase him but stopped in her doorway, imagining the cameras springing into action outside, capturing their altercation – maybe Steph looking down from above. The questions that would follow while Emma's legs were still trembling.

So she watched from her living-room window, as she had on so many occasions recently, but this time it was to see her son weaving a path through the journalists, pausing at one of the posters of Freya, glancing back towards the house before he was gone.

50

Chris

An engagement ring was visible in the photograph, glinting like a piece of treasure among earthquake debris. Except that the debris in the photo was treasure, too, in a way, the treasure of other people's lives: a set of keys on a dolphin-shaped key-ring; a treble clef cufflink; a red Prada glasses case. And the silver pillbox, which had been the first thing to tumble out of the glovebox that day, into Freya's lap.

What's with all the stuff in here? she'd said, as Chris had frozen, watching her sift through.

He'd just managed to think of an excuse – they'd been having a clear-out at home, he was taking these things to a charity shop – when she'd recognised the pillbox. It belonged to Jess's cousin, whom Chris also taught. Apparently she'd recently lost it and had been asking all her friends if they'd seen it because it was a christening present she'd had since she was young. Then Chris had been able to see Freya making connections, reading his own panic, understanding she'd discovered a stash of strangely personal loot.

Now Chris avoided his solicitor's bewildered gaze, the expectant eyes of the detectives. He stared down at his own hands on the desk. His veins seemed bluer than usual, as though his skin was thinning as he sat there.

'Freya hasn't paid for any driving lessons since December,' he said.

Ford's eyes narrowed. Johnson's fingers twitched as if she was ready to slap handcuffs on Chris.

'Why?' Ford asked.

Chris said nothing for a moment. Her one-word question hovered.

'Are you – or were you – having a relationship with her?'

'No.'

'Then why wasn't she paying you?'

Chris swallowed. 'She ... Well, I suppose you'd call it blackmail.'

'Blackmailing *you*?'

The scorn in Johnson's tone made Chris stiffen. *A grown man let himself be blackmailed by a seventeen-year-old girl?* Chris kept his gaze on Ford: she clearly didn't like him, but at least she never seemed to be laughing at him from behind her hand.

'She had something over me,' Chris said, praying they'd somehow let him skirt around the details. 'She threatened to give me away unless I let her keep her lesson money. She said she needed it to buy her own car. I was sure her parents would buy her one, but she acted so urgent about it.'

'Do you think she wanted to go somewhere? Did she ever mention a trip, or a plan to run away?'

He shook his head.

'Do you think the money might actually have been for something else?'

Chris jerked his shoulders. 'I just know she went to some lengths to get it.'

He thought of the little comments she would throw in as they drove the streets, reminding him of what she knew, how she could ruin him. The folded notes she'd leave on his windscreen. *Picked up anything nice lately? ... Still got the photos.* Sometimes she'd acted like a vigilante, doing a public service by keeping him in check. But really she was just a child who'd stumbled across an adult's secret and realised she could wield it like a weapon.

Up until the day she'd flipped open his glovebox and its contents had spilled into her lap, he'd actually liked her, despite her over-confidence in the driver's seat, despite his innate mistrust of glossy people. She had an edge, sure: she wasn't meek or strait-laced, but she was funny and interesting. And maybe the change had begun *before* she'd made her discovery about him. He recalled a distracted sullenness that had developed over a matter of weeks. Then, as she'd sifted through the items, it was as if something had clicked and she'd understood she could turn knowledge into power.

Chris shot a glance at Ford's iPad, his gaze lingering on the pillbox. It was the one thing Freya had managed to smuggle from his car after that day. Her leverage, she'd called it.

'What's the significance of these things?' Ford asked.

Ms Beaumont turned her upper body towards him as though hinged at the waist. 'Chris, we need to talk before you answer any further questions.'

'Just tell us why Freya took this picture,' Ford said, ignoring his solicitor. 'Why she was blackmailing you. Why you were driving away from Kingston with her on the day she disappeared.'

Chris felt a surge of pure terror. Was he actually going to be charged? Ms Beaumont tried one more time to convince him to consult, but Chris just wanted to get this over with now. He could only hope they wouldn't equate his confession with a motive to harm Freya.

'I steal things,' he said dispassionately. 'I take little tokens from my learners, whenever I can.'

Johnson was smirking again. Chris had never felt so pathetic. Ford was pushing up her sleeves. 'Do you sell them? Is business not exactly booming?'

It won't be after this. Perhaps it was crazy to think about his livelihood when he was on the verge of being charged with a crime, but he couldn't help envisaging the kind of future he'd have even if he did get out of there.

'It's not for the money,' he said. 'I s'pose it's a compulsion. Like I want a piece of their lives.'

They both stared at him. They didn't get it, and he hadn't expected them to. Didn't need them to, really. Only to believe him.

'So . . . you were stealing from your clients, and Freya found out?'

He gave a reluctant nod. 'She threatened to tell unless I let her off paying for her lessons. It was a small price to pay to keep my business and my reputation.'

'But soon you got fed up,' Ford said, her voice steely. 'Being blackmailed by a teenage girl just galled you a little too much. Maybe Freya started asking for more money, making bigger and bigger threats.'

'That's not—'

'What happened on March the fifteenth?'

Chris imagined he was looking down a long tunnel, with that afternoon at its end. He *had* become fed up. And nervous. His lessons with Freya would soon have to end: she couldn't drag them out indefinitely, and what was to stop her telling people his 'little secret' then? It was gossip to everybody else but it could destroy Chris. Worse: it could destroy Vicky, and he couldn't let that happen, not when she'd struggled so hard to make something of her life.

Chris set his jaw. 'I said I couldn't keep giving her money. And I needed to know she wouldn't blab about my . . . habit.'

'Did you threaten her?'

'No. But we argued. Anger just seemed to burst out of her and, to be honest, I wasn't sure it was all aimed at me.'

'What do you mean?'

'After a while it was like she was just venting. It didn't seem to be about the money any more, or my stealing. She seemed furious with life in general. She was driving erratically, not following my directions . . . That was why we ended up heading in the wrong direction when we should've been going back to her school. Eventually I persuaded her to let me drive.'

'Did you try to stop her making a scene?'

'I tried to calm her down.'

Ford leaned forward. 'How?'

'Not with any force.'

'Are you sure about that?'

'*Yes.*'

'So what happened after you swapped places?'

'She got out of the car.'

Ford wasn't blinking. 'Where was this?'

'Portsmouth Road. Out towards the river. I tried to call after her but she ran off. I assumed she'd make her own way back to school. I . . .' His words caught on the lump in his throat. 'I never thought that might be the last I saw of her.'

'Why didn't you come forward about this before?' Ford's face had turned thunderous, but Chris couldn't work out if she believed him and was angry he'd withheld information, or whether she still considered him their prime suspect. Johnson wasn't bothering to disguise his scorn. Ms Beaumont had the air of somebody who'd been excluded from a conversation and was silently raging.

'Because I would've had to admit the thefts,' Chris said. 'And I knew it would look bad – I was the last person to see Freya, she'd been blackmailing me, we argued . . .'

Ford trailed her fingertips across the darkened surface of the iPad. 'You're right,' she said. 'It does look bad.'

51

Paul

'I should get back inside,' Paul told Yvette, as a cold wind blew through the hospital car park, and he felt himself swaying under the crush of too many memories. 'Get home.'

Even as he allowed Nathalie back into his head, made her solid again, Steph and Freya gripped hold of him, calling him back to London. He couldn't even give Nathalie the dubious honour of being the love of his life. She was a wound in the corner of his heart while his wife and daughter had the rest, always would, and what he wanted more than anything was another chance to tell them so.

If Daniel hadn't taken Freya, who had? In Paul's mind, by now, his past mistakes and present crisis were utterly entwined. But he had to face the possibility: might this journey into his former life have been nothing but a devastating waste of time?

Yvette slipped her arm through his and risked accompanying him back across the car park. The buzz of evening visiting time was building around the hospital grounds, a smell of mass-cooked food drifting from the upper wards.

Paul's eye was drawn by a large black car parked at the entrance to his block. Something about its mirrored windows woke his instincts, just when he thought they'd been killed off again. He was almost unsurprised when the door opened and Tom Glover climbed out.

'Hello, you two.' He greeted them with a blank face. '*Yvette*. Fancy seeing you here.' He threw her a stony, meaningful stare. 'Mind if I borrow Paul?'

Yvette looked at Paul. Her eyes flashed concern but he gave a small nod.

'DS Nicholls can give you a lift back to work,' Glover said pointedly, gesturing at the car.

'No,' Yvette said. 'I'm fine.'

She glanced once more at Paul, before releasing his arm and finally walking away.

Paul didn't want to get into the car with Glover. Instead they walked in slow laps around the outskirts of the hospital grounds, passing smokers in wheelchairs and patients dragging their drips. His former boss was pretending he'd come to check how Paul was doing, but it was clear there was another agenda.

'Why don't you spit it out, Tom?'

Something complicated crossed Glover's face. He stared at a pair of doves that had found their way onto the site and were nesting on top of a Hospital Hopper bus stop.

'I've smoothed everything over with Nottinghamshire police. It never happened. You were never there.'

Paul stared at him. He didn't know why he was so shocked. Glover had a talent for erasing things from the record. Paul should have been relieved, he knew. But this felt like one more thing he wouldn't be held accountable for, which would catch up with him one day.

'What the fuck were you playing at?' Glover asked.

'How did you know I was there?' Paul shot back.

'You think I don't keep tabs on Sanderson even now? And you think I didn't anticipate you'd go off on a fool's mission? I didn't think you'd be quite so foolish as to break into his house and *stab* him . . . If I'd got here an hour sooner I could've prevented it all.'

'You should've helped me when I first came to you.'

'For God's sake, Paul! You know we can't draw any attention back to that bloody disaster of a case. We're going to have to buy Sanderson's silence yet again—'

Paul's head reared up. 'He's alive?'

'Well, yes. He's recovering.' Glover jerked his head towards the hospital building. 'He'll stay away from you from now on. And you have to stay away from him. *No exceptions.*'

Daniel had survived. Paul blinked slowly, taking it in. His throat loosened as though someone had just removed their hands from around his neck.

'It's essential we contain this,' Glover steamed on. 'If the public ever finds out we sent in a UC to infiltrate that family, or that Nathalie Sanderson died because she was seduced by that UC, heads will *roll*. There'll be a major inquiry. People will be incensed.'

'I don't care any more!' Paul's shout made a passing porter look their way.

Glover stopped walking and turned Paul to face him. His spicy aftershave was still the same scent as years ago, with its bitter aniseed edge. 'I'm thinking about the complications for you as well, Paul. I take it Steph still doesn't know about Nathalie?'

'No.' Paul was aware of a collapsing sensation inside him, then a spark of defiance. 'But maybe it's time it was all out in the open.'

Glover's mask of sympathy dissolved. Paul was reminded of that switch, on the day Glover had told him Nathalie was dead, that transformation from solemn deliverer of bad news to hard-faced guardian of the force's reputation. Paul had been staying in a safe house at the time. After Nathalie had found out the truth, and gone running with it to her brother, Paul had called Glover and a back-up team had rushed to pull him out. He'd been kept in hiding while things were brought under control. He still remembered the house's plaster-dust scent, hard mattress, and the endlessness of his thoughts, punctuated only by visits from Glover. Daniel had got himself a lawyer and was threatening to sue the police. And there were 'concerns' in high places about the way Paul had handled the operation. Concerns about his unethical sexual relationship with the suspect's sister.

A few days later, Glover had arrived at the safe house unable to look Paul in the eye. Paul had thought he was going to tell him his career was over, which he'd assumed anyway. Perhaps, even, that Paul would be given another new identity for his own protection, and would have to move somewhere Daniel couldn't find him.

But Glover told him that Nathalie had returned to the woods that had last seen her daughter, and added to their infamy by hanging herself deep within the trees. After he'd delivered the news, he'd seemed to lighten with the relief of having got the unpleasantness out of the way. Then he'd launched into his plan for 'damage limitation'. He'd said it could easily blow up into a scandal, that Daniel was raging, lashing out, and would no doubt go public about the 'misjudgements' that had led to his sister's death unless they paid him off in a big way.

Paul had stared at his boss, wondering what kind of man he'd put his trust in. He'd imagined Nathalie thinking the same thing as she'd looked at Paul and realised he was a stranger, a faker, a person with an agenda. The fact of her death would not sink in straight away. The guilt would come later, would cripple and change him, but in that moment all he'd felt was disgust, aimed at the man in front of him.

Disgust that was replicated now.

'I don't think you mean that, Paul,' Glover said. 'I don't think you want the truth to come out any more than I do.'

The subtext was as clear as it had been back then: *And I have the power to make sure.*

But Paul had a new kind of power himself. The unhappy power of someone with little left to lose.

Glover adjusted his collar, eyes hard. 'It would've made things easier if you'd let Sanderson bleed.'

Paul closed the space between them. 'You'd have liked that. Another convenient death on somebody else's conscience.'

He strode away, suppressing his limp until the hospital's automatic doors breezed shut behind him.

The corridors had become crowded. The jostle of other people's elbows and bags felt deliberate, personal. Paul could barely stop himself throwing out his arms and shoving blameless strangers out of his path. A roar of emotion was in danger of bursting from him, and a confession was crystallising in his mind, a sort of statement about Daniel and Nathalie and Billie and everything.

Just as he reached the lifts, a hand grabbed his wrist. He twisted his arm in an instinctive self-defence move, but as he did so, he saw who'd seized him. Yvette kept hold, looking apologetic but determined.

'Yvette? Are you okay?'

She pulled him to one side, out of the current of people. 'What did Glover say?'

'He wants me to keep quiet. Not cause any trouble. And he told me Daniel survived.'

'He did?' Yvette rubbed her lips together. 'Jesus.' She seemed twitchy and pale, her eyes glassy.

'Yvette? What is it?'

She turned her head and stared into his face. Her fingers grasped his wrists. 'I have to tell you something, Paul.'

52

Kate

Twenty-five years earlier

I'm in an interview room. The two policemen are opposite, their hands folded around huge white coffee mugs with drippy brown stains down the sides. One has very chunky hairy fingers and the other is rocking back on two legs of his chair – my history teacher would be barking at him to stop it if she were here.

Next to me is a woman from Social Services they're calling an 'appropriate adult'. Apparently she has to be present for my questioning because I'm under eighteen. I don't know what's so appropriate about her – her grey hair, her flowery blouse? – or what an inappropriate adult might look like in comparison.

As the questions begin, I see a ghostly twin of myself hovering beside me. The twin is telling the truth. Each part of her confession makes her lighter so she floats into the air, higher and higher like the part in *Mary Poppins* I used to love, where the old man levitates to the ceiling.

Except the real me is rooted with terror to her chair. Denying everything, as I'm pretty sure Becca's round eyes were urging me to do, before we were led to separate rooms. They ask me if I know what pills Becca was taking at the time, and it seems safest to say I'm not sure. They want to know whether Becca liked Nick. 'She thought he was okay,' I tell them. 'She didn't really know him that well.'

Then they want to hear all about that Friday night again.

'I went to meet Mum at Costcutter.'

'What time was that?'

'Um . . . probably about five?'

'Can anyone confirm you were out of the house at that time? Other than your mum?'

I'm struggling to grasp the significance of all their questions. I want to stick as close to the truth as possible – apart, of course, from the words my ghost twin is mouthing.

'Linda. We saw our neighbour, Linda Clarke, on the way home.'

The policemen write this down, then without explanation disappear from the room. Mrs Appropriate offers me a reassuring smile but the pink flowers on her blouse make my eyes ache.

At last the policemen return. 'Thank you, Miss Thomas. You're free to go.'

Really? I can go? What does that mean? What will happen next?

Mrs Appropriate rises to her feet. 'I'll show you back to reception, Kate.'

Mum's waiting, looking small and slumped in a black plastic chair against a big white wall. She was questioned just before me, by the same two policemen; we weren't allowed to talk to each other in between. She gives me a searching look as I approach.

'I'm allowed to go home,' I say.

'Good . . . that's good.' She pats my shoulder but her anxious frown sticks in place. 'Let's get out of here.' She stands up, glancing around. I think of my visit here almost two months ago. I'm glad nobody seems to recognise me from that.

'What about Becca and Auntie Rach?' I ask.

As if on cue, we hear Auntie Rach's voice. We turn to see her at the far end of the reception desk, leaning towards the woman behind the screen. Her words carry: 'I want to see my daughter.'

'What's going on?' I ask Mum.

'I don't know, love.' Mum walks forward and I shuffle along beside her.

Auntie Rach looks up as we get near. Her face is red and shiny, like a glazed cherry.

'They're keeping Becca in,' she says. 'I think I need to get her a solicitor.'

Everything smears. All I can see is a blur of light with the negatives of my aunt and Mum emblazoned onto it.

Mum and I come home while Auntie Rach stays at the police station. When we get back to the flat I turn freezing cold and can't stop shaking. Mum puts me to bed, brings me a hot Ribena, lays her hand on my forehead, like I've got flu. I think she's going to speak but she stays quiet, her palm a heavy blanket on my skin. I'm almost asleep by the time I hear my bedroom door hitch on my lumpy carpet as she closes it behind her.

Sometime during the night I half wake to the hiss of an argument. I swim up through layers of sleep, disentangling myself from a net of bad dreams, and I make out Auntie Rach's voice, and Mum's . . . but no Becca.

Mum saying, *Trouble ever since she got here . . .*

And then . . . *pills. They were Becca's pills, and they killed him.*

Sleep drags me back down. When I next open my eyes, the silence feels solid. There's a clear expanse of carpet where Becca's sleeping-bag should be. I haul myself out of bed to find that Auntie Rach is gone. So are all her things, Becca's too.

The news comes a few days later. Time has become elastic by then, a rubber band stretching from the point at which I stirred the pills into the beer and eggs, forever in danger of snapping back. Mum and I barely talk. Often I catch her looking at me sideways, a question in her eyes. She's as pale and tired as she was before he died and the weight's still peeling off her.

The home phone rings while I'm in the bath. I hear Mum's footsteps travel towards it but can't tell what she's saying once the ringing stops. I get out, pull on some clothes and venture into the living room. Mum's perched on the arm of a chair, twirling an unlit cigarette.

Her eyes slide towards me. 'Becca's been charged.'

'What?'

'With Nick's murder.'

'*Murder?*' The word burns. I can't swallow it, must spit it out, but it won't shift and I'm running out of air. 'But . . . no . . . that's crazy . . .'

'Is it?' Mum pinches each end of the fag, little crumbles of tobacco escaping. 'Becca's always been unpredictable. And she's had an obsession with Nick since she got here.'

I shake my head. 'No. The pills . . . he took them accidentally, surely . . .'

'Then why would she lie about her meds? Why would she change them, try to cover it up?'

There's a falling in my chest. 'I don't know.'

Tears shine in Mum's eyes: the first I've seen since Nick died. 'I should've made her leave when she started saying all that stuff about him.' She starts to sob, then folds over and cries so hard she can't keep herself upright.

I can't stand to see her so upset, can't stand to think of Becca in a cell, can't imagine what will happen once I've confessed. Because I have to now. How can I live with myself if I don't?

53

Steph

She was alone at last. George and the other police officers had gone, though their search continued and a helicopter still droned in Kingston's night sky. Even the journalists had dispersed for now. Heather and Brian were driving around rechecking places where Freya or Paul might be. Clutching at straws, really, and Steph shared their desperation but she hadn't joined them. She had her own leads to follow.

Her bare toes cut a route through the empty flat, into her own room and to her wardrobe. Her tailored dresses and silk shirts were like ghosts from a previous normality in which she'd worn make-up and gone out for date nights with Paul. She reached beneath the swish of hems, grasped the edge of a dusty shoebox, and slid it out from its long-term hiding place. There was another box concealed inside; she cradled the second on her knee, running her finger across the dried-out brown tape sealing it closed.

It seemed heavy in her lap. Almost hot with the memories it contained. She had to confront them now. Had to know whether she had done this to her daughter, her family.

Steph emptied the box onto the bed, its contents cascading out. The crumple of a newspaper article. The patent shine of a red ball. The photos that were aged and grainy, in contrast to the framed family portrait that smiled from the wall above.

Stretching up, she unhooked the newer photo. It left a square of bright wallpaper behind it, unspoiled by sun. She remembered the day it had been taken: Freya's fifteenth birthday. They'd let her get her ears pierced, then gone out for burgers afterwards. In the photo, her newly adorned lobes were pink and puffy, but she was beaming, a tall banana milkshake in front of her. Steph's favourite flavour, too, as a child.

She laid the picture on the bed among the other things, as though trying to slot her newer life into the old, trying to understand how the two might have collided. She envisaged more things in the gaps: the banknotes with her drawings on; the silver pillbox; the snaps of Freya and Zeb.

An image of Freya's bloodstained jacket cast a shadow over everything else. Where was it now? In a lab, with samples being scraped from the sleeves that were a fraction too short for Freya's long arms?

And where was Freya without it? Why would it be buried unless—

Steph caught herself, stamping out the thought before it could crush her. As she stuffed all the items back inside the shoebox, tears poured down her face. How could it have come to this? At what moment, precisely, could she have diverted the chain of events that had led her here? Because she was sure there must have been a moment. Perhaps several. A different choice or choices that might have kept *all* her loved ones safe.

She jumped off the bed, clutching the box, and left her flat in a daze. At the top of the stairs she paused, and turned back inside. Swerving into the kitchen, she tried not to think too hard about what she was doing: opening a drawer, groping for a sharp knife, holding it at her side as she hurried back through the flat, the box still under her other arm. *Just in case*, said a voice in her head, steadier than she really felt. She pulled on Paul's wax jacket and dropped the knife into one of its deep front pockets, where she could forget it was there, unless she needed it.

As she was stumbling down the stairs, she heard their letterbox clatter open, then snap closed. Reaching the hallway, she saw that a piece of paper had been shoved through. She stood staring at it, nerves stirring. The door to Emma's flat opened and her neighbour appeared.

'I heard something . . .'

Steph pointed at the note. Both women hesitated, as if unsure who should investigate it. Emma plucked it from the letterbox and Steph stood beside her, eyes zigzagging over the block capitals.

MOTHER OF THE YEAR?
TRY LIAR OF THE DECADE.
INNOCENT VICTIM?
NOBODY BUT YOURSELF TO BLAME.

Steph made a guttural noise in her throat. The shoebox slipped from beneath her elbow and its contents scattered, the red ball bouncing against her foot. It was the truth of the words that cut so deep. And it was the person who must've written them, the message Steph could no longer deny, not even the tiniest amount. She looked at Emma, who had turned pale too, and didn't even appear to have noticed the things Steph had dropped. She just seemed lost in her own reaction to the note.

Steph was about to start scooping up the items when it hit her. The note had been hand-posted. Its deliverer had been there only moments ago. Steph thrust open the exterior door and they spilled out into the sharpness of the evening.

'Hey!' Emma shouted.

Steph looked to where Emma was gesturing, and saw the silhouette of a figure down the far end of the street, wearing a baseball cap and a hooded jacket. Then suddenly they were running, chasing, and the person was bolting away, swerving trees and charging across roads. Steph felt Emma's arms knocking against hers, heard the other woman panting almost in unison with herself. When Emma stumbled, Steph flung out a hand to steady her. When Steph ran out of breath, Emma clasped her wrist and pulled her on.

It seemed to be a man. That was all Steph could make out. Her head was pulsing, her lungs screaming, so there was barely any room to process what was happening and who specifically the man might be. She just knew he must have been sent to threaten her . . . even summon her. And she had to get to him.

Driven by a blast of emotion, she pulled ahead of her neighbour. Then she heard Emma cry out as if she'd tripped. The man must have heard, too: he glanced briefly over his shoulder, but still Steph didn't fully glimpse his face.

'No,' Emma was saying from behind her. '*No* . . .'

Steph staggered to a breathless halt. Emma was lying on the pavement clutching her leg, but that didn't seem the main cause of her distress. She was gesturing towards the disappearing figure, shaking her head and sobbing.

54

Chris

'Can I make a phone call?'

'Excuse me – please. Can I have my phone call?'

'Don't walk away! I'm entitled to a call!'

Chris had no idea how long he'd been in custody. Inside the police station it was neither night nor day. He'd been charged with theft and perverting the course of justice. The Freya Harlow investigation was ongoing, they told him, so he wouldn't be released on bail yet.

He'd been locked in a cell with a man who was trying to pull off his own toenails. Chris felt he was inhaling human waste with every breath. Each time an officer appeared on the other side of the bars he asked if he could make a call.

Finally, someone came to fetch him and led him to the phone.

Chris dialled the hospital – he was fairly sure Vicky would be back on shift now – and was put through to her ward.

'Chris?' She sounded frantic when she came on the line. 'Are you still at the police station? What's going on?'

Chris imagined her standing beside a reception desk in her uniform, her dark fringe pinned back from her face, her fingers scrunching the blunt edges of her hair. Yearning swelled behind his ribs. 'I'm still at the police station,' he said.

'And?'

'I'm being questioned about Freya's disappearance. And I've been charged with . . . theft.'

'*Theft?*'

Chris was conscious of the custody officer, watching and listening. He had to choose his words carefully.

'Freya found out I'd been stealing things,' he said. 'She's been blackmailing me.'

'You . . .' Vicky trailed off and Chris imagined her glancing around her ward, checking who was eavesdropping. Her voice dipped: 'Found out *you*'d been stealing?'

'I'm sorry I didn't tell you.' Chris continued to speak cautiously but clearly, for the benefit of his guard. 'I'd been taking things from my learners, just bits and bobs, small tokens . . .'

Vicky fell silent. Perhaps she was utterly confused, or perhaps she was beginning to realise what he was trying to tell her: *Let me do this for you.*

What he really wanted to say was that he understood why she'd always felt the need to steal. From the other kids in her care home; from her flatmates at nursing college; now from the patients on her ward. He understood her desire for trinkets of other people's lives, knew she'd grown up feeling that nothing in the world belonged to her. But he couldn't articulate any of that right now. All he could do was try to put the message across: he would never betray her, no matter how strained things had become between them.

'I'd been keeping the stuff in my car,' Chris said, still hoping she was reading between the lines. 'I was going to get rid of it all, or even give it back to the people it came from, if I could. But Freya saw it and took her chance to get some money out of me.'

'You were keeping them,' Vicky murmured, and Chris knew his meaning was sinking in. The things he'd found in their bedroom, the things he'd immediately known she had stolen, which would lose Vicky her nursing licence if anybody discovered them . . . He'd panicked and shoved them all into his glovebox. And that was what Freya had discovered. Even the pillbox, which Freya had seen as confirmation of his thefts, had been a kind of confirmation for Chris, too. He knew Jess's cousin had had a brief spell on Vicky's old ward, having her tonsils out.

'They think you did something to Freya?' Vicky asked. 'Because of that?'

'I'm a suspect.'

'Oh, God—'

'It's going to be okay. Don't worry.'

'How can I not worry? You're in there because of—'

'Time's up,' the officer barked from behind.

'I've got to go,' he told Vicky.

There was another pause, during which Chris hunched protectively over the receiver, as though he could stop the policeman wrestling it from him.

'I'll come and pick you up,' Vicky blurted. 'When they let you out, I'll be there.'

Chris smiled again, and saw the officer shoot him a look, as if to say, *What the hell have you got to be cheerful about?*

'That would be good,' Chris whispered down the phone.

'Chris . . . thank you,' she said. 'And I'm sorry.'

He swallowed. 'You never need to say that to me, Vic.'

Then they were quiet, breathing in synchrony, until the officer snatched the receiver and hung it up.

55

Kate

Twenty-five years earlier

'Mum,' I say, my voice off-beat with nerves. 'There's something I need to tell you.'

I have no idea how I'm going to say it. How she's going to react. Once it's said, it's said. As irreversible as what I did to Nick.

She's still doubled over after her fit of crying. When she raises her chin, I'm startled to see blood leaking from her nose. 'Oh, Mum! You're having a nose bleed!'

She blinks and raises a hand to her nostrils. The blood ribbons over her fingers, across her chin, onto the collar of her grey T-shirt.

I dash to the bathroom for a wad of toilet roll. She tries to stem the bleeding, then tips back her head and pinches the bridge of her nose. 'Damn,' she murmurs, in a way that makes me think this isn't the first time she's had a nose bleed this bad. She doesn't seem surprised, just annoyed, frustrated.

But I'm scared to see her losing so much blood. Disturbed by the puddle of red on the front of her top. Uneasy, as I remember a different top, a similar stain. Scarlet against pale blue.

'You okay, Mum?' I ask, when the bleeding's stopped. She's slumped in the armchair, burrowing her feet beneath our scruffy flowery rug.

'Oh, Kate,' she says, in a strangled voice, shutting her eyes. 'What are we going to do?'

A tremor passes through me. 'What do you mean?'

Her tears brim again, slipping from beneath her closed lids. She opens her eyes but doesn't wipe them; pearls of water cling to her skin.

'Maybe Nick was right. I should've told you months ago.'

'Told me what?'

She massages her cheeks with the heels of her hands. There are clots of dried blood around her nostrils, like little splodges of paint.

'*What*, Mum?'

'Things are going to be difficult now, love. Nick's gone. Becca and Rach won't be coming back here. And it's going to be hard. Even harder than it would've been if I didn't . . . if I wasn't . . .' She leans forward, grasping my hands. 'I'm ill, Kate.'

Everything freezes. I feel a door swing shut in my brain as though it's rejecting this information, refusing it entry.

'It's called MDS, love. Myelodysplastic syndrome. It's a kind of cancer.'

Her words fall through me but still I can't speak. It's like my mouth is anaesthetised.

'I didn't want to upset you, love. Didn't want to jeopardise your GCSEs. I thought it was best . . .'

No, no, no. I would have *known*. My eyes roam her face, searching for some chink in her act. All I see is her white skin and jutting bones. She is sick. Cancer. Fear wells from my chest, like nothing I've ever felt before. 'Are you going to die?'

'The doctors are doing everything they can to help me.'

I don't like her answer. I didn't hear the word *no*. My face collapses and she pulls me into a hug. 'It's okay, Kate. We're going to stick together. Get through this.'

'When did . . .?'

'I was diagnosed at the beginning of April. Nick was the only one who knew, and I wanted to keep it that way as long as possible.'

'You should have told me!'

She says nothing and I feel horrible for shouting at her. I want to yell at *someone*, though. Want to hit something solid and knuckle-crushing.

'You're going to get better, aren't you?'

'I'm on drugs to slow the progress of the disease.' There it is once more: the non-answer. Some distant part of me is gathering up all these non-answers and rearranging them into what I want to hear. 'If they don't work, I might have to have some chemo. Possibly a stem-cell transplant. I'm staying positive, Kate, and you should too.'

I hug her tighter, craving the lily smell of the perfume Auntie Rach bought her, even the cling of cigarettes. Then I pull back, blinking at her stained T-shirt. Déjà vu returning.

She follows my gaze. 'Sorry if the nose bleed alarmed you, love. I'm getting used to them now. The illness makes me bleed and bruise really easily. And this crappy tiredness . . . It's a relief to tell you, really. I don't know how much longer I could've covered it up, especially now Nick's gone.'

My heart batters my ribs. Realisations are stirring, half forming.

Mum studies me as if she can see what I'm thinking. 'I know you picked up on the tense atmosphere sometimes,' she says. 'It's been so tough, dealing with the symptoms, the appointments, the decisions about treatment . . . I wouldn't have blamed Nick if he'd backed away completely, but he never did . . . and he respected my decision not to tell you, even though he felt pretty strongly you ought to know. We argued about it a lot. And maybe he was right after all.'

I press my hands to my mouth, tasting salt on my skin.

All this time she was being attacked by something I couldn't save her from. And I still can't.

As we fall quiet, listening to the buzz of the fridge that still threatens to clap out any moment, more realisations move through me. I can't fend them off now: they just keep coming, like waves of heat and ice.

He wasn't hurting her, was he? He was helping her keep the secret. I killed the one person she relied on. Killed him for no reason at all.

56

Paul

It was 10 p.m. when Paul finally limped towards home. His body felt broken, his mind lagging. He'd discharged himself from the hospital against medical advice, and Yvette had driven him to her place, lent him some of her partner's clothes, then dropped him off, at his request, around the corner from his house.

Leaving him to try to come to terms with a new, almost incomprehensible truth.

Half of him still could not believe what Yvette had told him as she'd grasped his wrists in the hospital corridor a few hours before. The other half had to acknowledge that her revelation made sense of everything. Shadowed thoughts that had been knocking at the back of his brain for years had emerged into the light as she'd spoken. But that hadn't made it any easier to take in.

She wanted to escape, Yvette had said. *From Daniel, from his hold over her, from whatever he may or may not have done to Billie. And ...*

And from me, Paul had finished for her, still not fully comprehending.

Yvette had looked down. *In a way, yes. She thought you'd try to follow her or track her down if you ever knew. She just wanted to disappear, and we thought we owed her that. A new life and some protection.*

Breathlessness had swept across Paul's chest as he'd begun to understand.

Nathalie hadn't killed herself.

Nathalie was alive.

I wanted to tell you, Yvette had said. *So many times, I almost did.*

Paul had realised, then, what had been gnawing at him, almost subconsciously, for a long time. The fact that nobody ever went near Chainwell Woods any more, not since what had happened to Billie, yet Glover had told him that Nathalie had been found hanging from a tree by a local dog-walker. It was a clichéd, lazy detail in the story. It had never sat quite right, but Paul hadn't grasped why until now.

Glover knows? he'd asked Yvette.

She'd nodded. *It suited him to get Nathalie out of the picture. One less person to expose the whole 'scandal'. But I didn't go along with it for his sake. It was for Nathalie . . . and you.*

Me?

You had to let her go, Paul. I knew you never would as long as you thought she was somewhere out there.

The words echoed in his head now: *somewhere out there.*

And yet he didn't know what to feel. Sadness? Relief? Fury? Deep inside, he knew that what Yvette had told him was *huge*. But he couldn't bring his reaction to the surface alongside everything else. He just wanted to nuzzle his face into his wife's hair, shut his eyes and open them to see Freya behind her, smiling and sleepy, in her polka-dot pyjamas.

Imagine if he got home to find her there. If there was an explanation so simple he'd looked right past it. Looked in the wrong direction.

As he neared the house, he noticed Steph's car wasn't on the street. Two police cars were parked in its place. That wasn't so unusual: police had been there constantly over the last few days, but something about them suggested a flurry of activity. One had its doors open, leaking the buzz of a radio. An officer got out of the other and headed towards Paul.

'Mr Harlow.' It was dark enough for him not to notice Paul's injuries. Paul stood as upright as he could, braced. 'There's been an incident.'

Paul's heart juddered. Would it be Freya? Before he could speak, the officer said: 'An abusive note was pushed through your door.'

'*Abusive?* Saying what?'

'It's been taken away for examination. But it said . . .' The man shone a torch at his book and read awkwardly, without glancing up: '"Mother of the year – question mark. Try liar of the decade. Innocent victim – question mark. Nobody but yourself to blame."'

Paul laboured to compute the words. Liar? Blame? Each one felt like a pendulum swinging hard in his skull.

Mother?

The officer cleared his throat. 'Mrs Harlow and your neighbour, Miss Brighton, chased a man—'

'*Chased* him? What? Are they okay?' He glanced to the left, where Steph's car should have been, and felt the churn of alarm that had become a constant companion. 'Where's my wife?'

'We . . . don't know.'

'What the hell do you mean?'

'Miss Brighton fell. An ambulance took her to hospital, and we arrived at the scene, but . . . Mrs Harlow had gone.'

'*Gone?*'

'Somehow, among all the activity, she disappeared. Nobody's answering the buzzer to your flat. Has she been in touch with you?'

Paul shook his head, cursing his smashed phone, his own distraction. The alarm was taking on a new colour now. More sinister, bewildering. But awakening, too. 'Who was the man?'

'He fled, I'm afraid. We're doing everything we can to track him down.'

Paul swore softly, turning towards his house. 'I'll check the flat.'

Letting himself in, he stopped and stared around him. There was a scattering of papers and photos on the floor of the shared hallway, a shiny red ball in one corner, a shoebox on its side. Paul crouched painfully to examine the items. Who were the people in these old photos? What was the significance of the newspaper clipping? Who had put these things here?

'Steph?' he shouted, as he used the banister to haul himself upstairs. The flat was cold and still. His parents weren't there either. He hollered Steph's name again into the empty living space.

In their bedroom, he saw the wardrobe doors flung open, pairs of shoes and bundles of scarves scooped out from its bottom shelf. Paul stepped closer but still couldn't make any sense of it.

What had happened while he'd been caught up yet again in the fallout from his past?

A drawer hung open in the kitchen. The drawer where they kept their knives. Paul's heart kicked as he tried to work out whether any were missing. He was fairly sure their largest kitchen knife was absent. He checked the sink and the dishwasher, a chill taking hold when he failed to find it.

The memory of sinking a blade into Daniel's shoulder turned him even colder. The idea of Steph doing anything like that was unimaginable, but perhaps she would have said the same about him, before all this. Had she been tumbling through her own destructive series of events, while he'd been miles away, diving headlong into his?

57

Emma

Emma lay on a trolley in a small curtained bay, surrounded by the hellish bustle of late-night A&E. The ache in her leg had been dimmed by strong painkillers, which also turned her brain swampy and her saliva to chalk. It wasn't clear what she was waiting for – an X-ray, a proper bed, a doctor?

One thing was clear, though, even through the fuzz. The memory of lying on a cold pavement, pain splintering up her side, finally seeing the face of the person she and Steph had been chasing. Emma had still been convinced it was Robin as they'd pursued him. He'd seemed the right height, right shape. She'd been about to scream his name when she'd tripped. For a split-second things had ground into slow motion. The figure had twisted back towards them and a streetlamp had shown her, unmistakably, who he was. As time had boomeranged back to normal speed, she'd landed on the concrete with a painful smack. Then the figure was gone and she'd been left winded, unable to believe it.

She remembered, too, Steph kneeling beside her as the blue lights of an ambulance had loomed. Grabbing her hand, putting her mouth close to Emma's ear. 'I have to go. I'm sorry.'

Emma had been groggy. 'What?'

'I can't come with you to the hospital.' Steph had spoken quickly and quietly, her breath hot on Emma's skin.

'Where are you going?'

She recalled the whites of Steph's eyes, incandescent in the dark. Strands of sweaty hair plastered to one of her cheeks from their chase, the smell of the wax jacket she'd been wearing.

Emma had wondered whether she'd recognised the person they'd been following, too.

'Are you going to that place? The address you gave me?'

'Don't tell anybody,' Steph had begged. 'Please don't tell the police. Tell them they have to look for Paul, though. I can't lose either of them. This is all my fault.'

'Steph—'

But a paramedic had arrived and Steph had leaped to her feet. A support had been slipped around Emma's neck: she couldn't move, couldn't lift her head even to watch Steph dash away. It seemed as though she'd just melted into the night.

Now the blue curtain swished and a nurse poked her head into Emma's bay. 'How are you doing?'

'I'm okay, but I really need to—'

'The police want to talk to you.'

'Oh?' Emma's stomach fluttered.

'They're at reception. They'll be here in a moment. Once they're done, we'll get you down to X-ray.'

Emma tried to sit up and compose herself, as two uniformed figures approached. One of them was the man she'd started talking to about the hate mail and silent phone calls, before the sight of Zeb had cut the conversation short. 'Miss Brighton, the incident tonight – Could you tell us what happened?'

'I . . . er . . .' She found herself acting more drugged than she really felt. Actually, her head was beginning to clear, and she realised she'd preferred the cushioning fog. 'Steph and I heard noises. We found a note had been put through the door. Outside, we saw a person running away . . .'

One of the officers nodded. 'We have the note.'

Emma nodded as well, glad of any information about how much they knew.

'So we chased him. Or tried to. I fell and I presume he got away.' She held her breath until the officers confirmed that they hadn't caught him.

'Did you see the man?' they asked.

Emma winced as if she'd had a twinge in her hip, trying to distract their attention from her face. She'd never been a good liar. 'It was too dark.' She mimed another pang of pain, hoping they'd take the hint and leave her to rest.

'Could you give any kind of description?'

'He was wearing a baseball cap.' She made her voice slow and dreamy. 'Normal height. Sorry, I . . .'

They exchanged a glance. 'No problem.' One of them laid a business card on her pillow. 'Please call us if you remember anything else.'

Emma sank into the pillow, feeling it deflate around her head, the card sliding towards her ear.

Zeb's words flashed back to her: *Dad wouldn't do that.*

'Miss Brighton, do you wish to continue with the concerns you started registering yesterday?'

She stiffened again, staring up at the ceiling. 'I . . . No. I got my wires crossed there.'

She heard them shuffle but didn't dare look at them.

'You don't think it's connected to tonight's events?'

'I don't think so.' She spoke too sharply. Anxiety had slain any acting skills she'd had in the first place. She didn't even want to think about the potential consequences of her lies. What choice did she have?

'Well, if you change your mind . . .' He nudged the business card closer, almost poking her jaw.

As they turned to go, Emma propped herself up. 'One more thing.'

They paused. Another look flickered between them, perhaps questioning her now-lucid voice and surge of energy. She tried to slide back into her out-of-it act.

'Steph Harlow,' she slurred.

That seized their attention. But Emma's words receded as quickly as they'd arrived. She recalled Steph's urgent voice in the darkness, almost drowned by sirens: *Please don't tell the police.*

'Is . . . she all right?' she substituted lamely.

'Actually, she disappeared from the scene, shortly after you were taken to hospital. We're still trying to ascertain her whereabouts. Do you have any ideas?'

Emma could remember the maisonette's address exactly. Could picture it in Steph's frantic scrawl. She didn't know what was there . . . but Steph was Freya's mother. Suddenly that seemed to dwarf everything else, seemed to give her, in Emma's mind, the right to do whatever she felt she must.

'No,' Emma said. 'Sorry, I don't.'

The officers gazed at her for a few more seconds and then, when they realised she had nothing more to add, walked away.

As soon as they'd disappeared, Emma let herself cry. She kept replaying that moment, the figure turning back under the lamplight, the shock as she'd glimpsed his face.

Zeb.

She'd looked away and then back, as if it might have been a trick, and in that brief window he'd sprinted out of reach. But it *had* been him. The question was, had it *all* been him? Eggs and dog shit and parenting books and vicious notes?

Panic was stacking up in her chest. She needed to speak to Zeb. And what was she going to do about the Harlows? What if Steph was in danger and Emma was the only one who knew where she was?

The more she thought about it, the more contacting Paul Harlow seemed her only remaining option. *I can't lose either of them*, Steph had said. *This is all my fault.* Was that true, Emma wondered. What about Paul's shadow on the stairs that first night, Steph hunched on the bottom step with a bleeding ear?

What about his raised voice the next evening, the smashing glass, the way he'd shaken off that woman on Kingston Bridge?

Were these images so vivid because Emma knew what it felt like to be threatened by a man? If she could just rinse Andy and Robin out of her system, would she be able to see clearly, know who to trust?

There had been plenty of strange behaviour from Steph as well. But Emma had felt an inexplicable loyalty towards her. Perhaps she'd idolised her, in a way, because she'd seemed like one of the golden girls Emma had never been at school, with a golden daughter to match . . .

She felt a sudden wave of exhaustion, trying to understand her neighbours, to untangle her life from theirs. Maybe Steph and Paul were really just two parents in absolute crisis. Maybe the only thing left was to drop all judgements and allegiances, and give them the chance to make things right.

Then she had to figure out how to do the same with her own child. And hope that the two quests weren't in conflict.

58

Paul

Paul thrust open his living-room window. A rush of night air hit his bruised face, widened his drowsy eyes. He slapped his cheeks to revive himself. His daughter and his wife were somewhere out there in this long, strange night. Paul had to expand his tunnel vision now, try to see the things his guilty conscience might have obscured.

Looking down at the newspaper cutting in his hand, he scoured the faded type yet again.

A poisoning, back in the nineties. The reporter had made a big deal of the controversial case: a young woman accused of murdering an older man.

He threw it down on the coffee-table and flipped through the photos that had also been scattered in the hall. One showed a teenage girl with bobbed dark hair and a confident smile. The same girl was in another picture, standing between an overweight woman and a bearded man.

And then there was the birth certificate. The paper was thin as he lifted it, trembling slightly in the breeze from the window. This document was the most baffling, most troubling.

Because the date of birth was the same as Steph's. And yet the name wasn't.

Had somebody left these items, deliberately, to be found? Were they a clue, a warning?

Their family liaison officer stuck his head around the living-room door. Paul saw his eyes flicker again over his cuts and bruises. Since he'd called George and asked him to come straight over, Paul had managed to dodge all questions about his injuries. He knew he'd have to answer them sooner or later, but right now there were more urgent things.

'I've asked the team to look for any information about Kate Thomas or Rebecca Fielding,' George said. 'They're looking into the case described in the article, too. And we've put out a search for Steph. The helicopter's looking for her and Freya now.'

Paul stared towards the window, at the starless sky bearing down on the suburban rooftops. Was that the helicopter's beam he could see, sweeping over the neighbourhood, illuminating its nocturnal secrets?

Where are you, Steph?

Who *are you, Steph?*

He couldn't help hearing Nathalie's voice, asking that same question of him, like a reversed echo through time. Couldn't stop seeing mirrors across present and past: Steph and Nathalie, Freya and Billie . . .

Steph and *Kate?*

Striding along the corridor into their bedroom, Paul stared at his wife's clothes in the still-open wardrobe, touching familiar sleeves and collars. His marriage was in these textures: years of feeling this silk shirt brush against his skin as he kissed her, or hooking his fingers into the belt loops of these trousers to draw her close, or vaguely registering the softness of a jumper as he sat next to her on the sofa, Freya on his other side.

It wasn't *possible* he'd been oblivious to something so big all these years. Yet fragments of memory were waking: questions that had stirred before, but had always been put back to sleep.

Paul had been obsessed with the life he'd had before meeting Steph and having Freya. The things he'd been forced to hide from them. Had that blinded him to the fact that Steph was evasive about her own past? Had he failed to see that he wasn't the only one capable of wearing different masks?

If he'd learned anything these last few horrific days, it was that the stories he'd told himself about his life – or others had told him – couldn't be relied on. They weren't rigid but fluid, different perspectives flowing alongside one another. He hardly recognised himself any more. Felt he'd changed as much in the last week as he had during three years under-cover. But Steph was supposed to be the constant. His anchor.

'Paul?' George reappeared. 'The team's found some information.'

Paul whipped around. 'Yes?'

George passed him his iPad and Paul scanned the email on the screen. *Epilepsy medication ... trial ... disappearance from the record ...* His vision was fuzzy, like when he was tired and should be wearing his reading glasses, that film across his eyeballs.

But *something* was winking at him through the mist, like a single point of light.

George's phone rang. He gestured apologetically and moved into the kitchen with it. As Paul continued to stare around his bedroom, the home phone also trilled. He broke from his trance and dashed into the kitchen to answer it.

'Hello?'

'Is that Paul?'

'Yes, who's this?'

'Emma Brighton.'

Their downstairs neighbour? She spoke softly, struggling to make herself heard over a background din that sounded, from Paul's recent experience, very much like a hospital.

'You're home,' she said, seeming relieved. 'Steph was afraid you were gone too.'

'*She*'s gone.'

'I think I know where she is.'

Paul clenched the receiver. 'Seriously?'

'And I . . . I think you need to get to her before the police do.'

His heartbeat ramped up. He listened for a moment to check George was still occupied in another room, then pressed the phone close to his lips. 'Where is she?'

Emma recited an address. Paul grabbed a scrap of paper and wrote it down. He'd never heard of the place, knew nobody who lived in that area. 'Why would Steph be there?'

'I don't know. She gave me the address yesterday. Asked me to nudge the police towards it in their search for Freya—'

'Freya?' He couldn't stop the soar of his voice, and feared he'd alerted George, but he could hear that he was still deep in his own conversation. 'Is she connected to this place too?'

'I'm not sure how. Steph didn't seem to want anyone to know about it. But then Freya's coat was found and things changed and I . . .'

Emma's words were fragmenting, but it wasn't the line: it was the thundering that had started in Paul's skull.

'Freya's coat was found?' he interrupted her.

There was a moment of silence. 'You didn't know?'

Paul gripped the back of a kitchen chair. 'When? Where?'

'Yesterday. In the countryside, somewhere near Slough, I think. It was . . . buried.'

Paul's breath left him. Why hadn't anybody told him this? Presumably George and the other officers had assumed he knew. Paul began pacing with the phone, short distances back and forth. 'Buried?' he echoed, and suddenly his cheeks were wet, his gut was hollow.

'I'm sorry,' Emma said. 'It – it had blood on it. But that doesn't mean . . . There was no . . .' He could almost feel her scrabbling for the right things to say. 'God, I'm just so sorry.'

She sounded like she was crying too. Paul closed his eyes. Why did his neighbour seem so invested in his daughter's fate all of a sudden? Everything was confused. He could hear George wrapping up his call. There was barely any time, but all he could think about now was a grave with his daughter's jacket in.

The only concrete thing was the address on the paper. It was a new focal point. A shred of hope. Paul shook his head forcefully, dislodging the despair that was trying to overpower it. He hung up on Emma and tiptoed out of the flat.

Outside the house, just as he was debating how best to reach the address without his car, he ran into his parents.

'Paul!' His mum threw her arms around his neck, her feet almost leaving the ground with the force of her hug and their difference in height. 'Where have you been? Are you hurt? What's happened?'

He disentangled himself. Her questions accelerated and he had to cut her off. 'Mum, Dad, I'm sorry but I have to go.'

'*Don't* disappear again, Paul,' his mum said, with fervour, almost anger. 'Stay here with us. We need each other, and Freya needs us all.'

'I'm sorry. Can I take your car? I'll explain later. Just please stall George for now. Make something up . . .'

'Paul!' His mum looked anguished, but she relinquished her car keys into his shaking hands.

59

Kate

Twenty-five years earlier

I'm wearing the same dress I wore to Nick's funeral. It's the smartest thing I own – it was either that or my school uniform. The dress is looser than when I last wore it: I drown inside the dark fabric.

We sit in a room with a rust-red carpet and panelled walls: me, Mum, and a man who works for the court. The man has already talked us through what will happen, and let us read our original witness statements as a reminder of what we said all those weeks ago. Now the air snaps with the tension of waiting, a feeling that seems to have held me hostage for so long.

The door whines and another man appears, a moustached clone of the one sitting with us. 'Kate Thomas, we're ready for you.'

I shoot a glance at Mum, who gives me a small nervous smile, then follow the man down an echoey corridor, my school lace-ups slapping the floor.

He opens another heavy door and we're in the high-ceilinged courtroom. Heads turn from all sides to watch me come in. My eyes sweep without focusing, and I catch sight of Becca in the dock with a glass screen around her. The whole place smells of furniture polish; it gives me a head rush like I've inhaled a vat of it.

'I do solemnly, sincerely and truly declare and affirm that the evidence I shall give shall be the truth, the whole truth and nothing but the truth.'

Details emerge now from the blurred crowd: a woman in the jury with a purple cardigan; a man scribbling in a notebook towards the back of the room. Auntie Rach's curly mop and wide shoulders, Uncle Jack's greying beard. And Nick, *Nick* . . . except it isn't him, of course, it's his brother Richard, sitting bolt upright, like he's on strings. The one who pushed for the case to go to trial.

I let myself glance again at Becca. Just long enough to see that her hair has grown and is scraped into a ponytail, that she's gripping her elbows as she hunches behind the glass. How must she feel being the one on trial while I'm on the witness stand, called by the prosecution? She has stuck to her tactic of denying everything, meaning she's never mentioned my involvement. There's nothing I can do but keep to the same story, and hope. And surely, surely, they can't prove that Nick didn't just take those pills himself?

Except now that I'm here, a tiny dot in the eye of this massive courtroom, I'm gripped by the same powerlessness as when I feared Nick would kill my mum. It feels like anything can be proven in a place like this, with clever people steering the ship, people who know far more about cases and evidence than Becca or I.

The prosecutor stands. She's wearing a swishy black gown that makes her look like a giant crow. She pats her wig and my questions begin.

Afterwards, it's like looking back on an exam and trying to work out whether I might have passed. I can't remember exactly what my answers were. Can't judge if they were the right ones.

The prosecutor was clearly trying to demonstrate that Becca was alone with Nick for a while during that Friday night, around the time 'the pills were mostly likely ingested'. She probed for other things too, asked whether there had been any 'bad feeling' between Becca and Nick while she'd been staying with us. Becca's lawyer yelled, 'Objection,' and said the question was leading. The judge agreed, so the prosecutor rephrased it, asking what the *relationship* between Becca and Nick was like. But the idea of 'bad feeling' was out there, and I wonder if the jury saw the heat in my cheeks.

Mum had told me, earlier, that I should go home after my bit was over. She wants me to stay away from the trial as much as possible, thinks it'll be too stressful for me. But she's not allowed into the courtroom until she's given her evidence, so she isn't there to stop me slipping into a corner of the public gallery and watching.

This is the second day of the trial. I don't know what happened yesterday, and I don't really understand how the legal system works, but I can see the prosecutor slowly spinning her case, seeding her ideas. And I can see the defence trying to dissolve the suspicions as they form, like popping bubbles before they land. Becca's lawyer has a round, scrubbed-looking face and is at least a foot shorter than the tall, striking prosecutor woman. His voice is quieter and less confident too. I wonder if that matters. And I wonder how Auntie Rach and Uncle Jack have managed to afford a lawyer at all.

The next witness is Becca's GP. My stomach twirls as he confirms that Becca did take carbamazepine, and that she came to him asking for a change of prescription. A murmur ripples through the courtroom as he's asked when this happened.

Eight days after Nick died.

She must have panicked. Must have gone back to Derby and decided she had to switch her pills, hoping it would somehow disguise the connection.

'Did she say why she was *suddenly* so desperate to alter her prescription?' the prosecutor asks.

'She said she was getting side effects. Nausea and dizziness. She was very keen to try something else, so I agreed we could.'

'The defendant's original statement claimed she was not taking any medication for her epilepsy at the time of the victim's death,' the prosecutor says. 'Were you aware of her stopping drug therapy, Dr Holmes?'

'No, I wasn't.'

'You didn't advise her to stop taking carbamazepine?'

'I wouldn't have advised that.'

'Why not?' The prosecutor has this way of sounding intrigued and almost surprised, even when the examination's clearly going the way she means it to.

'It's dangerous to stop taking it. It can bring on a rebound seizure. The dose needs to be lowered incrementally, and alternative medication introduced.'

The prosecutor asks the jury to turn to Document F in their evidence packs. There's a sound of shuffling paper followed by a moment of quiet.

'This is a copy of the defendant's medical records,' she tells them. 'You can see she was given a repeat prescription of carbamazepine only four days before she went to stay with her aunt and cousin.' The prosecutor turns back to Dr Holmes. 'Did she mention that she wanted to stop taking the drug, then?'

'No,' he says. 'It was my belief she would continue.'

'Do you know whether she took her carbamazepine pills with her to her aunt's flat?'

'I don't know that,' Dr Holmes says.

The prosecutor nudges the jury back to their evidence packs, pointing out the record for the later change from carbamazepine to sodium valproate. She draws their attention to the date again, and the phrase that Dr Holmes has apparently written in his notes: *Medication reviewed at the patient's request.*

After Dr Holmes, a few witnesses are brought in to testify about 'the defendant's character'. Somehow these shock me more than anything. One of Becca's old teachers says Becca was suspended from school in year nine for fighting, and in year ten for bullying. I didn't know about any of this. I glance at Becca: her head is down, warped reflections dancing in the glass that screens her. Her defence lawyer cross-examines the teacher to show that, both times, Becca claimed to be defending a friend who'd been threatened by the other people involved.

'We never managed to establish whether that was true,' the teacher says, 'so Becca was suspended.'

A girl around Becca's age is up next. Becca stares at her as she takes the stand. They were at school together, apparently. The prosecutor asks about the 'incidents' in years nine and ten.

The girl addresses the jury directly; she seems self-assured, her earrings tinkling. Or perhaps she's just avoiding looking towards Becca. 'Bec always liked to think she was defending people but she took it to extremes sometimes,' she says. 'She'd get it into her head that people needed to be taught a lesson. Think she saw herself as a bit of a crusader.'

I glance around, sensing people absorbing those words, *needed to be taught a lesson*.

It feels like the truth of what happened that Friday, and the weeks before, is just a toy to be bounced around and bent out of shape. The way the prosecutor presents the evidence is so clever, it plants doubts even in my mind. Is Becca the strong, protective cousin I've always looked up to, or the deluded 'crusader' they're making her out to be?

I screw my eyes shut and think about jabbing my fingers into my ears. Then I hear them announce my mum's name and my eyes spring open.

Seeing her from a distance, in these unfamiliar surroundings, makes me jolt. She looks so poorly. She's wearing a navy headscarf, knotted at the back, her skin paper-white in contrast. Her fingers are thin where she clutches the edges of the witness box, her face gaunt under the lights.

She's fading away. And this was all for her. I want to stand up and shout it: *We did it but we did it for a reason. We were wrong but we thought we were right.*

Something makes me glance to the left and, through a gap in the rows of people, I catch Richard's eye. It's almost as if he's read my thoughts and turned towards me at that exact moment. I burn with shame, wrenching my gaze away.

'Miss Thomas,' the prosecutor says to Mum, 'could you confirm your association with the victim and the defendant?'

'I was Nick's partner,' Mum says, 'And Becca, the defendant, is my niece.'

'Did you have a good relationship with Mr Wood – Nick?'

'Yes.' Mum's voice is shaky but formal. Her focus never drifts towards Becca or Auntie Rach, and I'm not sure whether she's spotted me. 'We'd only been together for eight, maybe nine months, but we cared deeply about each other.'

'What would you say Mr Wood's state of mind was like in the weeks preceding his death?'

'It was a difficult time. I'd been diagnosed with a form of cancer and he was the only one who knew.'

'Did you ever suspect he was suicidal?'

Mum considers. 'No. I honestly don't think he was. Distressed, yes. Worried about me. But . . . he wouldn't have left me to deal with everything on my own. We were both trying to stay positive.'

The prosecutor leaves a tiny lull, then her voice rises: 'How would you describe the relationship between Mr Wood and Miss Fielding?'

It's the same question I was asked. My heart canters as I wait to hear how Mum will answer.

'Becca spoke to me about Nick after she'd been staying with us a few days,' Mum says. 'She said he gave her *bad vibes.*

She even hinted that he'd behaved inappropriately towards her.'

'Did you believe that?'

'Not at all. Nick wasn't . . . He wouldn't. Becca was quite flirtatious towards him when she first arrived, but then she seemed to sour.'

It hits me properly, then: Mum wants to see Becca convicted. She believes she did it. Or maybe she's just grasping at the explanation, desperate for that closure.

Her *niece*, though. Her sister's daughter.

The thought flickers at the edge of my mind: *Better than her own daughter.* She hasn't once mentioned that I had 'bad vibes' about Nick too.

Over the last few weeks, waiting for the trial, I've been obsessing over the many wrong conclusions I jumped to. It's frightening how everything can be seen in a different light: the hidden arguments, the secrecy, Mum's altered personality and Nick's mood swings. The way he was always watching her, hovering close to her. And her reluctance to leave me alone with him . . . her anxiety that Becca and I shouldn't throw any accusations his way. She was scared, I think, that he might snap and blurt out the truth.

There *was* fear and threat under our roof – I felt it and I was right. It was just the cause I was hideously wrong about.

Sometimes I feel so angry that she didn't just tell me she was sick. I've since found out that even Nick's dad knew – that must have been what he and Mum went off to talk about at Nick's funeral. But, of course, it's myself I'm really furious with. For not realising. For being so catastrophically stupid.

After Mum leaves the witness box, the prosecutor nods towards the judge.

'The Crown rests.'

60

Steph

The Chertsey maisonette had never really looked or felt lived-in. No pictures on the wall; no plants to bring colour and life. Yet despite the scarcity of furniture or accessories (and Steph *had* made tentative offers to 'brighten up the place'), it had always felt claustrophobic, as if congested with something other than the normal stuff of a home.

Though the place was small, its rent and upkeep had cut harshly into Steph's salary over the last four years. The rent was particularly high, in return for a no-questions-asked land-lord, an agreement that she could pay in cash, and no official paperwork or real names involved. Occasionally, and asham-edly, she'd had to borrow from the account where Paul's 'sever-ance package' from the police sat barely touched, saved for Freya's university fees, wedding, house deposit. He'd asked her about a withdrawal once and she'd made an excuse about emergency car repairs. Paul had accepted her explanation, just as his original 'Did you take seven hundred pounds out of the savings?' had been more curious than interrogatory.

He'd trusted her. Even though he'd once been trained to be suspicious, observant. It seemed their daughter was the one with those attributes now.

Steph felt sick as she glanced up at the curtains of the maison-ette. She'd done the same thing countless times before, flicking her eyes towards the upper floor as she approached, always with mixed emotions. Sometimes she'd looked forward to the visits, in a strange way, but there'd also been apprehension, guilt, the suffocating feeling of a responsibility she'd never be free from. Now it was all heightened by fury, and fear . . . and hope. Dizzying hope that Freya might somehow be there.

A bloodied coat doesn't mean the end, she told herself yet again.

She just couldn't waste any more time.

It was this thought, and the memory of the note she and Emma had found, that made her take the knife from the pocket of Paul's jacket and slip it up her sleeve. She shivered at the metal against her skin, shed the heavy coat and got out of the car. Fleetingly, she remembered she'd left the shoebox and its contents in the hallway of their house. The exhibits of her past, which she'd guarded so carefully. She dismissed the thought before it could divert her. It didn't matter any more.

Opening the door of the maisonette was such a familiar action, pulling up the handle and wriggling the key, but tonight she had no idea what she'd find. The hallway smelt, as always, of old cardboard and dust balls. The lower floor was a steep staircase with a boarded-up shop to the right. Above was the place Steph visited regularly, the place nobody knew about. Except maybe Freya. Clearly she'd seen her mum heading this way when she should have been at work. And clearly she'd already noticed those lies about money and errands and working late. She'd known dishonesty when she'd seen it, though she'd been mistaken about the reason. According to Zeb, Freya had even wanted to buy a car so she could do her own detective work. Was that what the money in her jacket pocket had been for? *Had* she managed to follow Steph all the way here, and become tangled in something much bigger than she'd anticipated?

Steph's heart boomed as she climbed the stairs. *I can deal with anything else now. Just let me not be too late.* She should have come sooner, told the police, done everything differently. Denial and fear had paralysed her at first. Then, for a brief moment, she'd hoped she could keep her own secrets, hold on to her life *and* save Freya. Stupid, stupid, stupid. But now she was here and ready to sacrifice everything except her daughter.

She opened the door at the top to reveal a deserted living room. Her eyes picked out details in the normally tidy space: a desk drawer pulled out, coins dotting the carpet below. A scruffy holdall on the sofa, bulging with clothes.

A creak from the back of the house made her right hand fly to her left sleeve, finding the outline of the knife. Familiar footsteps travelled down the small corridor that separated the bedroom from the lounge.

61

Kate

Twenty-five years earlier

The next day, I know I'll go back. It's inevitable that I'll slip away from school, catch a bus into town, take the same seat in the gallery and bite my nails until warm blood trickles beneath my tongue. To my relief, Mum isn't there. Maybe she can't face Auntie Rach and Uncle Jack after the evidence she gave yesterday. Maybe she can't face any of it.

It's the defence's turn today: the short, round man, whose belly protrudes from his black gown so it won't hang closed. I glance towards my aunt and uncle, clasping hands on the other side of the gallery, and wonder if Becca's lawyer realises how much hope is resting on his curly-wigged head. In the solace of the school library this morning, I managed to find a book on English law. It said the defence doesn't have to prove anything, only show 'reasonable doubt'. I roll the phrase around my brain, trying to wring some comfort out of it.

Becca's lawyer questions Nick's GP first.

'Why did you prescribe antidepressants for Mr Wood?'

'He was going through a difficult period. Insomnia, feeling anxious . . . It was just a temporary measure.'

'Were you concerned about his state of mind?'

'I suppose so, yes.'

I can see what the defence man is trying to do. Reminding the jury of the *possibility* of suicide. Because possibility surely means doubt. But then the prosecutor stands up to cross-examine the doctor, and shoots to the heart of it: 'Did you think Mr Wood was a suicide risk?'

The doctor ponders. 'I can never rule it out, of course. But I actually got the impression he wanted to address his mental state so he could be there for his partner.'

'If Mr Wood was intending to commit suicide, don't you think he would have taken a large amount of his anti-depressants, or perhaps something like paracetamol, rather than a dose of unknown medication he found lying around?'

'Objection!' calls Becca's lawyer. 'This is speculation.'

The judge agrees. But, again, the prosecutor's logic trails in the air, like smoke.

And although I presume the defence lawyer knows what he's doing, I can't help feeling his suggestions contradict one another as he continues. Maybe Nick took the pills on purpose, maybe accidentally, maybe they were Becca's pills or maybe they weren't. We can't prove it, he's trying to insist, and sometimes he sounds convincing. At others the prosecutor smashes her manicured hand right through his theories.

My hope lifts and dives so many times I feel sick.

Then it's over for another day, and when I get home I think Mum suspects where I've been but she doesn't say anything. I make chicken nuggets and burned potato waffles because she's too tired to cook, and there's something comforting about the childish meal, something that makes me want to curl up on her knee.

Another thing I read in the law book from school was about the defendant giving evidence. The person accused of the crime has to choose whether to take the stand and be questioned themselves. My first instinct was *Why wouldn't you?* It's your chance to put your side across. But then I think about what that means, in Becca's case: clinging to a lie in front of all those people, being cross-examined by the Human Crow and scrutinised more closely than any of the other witnesses.

It keeps me awake for the next few nights, the possibility that she might break down and reveal everything.

I dream about the scene, and when I'm back in the public gallery on the final day, with the judge announcing that the last witness for the defence will be Becca, I feel as if I've been submerged in my own nightmare. The light in the courtroom seems hazy; people's voices are slurred; my legs sink into the wooden bench with dream-like paralysis. For a moment the only clear point in the room is Becca, stepping up to the box, taking her oath.

'Miss Fielding,' her defence barrister begins, 'can you clarify for the court whether or not you were taking carbamazepine at the time of the victim's death?'

Becca's voice is hoarse, as if she hasn't used it for a while. 'Yes, I was.'

'Why did you originally tell the police – at your aunt's home and subsequently at the police station – that you weren't?'

She clears her throat. 'I got confused. There'd been so much happening. And I *was* thinking of stopping because it was making me feel ill. But Dr Holmes had told me not to just stop.'

'Did you have some with you while you were staying with your aunt and cousin?'

'Yes.'

'Were they accessible to Mr Wood?'

'They were in Kate's room.' The mention of my name makes me breathe harder. 'They weren't locked away or anything. So I guess they would've been accessible.'

'And did you notice any missing after the evening in question?'

'No, but I didn't count them, just took my dose as normal.'

'Did you notice you were a number of tablets short at any point following Mr Wood's death?'

'No. I didn't get to the end of the pack before I changed my medication, though. If I had, I might've noticed if there were fewer left than there should've been.'

There's something rehearsed about the exchange. I wonder if it's only me who notices, perhaps because I know Becca so well.

'Did you administer your tablets to Mr Wood in any way?' the defence lawyer asks, making me freeze.

Becca replies firmly, 'No.'

'Did you get on with him?'

'Yes. I admit I had a bad first impression of him, but as I got to know him better, we got on fine.'

'So did you talk to your aunt and express concerns about him?'

'Just once. After that I changed my opinion of him.'

'There were no further disagreements?'

'No.'

When the defence's questions are over, I feel a fraction calmer. It's hard to tell, but I think it went okay. I try to imagine myself as a member of the jury: what would I be making of it all?

The prosecutor is on her feet, striding forward. The pace picks up. She asks her questions at speed, one after another, making waves in the courtroom.

'Why did you change your medication, Miss Fielding?'

'Because it was making me feel sick.'

'Not because Mr Wood died from a reaction to that particular drug?'

'I – I didn't even know that was what he'd died from. Not then.'

'You had no inkling?'

'How could I?' Becca's tugging at her own ponytail. 'I had no idea he'd even taken them.'

'You didn't try to cover up the fact that they were your pills?'

'Well, it wouldn't cover it up, would it?'

'You tell me.'

'I mean, it hasn't.'

'So your plan didn't work?'

'No – no, it wasn't my plan. But if it had been, it would've been a pretty stupid one.'

'I see.' The prosecutor arches one eyebrow. My head is reeling from the quick-fire questions. Becca looks like they're having the same effect on her.

'Why did you lie to the police about what medication you were taking?'

'I've already said, I just got muddled.'

'So, if I've got this right, you thought you hadn't packed *any* pills for your stay at your aunt's flat? Because you were, as you said originally to the police, "between medications".'

'That's what I thought—'

'Even though, as you've just confirmed, they were in your cousin's bedroom, where you were also sleeping, so you would've seen and taken them every day?'

'Of course I remember that now.'

'But when the police asked – *twice* – if Mr Wood might've had access to carbamazepine around the time he died, you said no.'

'I got muddled.'

'You weren't trying to cover anything up?'

The judge interrupts: 'Please move on. The witness has already answered these questions.'

'Of course, m'lord. I'm merely trying to get everything clear. I don't want the jury to be *muddled* also.'

She's having a joke now. Doing a victory jig even before the end. Tears prod at the backs of my eyes, but I force them away: it's not over yet.

Hold it together, I want to tell my cousin, who's visibly shaking on the stand. I remember what happened in my nightmare and a stream of cold air wafts down my back.

'Did Mr Wood make sexual advances towards you?'

'Um, no.'

'So why did you tell your aunt that he did?'

'I didn't. Not in so many words.'

'But you implied it?'

'Perhaps accidentally.'

'Did you get muddled again?'

Becca flushes. 'I . . . I just got a bad feeling about him at first and I wanted to . . .'

'Wanted to what?'

'To make sure.'

'Make *sure*?'

'Make sure Aunt Laura was okay.'

'And if she wasn't, what action did you plan to take?'

'I don't know . . .'

'You've responded violently in the past when you've thought people close to you were being treated badly.'

'No, I haven't.'

'We've heard evidence of fighting, bullying . . .'

'That's just school stuff! It's nothing to do with any of this!'

'And what is "this" exactly?'

'This – this case . . .' Becca's voice cracks, tears glossing her eyes.

'Objection!' her lawyer shouts. 'The witness is being intimidated.'

The prosecutor holds up her palms. 'No further questions.'

Becca seems to draw herself together, swallowing her tears. Just before she's led back to her seat behind the glass, she looks in my direction for the first time. Her eyes find mine, as if she's known exactly where I've been sitting the whole while, but panic makes me cast my gaze down to my lap. There's a hole in my school tights that I must have been picking at throughout the questioning – it gapes right across my thigh.

Energy swirls around the room like dust that won't settle. Becca's lawyer leaps out of his seat, as if remembering he's supposed to be doing something, and fluffs his words as he tells the judge that the case for the defence is concluded.

62

Steph

'What are you doing here?' Becca said, a blaze of fear in her eyes. Then she adjusted her tone, as if to sound casual: 'You're not due to visit until tomorrow.'

Steph was incredulous as they stared at one another across the living room of the maisonette. Was Becca really going to act like everything was normal? They hadn't spoken since Freya had disappeared, so officially her cousin was oblivious, but surely they were past that now. Hadn't Becca sent somebody with a note, only an hour ago, to summon Steph? To invite this confrontation and whatever it would lead to?

'You're leaving.' Steph gestured at the packed bag lying on Becca's sofa.

Becca opened her mouth, then pressed it closed again. Steph saw the familiar nervous blotches on her neck. Her cousin's hair was long and unstyled now, her skin dull from so much time spent indoors, her clothes plain. Steph always felt conscious of her own tailored work suits and salon-smooth hair when she visited. In a way she had become Becca, had borrowed her sleek style and social confidence as she'd built her new life.

'Where is she?' Steph rushed forward, the words spitting out. 'Where's my daughter?'

Becca backed off towards the wall. 'What?'

'I know you're behind this. I didn't want to believe it at first . . .' Steph's eyes scanned the room again, searching for any signs that Freya had been there.

'I don't know what you're talking about.'

'Then why are you running away?'

'It's best for both of us if I leave. You've got other things to think about than me.'

'You're lying.'

Becca suddenly stood firm, lifting her chin. 'Well, you're the expert on that, *Kate*.'

Steph flinched at her former name. Becca threw it at her occasionally, when she was having a bad day. Clearly Steph had underestimated the depth of her resentment all these years. There had been signs, of course: the times when the visits had felt strained, or when Becca had seemed barely there, turning her back to gaze through a crack in the curtains. But there had also been lingering affection. A sense that they had gone through a journey and that, whatever had happened, they were still family, still inescapably tied. *We did it together,* Becca had once said, the only time they had really discussed their crime, and her conviction. *Telling them you were involved wouldn't have changed anything for me, even later.* But maybe she'd been trying to convince herself. She hadn't looked at Steph as she had said it, hadn't wanted to talk about it for long.

'Tell me the truth.' Now Steph couldn't gauge her own volume: she might have been shouting or whispering. The knife slithered down her arm and emerged from her sleeve. Becca recoiled in shock.

Steph backed her into the wall, lifting the knife to her throat. 'What have you done?'

The air seemed to tremble around them. Becca mouthed something, as if afraid to speak aloud with the blade so close. Steph moved it even closer. '*Tell* me.'

'Oh, God,' Becca said softly.

'Tell me!'

'Please . . . it wasn't supposed to go this far.'

Steph inhaled sharply. For a second her vision went black. She grazed Becca's jawbone with the knife. 'What wasn't?'

Tears gleamed in her cousin's eyes. 'Freya's everything to you—'

'*Yes.*'

'You always avoid telling me too much about your life, but you can't resist gushing about Freya. That's how I knew she was the way to get at you.'

Steph's lungs seemed to crush up into her throat. Becca had gone after Freya. Because of her. The confirmation made her buckle. It took all her strength to stay standing.

'I only wanted to scare you.' Becca began to weep. 'To make you feel like your perfect life was vulnerable, it could be snatched away, like mine was . . .' Her words gathered momentum, flowing fast and angry. 'I've been your dirty secret, kept here in this house. Before that I was locked up for something *you* did, something I protected you from, out of loyalty, and *love* . . .'

'I—'

'I wanted to make you feel even a tiny bit of what I've been through. You haven't got a clue what prison's like! In all these years, you've never even *asked*. And I'm still a prisoner – I can't get a job, have any freedom. You keep control of me, make sure I don't interfere with your precious new existence . . .'

'You were the one who skipped parole. You could've rebuilt your life, stayed out of mine—'

'You don't get it, do you? My life was over the second I was convicted. There was no way to go back.'

An image came into Steph's head: Becca's pale, stunned face turning towards her as she'd been led out of the courtroom following the verdict. Quick on its heels, the moment Steph had strolled out of her comfortable home twenty-one years later, texting thirteen-year-old Freya to make sure she'd got to school, and stopped dead because Becca had been standing in front of her. Aged and dull-eyed. The embodiment of everything Steph had tried to escape.

Becca had skipped parole, left the halfway house where she'd been living since her release, and made it her mission to reappear in her cousin's life. She'd figured out Steph's workplace from a comment Steph had let slip the one time she'd visited her in prison, and from that her new name, eventually her address. And Steph couldn't turn her away, though she'd bundled her hastily into her car that first morning, out from under the neighbourhood's gaze. Of course she'd had to provide her with a home, money, a strange kind of companionship and protection. What she couldn't offer was a real place in her new family. If she had, maybe things would have been different.

As the years had gone on, Steph had continued to fund Becca's unofficial existence, sneaking off to visit her in the maisonette whenever she could. They'd fallen into a routine of small-talk and tea, as though Becca was an elderly relative Steph was dutifully checking on. But it had sat there between them. The injustice of Steph's freedom and happiness versus Becca's limited life.

'I wanted to turn Freya against you,' Becca said. 'To show her you weren't everything you claimed. That was all.'

Steph closed her eyes. Her other big mistake had been ever to utter her daughter's name to Becca. Her pride in Freya, her inability to shut up about her . . .

'You told me about the argument with Freya's driving instructor.'

Steph's eyes flew open. 'What?'

More scarlet blotches had broken out on Becca's neck. 'It made me so angry. That the biggest thing you had to worry about was whether your daughter's driving instructor was milking you. When you wouldn't even let *me* have a car until I begged like a child last year! Afraid of giving me too much independence . . .'

Steph started to protest but the words dissolved. Becca was right. The things that had once made her indignant seemed unbelievably petty now. And she *had* tried to restrict her cousin's freedom – not out of over-protectiveness, like with Freya, but out of fear for herself, a need to contain what Becca represented.

'I sympathised with the instructor,' Becca said. 'I imagined this poor guy on the receiving end of your demands and accusations . . . That was how much I'd come to resent you, cooped up here keeping your secrets. I'd reached my limit, I suppose. One day, I got so livid that I looked him up. And . . . and I called him.'

Steph stared at her. 'You called Chris Watson?'

Becca wouldn't return her eye contact. The defiance had evaporated. Tears spilled down her cheeks again. 'It was a whim. A reckless decision.'

'What did you say to him?'

'That I'd heard he was having a disagreement over one of his students. And that I was an interested party . . . with a proposition for him.'

Steph could hardly breathe. There was a thick, sour taste in her mouth. 'A proposition?'

63

Chris

His cell mate had been taken away. It was hard to tell whether it was a good or a bad exit. Home or prison? Afterwards, the silence of the holding cell was as cloying as the stench. Despite how lonely he often felt, Chris realised how little silence he actually had in his day-to-day life. In his car there was always the radio. At home there was the click-clack of Vicky's knitting needles or the chatter of her sisters. Now the silence felt dangerous, allowing his thoughts to roam.

Would they let him make another phone call? The need to call the number he should have erased, which he'd panic-dialled in his car only two days ago, was prickling over him again. It was an absurd idea to contact her from the police station. She wouldn't pick up anyway. He had to stop obsessing about her, the woman who'd dragged him into this nightmare, but she and Freya shadowed his every movement.

He'd let a stranger ruin his life.

If you'd asked him a few months ago, he'd have said there wasn't much left to ruin. A marriage that was haemorrhaging love by the day. A business haemorrhaging money at a similar rate. Family who didn't respect him, routines that made him heavy. But now he longed for all of that. He whispered into the silence that he would never complain about it again, if he could just have it back.

He'd felt brief euphoria after speaking to Vicky. He'd managed to do one thing right: nobody suspected she'd been the one stealing. She'd seemed so surprised and moved that for a moment he'd let himself believe he could go back to his marriage and be redeemed. But now, in this cold, stinking cell, the bleakness returned.

He could never go back. He didn't deserve to. All he wanted, now, was to purge all the hideousness he'd been carrying around inside.

It had started with the stolen trinkets, just as he'd told the detectives. When he'd realised Vicky had been stealing again, he'd experienced that sinking feeling, the familiar dread, but also a flame of determination. He had to protect her from her own habit, make sure it didn't do her any harm this time. And he might have pulled it off, if Freya hadn't stood in his way.

Their deal had made him uncomfortable, but it had served both of them in the beginning. Freya wouldn't tell anyone about the stolen goods, in return for him letting her keep the money her parents gave her for driving lessons. But as the weeks had gone on, Freya had seemed to become ruthlessly invested in their arrangement, as if it meant more to her than just a bit of cash or her own car. She'd started booking extra sessions, all at her parents' expense, until eventually they'd accused Chris of trying to cheat them.

That had really, really got to him. The one thing he still had was the integrity and satisfaction of his business, even if he was barely making a profit. Now a teenager was stripping him of his money and her well-off parents were accusing him of fraud. The Wholesome Harlows, who literally looked down on him from the wide windows of their John Lewis-sponsored apartment.

The day he'd got the phone call, he'd been boiling with resentment. Vicky had criticised his loading of the dishwasher that morning and he'd been so close to screaming, *Do you know what I'm going through because of you?* But she'd walked away before he'd been able to utter a word. And maybe he wouldn't have said anything anyway, because he never did.

He just let the resentment grow while congratulating himself on all his sacrifices.

He'd stormed out to his car to find that Freya had left him another note. One of her taunting reminders that she still had something over him: not just knowledge but photos, too, and the pillbox. Just to add to his sense of worthlessness, he'd left the house to go to work, then remembered he had no learners booked until the afternoon. He would spend the morning driving the streets, using petrol he couldn't afford, letting fury expand into every part of him.

The call had come through on his work phone. If the woman had caught him on a different day, perhaps he would have dismissed her as a crazy person. But that morning she'd spoken directly to his state of mind, whether she'd known it or not.

'I hear you've been having some issues with the Harlow family.'

'What?' he'd said. 'Who are you?'

'Someone who'd like to teach them a lesson too. I think we could be of use to one another.'

He'd been intrigued. Excited, even. Like this ally had been sent to him by some weird dark angel. When she'd offered him money it should have aroused his suspicions, but on that day it had just made him more convinced that this stranger could solve *all* his problems. Re-living that turning point, he was ashamed of how easily persuaded he'd been. How much agony he could have prevented by cutting off the call.

To begin with, the plan was nothing earth-shattering. The woman, who said she'd known Steph Harlow years ago, wanted to dispel her daughter's illusions about her mother.

'She tells lies to her family.' The woman's voice had been soaked in bitterness. 'I just need you to make sure Freya sees that.'

She'd given him times, locations. All he'd had to do was hit the right spots at the right moments during Freya's lessons.

Sometimes he'd mistimed it of course – it was hard to be precise. But one lesson, they had ended up a few cars behind Steph Harlow's BMW, and had seen her speeding off down a slip-road towards the motorway. Freya had straightened behind the wheel, her foot easing onto the accelerator.

'I knew it,' she'd said, under her breath, but with such passion it was as if she'd shouted.

Chris had realised, then, that Freya already suspected her mum of some kind of duplicity. Did that explain her recent personality transformation? The blackmailing, the anger? Suddenly he'd noticed Freya veering towards the slip-road, too, and he'd had to slam on his own pedals to stop her. 'The Woman' had told him not to let Freya trail Steph to her destination, only glimpse her somewhere unexplained. Chris would never forget the determination in Freya's posture, her torso slanting forward, fingers bone-white on the wheel. She'd been desperate to know where her mother was going, and now that desperation seemed crushingly sad. He couldn't believe he'd colluded with a stranger to prey on it.

They should have stopped it there. Should have been satisfied that they'd upset the equilibrium of the Harlow family enough. But the woman on the phone never seemed satisfied.

And him? Was it the offer of more money? Had he wrecked lives for the sake of a few hundred pounds? Or had there been something addictive about the scheme, once they'd started? Had it made him feel like he was taking back some power?

64

Steph

Steph pressed again with the blade, hard as she dared without splitting the skin over Becca's collarbone. This was the person who'd shown her how to do a French plait, told her what it was like to kiss a boy, comforted her when she'd been sad. The person whom Steph had looked after during seizures, who had always protected her in return. Now Steph was holding a knife to her throat.

'Keep going,' she said.

She had to hear it all, no matter how much it hurt. The guilt felt physical, piling on top of her. And a new horror was seeping in, now that Becca had revealed she'd paid Chris Watson to help her. Becca's only source of cash was Steph. Had her own money funded this? Her mind raced over all those times Becca had asked her for a little extra to buy chocolate or beers, things to brighten her isolated days and nights.

Becca could hardly speak through her tears. 'A couple of times we were able to fix it so Freya saw you on your way to visit me. We hoped if she kept spotting you in places you shouldn't be, she'd think you were having an affair or something. And, as it turned out, she'd already got suspicions . . .'

The guilt hammered down harder. How could Steph have thought that her secrets would have no impact on her family? That she could live a double life without them ever sensing something amiss?

'That was all it was supposed to be,' Becca said. 'That was all I wanted to do, but . . .' A sob jerked her body and caused the knife to break her skin, a tiny cut that sent a trickle of blood down her still-blotchy neck. Steph watched it run over the soft creases. They'd both aged, yet time had healed nothing, it seemed.

'It wasn't enough,' Becca said. 'I *needed* you to suffer.'

'So you made *her* suffer?' Steph cupped her hand beneath Becca's chin and thrust her head back against the wall.

She could see the tension in Becca's stretched throat, the hyper-awareness of the blade. Her cousin's voice came out strangled: 'Chris was only supposed to take her away for a couple of days. Just long enough to put you through hell.'

Steph banged Becca's head against the plasterwork. 'He kidnapped her?'

'He was meant to bring her back, no harm done. It was *not* planned this way. You have to believe—'

'Why should I? How could you do this? Freya's innocent. She was your family—' Her unintentional switch to the past tense made something snap inside. And Becca's *no harm done* was loaded with the message that the opposite was true. The message that a jacket soaked in blood might represent exactly what it seemed to. A foregone conclusion that strangers watching the news had probably already reached, because assuming the worst wouldn't bring down their whole world.

Steph's left hand pushed into Becca's face, clawing soft eyelids, the squashy cartilage of a nose. There was white noise in her head and she was dimly aware of her cousin moaning; Steph was hurting her but she didn't know how badly or whether she'd be able to stop.

Becca began to fight back. Steph felt her cousin's hand against her chest, trying to shove her away. Her own hands were around Becca's neck now, the knife jutting at an angle from her right.

'Please, Steph,' Becca gasped. 'You don't . . . she . . .' Her left arm flailed, swiping for the knife. Steph jerked the blade away, then grabbed Becca's hair and pulled: a childish act of violence as if they were teenagers again. Becca cried out, and Steph felt herself splitting in two: one part wanting her cousin to feel all the pain that was gripping her own heart, another horrified at the prospect of harming her. Steph had killed for her mum all those years ago, and now perhaps she would kill for her daughter, destroying what was left of her own life in the process.

She shifted her palm back over Becca's nose and mouth. Becca thrashed again with her left hand, shouting something incoherent, and Steph imagined she was driving her into the wall, through the bricks, making her disappear.

Then Becca became still.

Steph's eyes snapped open. She hadn't even realised she'd screwed them shut. Becca's head lolled against the wall, her face slack and grey. Steph eased her grip and the knife clattered to the floor. Her mind wouldn't clear enough to be sure of what she'd done.

Becca twitched beneath her hands. And as Steph looked again at her face, she realised she hadn't smothered or strangled Becca. Her cousin was having a seizure. As far as Steph knew, it was her first in over twenty years. She'd shunned her medication while in prison, but had remained seizure-free. Apparently that could happen: epilepsy could absent itself without any obvious explanation. Becca had told Steph, during one of her more candid moments last year, that it was almost as if she'd dreamed her condition: *It's like I dreamed it all. Mum, Dad, hairdressing, epilepsy . . . life.*

Becca wasn't convulsing like she'd done during seizures in the past. Her eyes were rolling, though, that left arm still raised as if stuck. Steph lowered her to the floor. The seizure gathered momentum and Steph was back in her old kitchen, or perhaps in Auntie Rach's garden, anxious to help her cousin. Old habits took over: she slipped her hand beneath Becca's head and, for a confused time-slip of a moment, she flooded with tenderness.

It was as if things were on pause for the length of Becca's seizure, and then reality would be back, choices would have to be made, truths confronted. In her mind's eye, Steph saw the wingspan of a plane with a rippling backdrop of stars. She felt breeze on her face, a swooping sensation inside.

The room suffused with bleached light. It skated across the carpet, turned the walls into bright blank screens. Everything was awash with it: the second-hand furniture that Steph had bought for Becca; the sofa where they'd had so many strained conversations, but also where they'd laughed and reminisced, even in recent times.

She became aware of her name being shouted. Then somebody else was in the room, running towards her. The white light had gone, and Steph realised it must have been headlights from the street below.

Turning to her left, she saw Paul.

Paul is here. Kneeling beside her, staring at Becca stretched out on the floor with her eyes closed. Steph had never thought her husband and cousin would be in the same room. She'd spent the last four years doing everything she could to keep them apart.

'Steph, are you . . .? What *is* this place? Who's this woman?'

His questions flowed over her.

'You've got blood on you. Is it yours? Is it hers? Is Freya here?'

She swayed towards him and he shot out a hand to steady her. Her neck was covered in tears. 'This is my cousin.' She pointed at Becca. 'She and Chris Watson did this to Freya. Because of me. It was all because of me.'

65

Emma

'Are you sure you won't come and stay with me?' her mum asked, slowing the car as they approached Emma's street.

The dark road swarmed with even more police. Lights flashed, officers gesticulated to one another. The windows of Emma's flat peered out, like scared eyes.

'It's not the ideal environment for rest and recovery,' her mum pointed out, as she parked, then helped Emma out of the passenger side. Emma was still getting used to the crutches. She hobbled along the pavement, convinced that a distracted police officer would kick a crutch from under her. Walking beside her, Julie gaped at the chaos that had engulfed the neighbourhood.

Emma kept her ears pricked, listening for information on the crackling police radios. She heard the Harlows' names. Something about a search. *Paul Harlow's car tracked as far as* ... The rest of the sentence was inaudible.

'I think we should go back to mine,' her mum said. 'I've got some leftover gnocchi in the fridge. I could whip up a sauce. You must be starving.'

'I'll double my body weight if I stay with you, Mum. And it's one a.m., not exactly gnocchi hour.'

'You're looking too thin. The cookery gene did seem to skip a generation with you, Em.'

Emma ignored this and looked up at the Harlows' flat. It had an air of stillness that contrasted with the flashing, simmering energy of its surroundings. She wondered where Steph and

Paul were. She hoped they were together, and safe, pulling Freya into a tearful embrace at this very moment. The decisions she'd made sat like indigestible rocks in her gut. Would she ever know if they'd been the right ones?

Her eyes fell to her own flat.

'It'll be good for me to be alone for a bit,' she told her mum. 'I need to think about my future.'

'Well,' Julie said, 'I wouldn't bank on the "being alone" part just yet.'

'You don't have to stay with me.' Emma was half alarmed and half comforted at the thought that her mum might move in until her hip had healed.

'I didn't mean me.'

Julie was pointing down the road. One of the parked vehicles wasn't a police car: it was a small white van.

Standing beside it was Zeb.

Emma squeezed her crutches closer to her body as though they might prop up her courage, too. She ached when she looked at Zeb, his curly hair falling into his face, his eyes wary. Maybe it was all a misunderstanding. Just because he'd been running away didn't mean he'd posted the note or done the other things. Just because he'd been evasive about his friendship with Freya didn't mean he had more to hide.

She jumped as she registered the long-haired man behind him. Her crutches almost gave way. *Robin.* He seemed to be smirking at her – or was she imagining that? If she glanced down, maybe her chest would have flattened and her skinny knees would be knocking, and there'd be an Alien Girl cartoon shoved down the front of her top.

She found herself shuffling backwards, almost clobbering her mum in her urgency to get away. Julie looked at her in surprise, and Zeb rushed forward. Emma couldn't stop shaking her head. 'I don't want to talk to you,' she said to Zeb, the words spilling before she could filter them. She flung a glance at Robin. 'Either of you.' That panicky sensation climbing up into her throat again.

'What's going on?' Julie asked.

'Please, Mum,' said Zeb. 'Let me explain.'

'I don't even know what to say to you, Zeb.' She wished she'd had more time to decide how to handle this. Her emotions were spiralling.

'She asked me to do those things,' Zeb said. 'That's how it started.'

'What?' Emma glanced around. 'Who?'

'Freya.'

The mention of her name made a police officer turn their way. Emma seized Zeb's arm. 'You'd better come inside.'

She pushed him towards her flat, aware of her mum and Robin looking uneasily at one another, never having met before.

'Dad needs to hear this as well,' Zeb said, making Emma freeze.

She couldn't have Robin in her flat. Sitting on her sofa, drinking from her cups . . . *no.*

'Please, Mum,' Zeb begged. 'I want to talk to both of you.'

'Emma.' Robin spoke for the first time. Hearing him say her name made the hairs stand up on her neck. It used to shock her when Andy called her Emma rather than Alien Girl. It was like an alert: was he going to be nice to her that day? Or was he lulling her into a false sense of security?

She remembered Robin whispering her name into her ear on the night they'd made Zeb.

'We could sit in the van, or go somewhere else, if you'd be more comfortable,' he said now.

His voice was deeper, more pronounced. More his own, perhaps, now that he wasn't just parroting Andy. She knew his appearance was different, too, but she couldn't look at him straight. Couldn't help wondering what he was noticing about her, how changed she was, how bedraggled from a night in hospital.

She pulled back her shoulders. There was no way she'd let him see her break down.

'Let's go inside.' She nodded towards her flat. Maybe she'd feel more in control on her own turf. She had to admit she was relieved when her mum followed them in.

It was as strange as she'd thought it would be, having Robin among her things. All the photos of her and Zeb from their years without him. The boxes of stock that made her life look as if it was in some kind of chaotic transition. Gilbert was awake and seemed to be rearranging his nest, a flurry of industrious noises coming from the cupboard. Emma urged everybody into the kitchen. Zeb sat between his parents – for the first time ever – while Julie busied herself making tea.

Everything about the situation felt wrong, wrong, wrong. This was a conventional family set-up, but not for them. Not for their family.

Zeb stared at the table. 'I've fucked up.'

'Tell us, mate,' Robin said, and Emma squeezed her fists, trying not to succumb to the rage she felt, hearing him address her son like that. Watching him parent.

This is about Zeb now, she told herself, pinning her eyes on her son's face.

'The night Freya and I got drunk in the park,' Zeb said. 'You were right, Mum, it wasn't the only time. We bonded that night because we were both pissed off with life. After that we started sneaking out, just to talk, drink . . . It was good for me at first. I didn't want to tell you because it was my thing, my way of dealing with how I was feeling.' He glanced at Robin, then back to Emma, then down again.

'I would buy the booze and bring the music, she'd lend me books. Sometimes we'd just listen to podcasts, trying to

relax. But sometimes she'd be angry or upset, and sometimes I would be. She told me her mum was having an affair
and she was planning to get proof. But she also . . .' He
paused and coughed into his sleeve. 'Well, she kind of
recruited me.'

'How do you mean?' Emma asked in alarm.

'She was so fuming and hurt because she'd idolised her
mum so much, and she'd always been sold this idea of their
family being so close – "three sides of a triangle" or something.
And she got me all riled up, too, even more than I already was.
She convinced me to help her mess with her mum . . . Like, she
had this idea of targeting their perfect house. She said it would
be like irony or something—'

'But it's your house, too, Zeb!'

'I know, Mum. It was a shitty plan. But I was in a shitty
place . . .' He tapped between his eyes. 'I was furious with you
for keeping me apart from Dad. I wanted to punish you, too
– it wasn't just about Freya's mum. And once I'd started doing
all that nasty stuff, it got weirdly addictive. That's why I kept
phoning you, I think. I wanted to confess, wanted you to make
me stop. But I always chickened out.' He flattened his palm
against his brow and seemed to press hard.

'Mate—' Robin began, but Emma cut him a look that
silenced him. Except she didn't know what to say to Zeb.
Whether to scream at him or console him.

'What about after Freya disappeared?' she said. 'How could
you have kept doing those things, knowing what her parents
must be going through?'

'I *didn't* know, at first. I was living at Dad's, out of the loop,
but I kept on with the plan Freya had made. When you told
me she'd disappeared, I thought she'd taken the plan to a
major new level. I felt like I should step things up, too. And
every day I seemed to get angrier towards you, Mum, not
calmer . . .'

Emma remembered the foul smell of dog dirt in their foyer. Her son had done that. Her son, who'd never done anything like it before, as far as she knew. She'd ignored the signs, though, hadn't she? The recent temper that had led his teachers to suggest 'a few anger-management sessions, nothing to be too concerned about'. The change in their relationship since she'd lied to him.

'Then, when I came here and saw it for myself – the police and the posters and everything – I realised there was no way she could be messing about. She really had gone.' Zeb's voice cracked and Emma instinctively grabbed his hand. On his other side, she saw Robin take his arm. Her mum had stopped making tea and was standing very still by the boiled kettle.

'My anger just . . . exploded,' Zeb continued. 'I think it was the shock of realising this was real, she was *missing* . . . and then you and I argued, Mum, and you refused to even acknowledge you'd done anything wrong. And I know *I* was in the wrong, too, but I couldn't think straight. I wrote that note and I . . .' He broke down into sobs, dropping his head into his hands.

'The last note was aimed at me?' Emma asked, choked with tears, too.

'I wish I could take it back. All of it.'

Emma jumped to her feet, her own hurt overtaken by the sight of him so distraught. He hadn't cried like that since he was tiny. She hugged him from behind, burying her face in his hood; it smelt woody, like a bonfire.

'Oh, shit,' Zeb kept saying, swiping at his eyes, 'Shit.' Eventually he stood and ran out of the kitchen, towards the bathroom.

Emma looked at her mum, mainly to avoid looking at Robin. 'What are we going to do?' she said.

For once, Julie seemed lost for words. Her gaze flicked to Robin as if to imply that she wasn't the person Emma should be asking. Emma felt Robin's eyes on her, and in her mind it was that blank stare from across a classroom as he'd failed to stick up for her, even after he'd been inside her.

But she made herself look back at him. At first, all she saw was an older version of the boy who'd followed Andy's every cruel command. Longer hair, and the freckled, mildly weathered skin of somebody who worked outdoors a lot. After a moment or two, though, she couldn't help but see Zeb in him. And she had to acknowledge he looked as sad as she felt.

'Emma,' he said, and still she shuddered at her name on his lips. 'We need to be there for him.'

'No, *I* do.'

'Emma.' God, she wished he would stop saying it. 'I'm so, so sorry for how I treated you at school. I was a coward. Unforgivable. But if it makes any difference at all, I really did like you. You didn't follow the crowd the way I did. The way I followed that scumbag Andy.'

Emma made a noise of disbelief. Robin kept going: 'I'm not making excuses. I was an utter bastard. But I swear I'm not that guy any more. It keeps me awake at night, thinking about everything Andy did, and how I let him. Then finding out years later that I'd got you pregnant . . . It was the shock of my life. I can't blame you for not wanting me to have anything to do with Zeb . . . but you've done an amazing job. He's funny, smart, passionate, artistic . . . Basically, from what I can make out, he's you.'

Despite everything, Emma flushed with pride. Her stubborn streak bristled, of course (Zeb had *that*, too): *I don't need you to tell me I did a good job.* But she had to admit it was gratifying to hear, especially when she'd been doubting herself so much. In the background, her mum nodded manically in agreement.

'The way he's been acting, though,' Robin added tentatively, 'all this bizarre stuff he's done . . . surely it's telling us something.'

Emma blew out another sigh. The lights of the police cars outside made her whole flat seem to flash and pulsate. Sounds from upstairs were strikingly absent. She thought of all the times she'd heard the Harlows' footsteps and voices, their apparently perfect life rippling above. Now upstairs was empty, yet she had the chance to salvage her own family.

She was grown-up now. So was Robin. Their son was standing in the doorway of this kitchen, looking from one parent to the other for help. How strange it must be for him, never having been in a room with both of them until tonight. And how lucky they were that he was here, and safe, with a whole life in front of him that could be better all round, if maybe they just called this their new Day One. Got reacquainted, without any secrets.

'I heard that,' Zeb murmured.

'What?' Emma asked, trying to collect herself.

'The stuff Dad said, about being shitty to you at school. About how hard everything's been for you.' His eyes were wide. 'I didn't know all that.'

'Because we didn't talk about it,' she conceded.

Zeb sniffed again. 'It might've helped me understand things . . . you know, from your point of view.'

'I did think about telling you myself, Zeb,' Robin said quietly. 'But I assumed there must've been a reason your mum hadn't. And, since we're being honest, I was worried it would kill our relationship before it even started. I wanted you to get to know me a bit, first.'

'Well . . . I can't exactly judge you,' Zeb said, twisting his cuffs. 'I'm the worst person in the world.'

'No!' three voices protested in unison.

Emma, her mum and Robin shared a glance before Emma pressed the point home: 'You're not, Zeb. You made some questionable choices when you were angry. It doesn't make you a bad person.'

She remembered what he'd said during their last argument,

exasperated with her for refusing to give his dad a chance. *Is it one strike and you're out with you?* He didn't realise that he, Zeb, was the one person who could have endless strikes with her.

Emma dried her eyes, smoothed her hair. 'We can fix this. It might be tough but we can try to fix everything . . .' Letting her gaze flit towards Robin, she took the plunge and added, 'All of us.'

As she said it, she felt an unexpected bud of hope. Maybe this really could be a fresh start for them. Maybe, once they'd got through this, she could even try again with the shop, rebuild her confidence, the vision she'd had . . . After all, she was still the owner. Perhaps there was a reason she'd procrastinated over letting the estate agent relist it.

Her optimism grew a little stronger: maybe Freya would be found, too. Emma would go back to hearing laughter from above, smelling bakery bread and Friday-night takeaways. And she'd feel differently about it, now. Not envious or obsessive or excluded, but relieved, and sorry for her own part in their ordeal, and connected to her neighbours because they'd both lost their children and got them back, in the end.

66

Chris

He felt an avalanche of release once he'd made the decision to confess. The weight lifted from his chest and, for a fleeting moment, he was almost elated. He didn't realise he was crying until he felt the moisture on his collar and saw Johnson watching him with that scathing expression.

They were back in the interrogation room, camera rolling, Chris alone on his side of the table. The elation crashed away, but he knew he had to go through with it. For his own sanity, for Freya's parents, who were trapped, not knowing, not deserving *this*. For Freya herself.

Ford recited the date and time and other details. Chris wished he could just open up his brain and show them the memory of that day, rather than have to describe it in words.

'We've established that Freya Harlow had been blackmailing you,' Ford summarised brusquely, 'and that you were contacted by an unknown woman who offered you money to make Freya think her mother was having an affair. This woman then offered you more money to take Freya away.'

Chris nodded. He couldn't stop imagining Vicky's reaction if she could hear this. The hope he'd dared to feel when they'd spoken on the phone seemed absurd now, as did all his attempts to hide what he'd done. He would release Vicky from any obligation to him. He didn't want her to visit him in prison, wait for him, put her life on pause.

'Which brings us to March the fifteenth,' Ford said. 'Tell us what happened.'

Chris sat up as straight as he could. His body felt soft, withered.

'I planned to get us "lost" during the driving lesson, and somehow lose Freya's phone as well, keep her out of touch long enough to panic the Harlows . . . To be honest, I wasn't sure how I was going to pull it off, and I was having serious second thoughts.

'In the end, Freya and I argued before I had a chance to do anything. Like I said before, she seemed generally angry, and she started shouting, driving crazily. So I forced her to pull over and swap seats with me before she killed us both.' His own turn of phrase lurched through him.

He made himself continue.

'I pretended I was going to take her back to school but I drove out of town. When she realised we were going the wrong way she started screaming and trying to get out of the car. She grabbed the wheel a few times. I only just managed to stay in control.'

He remembered how his mind had blanked. He was no longer thinking about what he'd been paid to do, no longer deliberating about whether he could go through with it, or how to execute the plan. He was just trying to keep the car from crashing. It had been a relief, in a way, to be able to focus on something so immediate.

'At one point she was fighting me for the wheel, making the car swerve. We were on a quiet road by this point but we could easily have hit a tree, and if anything *had* come in the opposite direction . . . I was shouting at her to stop but she wouldn't let go, and I swear I thought, I've just got to keep us alive and then I'll take her home. I knew things had gone too far.'

Chris put his elbows on the table and buried his face in his hands. His palms were burning hot.

I really was going to bring her home.

He realised he was speaking to Vicky in his head, saying the thing he most wanted her to know.

'She just wouldn't let go of the wheel,' he said into his palms.

'Could you speak up, please?'

He lifted his head and looked at the camera. 'She wouldn't let go so I shoved her away. Her head hit the window . . .' He shuddered, the sickening crack reverberating in his mind. 'It knocked her unconscious. As I was looking at her, trying to see if she was okay, I realised we were about to hit a road sign. I swerved . . . but because she was unconscious and not wearing a seatbelt, she slumped forward and her head smacked the dashboard . . .'

Chris began to splutter, as if choking. The air in his lungs felt noxious.

After that second blow to the head, he'd known she was gone. But all he'd felt able to do was keep driving. He'd driven like a robot as Freya had crumpled down, blood oozing from her head. The sight that would never leave him.

He'd pulled over down a deserted lane and called The Woman. *It's gone wrong*, he'd told her, in a voice he'd never heard himself use before. *Very wrong.* She'd asked him where he was and told him to stay put. When she'd arrived in an old Fiesta half an hour later, he'd still been in shock. He hadn't yelled at her, like he had in his head a hundred times since. Hadn't asked who the fuck she was. She'd been wearing a hat and scarf so he couldn't see her whole face, only watery green eyes. When she'd caught sight of Freya she'd let out a low, pained moan, and chanted softly to herself as she'd felt for a pulse, inspected the head wound, gestured for Chris to help her move Freya into her car. Seconds later she'd been gone, leaving Chris to fall to his knees at the side of the road.

He wasn't sure how long he'd stayed there, kneeling, in denial. How long it took him to emerge from the fug and realise that Freya's jacket was still on his passenger seat, that there was blood everywhere, that he had to deal with these awful, awful facts, and then return to his house where Freya's parents also lived.

'I'm so sorry,' he said out loud, feeling as if he was breaking into tiny pieces, disintegrating all over the desk. He was no longer sure whether he was apologising to Freya or the Harlows or Vicky or himself. All the lives he'd destroyed.

The only crumb of hope was that Vicky would recover. That her life could still be good. Chris would set her free, and Di and Jane would look after her, and eventually, hopefully, she would forget she had ever known him.

67

Steph

Steph stared at her husband as they knelt next to her semi-conscious cousin. His face was covered with bruises. And it looked like it was in collapse, like his muscles had forgotten what to do. Was he in shock? Was she? The popping in her ears, the sense that the air she was breathing was getting thicker.

She dared to glance at Becca and saw her eyelids starting to twitch, her chest rising: signs of recovery that Steph had often watched for in the past.

'Where is Freya?' she whispered to her, leaning in close. 'You still haven't told me.' The idea struck her, with an inward scream of pain, that what was left to find might be her body.

'*No*,' she cried softly, to herself now, pulling back from Becca and lurching to her feet.

'Steph?' Paul stood up too.

Steph reeled on the spot for a second, then turned and ran towards the back of the maisonette. The small kitchen was bare, the tiny table and all the surfaces wiped clean. She continued along the corridor to Becca's bedroom, shouting Freya's name, her fingertips trailing the cold walls. The bed was unmade, the curtains drawn. A week-old newspaper, which Steph had brought on her last visit, lay unopened next to the bed.

Steph raced on to the spare room, freezing as she tried the handle.

The door was locked.

Her whole chest became a drumbeat. She rattled the handle and pressed her ear to the wood, willing her heart to quieten so she could hear.

'Steph?' Paul appeared beside her but she shushed him, listening hard.

Then she reared back with a hand over her mouth.

'Someone's in there,' she said, through ragged breaths.

She'd heard a moan. Hadn't she? Could she have imagined it? Steph threw herself against the door, pounding with both fists. 'Freya! Freya? Is that you?'

There was no response, but she thought she heard another noise, barely perceptible. Steph ran back to the living room. There had to be a key somewhere. She yanked out drawers, spilling their contents onto the floor, shouting to Paul to search the bedroom at the same time. Finding nothing, Steph returned to her stirring cousin and frantically patted her pockets.

As she did so, she found herself fixating on Becca's left arm, still stretched out across the worn carpet. She remembered it flailing to intercept the knife, flailing again at the start of her seizure. Now the hand was in a loose fist. The first finger sticking slightly out.

Becca wasn't just thrashing.

She was pointing.

Trying to tell me Freya is here?

Had Steph been blind once again? Wasted yet more time?

'Paul!' she screamed, 'We *have* to get into that room!'

She heard the sound of his rapid footsteps, then a thud. The noise was repeated as Steph rushed back down the corridor, to find Paul slamming his shoulder into the spare-room door. He gasped in pain but braced himself and tried again. In different circumstances, Freya would have been tickled to watch him enacting this police cliché. *You've obviously done this before, Dad. You were a bit younger, though, right?*

On his third attempt the door gave way. They both flew into the room. Steph's vision smudged, unable to take in the scene. For a moment she was so overwhelmed that everything fragmented and slowed.

Then she saw the figure on the bed. The tangle of greasy blonde hair on the pillow. Freya was curled up, eyes closed, her skin pale and sweaty with a weeping red wound on her head.

'Oh, my God.' Steph and Paul almost tripped over each other in their desperation to get to her. Steph grasped her hand, touched her cheek, said her name over and over. Becca, or somebody else, had evidently tried to treat Freya's injury – there was antiseptic by the bed – but it was obvious that she was very ill.

But she was breathing. Beautiful. Her cloudy eyes were opening now, almost focusing on Steph's face. Her dry lips moving.

'Oh, my darling.' Steph kissed her daughter's clammy fingers, then her forehead, wetting her skin further with her tears. 'Oh Freya oh Freya oh Freya. Thank *God.*'

'Mum?' Freya croaked.

'It's me. It's us.' Steph reached for Paul and he leaned in close. He gathered Steph and Freya's hands inside his own and brought them up to his lips, his eyes streaming.

'We're here now, Frey,' Paul said. 'It's going to be okay, sweetheart.'

'We're so, so happy to see you.' Steph broke down completely, and the release was like something leaving her body, something she'd held in for years and years and years.

68

Chris

He was now sharing his custody cell with a brutal gang of memories. They wouldn't allow him any peace. Knew all his weaknesses and wanted to see how fast they could break him. Was this what prison would be like? Peopled not just by angry criminals, but by all the thoughts he could no longer distract himself from?

Vicky was in here, the younger Vicky who'd first admitted to him, *I have a bit of a habit . . . of taking things that aren't mine.* The fear and challenge in her face: *Does this change your feelings for me?*

And Freya, on her first ever driving lesson, asking if they could have Radio Five Live on because Arsenal was playing Spurs.

Steph, when they'd returned, hovering outside her house and laughing at herself as she admitted she'd been fretting the whole hour. *But she looks happy. And your car's in one piece! And I clearly can't do this every time—*

'Watson.'

The appearance of the custody officer made the memories scatter, like prison bullies caught out. Chris knew they'd return the second he was alone again. And they'd be crueller next time.

'Follow me,' the officer said.

'Where to?'

He was answered only by a glare. They were all treating him with distaste since his confession. Chris felt as if everything about himself had been removed, just like his belongings relinquished into that small box at the police station reception, and all that remained was the label *murderer*. He would be treated accordingly – deservedly – from now on, by everybody who already knew him and everyone he was yet to meet.

The officer led him back towards the interview rooms. As he walked along the corridor, something caught Chris's eye and made his heart stop. He stopped walking, too. The custody officer urged him on with an impatient bark.

Chris shuffled onwards but looked back over his shoulder, wondering if it had really been her, disappearing into one of the other interview suites. He'd never seen her whole face but he felt he'd know her anywhere: the unbrushed waist-length hair; the thin arms that had managed to lift Freya's upper body while he had gripped her legs.

The Woman.

His mind wheeled as he sat down again opposite Ford and Johnson. He could hardly take in what they were saying to him. All he could think was *They found her? Does that mean they found Freya's body too?* Flashes of her rolled-back eyes and the fountain of blood from her head.

'You've confessed to the murder of Freya Harlow,' Ford was saying.

Chris nodded. There it was again. *Murderer.*

He'd been a son, a schoolboy, a smoker, a drop-out, a boyfriend, a driving instructor, a husband, an ex-smoker, a homeowner, a business owner. Now a murderer.

'Freya Harlow has been found alive at the home of Rebecca Fielding.'

Chris's head ricocheted back. 'What did you say?'

'Freya is in hospital being treated for a serious head wound and a resulting infection.'

'She . . . *What?*'

'She's alive.'

But she was so still. Heavy and cold. The Woman took her away. She was dead.

'Is this a . . . trick?' he asked.

'No.'

'She was dead.' He felt his mouth contort, his eyes get wet.

'Well, she isn't,' Johnson said bluntly. 'Rebecca Fielding took her back to her house after you parted ways and she regained consciousness. Fielding locked her in a room and, according to her, tried to care for her as best she could until she'd decided what to do. Did you have any contact with her during this time?'

Chris was kneading his cheeks. The Woman had a name. Rebecca Fielding. It didn't matter. It did. The room was revolving. 'I called her a couple of times but she didn't answer. I thought . . .'

'We know what you thought. But Freya Harlow is not dead.'

The words seemed to penetrate at last.

'You've still committed multiple crimes,' Johnson reminded him unnecessarily.

But he hadn't killed a teenage girl. Hadn't cut her life short and turned the light out on her parents'.

Maybe he didn't deserve this redemption, but he strained breathlessly towards it.

He should have known that Freya Harlow, with all her talents, her tricks, all her energy and anger, would bring herself back to life.

69

Paul

Paul couldn't stop gazing at Freya's sleeping face, the halo of her hair on the hospital pillows. He was afraid to look away, or close his exhausted eyes, in case she was gone when he looked back. There were cuts and bruises on her skin and an antibiotic drip attached to her arm, but the steady beep of her heart monitor was the most comforting sound he'd heard in a long time.

Stop staring at me while I'm asleep, Dad, she might say if she woke now. *It's weird.*

This is how it's going to be from now on, Frey. Mum and I are never letting you out of our sight again.

Oh, God. That's worse than nearly dying.

Maybe they would get through this by making light of it, but it was hard to imagine a time when the tension would melt from his muscles. Paul felt like he'd been catapulted through a week-long war. And he was somehow on the other side, sitting dazed amid the debris, trying to get his breath back and understand what had happened.

'I'm so sorry, Paul,' Steph said, beside him. 'More than I can ever say.'

Paul turned to his wife, who looked every bit as shell-shocked as he felt.

His wife, who was not really Stephanie. Who had killed a man when she was just a teenager and indirectly caused all of this. These facts staggered inside him each time he tried to make them seem real.

'I let you assume this was your fault,' Steph said, through tears. 'I even assumed that, too. I didn't want to believe it could be anything to do with me. I never thought Becca would . . . I didn't think she had the resources, let alone that she would want to hurt me this badly . . .'

Paul twisted his hands in his lap, his emotions seesawing. 'It could've been either of us, Steph.'

She stalled and dabbed at her eyes. Freya's green scarf was still wrapped around her neck, filthy now, but Steph wouldn't be parted from it.

'In the church,' she said. 'When I asked if you'd killed someone. It was because I recognise something in you. Always have, I suppose. I think that, like me, you know what it's like to carry the darkest kind of guilt.'

Paul looked steadily back at her and, for just a moment, her face was Nathalie's. He could still hardly process the fact that she wasn't dead. But one day he would, and then maybe he'd allow himself a glimmer of relief.

He hadn't asked Yvette anything about her whereabouts. She wouldn't tell him where she'd fled to, he was sure, but that wasn't why he'd resisted asking. *Somewhere out there* was more than enough, now. He just prayed she'd found some happiness, some peace. Perhaps Billie was *somewhere out there* too. Poor Billie, who would probably remain a tragic unanswered question for ever. Had Paul been wrong about Daniel's role in her disappearance? It was possible, he now saw. They'd hated each other from a distance for too long, wasting energy, wasting their lives.

Paul slipped his hand into his wife's and her fingers curled around his. All these years they'd been carrying similar burdens. Guarding their secrets, burying their pasts. It had almost lost them everything.

'You're right,' he said. 'I caused a death, too . . . or thought I had. Someone I loved, and lied to. Someone I didn't want you to know about.'

Steph closed her eyes. He wasn't sure if it was with distress or relief at finally hearing this.

'I know what it does to you,' Paul continued. 'How you want forgiveness but you don't feel like you deserve it, only punishment . . . except you can't ask for that either. And you want to tell the people you've been lucky enough to find a new life with . . .' He gripped her fingers '. . . but you're terrified they won't love you any more.'

Steph's eyes were still leaking. 'Even when my punishment came, I didn't recognise it straight away. Now we've all been punished, Freya worst of all.'

'But we're all still here.' Paul shuffled nearer to her, and they both looked at Freya again. 'We can forgive each other. We have to, don't we?'

Steph laid her face against his shoulder. Her hair, though unwashed in five days, still smelt faintly of vanilla. She was still the same person, despite the name change, despite the part of her life he hadn't known – just as she'd been oblivious to a part of his. Paul felt a blast of sympathy as he pictured her as a frightened young girl, making a mistake that would haunt her entire life.

Of *course* he knew what that felt like. They could have forgiven each other, maybe even themselves, a long time ago.

Freya's eyelids fluttered and Paul was overcome with love. The memory of finding her at last, in that tiny locked room, kept bowling into him. Somehow he'd been given a third chance. And this time he wouldn't squander it with half his head still in the past. He would be present. Grateful. Real.

He wrapped his arms around Steph. Their breathing evened out as they sat there, eyes closed, lulled by the musical beeps of their daughter's heart.

70

Kate

Twenty-three years earlier

Heathrow is a bubble of suspended reality. People drink fizzy wine and eat burgers at 6 a.m., brush their teeth in public toilets and snooze on plastic chairs surrounded by strangers. Some are moving between different time zones – they've flown in from tomorrow or will land yesterday. There's a feeling of anonymity, even though everyone's had their identity rigorously checked.

I weave among it all, cleaning toilets, glad to be pretty much invisible. I hear spurts of conversation, snatches of lives, the constant drone of flight announcements in multiple languages. My skin smells of bleach and my fingertips are cracked.

Often, I think about the day – two years ago, almost exactly – when I stood on the boundary of a different airport, watching planes rising into the dusk, holding my breath as one swept overhead. I remember how, in the months that followed, I clung to the image of that fluid starry sky whenever I couldn't stand to be in the new reality I'd created for myself. The one in which I was a killer and a coward.

And I'm still both of those things. I hide here among the daily swarm of travellers, then go home or to the hospital, my head ducked to the outside world. Sometimes I think I'm as much a prisoner as Becca, but then I feel even more guilty: how would I know what she's going through? Just once have I had the guts to visit her in prison, and her flinty gaze cut right through me.

By now I know the length and rhythm of the journey from Heathrow to the hospital. When we first moved here, it took me a while to get used to the rush and crush of the Underground. I'm not sure why Mum thought London would be a good place to start over. She talked about the specialist hospitals, but maybe she thought it would be somewhere to blend in; maybe she realised I wanted to hide. I still wonder how much she suspects about what really happened to Nick. She accepted the idea of Becca as a killer so wholeheartedly. But if some pushed-down part of her *does* know I was involved, what does that mean? Does motherly love trump what she had with Nick – enough to forgive me, even protect me?

Auntie Rach and Uncle Jack never turned their backs on Becca. But Becca pushed them away, refused to see them. Mum reckons Becca blames them for her shoddy defence lawyer, but I think there's more to it. I don't know if I'd want Mum visiting me in prison, either. Sitting across a table from each other, like we used to in our flat after school, except surrounded by other prisoners, watched by guards. I'm not sure I could stand it. To this day I'm still anxious for her to be proud of me.

I arrive at the hospital and my nose detects the alteration from one chemical smell to another. Lemon bleach to alcohol hand sanitiser, cleaning fluids to something more potent being pumped into my mum's blood. Our landlady, Dominique, is sitting with Mum, her long grey hair giving her the look of a kindly witch. We wouldn't have coped without Dom, especially since Mum's MDS has developed into leukaemia. The first day we moved into a tiny flat in Wembley, it was like Dom sensed we were a desperate little unit of two, in need of a crutch. She checks on Mum when I'm at work, takes her to chemo when I can't, holds her hand till I arrive. There are good days sometimes, when we joke about the doctors or flip through magazines. But there are dark days too.

I have to keep going, have to put one foot in front of the other as I walk through this brightly lit ward. Mum is counting on me.

Another two years from this day, Mum will be dead. I will have nothing left, nobody to care for, and I'll know the time has come to confess.

I'll put it off, though. I'll keep working hard, as many hours as I can get, leaving myself no time to think about the past. My bosses will promote me from cleaner to server, and then to the first-class lounge, recognising me as someone who's never off sick and never turns down a shift. Every day I'll watch the travellers and wonder what it's like to be them. Eventually this game of displacement will consume me and I'll reinvent myself bit by bit as Stephanie Shaw, a name glimpsed on a boarding card during a transaction. A name that sounds like a character from a book.

'Stephanie Shaw' has always lived in London. She's independent, lives alone by choice. Though it'll break my heart to leave Dominique, I'll move into a flat closer to the airport and one day I'll make it official: I'll legally become Stephanie Shaw. Kate Thomas will no longer exist.

Then, without meaning to, I'll meet a man. I'll be drawn towards him, sitting lost in his thoughts in the first-class lounge. Perhaps I'll sense that, like me, he's both a blank sheet and a labyrinth of secrets. I'll fall for him so quickly I'll barely know it's happening, and I'll let myself be happy for a while.

Then the guilt will return, even stronger. How can I lie in a comfortable bed, in this man's arms, while Becca's in prison? I'll feel it again: the certainty that I have to turn myself in, and the fear of everything that will follow.

Because there's still something only I know.

The effects of the carbamazepine were not just increased because of anti-depressants and alcohol. The level in Nick's blood appeared higher than the dose Becca and I agreed to give him because, quite simply, it was.

I was so scared it wouldn't be enough. Scared that two small white pills would have no impact on tall, broad Nick. So as he was waiting for Mum to get ready, sipping a second beer between ordering a taxi and packing last-minute things, I snuck two more tablets into his drink.

This is the part I've never told a soul. The part that might get Becca out of jail, switch our places, reverse the courses of our lives.

But just when I've gathered every scrap of courage from every corner of myself, I'll discover something that changes my whole perspective.

I'll discover I'm pregnant.

My life will become about that baby instead. I'll realise that whatever I tried to do for Mum in the past, whatever I know I should do for Becca, it doesn't compare with what I would do for her, my daughter, my Freya.

71

Steph

'Are you warm enough?'

'Yes.'

'Do you want my coat?'

'I'm fine.'

'Is your head hurting?'

'A bit.'

'How much?'

'A bit! That's as precise a unit as I can give you, Mum!' Freya rolled her eyes but she was half smiling, and both expressions made Steph want to weep with relief. She was back and she was still Freya. Probably shaken and scarred in ways that were yet to reveal themselves, but still Freya. And they were driving her home after the longest ten days of their lives.

Steph thrummed with nerves as they drew close to their neighbourhood, gripping Freya's hand for her own sake now. She and Paul had slept in a cheap hotel near the hospital for the last five nights, wanting to stay close. Now this had the momentous feel of a homecoming after years abroad. Surely everything would be different, strange.

I'm so sorry, she said again, to her daughter and husband, but in her head this time, because Paul had banned her from repeating it. She wanted to say it every day for the rest of their lives, and she was reminded of feeling the same after Becca had gone to prison.

Her cousin was in custody. Again. And Steph, like her sixteen-year-old self, was back to waiting and wondering whether she would incriminate her. So far, no officers had threatened to take Steph away from the family she'd only just been reunited with. The questions they'd asked hadn't touched on her involvement in Nick's poisoning, or that she'd been harbouring somebody who'd broken parole. They'd told her Becca was being tight-lipped about her motivation for trying to damage the Harlows' life. She'd cited jealousy, old grievances, nothing specific. So perhaps she was still keeping Steph's secrets, even after everything.

The idea sat uneasily with Steph, despite the anguish Becca had caused. Hadn't the time come to tell the truth? Hadn't other people suffered enough for her mistakes? But then she would look at her family and think, *How can I leave them?*

Her dilemma was knocked from her mind as they turned into their street. She and Freya were sitting together in the back, Paul driving, and Freya began to giggle. 'We're like royals and Dad's our chauffeur.'

'I live to serve,' Paul said, from the front, doffing an invisible cap.

Nervous laughter bubbled out of Steph, too. She caught Freya's eye and they were off, Paul joining them, the joy of it like a drug. Steph couldn't help thinking of the giggling fits she used to have with Becca over practically nothing. She and Freya were the same sometimes, or had been before Freya's faith in her had been rocked. A pang dented Steph's laughter. She couldn't give this up.

They laughed harder as Irene from number 12 came rushing out of her house to wave, and Freya performed a subtle royal wave in return. But their amusement faded as they progressed along the street and saw other neighbours emerging onto the pavement to welcome them home. Clearly word had got around that they were due back. People were clapping. Crying. Somebody had had the foresight and the kindness to remove the MISSING posters from the trees.

A lump expanded in Steph's throat. She glanced at Freya and saw the shock in her face, the sudden childishness of her blinking eyes. Perhaps she hadn't realised how many people had willed her to be found. If she was honest, Steph hadn't realised either, in the whirl of it all. She didn't allow herself to look towards Chris Watson's basement, to wonder whether Vicky was watching, how she must feel. The darker shades of their street, and of their story, could be held at bay for this moment of slow-motion happiness.

Emma was there, too, as they stepped out of the car. Standing on crutches, with Zeb, in front of their railings. She was wearing the baby-pink 1960s coat that Steph had often admired, and her hair was a turbo-charged shade of blue, as if freshly dyed. Steph held her gaze, and thought she saw Freya catch Zeb's eye, something unsaid momentarily connecting them all. It seemed that one of them might speak, like maybe they all wanted to, but Emma just smiled and stuck close to Zeb, and Steph looped her arm around Freya as they moved towards their front door.

Then she noticed the sign. TO LET.

Steph's stomach corkscrewed with jittery relief. Vicky was leaving, of course. Would she start again, like Steph had once? Would she spend her life trying to forget what her husband had done, or would she stick by him?

Steph blinked, though, as she registered what the sign actually said: *Two-bedroom ground-floor flat.* She swivelled back to Emma. 'You're moving?'

Emma flushed a little, and nodded. 'It's all happened quite fast. I'm giving my business another go, fingers crossed . . . but until I start making money I can't afford the rent on this place as well. So I'll live above the shop temporarily. Zeb's going to stay with his dad a bit longer. They're helping me spruce up the shop . . . and then we'll see.'

Steph wasn't sure what to feel. It seemed her relationship with Emma – however she might define it – probably wouldn't evolve beyond the intensity of this period. And maybe it never would have, because where was there to go from here? It was already becoming dreamlike: Steph trusting Emma with the address she'd kept secret for years; running beside her in pursuit of a man who was still unidentified. Now they'd reverted to two neighbours in the street, talking politely, their children beside them.

'Well, that's great,' Steph said. 'Good luck.' For old times' sake, she added: 'Your earrings are spectacular.'

Emma touched the dangling peacock feathers. 'If you fancy something similar, swing by the shop in a few weeks.'

'Not sure I could pull them off,' Steph said, and Emma smiled in recognition of their familiar script.

'Welcome home, Freya,' Emma added, turning to her, a sudden dampness in her eyes. 'It's such a relief to see you.'

Freya murmured her thanks, seeming overwhelmed. Zeb nodded beneath his curly fringe, and a moment of quiet settled. It was Paul who broke it, suggesting they should get Freya inside to rest.

Steph glanced towards the basement steps, just for a moment, before she urged Freya into their cool, quiet hallway.

At the entrance to their flat, Freya stopped and breathed in. Unmistakably, there was a smell of Elizabeth Arden perfume. And homemade ginger cake. The source of both scents ran out from the living room with Brian behind, then Jess. They gathered Freya into their arms. Heather kissed her all over her face, Brian cried almost as much as Jess, and Paul was sucked into their messy, teary huddle too.

Steph found herself hanging back. She watched her family and imagined, in different circumstances, two extra people: her mum and her cousin. Alive and free, driving each other mad, but with nothing huge to forgive or be forgiven for. Would her mum and Heather have got on?

Would her cousin have become Freya's Auntie Bec? What was the use in wondering?

Freya turned to look for her, and Paul held out his arm to bring her into the fold. Steph shook off her sadness and stepped towards them. This was another moment that shouldn't be tainted, another outbreak of joy before the process of putting their lives back together had to begin.

That night, Steph climbed the attic stairs. Halfway up she paused and looked down, seeing Paul through the living-room door, in his usual armchair wearing his suede slippers. How quickly they'd rediscovered their routines: their places in front of the TV and round the table, Freya's favourite cheesy pasta for dinner. Ordinary things made extraordinarily precious.

Paul glanced up and saw her watching him. He smiled, and Steph's stomach fluttered with love, and gratitude, and residual guilt. While they'd been staying near the hospital, they'd talked and talked about their lives as other people. Yet there was still that one part of her own story she hadn't shared and probably never would. It wasn't a chapter, not even a page, only a paragraph, a line. But it was the axis upon which the story spun. The two extra pills that might have made the difference between Nick living and dying.

She pointed to indicate that she was going to check on Freya. Paul nodded, and Steph tiptoed up the last few wooden stairs to knock on her daughter's door. Still part of her expected a furious '*Leave me alone!*' but Freya invited her in. Steph paused a beat to appreciate, again, the miraculous fact that her daughter was back where she belonged.

The room was warmly lit by the bedside lamp. Freya was in bed cocooned by pillows. As she took her headphones out of her ears, the murmur of a Harry Potter audio book seeped from them. Steph glanced at Freya's other books, her Agatha Christies and Conan Doyles, and thought about her daughter playing detective, emulating her dad or her favourite characters, but going to extreme lengths. Blackmailing her driving instructor, behaving in unrecognisable ways. *Why didn't you just ask me, Frey?*

But why hadn't Steph asked *her* if anything was wrong?

Why hadn't she asked Paul about his past?

It wasn't always easy to ask the question.

Steph perched on Freya's bed and brushed her hair back from her face, checking the dressed wound. She couldn't help picturing, for the hundredth time, the moment of Freya's head hitting Chris's dashboard. Freya couldn't remember it, or much of her four delirious days in Becca's spare room, kept hidden but alive. Apparently, just before Steph had arrived at the maisonette, Becca had been planning to alert the police to Freya's whereabouts and then disappear. She was denying sending the note or the book. A question mark still hovered over those things.

Steph let Freya's hair fall back into place. Then she opened her mouth and suddenly she was telling her daughter the story of a girl called Kate Thomas. A girl only a few months younger than Freya was now, who had thought she'd understood something, thought she could fix it. Much like Freya had.

It was a twisted bedtime story. Steph felt herself dividing as she told it, the same as when she'd first been interviewed by the police with her appropriate adult beside her. The version of herself that owned the whole truth was floating towards the attic ceiling, disappearing through the skylight with those extra pills in her fist. It was Kate, carrying away the snipped-out portion of the tale, leaving Steph on the bed with her daughter, sharing only as much as she could bring herself to confess. Only as much as she had told Paul.

Freya stared into space as she listened. Then her eyes moved to Steph. She looked calm, but her neck had reddened, like Becca's did when her emotions were rising to the surface.

'You never even told Dad your real name?'

Steph shook her head. 'I wanted to be Steph Harlow. And when I was with you and Dad, I was. You made me better. Helped me forget.'

'You killed someone.'

Steph swallowed. 'Yes.'

'Did you mean to?'

Steph tensed. She'd never actually had to answer that question before. She thought of the adrenalin that had exploded through her as she'd snuck the additional dose into Nick's drink. The thud of despair when she'd returned from Costcutter to find him unharmed. Later, when her mum had called from the hospital, the reality of what she'd done had ripped into her. But up to that point, deep down, had she wished him dead?

She met her daughter's eyes, which seemed to brim with a kind of troubled fascination. Steph couldn't let Freya think of her as a killer. She'd never really come to terms with the idea that her mum might have seen her that way, underneath their pretence.

'No,' she said. 'I was scared, and desperate. But of course I didn't want to kill him.'

Freya plucked at her bedclothes. Steph knew her face was going to crumple even before it did, and she shuffled closer to hug her, stroking her back as she cried.

'I'm sorry,' she whispered into her hair. 'I love you so much, Frey.'

'What's going to happen?' Freya asked. 'You won't go to prison, will you? You and Dad aren't going to split up? Will I get into trouble for blackmailing Chris?'

'No!' Steph rushed to promise her. 'None of those things are going to happen.'

She checked herself, remembering all the times she'd over-promised in the past, convincing both Freya and herself that their charmed life was untouchable.

'At least, I'll try my hardest to make sure they don't,' she amended carefully. 'There might be some things out of our control. But Dad and I are solid. And all three of us made some mistakes but we've paid for them pretty thoroughly already, don't you think?'

Freya nodded. 'I . . . I did other stuff, too.'

'What stuff?'

'The eggs, the banana skins, the stupid parenting book . . . Well, Zeb did them, but it was all my idea.'

Steph couldn't stop her mouth twisting with this final shock.

'It was all part of my anti-Mum campaign,' Freya said, 'once I'd got it into my head that . . . but I *don't* think you're a bad mum. The opposite, actually.'

It was one more thing to absorb. It made Steph's limbs feel heavy. She sank down next to her daughter and Freya shuffled to make room for her on the bed. A rectangle of star-peppered night hovered above them. Steph pictured the sky rippling and churning, and her breathless teenage self, watching the turmoil without knowing her life was about to be thrown into similar disorder.

'I don't want Zeb to get into trouble,' Freya said, as they looked up. 'But I just want to be completely honest with you, like you have with me. Get it all out in the open.'

Steph squeezed her hand. Her overwhelming feeling, now, was a desire to give in to a dreamless sleep. The stars were hazy and the wind was a lullaby. She remembered all those times, as a worn-out young mum, when she'd put Freya to bed and ended up dropping off beside her. Paul used to do the same on his turns. She'd discover him snoring peacefully, as he would no doubt discover her in an hour or so, creeping up to check where she'd got to.

Hopefully, he would leave them to sleep. When Steph woke, spring sunlight would be pouring through the windows, and Freya would still be close.

'I . . . haven't been completely honest,' Steph murmured.

She closed her eyes, listening to the wind, the missing scenes of her guilt playing out behind the lids. But she had spoken softly, almost under her breath, and she knew Freya was already asleep.

Acknowledgements

I've been incredibly lucky to have so many talented and supportive people helping me, and my book, along the way.

To my brilliant agent, Hellie Ogden: a huge thank you for all your support, wisdom, advice, inspiration, and for always keeping the faith! You really have brought me a long way. Thank you also to Will Francis, Kate Longman, Kirsty Gordon, and all of the fantastic Janklow & Nesbit team.

To my incredible editors: Kimberley Atkins at Hodder, for your vision and enthusiasm from day one, and Danielle Dieterich at Putnam, for all the extra insight you brought. You two have an astonishing talent for bringing out the best in a book. Thank you for taking so much time and care, and for giving feedback that made me excited about re-writing! Thank you also to Helen O'Hare for seeing the book's potential in the US and for your invaluable input in the early stages of editing. Thanks to Hazel Orme and Madeline Hopkins for the perceptive copyediting, Amy Batley at Hodder for all your help, and Rebecca Folland and the rights team at Hachette. Thank you to Lewis Csizmazia, Libby Earland, Myrto Kalavrezou, Callie Robertson and to everyone at Hodder, and at Putnam, who have made the whole process extremely enjoyable.

To Anna and John Cotton, and Charlotte and Sam Strong: your feedback helped shape this book in the very beginning, and our writing group sessions were a great source of support and fun. (The pizzas were nice, too.) A heartfelt thanks goes to all the friends and family who have kept asking about my writing over the years, cheered me on, and celebrated with me – you know who you are and I hope you know how much it has meant. Thank you to Jimmy for being endlessly supportive, for hours spent decorating my office, and for answering questions about cars and flooring for the book! And thank you to Mum, Dad, and Gramms, who have bought, read and shared everything I've ever had in print; to Christine and Yass for inspiring the setting (and the mentions of Harry Potter); to Daisy for insights into Snapchat and other things I'm too old to know about; and to my nephews just for making me smile.